ABDULRAZAK GURNAH is the winner of the Nobel Prize in Literature 2021. He is the author of ten novels: *Memory of Departure*, *Pilgrims Way*, *Dottie*, *Paradise* (shortlisted for the Booker Prize and the Whitbread Award), *Admiring Silence*, *By the Sea* (longlisted for the Booker Prize and shortlisted for the *Los Angeles Times* Book Award), *Desertion* (shortlisted for the Commonwealth Writers' Prize), *The Last Gift*, *Gravel Heart* and *Afterlives* (longlisted for the Walter Scott Prize and shortlisted for the Orwell Prize for Political Fiction). He is Emeritus Professor of English and Postcolonial Literatures at the University of Kent. He lives in Canterbury.

BY THE SAME AUTHOR

Memory of Departure
Pilgrims Way
Paradise
Admiring Silence
By the Sea
Desertion
The Last Gift
Gravel Heart
Afterlives

DOTTIE

ABDULRAZAK
GURNAH

BLOOMSBURY PUBLISHING
LONDON • OXFORD • NEW YORK • NEW DELHI • SYDNEY

BLOOMSBURY PUBLISHING
Bloomsbury Publishing Plc
50 Bedford Square, London, WC1B 3DP, UK
29 Earlsfort Terrace, Dublin 2, Ireland

BLOOMSBURY, BLOOMSBURY PUBLISHING and the Diana logo are trademarks of Bloomsbury Publishing Plc

First published in Great Britain 1990
This edition published 2021

A catalogue record for this book is available from the British Library

ISBN: PB: 978-1-5266-5346-8; eBook: 978-1-4088-8565-9;
ePDF: 978-1-5266-5420-5

2 4 6 8 10 9 7 5 3 1

Typeset by Newgen KnowledgeWorks Pvt. Ltd., Chennai, India
Printed and bound in Great Britain by CPI Group (UK) Ltd, Croydon CR0 4YY

For Abadi and Ahmed who have both travelled well

The First Journey

1

Dottie first heard the news of her sister's labour on the factory Tannoy. The voice booming through the public address system did not say that she was being urgently summoned to attend a birth, but Dottie knew. She hurried away with a feeling that this was a moment she had already lived through. In the office she was told that the hospital had rung with a message. Sophie had collapsed at work.

In the cab to the hospital she wondered if there was something she should do, some preparation she could make. It was a short journey from Kennington to Tooting, but the traffic was heavy and their progress was slow. At last the taxi came to a shuddering stop at the hospital entrance, and Dottie stepped out into a patch of autumn sunlight that had evaded the buildings around her. The ward sister smiled and told her that she was too late. The baby had already arrived. Sophie must have been in labour for a while before she collapsed, the sister said as she guided Dottie to the patient's bedside.

Sophie's exhaustion was plain in her face, but through her tiredness shone a small smile of triumph. Haltingly, searching for words, she told Dottie how she had been rushed into a cab from Kimberly Street in Waterloo. The cab driver had refused payment, she said, telling her she would be his good luck. At the hospital, the nurses had been kind. They had washed her and shaved her, and Sophie had been ashamed because she had made the bath water filthy. Then the baby came and it was so perfect. Didn't Dottie think so? To her surprise, the nurses asked for a name for the baby. She had not thought they would ask her straight away, had thought she would have time to talk to Jimmy first. But the nurses became annoyed, Sophie said, and after they had been so kind. So she gave them the name she had been thinking of.

'I called him Hudson, Sis,' she said, looking at Dottie with uncertainty.

Dottie said nothing for a while, and then talked about the baby's perfection, and the pain her sister must have borne for so long. She sat beside Sophie and watched the baby sleeping in his metal cot. She made cheerful conversation about their plans, knowing that her sister was waiting for her to say something else. Sophie's hand lay in hers and she stroked it absently, tutting at the groans of pain that her sister made now and then. She knew that Sophie wanted her to say how pleased she was about the name. It was their younger brother's, and Sophie was waiting to hear her say that naming the baby after him was right because they had loved him so much. Dottie watched the baby and stroked Sophie's hand abstractedly, smiling with an unconscious wince whenever she caught her sister's eye, or whenever Sophie moaned with the pain in her body and between her thighs. She hoped that Sophie would soon fall asleep. But although she dropped off for a short period, her eyes flew open with sudden anxiety and turned blearily at Dottie.

'It's a lovely name, and the baby looks just like Hudson,' Dottie said at last, and heard Sophie gurgling with pleasure and relief.

'Does he really look like Hudson?' Sophie asked, grinning with delight.

'Just like him,' Dottie said.

In a few moments Sophie was asleep. Dottie sat silently beside her for a long time, grateful for the solitude. Out of the corner of her eye she saw that her sister's hand was stirring uncertainly, and she reached out and held it again. Sophie sighed heavily in her sleep.

2

Dottie was the elder by two years, although she and Sophie had been born close enough to each other to be christened in the same church, Our Lady of Miracles in Leeds. That was how she remembered it, although she was not certain. Sometimes she thought it was Our Lady of Sorrows, but that sounded melodramatic, as if she was trying to make a case of herself, and she preferred the brighter name. There was an old disused well in the church-yard, she remembered that, and remembered the terror it filled her with as a child. She had carelessly glanced down into its giddy depths once, and even now, whenever she thought of it, she felt again the hand that had clutched her shoulder with a cry of warning. She could no longer hear the voice, and could not say if it was her mother or someone else. *Be careful, don't you know the hump-back lives down there?* When the explanation came, it was always in a man's voice, *his* voice. For years she dreamed of falling in and finding herself in the clutches of the creature who lived at the bottom of the well and who came out at night to gaze with longing at the living world of the church-yard. It was such a long time ago that she could not be sure how many of the details were true and how many she had altered to suit her needs. The stories jostled each other in her head despite her. Sophie often told her that she made these things up, to make an argument and be unpleasant.

Dottie had been christened Dottie Badoura Fatma Balfour. They were names she relished, and she sometimes secretly smiled over them. When she was younger she used to imagine and fabricate round the names, making childish romances and warm tales of painless sacrifice and abundant affection. In her absorption, she sometimes played the games in a soft whisper and was mocked and told off for talking to herself. She persisted in her games despite the ill-tempered correction that was administered for her own good. They told her, those teachers or whoever they were, that all people were the same, and that she would do best to realise that she now lived in England, and she should determine to do what she could to make herself acceptable. She could do more to help herself to that end than behave in such an obstinate and dreamy way.

Her whisperings might give the wrong impression, a kindly teacher warned her. They might make people believe that she could not cope. Don't play with fire. Don't tempt fate. When in Rome you have to do as the Romans. Pull your socks up. She heard that from them several times. We don't do that in England, dear, they told her when her ignorance caused offence. The criticism made her feel like a sinner, or like a traitor.

Yet it was not because she attempted to assert herself that these criticisms descended on her. She would not have dreamed of protesting against the proper pre-eminence of England, nor had she for a moment considered questioning or challenging its rectitude. So all that Dottie could assume, in those early days, was that they knew of the secret hours she spent dwelling over those beautiful names. The whole world must have found out about her secret vices and taken them for treachery. In reality, the circumstances of her life had turned her into Dottie long before she was in any condition to protest, long before it might even have occurred to her to think otherwise. She would not have thought of claiming that the childhood life she led was her own, let alone that she should be able to give a name to it.

She frowned now as she sought to control her worry, and the fear that she felt for the child that Sophie had brought into the world. As if things were not hard enough. As if Sophie herself was anything more than a big, fat child! That she should call the boy Hudson …

3

Dottie thought of herself as having failed with Hudson. It was not that anyone had expected anything different from her, but it had fallen to her to look after him from an early age. And she had failed to prevent him from self-destruction. When they were children, their mother was often ill, and when she was not ill she had other things to attend to. Dottie had learned to do things in the house, and look after her sister and brother. Hudson was difficult, and she herself was too ignorant to be of any real help to him. She had watched Hudson grow angry with them as he grew up, despising them for the cruel blows life rained on them, as if there was anything any of them could have done about it. They did what they could for him, bore for him whatever burdens he could not carry. Hudson took whatever they offered him with sulky ill-grace, suffering the adoration that his mother and his sisters lavished on him, and allowing them to spoil him with their devotion. Sophie showered him with love, fondling and kissing him whenever he let her. More often than not, he fought her off, shouting and complaining about her fumbling embraces. On rare occasions he allowed himself to be taken into her arms, reluctant and tense at first, then slowly allowing himself to melt, curling up against her girlish plumpness with long-suffering sighs.

By the time he was eleven, it was no longer possible to compel him to do anything he did not want to do. It was no use appealing to his better nature since he was in the process of training himself not to admit to one, and had learnt to pre-empt criticism with torrents of abuse. If Dottie attempted to force him he ran away from her, or if he could not he screamed with frightening abandon. She could not bear the screaming. It sounded like a person being slaughtered.

He became obsessed with being an American, and started to talk with a clumsy imitation of an American voice. He was different from all of them, he said. His father was an American Negro. In Hudson's story the father was a fabulous creature who was part of the glamour of America: a tap-dancing, smiling man in a suit who rode in huge white Cadillacs and spent his days going from hotels to apartments, as everyone did in the movies. Nobody talked of who Dottie's father was, or Sophie's, he reminded his sisters. Nobody knew, not even their mother.

Sometimes their mother caught her breath as she looked at one of them, reminded of something in the way they looked, but it never came to anything. Their mother's life had become so confused. She would shake her head and smile because she could not remember. Hudson taunted his sisters about that, calling them bastards and making monkey noises at them. Once he found a picture of a cannibal chief in a *Tarzan* comic and went running up to Dottie, crying, 'I've found your daddy! Look, look, I've found him.'

Dottie slapped him across the face and dragged him to a mirror. 'Who do you think you're laughing at?' she asked him. He wept at the humiliating explanations she offered him.

'My daddy is an American, not a savage!' he cried, squeezing his eyelids to shut out the pain. 'Your daddy's a savage. My daddy has a green car and lives in a big building in New York. He's tall and rich, not fat and ugly like Sophie. And Sophie's daddy is a savage. But my daddy is a soldier and lives in America. I'm not a bastard. I'm not a bastard like you. When I grow up ...' There he halted in his tracks and glanced guiltily at Dottie, overcome by his inability to imagine his grown-up self. He glared at his sisters with unfeigned bitterness, wounded by the indignity and the childishness of his protest. When he was older he would go to New York to find his father, he declared, and ran out into the street.

4

The fabulous American had been among the black GIs who had been sent over to England from 1942 onwards until the end of the war and beyond. The early contingent caused havoc in quiet English towns and raised the bogey of bestial couplings of the ape-like monsters with milk-skinned English maids. Hands and hearts were wrung in the letter columns of national newspapers. Questions were asked during Prime Minister's Question Time. Discussions took place at the highest levels, at Cabinet meetings and over state banquets. Her Majesty's Secretary of State for War, Sir James Grigg, prepared guidelines to British officers to instruct that troops, especially the ATS, avoid intimate friendships with black soldiers. The War Cabinet approved the guidelines, on condition that they were kept confidential. The British press were asked not to refer to them. So, accordingly, directives were issued by government officials that black troops were to be kept strictly away from white female service personnel, whom they could easily rupture with their huge members, causing havoc to the logistics of war. They were not to be admitted in restaurants and bars that were frequented by white American soldiers as this would cause problems when or if they returned to the United States. Some restaurant managers, their zeal for the war effort fired up by their greed for dollars, excluded *empire* soldiers and officers as well, despite the emblems these foreigners wore in the service of the King-Emperor.

Hudson's father would not have been surprised by any of this. He was quartered in Carlisle, and accepted the antagonism of English people with a cynical pretence of indifference. None of it was worth spending years in a military prison for. It was in Carlisle that he met Dottie's mother. Her name was Bilkisu, but her children had not known this. She called herself Sharon. They knew she came from Cardiff and that she had run away from home when she discovered that her parents were planning a marriage for her with someone she had only just met. She had told her children often, when her despair had mellowed with drink, how she had never been back to that cruel city.

She had once known the name of the village where her father was born and could recite the names of her mother's family to fifteen generations, she told them, but she had forgotten all that as she had so much else from those times. Sometimes she talked bitterly of her father, and blamed him for the way her life had turned out. At other times, her face wreathed with smiles, she told them of his eccentric kindnesses and his transparent masquerade of the fierce patriarch from the mountains. She kept these tales of her father deliberately vague, sometimes mixing up details and pretending to have forgotten something important. She did not want her children bothered with all that stuff. She did not understand until it was too late, and perhaps not even then, that her children would need these stories to know who they were. The children, in turn, learned not to ask questions, accepting with instinctive courtesy that these were not things their mother could happily talk about.

5

So they did not know that Bilkisu's father was a Pathan called Taimur, and that he had had youthful adventures that were like the wildest fantasies. At the death of his father, whom he could only remember as a large beard, he had been taken away by his half-brother to herd sheep on a distant mountain pasture. He was his half-brother's share of the inheritance, along with the sheep and a large trunk containing brass goblets of many designs which the old man had had a life-long passion for. Taimur cried a lot at first, missing his mother, but his half-brother beat him severely and taught him that he should bear life's burdens without grumbling.

Taimur begged to differ, and as soon as he had learned the general direction of his home he set off in search of his mother. His half-brother caught him quite easily and took him back to the sheep. He told him stories of the Devil that lived in the mountains, to frighten him and keep him from running away. The Devil took many shapes, sometimes a wheeling hawk or a mountain antelope with a shaggy, silvery pelt, but its favourite shape was that of a beautiful woman with long black hair and ruby lips. She frequented the mountain paths, pretending to be lost. With her hair windswept and dishevelled and snagged with thorns, with tears streaming from her hazel eyes, weeping bitterly of her loneliness and homesickness, she would ensnare the traveller into stopping to aid her and then turn him into her slave. Instead of being frightened, as he was intended to be, Taimur grieved for the poor abandoned Devil while his half-brother gnashed his teeth at the creature he was describing. As he moved from pasture to pasture with the animals, Taimur kept his eyes open for the woman with ruby lips but never once caught sight of her.

The next time he was ready to run away, he took the precaution of giving his half-brother a good crack on the head with a sharp stone before leaving, to give himself a decent start. He reached his old home to find that his mother had been taken as wife by a man from another village, and that his half-brother was already around, looking for him and spreading stories of Taimur's treacherous attack. He realised then that it was his half-brother who was the real Devil in the mountain. And if he allowed himself to be found, if he did not escape at once, he would be a slave all his life. He set off on motherless wanderings across wild mountains, where petty chieftains ruled the face of the earth to their autocratic pleasure, with the power of life and death over their subjects. At night he lay under a wild, chaotic sky and felt the world hurtling underneath him, and thought the stars only existed because he was there. If it were not for him, lying on the hard earth, neither sky nor mountains would be visible. Nor would the sun or the hazy scrub of the granite foothills appear in the morning.

His wanderings came to an end when he was adopted into the family of one of the great chieftains who ruled the waking world. He lived in the chieftain's household for several years, looking after the goats and tending the orchards. He served the family joyfully in return for food, and he knew that he could live with them all his life and there would always be something for him. When there was no work in the fields he helped with repairs in the houses, or the stables. He was adept at all the tasks required of him, and his unfailing enthusiasm endeared him to his adopted suzerain. Sooner or later his master would help him find a wife, and would pay for the modest hospitality to celebrate it. Members of the family were already teasing him about a wedding and children of his own. The wife-to-be would not have long black hair and ruby lips most likely, but she would be a companion to him as he grew older and fell ill.

One night, after many secret struggles, he succumbed to his wanderlust and set off once more on his journeys. He was so filled with guilt that he did not say goodbye to his benefactors. He travelled south to Punjab and Sind and eventually took ship down the Arabian Gulf to the land of the Mahara. At the outbreak of the 1914 war he found himself working as a sailor on a Royal Navy ship, the *Argent*, in the Shatt el Arab by Basra. One day the Turkish forces sent fireships drifting down the Euphrates. It was like a scene from the Trojan War, wooden barges laden with naphtha that blazed remorselessly despite all attempts to extinguish the flames. Several British crafts were damaged, and many of the sailors were burnt or overcome with smoke. Taimur Khan fought so bravely and with such resourcefulness that the captain of his ship noticed and commended him. The captain declared that by his courage Taimur Khan had acquired the right to call himself an Englishman. It was less than Taimur Khan had expected. When he had seen how delighted the captain was with his endeavours, he had begun to hope for a small purse of rupees or a handful of guineas.

But waste not, want not. When the time came to pay off the ship's crew, Taimur Khan held the captain to his word and insisted on being repatriated to England. The captain laughed delightedly and endorsed Taimur Khan's request. He arrived in London in April 1919, and took a train to Cardiff with a Malayan whom he had met on the journey. The Malayan had also been a sailor, but had been working for the American Army in France during the last months of the war, digging trenches and laying pipes. He told Taimur that in Cardiff there were many black and brown people, some of whom had been living there for decades and generations. Many of them were Somalis and were Muslims, the Malay told him, so he would not lack hospitality. There were also some Malayan and Javanese families, but the ignorant people of Cardiff called all of them Arabs.

By this time Taimur Khan had learned to bear life's burdens without too much grumbling, and the months of his journey from Basra to Europe had opened his eyes to many things. In Cardiff he went about his business with as much dignity as he could manage, suffering the petty persecutions his hosts inflicted on him with smiling tolerance. They were foreigners and nasrani as well, and could not summon the discrimination to tell a Somali from a Malay, so one could not expect too much from them. In any case, where had he been where strangers were not treated with high-handed mockery? He found work in the docks, and lived near by, where all the black and brown people in the city also lived. The house belonged to a pious Somali, who had seven other tenants. Taimur had tried to find a less crowded house, where the call to prayer did not take precedence over all else and where the praises of the prophet did not run into scores of verses, but he had failed. He did not try to find a room in another area because he had been warned that the white people did not take foreign lodgers, so he had no choice except to squeeze in where he could and attend to his immortal soul with what grace he could muster.

Despite these small discomforts, he relished his new life. Some evenings he attended classes to improve his knowledge. They were free and were a respite from the interminable prayers at the house. The classes were held in a local school, and Taimur had learned about them from an exasperated fellow worker at the docks who had completely lost patience with his poor English. They were run by a young lawyer who was always talking about justice and equality, noble words that Taimur revered. The lawyer called him Ali Baba and sometimes cited him as an example of something he was explaining – *we can ask our good friend Ali Baba what the Eastern point of view on justice is* – but Taimur Khan did not mind. It was a chance to improve his knowledge. He knew that the people in the city were angry with foreigners, although he was not sure why. Perhaps there were hardships in the community – that would not be such a surprising thing. Children shouted at him in the streets, telling him to go away, but he smiled to himself and ignored them. The worst thing you can do with such rude children is take any notice of them.

The lawyer had hinted at an explanation now and then, but he talked in riddles which made the other people smile but which were too complicated for Taimur Khan's grasp of the language. He used words like utopia, feudal, occidental. Taimur felt the power of these beautiful words but did not have an inkling of their meanings. Even though he did not understand the lawyer's explanation, he knew it was something to do with him, because of the way they looked to see how he was taking it all.

What the lawyer sometimes said, and which Taimur Khan could not understand, was this: The mind of the Muslim man is unable to function rationally. It is obsessed with visions of sensual utopias and arcadias. Its idea of Paradise has no spiritual dimension, and consists only of thousands of houris ministering to basic physical needs. His processes of thought cannot resist atomising experience, so each event is concrete in itself and does not contribute to a larger whole. It is a feudal view of the world, which the occidental world advanced from during the glorious years of the Renaissance. The inability to function rationally, or recognise the general utility of individual action, therefore, has its explanation in the way the Muslim imagination takes experience to be discrete and atomised. That is why, the lawyer summarised, your run-of-the-mill Muslim cannot arrive at an intelligent generalisation of experience.

Taimur also knew that the people of the town were angry with foreigners because of the women. Their faces became tragic when they said *our women*. To be truthful, *their women* seemed a shameless crowd to him, brazen and half-undressed in the unaccustomed heat of that year. He himself was already courting the daughter of a Lebanese shopkeeper who lived two streets from him, and he could understand the people's irritation with the uncouth sailors who were always being disrespectful to women. Perhaps it would be better if the women did not always seem to be flaunting their bodies. The woman he was courting was called Hawa, and he had received enough encouragement from her hazel eyes to know that his endeavours would not be in vain. He had decided that Cardiff suited him, and had all but given up the idea of moving on to Argentina or the United States. He knew that he had done nothing to deserve the good luck that had attended his miserable existence, and he thanked God for having preserved him through the carelessness of his youth. He was ready now to accept the stroke of fortune that had landed him in this foreign city. If Hawa would have him, if she would honour him, he would give up his roaming life and stay with her.

He was tempted to tell the lawyer about her. Taimur had a habit of hanging around after classes, paying homage to his teacher and delaying the moment when he would be forced to return to the crowded house. At the end of the evening during which the lawyer had discoursed on the Muslim mind, Taimur was shyly loitering in the class-room when his teacher asked him how soon he would be going to sea again. 'Once a sailor always a sailor,' he said. 'When will you be off again? Although you'd be lucky to get a berth the way things are.' The temptation to speak about Hawa was almost irresistible, but a sense of the ridiculousness of his language made him reticent. He shook his head, saying that his language was bad. The lawyer at once resolved that Taimur Khan should talk to the class, recount something of his travels and experiences. So the following evening he told them about the fireships down the Euphrates, and how they lit up the sky with enormous tongues of smoke-fringed flames that shot glittering sparks over the water. He spoke so badly that when he told them what the captain had said about him being an Englishman, they laughed at his broken English until tears streamed down their faces.

The anger that the people of Cardiff felt against the foreigners could not be contained for ever, and in the end they ran riot and tried to hurt or kill as many of the black and brown people who lived among them as they could find. For two hot days in June the fighting raged. The Somali hotel in Millicent Street was attacked by soldiers and citizens, and was then set on fire. Lives were lost. Taimur Khan himself was chased through the streets by crowds of people carrying sticks and shouting abuse. He ran towards the docks and threw himself in the water. Hundreds of people stood on the water-front, at times thousands, rising and falling in the red-dimmed tide of his vision. They waved their fists and threw stones at him. He knew he was in terrible danger because he was not a good swimmer, so he could do little to escape the well-aimed stone. He had already gone as far out as he dared. In his terror, he shouted back at them, thrashing in the water and only attracting further attention to himself. Some yards away was a Somali man who must have already been in the sea when Taimur jumped in, and he angrily advised Taimur to calm down before he had both of them killed. The crowd saw him too, and began sharing out the missiles between the two men in the water.

Suddenly a stone hit the Somali on his forehead, making him roll back and twist in the sea. Taimur saw the crowd turn their whole attention on the wounded man, and hurl rock after rock at him. Every time he rolled under, a roar of joy went up from them. Taimur made one attempt to reach him, but he lost his footing and attracted a hail of stones in his direction as he struggled to recover his balance. He waved a defiant fist, thinking his time would soon come too. But the police arrived before either man was seriously injured, and persuaded the crowd to leave. They laughed as they dragged the two men out of the water, slapping them on the back and telling them to send prayers of thanksgiving to their Almighty Wog-Wallah for their deliverance. Taimur and the Somali, whose name was Salla, were taken to the police station, to join the other people already under arrest. They were told it was the black and brown people who had caused all the trouble, and a few of them were put in prison. 'East is East and West is West,' the trial judge said, 'and never the twain shall meet.' Many white people were arrested as well, some arraigned for murder and assault, but everyone knew how sorely provoked they had been. It would have been adding insult to injury to punish them too severely. Most of the foreign people who were arrested were sent away, first to Plymouth and then to their own countries. Taimur Khan was allowed to stay because the lawyer helped him and spoke for him.

6

That was the story that Bilkisu used to hear when she was very young and was still allowed to sit in her father's lap while he traded stories of his travels with the other people among whom they lived. Her mother Hawa never said anything but later she would tease him for exaggerating the hardships. *Times are harder now*, she used to say. Bilkisu's father used to call Hawa his Devil, because of her black hair and red lips. In Hawa's hearing, he told Bilkisu the story of how he came across her on a mountain path, abandoned and crying, surrounded by tumbled rocks. In her hair were thorns and poison berries, and her beautiful hazel eyes streamed with tears. He stopped to speak to her, and offer what help he could. He soon discovered that he could not leave for the rest of his life, and so he stayed with her and Bilkisu. In Bilkisu's hearing, Hawa called him an iblis for telling such stories, and if she was near enough slapped him hard on the back for his fierce jokes.

The trouble between Bilkisu and her father started when boys began to look at her. At first he only scolded her and asked her to remember that these were the children of the same people who had chased him through the streets, and would have killed him if he had not run faster than them. Then he had threatened to take her out of school, had forbidden her to go out after dark, and had started to talk of marriage. Bilkisu could barely bring herself to say anything affectionate to him any more, and he constantly found fault with her. In the end he became obsessed with the thought of finding her a husband. He was so disappointed in her that he was sure she would bring home a man who would exploit and ruin her. Hawa begged him to leave her alone but he could not, unable to hide from his wife the pain Bilkisu's rejection caused him, unable to stop thinking of the shame her behaviour could bring them.

Two things happening at once persuaded Bilkisu to flee. When she was seventeen she slept with a boy for the first time, and for a few days of terror at the end of the month she thought she was pregnant. At the same time her father began talking about a sailor from Karachi who was interested in her. He was a tall, fleshy man with a carefully trimmed moustache and a soft-looking pot-belly. When they met he smiled at her through a mouthful of the tobacco he was chewing, and the next morning she was gone. She could not bear the thought of that man's mouth on her. In any case, she was terrified of her father's wrath when he discovered that she was pregnant with a white boy.

She called herself Sharon, the name of her one true friend in Cardiff. She passed herself off as a Christian, contemptuously tossing aside the loyalties that her father had pressed on her. She took the name Balfour as a deliberate act of defiance. Her father had ranted about him, describing the

British Foreign Secretary as the perfidious agent of anti-Islam for giving the holy lands of Palestine to the Jews, and for dispossessing the Palestinian people of their homes. Even in his prayers Taimur Khan remembered to ask that God's curses should fall on Balfour for his treachery to the Palestinians. When he saw the Minister's name in the newspaper, his face would grimace with scorn. *Balfour! Laanatullah alaika!* he would cry, in a voice filled with rage. Bilkisu gave up her father's name for a name he loathed more than any other, rejecting Taimur Khan and the life he had tried to force on her.

She never went back to Cardiff, afraid that he would kill her if ever he caught sight of her. Instead she roamed the cities of England and Wales, attracting men with her dusky looks and her red lips, and fulfilling for them their prurient fantasies of A Thousand and One Orgies. When she was lucky, she had a regular man for a while, sometimes for months. Hudson's father was a man like that. She was *his woman* for two months before he went away to France and then she never saw him again. She had already had Dottie and Sophie by the time she met him in Carlisle. She was then twenty-four and beginning to put on weight.

For three years before moving to Carlisle, she lived in Leeds, but she had to escape hurriedly from there too, taking the train without thought or care of where it went. She ran because of a man called Jamil. His name meant beautiful and to Bilkisu he seemed like a prince. He had been seeing her for several months, and had just started to talk about being a father to her children. He told her things she had never heard of, and made her feel things she had forgotten about. One night he told her the story of Princess Badoura of China and the Ajemi Prince Qamar Zaman, who met each other in their sleep, brought together for one night while rival spirits quarrelled over which of the two of them was more beautiful. One of the spirits, Maimuna binti Damarat, favoured Prince Qamar Zaman while the other spirit, who was called Dahnash, preferred Princess Badoura.

The Prince is like a burst of sunlight in a dark forest, Maimuna wept, *streaming down the trunks and pouring off the leafy canopy like liquid fire. The moisture in his mouth is like the finest honey.*

In his turn Dahnash exulted: *Badoura's hair is like the nights of emigration and separation, and her face is like the days of union. She spread three locks of her hair one night and I saw four nights together. And she turned her face to the moon in heaven and I saw two moons.*

Maimuna hovered over the sleeping prince, her fingers almost touching his face. *His lips are like carnelia. Words fail to describe his other charms,* she murmured. *His beauty is that of God.*

Dahnash glowered but kept his irritation in check. Instead he knelt beside Princess Badoura and cried softly: *No one compares with her.*

In short, they could not agree. In the end they summoned the ugly hump-back who lived at the bottom of the well in the courtyard, and asked him to judge. He was sometimes called Cashcash, a name he hated, and Maimuna flattered him when he appeared among them by addressing him with his courtesy name of Dhamana, which meant Responsible. He squatted beside the Prince and Princess and gazed at them. His grotesque body, covered with scales and fuming with putrefaction, shook with amazement at the sight of such beauty, but he could not decide between them either. In desperation, the three spirits, Maimuna, Dahnash and Dhamana, were forced to wake the Prince and Princess one at a time, to see which of the two would show greater amazement at the beauty of the other. When that failed to resolve the matter, the three spirits in turn kissed the young people between the eyes and sang odes of praises to their beauty. Then Dahnash returned Princess Badoura to her home in China, and Qamar Zaman was whisked back to Ajemi, and the spirits returned to their crowded world to continue their arguments. The young people were stricken with love, and knew no way to find each other. Jamil told Bilkisu the story of their separation, and how their love overcame all obstacles until they found happiness. She did not tell him, because she did not know how to, that the story filled her with such joy that she felt that life was not impossible after all.

Jamil was from Jamaica and his father worked as a postman in Leeds. Jamil himself was an electrician on the railways, which was why he was not in the war, his job being considered important enough in other ways. He was only a few months younger than Bilkisu, but his face was still bright with optimism. She wondered, at times, if she was taking advantage of his innocence, if that was how it seemed to others. But she knew she would be good for him!

His family called themselves Syrians. They were Christians from Tripoli, but had been living in Kingston for three generations. It was Jamil who persuaded her to have the children christened in the church of Our Lady. He thought this would remove one of the objections that he could anticipate from his family. It did not matter, in the end. Jamil's father sent two men to see her and beat her about, friends of the family. They told her to leave before there was trouble. They were ambitious for their son and did not want him to be ruined by a woman like her. The men did not give her much time, telling her that if she was there the following morning they would give her more of the stuff she liked, and might even give her little daughters a taste of it as well. She waited up all night, thinking Jamil might come to tell her that all was well, that they too would find happiness like Badoura and Qamar Zaman. She would have told him, had he come, that fathers are tyrants. They can't help being like that. But Jamil did not come, even though she knew he was in town. She waited until it was light, in case he had been afraid to come in the blackout, but still he did not come.

She went for the train in the late morning, getting off at Carlisle because the guard discovered her without a ticket. He assumed she was going to Carlisle anyway because of the black soldiers. He looked sneeringly at her, and shook his head over the two little ones who would sooner or later walk down the same road. He took her to be a prostitute but Bilkisu liked to think that she had not yet sunk so low.

Carlisle taught her otherwise. The black soldiers treated her as a whore, bargained and argued with her in public. Business was brisk. The war had freed everybody from constraint, and the soldiers behaved as if they were on holiday or on a school trip, singing joyfully the crudest songs they could manage. Hudson's father had been one of many, black and white. Their money smelt the same, she used to say. But he came to her often and she became fond of him. It was his talk of the Hudson River, along the banks of which he had lived and played as a child, that made her call her son by that name. Long after the GI had gone, Bilkisu called him Hudson as well, and in the end pretended she could no longer remember his real name.

In the years after the war they moved several times, rarely staying more than a few months anywhere. Bilkisu was often unwell, and found it increasingly difficult to get any kind of work. They circled south towards London, living hand to mouth while Bilkisu fought a ragged rear-guard against humiliations. They always found something in the end, somewhere to stay for a few weeks, some kind of work, social security. But it was a losing battle. Bilkisu was now very ill and could do nothing to make herself better. She was too ashamed to go to a doctor. The abuse of her early years had caught up with her.

At the age of thirty-six she was a derelict, tortured by a vile disease whose name she dared not even utter to her children. She was broken by misery, and filled with despair at her wasted life. By then they were living in South London and Bilkisu's mind was constantly wandering back to her childhood. Often now she talked of returning to Cardiff to die, and it would fall to Dottie to comfort her. *I don't even have a name*, Bilkisu would cry. *How can I go back to Cardiff without a name?*

This was just at the time of Suez, when the consequences of Balfour's policy were being enacted across the lands of the Middle East. The Israelis attacked Egypt, under the frightening leadership of their one-eyed chief. They conquered at will, humiliating the atomising nomads and their incompetent, pseudo-modern bashaws in engagement after engagement. Eden sent in the British forces to teach Nasser an unforgettable lesson, and the French joined in the fun too. Whenever anyone mentioned Eden's name, Bilkisu exploded into curses: *Laanatu-llah alaika Anthony Eden!* She no longer remembered what the words meant, but that was what her father used to say about Balfour. In those times, abandoning Taimur Khan's name for Balfour seemed even more like treachery.

Bilkisu became too ill to do anything but sit waiting for the torment to end. Much of the time she was confused, then her mind cleared and for a while she seemed to be getting better. She would surface from the suffering with stories of Cardiff and her parents, and would wail at the fate that had befallen her. It was too late for her children to understand what she was telling them, their minds numbed by the wretchedness and squalor in which they lived. Bilkisu had become obese with age, and her illness made her retain so much fluid that she looked waterlogged. She lingered for nearly a year, trying to hide from her children the pain and degradation of her disease. They shared two rooms in Stockwell, and both were filled with the stench of her rotting body. The landlord came to demand rent but was driven away by the unspeakable vileness of their lives. He was a short, skinny Cypriot who made money out of renting dirty rooms to desperate people, but he was not without feeling. He shouted his warnings of eviction and police at the disgusting woman and her children, and fled. She would not go to the doctor, even to the bitter end.

She lived long enough to see the hated Sir Anthony Eden removed from office, but in the late spring of that year she died. One of the neighbours called the police because the groans of the fat woman and the angry yells of her young boy were frightening. It was too late then. They did what they could for her at the hospital but her body was so full of poison that they could not save her. In her uterine canal they found a pair of nylon stockings that was green with slime.

A Common Failing

1

Hudson took it badly, despite all that Dottie could do. He was then twelve years old, and frantic with loathing for the way they lived. That was what mattered to him above all else, that he had been forced to be part of the mess. He was inconsolable, not because he grieved for his mother so much as for himself. During Bilkisu's last months, he had avoided her. And when he could not, had sat sulking tensely while his mother tried to tempt him nearer with endearments and small bribes. If he succumbed, which he did disgustedly and with his eyes shut, he had to submit to her fumbling embraces and the vile smell she gave off. If he resisted her, she laughed at him like one of the demons in his nightmares, her face doughy and rubbery with evil. She mimicked different voices: the lost little girl, the indignant matron, the well-intentioned grown-up, and then laughed to see his agony. At least she was bed-ridden, and could not pursue him with her crazed malice. She had become a monster. Her face had swollen so that she was almost blind in one eye, and the strange lumps that had appeared made the open eye seem as if it was slit upwards. Her skin had become so diseased that Hudson sometimes imagined it giving off fumes.

On the morning she died he had stayed behind from school because Dottie had asked him to, in case his mother needed anything. He hardly ever went to school anyway, and usually came home at about lunch-time, after wandering the streets for several hours to get away from her. It was boring, but at least he did not have to listen to teachers hectoring him, or suffer the humiliations and beatings of the playground. On the morning his mother died, he had heard his sisters getting ready to leave as usual, Dottie to go to work and Sophie to go to school. He had pulled his blanket tightly over his head, hiding from their grumbles, and grunted an answer when Dottie became persistent. Yes, he'd stay behind and keep an eye on her.

His mother had lain in her bed, groaning with such deep anguish that Hudson had nearly gone mad with irritation and the strange pain her cries caused him. He crouched in the farthest corner of the room in which the children lived and slept. The other one was now the sick room, and he never went into that stinking pen unless it was *completely* unavoidable. Dottie had left the door open a crack so that Bilkisu would not need to shout to be heard, and Hudson was afraid to shut it in case she saw him and started to call to him in her demon voices. Every now and again she would catch her breath like someone sobbing, croaking her death-rattle through bubbles of phlegm, and then she would fall silent. Once the silence stretched for minutes, and Hudson stood with fists clenched, hoping that she had gone to sleep. He tiptoed gently towards the open door, allowing himself to entertain the beginnings of relief, feeling a smile spreading on his face. Suddenly, just as his suspicions were almost overcome, she started again. Stop that! he yelled, convinced that she was deliberately tormenting him. He ran to the window and pushed his head out, screaming with rage and terror. When the police came, they found him sitting under the window with his hands over his ears, yelling with pain while tears poured down his face.

He took to sitting on the floor, rocking backward and forward and staring before him. He refused to speak and showed no sign that he had heard when anybody spoke to him. Sophie tried to cuddle him while he sat on the floor, but whenever she touched him he shut his eyes and screamed, flapping his arms in a fury. Sophie laughed at him, unable to resist his melodramatic rages, and stole swift kisses whenever he became careless. She danced round him, singing a playground song, and tried to drag him to his feet. Hudson shouted and hit out at her, making her laugh even more as she skipped away from him. When she tired of tormenting him, she prepared little trays of dainties which she slid along the floor to him, singing soft praises and sighing endearments as she did so. Hudson would ignore the gifts at first, but when left to himself long enough he would take a piece of flapjack or jelebi, and then another piece and another because he could not resist them.

After a few days he became less obsessed with his feelings of outrage although he was still impossible to approach. He pouted and sulked with unabated ferocity whenever he felt anyone's eyes on him, and only listened to Dottie, only let *her* touch him, and then only lightly as if by accident. Dottie tearfully apologised to Hudson for leaving him alone, and begged him to stop acting so strange. They would take him away somewhere if he carried on like that, she warned, but Hudson was not to be frightened or mollified. Nothing could frighten him now after the months with the horned and claw-footed beast with whom they had been living, whose rotting smell still lingered in the air. Hudson dared not mention how he felt, so he raged and sulked, inviting his sisters to comfort and succour him. Dottie was afraid that they would be separated, fostered out to different families. She was working in Woolworth in Vauxhall at the time, and she knew that the pittance she got from there would not be enough to look after all three of them. In any case she was too young to have the legal care of her sister and her brother. The woman from the council told her that.

She had come with news of what Dottie had feared, pulling papers and files out of her case with the sudden whisper of swooping wings. Her eyes ran quickly round the room as she composed herself, taking shallow, silent breaths. Her name was Mrs Brenda Holly, she told them, making them read her name on a card that she showed them, and then smiling and waiting to see if they had an objection to this piece of news. She was a tall bony woman with short red hair and bright blue eyes. There were sharp, longitudinal creases of skin on either side of her lips, like tribal scars. When she smiled, which she did generally and not at any one of them in particular, the creases rippled tremulously, suggesting an uncertainty which her manner belied.

She told them that Sophie was to be sent to a special girls' school in Sussex because she was backward. Hudson was to be fostered out to a family in Dover. Dottie was to be left to fend for herself since she had a job and was nearly eighteen, but she was not to worry because Mrs Brenda Holly herself would come and check that she was all right. It was not that she meant to sound brutal, she told them, dropping her eyes and shuffling the papers in her file, but that she wanted to be honest with them and not pretend anything, because comforting lies were not what they needed. They were poor little mites who had suffered needlessly because of the ignorance of their mother. A mother should love her children without beginning or end, which was not what had happened to them. What a mess they had been left in!

Dottie tried smiles at first but the tall woman was not to be persuaded to go away and leave them alone. Dottie could see that the woman had her papers in front of her, and in them she had written down their lives and what was to happen to them. The smile Mrs Holly gave her was intended to say that Dottie could protest if she wanted, indeed it would be better if she did since that was the decent thing to do, but it would not do much to change things. Life was not like that. Her hands were folded over the file in her lap as she listened to the young woman's unavailing protest. When she had heard enough, Mrs Holly raised both hands suddenly, making Dottie wince with surprise.

The school in Hastings was a reputable place, she said, and quite used to handling children like Sophie. It had made a name for itself, as a matter of fact. She had made a point of checking that they had some experience of foreign girls too, so there was nothing to worry about. She would be looked after and given the rudiments of the skills she required for survival.

The family in Dover was reputable too, and Hudson was very lucky to have been taken by them, Mrs Holly said, raising her hands again to stop Dottie from protesting. The foster father was a headmaster at a local primary school, and the mother was a teacher too. The family had specifically asked for a foreign child. It was not easy to find good foster parents for black boys, and Hudson could not have done better than find such an eminently qualified family to look after him. She might add that Dover was a very interesting place, and so near France.

Dottie pleaded with her, promising that they would manage somehow, asking that the judgment against them be withdrawn. Mrs Holly shook her head and looked away, shutting her eyes firmly for a moment. In the end Dottie screamed the dirtiest abuse she could think of at the social worker. She reached for the papers that the woman cradled so grotesquely in her lap, but Mrs Holly was quicker and clipped Dottie's wrist sharply with the spine of the file. None of Dottie's protests did any good. Mrs Brenda Holly looked hurt and her face went red at the ingratitude, but Sophie and Hudson were still taken away. Dottie thought herself lucky not to have been sent to the police by the bony, red-haired woman who had such power over their lives.

To Dottie's astonishment, Mrs Brenda Holly returned a few days later, accompanied by the Cypriot landlord. He had come to tell her that she would have to move, which was what she guessed as soon as she saw him. She knew her mother had owed him rent, and had heard the man ranting at her, standing at the door in his stylish clothes. She now discovered that her mother had not paid any rent at all, apart from the month in advance that the landlord had demanded at the very beginning. *Nothing at all*, the skinny landlord declared, clapping his hands together and then holding them out to show that they were empty. He nodded his head tragically, asking for Dottie's understanding. Dottie smiled with pride that her mother had not paid the nasty man. The landlord mistook the smile and shrugged to acknowledge the sympathy she was offering him.

'I know you don't have anything to give me,' he said, glancing at Dottie's skinny and undeveloped form. 'But you got to get out of my house. Your family has cost me a thousand pounds already. A mother's memory is sacred so I won't say anything about her. It's a sin against God to abuse the memory of a mother. I know that, you don't have to tell me about that. She carries us for nine months and suffers so we can be born. Then day after day she washes and she cooks, and she cleans and she sews so we can grow up. I know the sacrifice a mother makes, I can tell you that. Whatever a mother does she can never do wrong in the eyes of her child. But I'm a businessman, and if I run my business with my heart I will always be a poor man. So I want you to get out of my house!' The landlord was almost pleading by this stage, and Dottie suspected that the performance was not intended for her but for the social worker. The cringing man disgusted Dottie, but with a victim's intuition she delayed making a reply, driving the landlord into a frenzy of frustrated impatience.

'All right, all right,' he said at last, dropping his voice and straightening himself to his full height. 'Your mother never paid me any rent. When I came here she abused me. The house is like a pig sty. All right, but I'm not without feeling. One day my heart will ruin my business. You can have a room in another house of mine in Balham for a reasonable rent. You can afford it easily if the council gives you a rebate. That's the best I can do. But I want you out of here!'

Dottie nodded at last, and earned an approving little smile from the social worker. That's the way to treat the cringing knave, her smile seemed to say. The landlord raised his eyes to heaven and muttered under his breath.

'There'll be no problem with the rebate,' Mrs Holly beamed at her.

The two sisters and their brother wept bitterly as they were separated. Dottie vowed that she would get them together again soon. But on a Sunday morning in late August, Dottie found herself on her own. With her few belongings tied in bundles like a beggar, she walked from Stockwell to her new room in Balham. The room was in the back of a large terraced house in Segovia Street, gloomy and overshadowed by a huge elm tree. The wallpaper had been stripped, as if in preparation for decorating, but nothing further had been done. There were damp marks on the outside wall and one of the window-panes was broken. The hand basin was cracked, and crusted with green sediment round the base of the taps. A powerful smell of drains filled the room and made her nauseous. Pushed against the inner wall was a metal bed, and hard up against the foot of it was a table and chair. It was like many other rooms they had lived in, bare and damp, with a layer of grime and grease over everything. From the bits of furniture and the walls themselves came soft gasps of despair. Dottie felt their hot breath on her and felt her heart sink with resignation. At least it was big enough, she thought, to have Sophie and Hudson come to stay now and then.

On her first night there, late at night, she heard laughter coming from one of the downstairs rooms. She wedged the door-handle with the chair and pushed the table up against that, barricading herself in. The laughter frightened her, for it reminded her of the drunken revelry that used to take place in their rooms when she was small, the noise of drinking men and the abandoned yells of paid women. That was the music that accompanied them when Sharon was alive, she thought. She always called her Sharon, to her face, when neither Sophie nor Hudson were allowed to. It was a privilege that her mother had foisted on her as an admission of her dependence. She realised as thoughts of her mother started to come back to her that she had not thought very much about her since her death. At first she felt guilt for her neglect, but as the memories came back she knew that she had been expecting her mother's death for months, had been waiting for it, desiring it. Although it was a shock when it came at last, as death always is, and the news filled her with sudden anguish, the need to assuage Hudson's terror had saved her from further thought about her mother.

Now, as she lay listening to the cruel rumbles of men's voices and the infrequent raucous hoots of the woman's laughter, she knew that she had resisted her mother in those last months, had fought off the burden of guilt and shame that Sharon seemed to be wanting to pass on to her. All that talk of Cardiff! All those names that she was to remember! She had paid no attention, remembering instead the countless times her mother had told her, when she was less feeble and crushed, that she should never allow past things to tyrannise her, that religion and culture were stuff and mumbo-jumbo for old people to force those who come after them to toe the line. Yet even as she thought this, she could not prevent herself feeling some blame for the misery of those last years, could not help feeling that there was more she could have done. Perhaps if she had tried harder she could have persuaded her to a hospital. It was wrong of her to feel revulsion, to wish her dead. Dottie's first night in her new room turned out a long and sleepless one. She rose every little while to check that the chair was firm under the handle, and in the end moved her bed up against the table. Also, once she started thinking of her mother she could not stop. Whenever she lay down, after another small adjustment to her barricade, her feelings of guilt instantly returned.

2

True to her word, the social worker came to see her every one or two weeks. At first Dottie said nothing, looking away from the woman with a blank expression on her face, and suffering her fussy ministrations with the dumb surliness of the oppressed. She was afraid of her, as she had been of the teachers and the supervisor at work and the policewoman. They talked to her so firmly, and made her feel silly and inept. It was worse than that, really, she thought. They made her feel dirty: grubby and covered with mud and ochre like the savage. And although she knew nothing, or only a little more than nothing, about her history, she was ready to give it all up to escape that kind of contempt. Somebody else could have all that. Why could she not be the same as everyone else?

While the woman was there Dottie listened to her questions and her words of encouragement without bothering to make a reply. Afterwards, when she had gone, she thought of her own cowardice with remorse and self-pity. The woman made her feel so small and pathetic that she had been ready to feel contempt for what she was, to wish herself one of them. It was wrong of her to wish that, she told herself. It gave in to their injustice of wanting to exclude her, of wanting to make less of her than she already was. She belonged here. So did Sophie and Hudson. And they all belonged as they were. Yet in her heart she had conceded to them, and had agreed to let them make her a foreigner. She tried to remind herself that she belonged here when the supervisor at work was telling her off for sitting down when she was tired. *You people can't be trusted to do anything right.* Dottie tried to take no notice of the she-goat, but she could not help dropping her eyes with shame.

One Saturday in the autumn, the social worker brought news of Hudson. Dottie had been sitting by the window, feeling wretched and alone as she watched leaves torn from the elm tree swirling in the high winds of the season. Mrs Holly said Hudson had started in his new secondary school and was having a good time in Dover. She showed Dottie a letter from the foster mother with a photograph of Hudson on a donkey. Husdon was grinning from ear to ear, holding a stick high in the air as if he was a jockey. The social worker left the photograph behind, saying that it should go in the file really but Dottie could have it for a while. She studied it carefully when she was on her own.

It must have been taken on the cliffs earlier in the summer, she thought, because she could see the sea in the background. The sun was shining, making Hudson squint in one eye as he looked into it. Another boy about Hudson's age was holding the donkey's tether, and he too was grinning. She thought it was a lovely picture and, even though she could not fully dispose of her suspicions that perhaps the photograph had caught the only happy moment Hudson had had since being taken away from London, she could not resist a smile whenever she looked at it. She hid the photograph in the biscuit tin that contained her meagre hoardings, birth certificates and one or two old photographs, hoping that the social worker would forget about it. Mrs Holly did ask for the photograph back but Dottie said she had lost it. The social worker gave her a long look, and then shrugged with exaggerated indifference. Dottie saw the beginnings of a sly, friendly smile on her face and could not supress her own grin.

Mrs Holly had brought with her an abridged copy of *David Copperfield* which she had taken out of the library. She told Dottie the outline of the story, how the unhappy orphan boy was taken in by a relative who lived in Dover and grew up to find fame and fortune. 'Just like Hudson will,' she said, her nostrils flaring with emotion. The book was illustrated, and Mrs Holly opened it on a page that showed a picture of a thin woman chasing a boy on a donkey across the cliff. Behind her the boy David was watching the scene with a comical look of horror on his face.

The picture of Hudson on a donkey made me think of the book. I had a vague memory of that illustration,' the social worker explained. 'And both boys are in Dover.'

'Is that David Copperfield?' Dottie asked, pointing at the picture of the horrified little boy. She smiled as she thought to herself how like Hudson he looked.

'That's better!' cried Brenda Holly. 'You should smile more! Do you know that's the first time I've seen you smile since … oh, I don't know when!'

Dottie wiped the smile off her face and waited for Mrs Holly to go. Once she started the book she read it all the time she could spare: in her room in the evening, on the bus to work and on her way home. There were times when she was so angry with the way that everybody was mistreating David that she shut the book and shook it with frustration. She did not like Mr Micawber one bit, thinking him a useless old man who was always bombasting about things and then getting into debt. She was not too delighted with Emily or Dora either, such useless creatures, although the latter was saved from Dottie's utter contempt because her love for David was so true. She was filled with joy when the poor boy became a rich and famous man. Just like Hudson would. She had had no idea that books contained such riches. It took her a few days to work up the courage, but one Saturday morning after buying her vegetables and meat at the market, she walked across the road and joined the library. She had meant to do this before, and seeing the library there every time she went shopping made it easier in the end.

She borrowed other books by Charles Dickens and was at first delighted by their size. They turned out much more difficult to read than the abridged *David Copperfield*. She tried taking out smaller books but they were just as difficult. In the end she asked the social worker for advice. Mrs Holly flushed with a mixture of pleasure and embarrassment, her smiles jostling with her anxiety about the answer she had to give. She told Dottie that she had found the book in the children's section. Dottie swallowed her pride, and the following Saturday went to the children's section to look for books she could read.

A kind of friendship began to grow between them. Sometimes Mrs Holly rushed in on her way to somewhere, with a small present or just a word of greeting. She found Dottie a better paid job in a factory off Kennington Park Road. She made the Cypriot landlord decorate the room and repair the window. He had, in any case, taken to treating Dottie as one of his charitable enterprises, and brought her gifts of philosophy and whatever worldly wisdom he could spare. He told her his name was Andreas, and he came from a beautiful fishing village not far from Larnaca. He and his brother left Cyprus to make their fortunes. The brother went to Canada and now cleaned toilets in Toronto. Nobody heard anything from him any more. He, Andreas, had become a businessman, with seven houses from Camden to Brixton, and without his help a whole crowd of useless relatives in Cyprus would have to work for a living.

Now and then Andreas brought small things for the room: a framed picture of an Arctic landscape which had been left behind by a tenant in one of his other places, a porcelain figurine of a country girl dancing which he had picked out of builder's rubbish in the street. He never came into the room, but delivered his discourses and his gifts at the door when he came for rent. Before he departed, he usually managed a gallant remark, more as an expression of his virility and manliness than because he admired any of Dottie's meagre attractions. Mrs Holly encouraged Dottie to make the most of the landlord's goodwill, but Dottie found it difficult to overcome her mistrust of him.

With Mrs Holly, sooner or later in their conversations, Dottie would bring up the subject of Sophie and Hudson. When were they coming back? Mrs Holly tried to argue with Dottie, telling her that the present arrangement was for the best, that Dottie should take the opportunity to sort something out for herself instead of looking to shoulder those old burdens. 'Honestly, my love, they are better off where they are,' she pleaded. But she saw the grim look return in Dottie's face and knew they would have to talk again.

Mrs Holly got an invitation for Dottie to spend Christmas with a Quaker family in Wimbledon. They did not know Dottie, they just wanted someone who was on her own over Christmas and who would appreciate company. Dottie refused, saying she wanted to spend Christmas with her family. She was eighteen, she had a good job, a place to live. Why could her brother and sister not come to live with her? Mrs Holly left without a word, leaving her present for Dottie on the chest of drawers as she went out. It was a pair of pillow-cases and a bed-sheet. Inside the folds of the bed-sheet was a Penguin paperback copy of *Brave New World*. She wrote her name proudly in it – Dottie Balfour – and spent a lonely Christmas reading and then re-reading the book, weeping whenever she reflected on the sadness of her life.

By the late spring Brenda Holly was weakening. Dottie had been living on her own for nearly a year, and had shown every sign of being able to cope. In all that time she had not been allowed to see her sister or her brother once. She had not been *allowed*, she reminded Brenda, when there was not one good reason to justify this prohibition. Mrs Holly could not resist in the end, and she arranged for Dottie to visit Sophie in her school in Hastings. The school's matron – matron was preferred to headmistress to emphasise a caring ethos – did not approve of the visit, and only agreed to allow Dottie to come because she was persuaded that the elder sister was on the point of cracking up for a sight of Sophie. The matron thought they had done a good job of saving their charge from the wayward ways of her past, and she did not want her upset by reminders of that life so soon after her redemption. In her Sussex school, Sophie had found God, although she could hardly have missed Him in an institution run by the Church of England. This knowledge of God, however, had not done anything to disturb the normal tranquillity with which she regarded the vicissitudes of life.

The school was a long, converted terrace of small, three-bedroomed houses. Most of the front doors and back doors had been pulled out and bricked up. The doors that remained, one at either end and another one in the middle, had been widened and been made more grand. Above the middle door was a stone plaque carrying the name of the institution, the Archbishop Lanfranc School for Girls, but none of this diminished the appearance the school had of being jerry-built and insubstantial. Rows of small-paned sash windows were fixed at frequent intervals in the brick wall. The small gardens in front of the terrace had been joined together to make a long narrow strip of lawn, cut off from the pavement and the road by an ornamental chain. The front obviously did not receive much sun, for the lawn was bare in places and covered with moss. Dottie had been preparing herself to expect a prison, with blank walls and barbed wire, to be intimidated by guards and iron bars across windows, perhaps even fierce dogs patrolling the courtyards, but was faced instead with this grubby and dingy block that looked more like the offices of a small family business than a prison.

She used the middle door and found herself standing in a cramped hallway with a door leading off on either side. Against the inner wall and facing the front door was a gas fire, burning fiercely and very quickly making Dottie steamy in her damp coat. The door on her right was labelled *Office*, and below that label was another sign that said *Please Knock and Enter*. A notice board beside the door displayed a copy of the fire insurance and details of mustering points in case of fire. An assortment of other notices enjoined their readers to brush their teeth, join the St John's Ambulance, and to be sure to wipe their feet when entering the building from outside. The floor-boards rocked under her feet as she moved forward, and she thought she heard a movement behind one of the doors.

Dottie knocked on the door that said *Office*, and after a moment a short, pleased-looking woman appeared. She smiled brightly, her eyes twinkling as she shook hands and introduced herself as the matron. 'Of course Matron is not my real name. My name is Mrs Temple, but I've given up trying to tell the girls that and now I call myself Matron with what grace I can manage. It's a terrible day for May, isn't it?' she said, unbuttoning Dottie's coat without further ado. Dottie was taken so completely by surprise that she made no protest, and forced herself not to cringe as the Matron's fingers fumbled with the buttons. 'You must've had a terrible journey, my dear. All the way from Sidcup or something, wasn't it? Come in here and sit down in front of the fire. You must be frozen!'

Another gas fire was roaring even more fiercely in the matron's office, in front of which an old and fat corgi was stretched out. The dog turned its head round curiously, then as if it had recognised Dottie it got up and waddled over to greet her. Dottie froze while the dog sniffed round her. 'Go back to sleep, Issy, there's a good boy. Go on, you lazy old brute!' the matron said, leaning down to slap the dog affectionately before pushing it away. 'You wouldn't know it to look at him now but when he was a puppy he had such a fur on him that we called him Isfahan. Like a Persian carpet, you know. Have you ever been to Persia, my dear? My husband went there once, just a private visit. He brought back one of those beautiful rugs from Isfahan. No, Issy, I wasn't calling you. Look at the poor old boy, he's so threadbare and tired. Sit down, my dear. Don't be frightened of him, he's nothing but a big baby. Nearer the fire, don't be shy.'

Having settled her guest comfortably, the matron sighed with satisfaction and offered Dottie a gentle smile. She sat like this for a long moment, her face inscrutable with kindness. Dottie found the pose intimidating, and began to wonder if she was expected to open the conversation. The fire was making her hot and the air in the room was stifling, a fug of dog smells and old carpets, and underneath that just a hint of perfume or medicine. At last the matron smoothed the smile from her face and leaned towards Dottie. 'Now then, you've come to see Sophie, haven't you?' she said. Like someone writing a title at the top of a page and underlining it, Dottie thought. 'She is such a sweet creature, such a friendly, natural child. The other girls have been magnificent with her. They've adopted her as a kind of mascot, I think. She seems to be very popular, and is always surrounded by crowds of them. I thought you might like to know that. At this school we believe that the most effective remedial therapy we can offer our children is affection and care, and we encourage that creed in all the girls at the school. I am glad to say that Sophie has taken to it with pleasure, and has benefited immeasurably from the experience. I know you'll be as pleased with that news as we are.' The matron paused in what she was saying, her eyes smiling distantly.

'Which brings me to what I have to say next,' she continued after a moment. She leaned forward to stroke her dog, which growled playfully as if it had been disturbed in tricky reveries. The matron glanced at Dottie to see if she had noticed Issy's mischief. Then she picked up a file that was lying on a table beside her and opened it. On a label pasted on the front of it were the names Sophie Balfour, written in a large flowing hand. The matron glanced at the label, then put the file down beside her. In the dramatic silence that followed she sat still for a moment, then looked up and started to speak. 'I won't pretend anything with you, and I hope you won't mind what I have to tell you. I was not pleased when I heard from your social worker. I knew that in due course such a meeting as this was bound to take place, but I feel that now is too soon. I think Sophie is doing very well here and I am not convinced that she has had enough time to pull herself together after all those years of being neglected. This is no fault of yours. You yourself were as much a victim as poor Sophie, perhaps even more so. From what Sophie has told me, I can tell you that you have my warmest sympathy. It must have been impossibly difficult for both of you.'

The matron glanced at Dottie's scrawny frame with mild pity, and looked into her eyes briefly before looking away with a sigh. 'I understand why you want to see her. You are her sister, after all, and I can tell you she is terribly excited at the thought of your arrival. None of which is at all surprising, of course. Don't imagine that I am unable to understand that … However, I still feel that for Sophie's good you should make such visits extremely infrequent, until the poor child is completely out of danger. I hope you understand me, my dear, and will see that my sternness is for your sister's own good. And perhaps, if you don't mind my saying so, for your own good too. Your social worker speaks highly of you, but I know that she too is concerned that this meeting is taking place, when your own circumstances are so fraught with uncertainties. Of course, you are not my problem, your sister is. You are probably aware that Sophie is a little backward. This is nothing to be ashamed of. We can't all be the same. She will not become a great inventor or anything wonderful like that even if she stays with us for a hundred years, but there is no reason why, with proper remedial care, she should not be able to learn to look after herself. But she needs expert care! And she needs time! So forgive me, my dear, but I must absolutely insist that your visits, such of them as I may allow, should occur only rarely.'

The matron had got progressively sharper as she spoke, so that when she reached the end of her speech, her teeth were bared slightly and her eyes were flashing with anger. Dottie nodded meekly, although what she wanted more than anything else was to reach across and slap the woman across the face for the cruel things she was saying. She should have somebody *my dear* her while she listened to a sermon about her useless sister and why she should be locked up in a prison and see how she liked it. Dottie kept silent, afraid to reply in case the matron refused to have Sophie meet her. After another moment's silence, the matron shook her head. 'Did you understand what I said to you, my dear?' she asked, her voice a mixture of perplexity and kindness. Dottie guessed that she was not expected to notice the meanness that lurked under the fussy warmth of the matron's manner.

'Yes, ma'am,' Dottie said. She knew more was expected of her, a cringing vow of good behaviour or a promise that she would be good and never trouble the good matron and her school more often than absolutely necessary. As the silence stretched between them, the dog turned nervously round, its eyes large with anxiety.

'Very well,' the matron said, rising abruptly to her feet. She went away to fetch Sophie, leaving Dottie alone with the corgi. The dog growled softly and gave Dottie a wondering look before returning to its slumbers.

Sophie had put on weight in the nine months since Dottie had seen her. That was the thought that flashed through her mind before Sophie threw herself at her with a cry of 'Oh Sis'. Despite the matron's disapproving stare and her attempts to intervene between them, Sophie clung to her sister and sobbed with complete and absurd abandon. When Dottie could find the presence of mind, after Sophie had exhausted the first crescendo of her passion, she moved both of them away from the fire and noticed that the matron and her dog had left the office. They sat on the floor and held on to each other, Sophie weeping bitterly while she told her sister how much she hated the school and how the other girls tormented her. During the day they made her fetch and carry for them. At night, they dressed her in mocking finery and made her into their dark queen. She could not escape them, could not even sit by herself without being bothered. Someone always came by to say something or play with her hair, or make her into a butt of one of their endless jokes.

When the matron returned she brought them two cups of tea, but Dottie was ready for her. She looked the older woman in the eye and allowed her to see all the dislike she felt for her, allowed her to feel the challenge that she was making. 'I want to take my sister away,' she said.

The matron raised her eyes to heaven, and put the cups abruptly down on her desk. 'Come along, my dear,' she said, ignoring Dottie and bustling Sophie out of the room. 'Let's get you back upstairs.'

'I ain't afraid of you,' Dottie said, and saw the matron smile. 'You want to keep her here like a circus animal, but I'll be back for her. Then she can come and live with her family.' Dottie had to wait until the matron returned before she could finish what she wanted to say. 'You're a cruel, bad, bad woman.'

For a moment it looked as if the matron would burst into rage, shout at Dottie or even attack her. She caught her breath and turned red, then slowly her eyes shimmered and the corners of her mouth lengthened. 'Thank you, my dear,' she said, her chin raised and her fists clenched in the effort to control herself. 'If you've quite finished. Your sister is here because she can't manage outside. This is in the judgment of people who are your betters in every respect, and who only have your sister's well-being at heart. They sent her to us because they thought we could be of use. We've done our best to give your sister the help we could and that we thought she needed.'

'No, you're treating her like an animal,' Dottie cried. 'You should ask her …'

'We're doing this out of charity to our fellows,' the matron said, raising her voice and interrupting Dottie, determined to complete what she wanted to say. 'Both for the love of God, who sent His son to redeem us, and for the love of man and the kindliness that we think is proper in his converse with fellow men. We charge no fees and make no profit from this activity, and our institution is governed by the church and funded by the local authority. In your eyes we run a circus, and you think me a cruel, bad person. You are entitled to your opinion in both cases. But by everything you have done, you have revealed nothing so much as your lack of charity and humility, and I regret that you were too old when they found you to be able to benefit from similar preparation as your sister is receiving, if I may say so. I knew this was a mistake. I should never have allowed it. Now if you don't mind, my dear, I must ask you to leave and to make no further arrangements to visit here.'

It was Dottie's turn to smile. 'I'll be back for her,' she said.

3

She gave Mrs Holly no choice when the latter came round. Help me get Sophie back or leave me alone, she demanded. She told her about the speech that the matron had made. Brenda Holly shook her head and sighed, then gave her a knowing, maternal smile. 'There's no need for such ructions, love,' she said. Dottie snorted with contempt, for she could sense that Brenda was not convinced. She told her about the treatment Sophie received at the hands of the other girls, and saw Brenda Holly's face cringe with distaste.

'Are you sure?' she asked.

'We can have a row about it if that'll convince you. Help me get her out of there! Let her come home before they do terrible things to her!' Dottie cried. 'Just you listen to me, there is no one there who cares what a fat black girl feels or wants. Now they dress her up, I don't know what they'll do to her tomorrow.'

'It's all right. It's all right,' Brenda Holly said, taken aback by the tumult, shocked by the feeling in Dottie's words. She wanted to reach out and touch the young woman who was burning up with bitterness and anguish. 'I want to help you, my love, but ...'

'Then let her come home,' Dottie interrupted her, staring at Brenda Holly with a coolness that the latter found painful.

'It's not a joke, you know ... what you're asking for. You can't just do things and undo them like that,' Mrs Holly said, resenting the unspoken accusation. Dottie looked away from her without a word, and they sat silently for a long time before Mrs Holly sighed deeply, then nodded with sudden decision. 'I'll have to look into it,' she said, and saw a small, fragile smile of relief appear on Dottie's face. 'I am sure the matron means no harm, but perhaps the school isn't doing Sophie any good. We can try and find her somewhere nearer, so she can live at home. I thought it would be good for her ...' She stopped and looked at Dottie for a moment.

From the look in her eye, Dottie guessed that she was trying to find words to say sorry, so she smiled and thanked her. Her mind was on the victory she had engineered, and she was not that attentive to the warnings and cautions Mrs Holly was reading out to her. Dottie no longer thought of her as the powerful arbiter of her life, but the decent aberration that even cruel systems throw up. If she was careful, she should be able to use her to achieve her own ends, she thought, and get Sophie and Hudson back so they could all live like a normal, happy family.

After Mrs Holly had gone, Dottie lived again through her moments of triumph, and this time she saw the look of hurt on Brenda's face. As the memory sank in, she thought of the older woman with just a slight stirring of shame in her breast. It had never occurred to her to ask what miseries tormented Brenda Holly's life, or what cares her life imposed on her. Then just as quickly as the thought had entered her mind, she shrugged it off and forced it away.

The weeks of the summer passed slowly, and she knew that Sophie would spend her seventeenth birthday in captivity. That was how she thought of it and, despite her visit to the Archbishop Lanfranc School for Girls, the image that flashed across her mind when she thought of her sister was the same one of prison yard and guard dogs that she had carried with her to Hastings the first time she went there. She would be out by September, Dottie promised herself, and then they would celebrate Dottie's nineteenth birthday together. The thought of her sister's return so filled her days now that her loneliness was close to being unbearable. She was too afraid of her neighbours in the house to speak to them, but she spoke about Sophie's return to some of the women at work. She even told her landlord, who smiled wickedly and said he would have to charge another rent. When Dottie protested, his eyes wandered absently as he gave her body his usual scrutiny. It was obvious that what he saw there did not thrill him, but none the less he made the ritual pass at her. If she felt she needed a bigger room, now that her sister was coming, they could come to an arrangment. He could come by one evening and they could talk all about it.

Dottie spent hours sitting by her window, watching the shadow-play of the leaves on the elm tree and reading. She read with a relish that she found in nothing else. Each new piece of knowledge suggested the next, so she moved from one book to another with the rightness of logical discovery. Sometimes she tried to write down what she had found out, but it took her too long to do this, and even then what she wrote came nowhere near what she wanted to remember from the book she had read. So she took her chances, thinking that in the long run she would retain what her mind found memorable. She wrote down the titles of the books she read in an old exercise book, and took pleasure in this growing list of the trophies that she was collecting from her forays into the fabulous world of books and learning. It was not, she admitted to herself, a very impressive list. She still could not read the large Dickens books she had once taken out of the library, and at times she despaired that she ever would. In her mind that had become the test of her advances. How could she ever think of herself as learning anything when a whole row of large Dickens novels stood on the library shelf, looking down at her? And Dickens was not the only one to mock her with her ignorance. Everywhere she went, everything she did announced her stupidity to her. She did not even know who Archbishop Lanfranc was, or what he did. Everybody else in the country probably did. Nor did she know the meaning or condition of her presence in a place that had no use for her. What did she know, poor Dottie? At least, she consoled herself, she no longer needed to take books out from the children's section. She had learned enough to escape that small indignity.

There were two black men she sometimes saw in the library. One was a short, glistening-black man, round-featured and solemn. He sat at one of the crowded tables near the window, surrounded by large books erected into a shallow, three-sided barricade. He kept his head lowered inside his fortifications, completely absorbed in what he was doing, and only glanced up absently now and then. She took him to be a student of law or medicine, because of the size of the books, but he looked quite old to be a student, and his manner seemed too opinionated for the disciplines she had chosen for him. There was a hopelessness about his appearance, she thought, and his intensity was a kind of play-acting, as if he had already recognised that the odds against him were too high. She felt embarrassed for him, because his busy and arrogant manner was so obviously a fake.

The other black man she saw sometimes was grey haired and old, with large features and tortoiseshell spectacles. He sat at the back of the library, where the fiction shelves faced the sets of encyclopaedias. Whenever she saw him he was reading a news paper, with his coat and hat still on, hunched forward to peer at the print. She stood and watched him one day, pretending to be browsing through the 'T's. He made small movements now and then, as if to intensify concentration. Suddenly he looked up and saw her. His face quivered with surprise, then after a long moment opened in a wide, joyous grin. With obvious effort but none the less surpassing grace, he half-rose from his chair and lifted his hat off to her. She grinned back and fled, filled with confusion. It was the look of pleasure she had provoked on that gnarled old face that had surprised her into panic, because in that sudden warmth in which he had bathed her she knew again her isolation and loneliness.

July had turned into August before the news came that Sophie would be coming home in time to start school in September. Dottie bought a new iron bed for herself, thinking to give the older, sturdier one to Sophie, who needed something stronger for her weight. Brenda Holly donated three saucepans and a motley collection of cups and saucers. The landlord brought Dottie a smoked-glass flower-vase and a jar of crystalline ginger. He also gave her a threadbare old rug he had picked out of a heap left for the dustmen. Dottie begged him for a cooker, saying that the hot-plate was next to useless, and she had nearly killed herself switching it on. And could they not have a comfortable chair in the room? After much resistance the landlord turned up with a Baby Belling, which he wired up himself. She flattered him shamelessly, in the hope of getting more furniture out of him, but he reminded her that, despite his undeniably powerful feelings, he was a businessman. More furniture would mean more rent.

When the day of Sophie's return finally arrived, Dottie wanted to go back to Hastings and collect her herself, so she could stare the matron in the face and tell her that she had kept her word. Archbishop Lanfranc would be ashamed of you and your school, if he were to come upon this prison you run in his name, she would be tempted to say. You are nothing but a joke, Matron Temple. She knew Brenda Holly would not sympathise with her gloating fantasies, so she tried to make an outing out of it, affecting a tone of girlish innocence. It was a lovely day, Dottie said, just right for a train ride down to the sea-side. I don't really know Hastings. It's a very pleasant town, I hear, and so near France. Brenda Holly looked wise and shook her head. She thought the matron deserved better than that, and suggested that they leave her to make the travel arrangements herself. Dottie admitted to herself afterwards that she probably would not have been able to say all she wanted to the matron anyway. They met Sophie at Victoria and took her home in a cab. It was the first time either of the two sisters had ridden in a London cab.

4

'Now we'll have to get Hudson out,' Dottie said to Sophie later that night. She explained how they had to be careful not to panic Brenda by making too many demands at once, that they had to show her they could manage first. She showed Sophie the photograph of Hudson on a donkey and they laughed so much at the look of happiness on the boy's face. 'Let's get him back soon, Sis,' Sophie cried, rocking herself slightly from side to side. Later, when they were lying in their beds in the dark, Dottie asked her if she was all right. After a silence, during which Dottie had begun to think that her sister had fallen asleep already, Sophie answered that she was very happy, because now she was home. The last few weeks had been difficult ... waiting for the day. No, she said to Dottie's question, she had had no trouble with the matron, and the other girls had been very kind, saying how sorry they were to see her go, because she was always a good laugh. The gardener's boy had pestered her, saying that she should come and visit him in the shed before she left. One day he surprised her on the far side of the playing field and became rough with her.

Dottie shut her eyes in the dark and held her breath. 'What happened? What do you mean rough?' she asked gently, trying not to frighten Sophie into silence.

'He was squeezing me and trying to push me on the ground.' Sophie chuckled in the dark. 'I screamed. Just like Hudson used to do ... with my eyes shut.'

'And arms waving?' Dottie asked, already laughing.

'Yes, everything. When I opened my eyes he was gone. The next time I saw him I threw a stone at him and he ran away. But he said he'd get me one day. He'd bring his friends ...'

'Hush!' Dottie whispered. 'You're home now.'

Many other stories about the school surfaced in the days and weeks that followed, describing small misuses and abuses of other victims as well as Sophie. Dottie felt they vindicated the urgency with which she had sought Sophie's return. She was not slow to tell Brenda Holly this, and to use it as the pretext for reopening her campaign to win back Hudson. Brenda smiled and blew Dottie an affectionate kiss. 'You're a wily little devil, but it won't work. We've had an excellent report on Hudson … I told you about it.'

'That was last year,' Dottie interrupted. 'You don't know what's been happening to him since then.'

'We would've heard if anything had happened. He's in a good home … and he's lucky to be there,' Mrs Holly said, raising her voice to stop another interruption that she could see coming. 'You've got enough troubles as it is, and there is no sense at all in looking for more. Now listen to me, my dear, you know I'm on your side. You've got a lot of things to sort out here. Take my advice, and try and make things better for yourselves first. Sophie needs all the help you can give her … and I think it's best for Hudson to be where he is.'

Dottie smiled mirthlessly. She did not say anything, because she did not need to remind Brenda Holly that that was what she had said about Sophie. It was obvious from the obstinate look in Dottie's eyes that this was only the opening skirmish in a long campaign.

The Maiden's Return

1

The landlord smiled when he saw Sophie. His eyes, which normally clambered graspingly over everything, softened and melted. 'This is the little sister. We've been waiting for you for a long time! You've grown up, darling,' he said, talking to her as if he had known her all her life. He took her hand and patted it with affection. When Sophie smiled, the landlord hunched his shoulders up playfully, pleased that he had amused her. He looked around for somewhere to sit, but there were only the beds. He drew Sophie with him to one of them, gently tugging her hand to make her follow him. When they were sitting, he held her hand in both of his, stroking her as he talked. 'Are you happy to be home? Does your sister look after you all right? You tell me if she doesn't. If you need anything, just ask for it, darling.'

Sophie nodded and glanced at Dottie, who was standing by the door watching the landlord. Usually they talked at the landing, unless there was cause to invite him in to witness some new dereliction that needed repair, but he had slithered past her as soon as he caught sight of Sophie. Dottie's instinct would have been to step in between them at once, to chase the predatory man away from Sophie. Her body was poised to move forward, but she could see that Sophie was amused by the attention the man was paying her, and the landlord seemed genuinely pleased to meet her.

Dottie rocked back on her heels, studying the small, skinny man who had filled her with such loathing the first time she met him and wondering that Sophie was not frightened of him. His features had something of the starved, malformed child, she thought, which gave his face a look of physical fragility, so that despite his indisputable greed and cynicism, and the constant tokens of his lust, there remained traces of child-like innocence in his appearance. The landlord smiled, and Dottie saw his teeth bared in a kind of grimace and his skin crease across his shrunken face. It made her shudder to think of any kind of intimacy with him.

'Do you like going to the cinema?' he asked Sophie, his eyes consuming her with a look of agony.

'I love to!' Sophie said, her face bursting into smiles. 'But I haven't been for a long time. Sometimes at the school they showed us a film.'

'Haven't been? Don't you worry, my darling. Next time I come for you. And you can have chocolate and ice cream. You like chocolate?' the landlord asked eagerly. He leant forward and nearly fell on Sophie, hardly able to contain his passion.

'Excuse me, Mister Landlord!' Dottie shouted.

'All right, all right,' the landlord said, grinning with triumph and keeping his eyes on Sophie. 'You call me Andy, you understand? Andreas. But you call me Andy, anytime.'

'Please take your rent,' Dottie said, holding the money out and wanting him to leave.

'You can come too,' the landlord said, his look changing to mischief as he spoke to Dottie. He rocked from side to side, holding his arms out at half-cock in an absurd display of his manliness. 'Or if you need anything for the room, or a little present or something like that. What's the matter? Don't I bring you lots of presents? You can trust me, darling. Anything you like. I can give you a lift to work sometimes … maybe if we have another bus strike like this one. What a strike, eh? The Englishman doesn't want to work any more. He just wants to rule the world in peace, and have a full belly and be civilised. He brings in niggers like you from Jamaica to do the dirty work. Everywhere you go you see them: Stockwell, Hackney, Tottenham. Last week I went to see my brother-in-law in Margate and I saw one nigger there. It is a big surprise to me to see a nigger in Margate. English busmen go on strike for three weeks, and their brothers bring in the niggers to take their jobs. Capitalists have no … mercy,' he said, frowning for a moment as he searched for the right word. He took the rent money from Dottie and counted it while he talked, glancing at Sophie now and then in anticipation of the pleasures to come.

'They will be sorry, these Englishmen,' he said. 'I'm telling you that. Maybe now they can get the buses running without paying big wages … but what about later? What will they do with these nigger people? These are dangerous people, I don't have to tell you. They will steal white women, and rob the Englishman's house. They are criminals. England will be ruined. They make everything dirty. I have some of these Jamaican niggers living in my house in Brixton. A nice house before I take them in! I take pity on them. Everywhere they go the landlords say no. No Dogs, No Children, No Niggers. They come to me, and I take them in. As you know, my one problem is too much feeling. I can't shut the door on this homeless people. I can't tell them to live in the street. But they turn my house into an African village. They cook in the hall, they hang their washing out of the window. The garden they make into a backyard and they throw rubbish into it. The toilet is no good now. Too full, too much … dirt. Every time I go there they are drinking and beating each other. I'm afraid to collect rent for my own house!'

Dottie swallowed but did not know what to say. It seemed cowardly not to speak. She was not a Jamaican, and she had not met any yet that she knew of. She had not seen the landlord's house in Brixton, and she could not just accuse him of lying. She had seen enough squalor in her own life to find his description quite believable. None the less she was pained by what the man was saying. It was that way of talking about people like her, for she knew that *Jamaican niggers* could be effortlessly stretched to include her, as if they were primitive and criminal, only capable of soiling and destroying whatever they had anything to do with. How could that be true?

'Don't worry, darling,' the landlord said, seeing the misery on Dottie's face. 'You're not very black, not like them Jamaican niggers.' He retreated hastily when he saw the look on Dottie's face. For a moment he seemed puzzled, then shrugged and laughed good-naturedly, and called out a farewell to Sophie.

2

Dottie had heard people at the factory talking like that, although most of them treated the arrival of the black workers as something of a joke. She thought they pitied themselves, like condemned prisoners who were resigned to their fate but tried to keep their spirits up with humour. The women she worked with made remarks about finding themselves a decent dancing partner at last, or made crude jokes about warming their beds with *one of 'em buck niggers*, and availing themselves of their giant physiques of global fame. They told stories and anecdotes of their brushes with these creatures. A couple of black men, for example, turned up at a local dance and tried to find themselves a partner. They were saved from injury by the manager, who intervened to stop what he could see his regular patrons planning. The manager suggested to the two men that next time they should bring black women, for white women found their odour offensive. Another of the women at the factory told a story of a black boarder that her aunt had taken in. One of her rules was no guests, and she could always tell if anyone was breaking the rule because her living room was by the stairs. After several weeks of suspicion – the noise of a creaking bed was unmistakable in a small house – she caught her black boarder smuggling his woman in, carrying her up the stairs on his back.

Yet many of the women had also been pleasant to Dottie, and even as they told their stories they smiled to reassure her. *Let them come, I say. They can't be worse than this lot we've been lumbered with for donkey's years. I don't expect they'll be any better, and I don't expect they'll be any worse. Just the same effin' buggers that men always is, pardon my French.*

The men were inclined to be more serious, shaking their heads at the ignorance and equanimity of the women. Given half a chance they began quoting tales of their wanderings with the forces, when they had seen the shocking propensities of black men and brown men in their natural state. They told stories of whole gangs of labourers falling asleep under trees when left unsupervised, of teeming populations whose slowness of understanding staggered the imagination. They described the deep cunning of these sullen peoples, their incredible strength, which combined with a brutish nature made the nig-nog something of an unpredictable handful. So sure were these men of their judgment and understanding that they did not think to drop their voices for fear of being overheard by anyone who might know better or who might feel forced to take issue with their summaries. They nodded sagely at their words, gathering into a huddle to comfort each other with presages of doom.

'I couldn't agree with you more,' one of the charge-hands said. 'Not that I have anything against them personally.' His name was William Hampshire and he liked to think of himself as a decent man who took everything with a healthy dose of scepticism. People he worked with sometimes spoke of him as a philosopher, and he always tried to be wise whenever he made a contribution to a conversation. No one took any liberties with him to his face, yet quite evidently there was nothing frightening in his manner or appearance. He was short and plump, and when he smiled, the light twinkled off the lenses of his dark-rimmed spectacles and his soft cheeks glowed. His hair was slicked back stylishly, but with enough exaggeration to suggest self-mockery. The women were fond of him because he was polite and gentle, and could put up with any amount of teasing. And because they took pity on him. He was close to fifty and still lived with his mother, and rode to work on a moped. Hampshire had not been out of England in his life and saw nothing to be ashamed of in that.

He had spent the war years as a clerical officer at the Moorfield Hospital, first in the ambulance station and then in the sterilising unit. When he was called up, he told the recruiting office straight out that if they put him in a combat unit he would declare himself a conscientious objector and go to jail if necessary, so they made him a medic and posted him to the Moorfield, if that was all right with him.

He was not afraid to say that he was more comfortable in the company of women than men, and he had unconsciously adopted their gestures and mannerisms. To someone who did not know him, his bearing would have seemed like an inept parody of effeminacy. He tossed his head when he was irritated, and he had a habit of holding his arm out when he was in a hurry, as if he was lifting up a skirt that was impeding his calves as he swept out of the room. When he had to say anything unpleasant, he lifted his chin and raised his eyes towards the ceiling, so he would not have to look at his listeners. He did this as he spoke about the black workers, looking away from Dottie who was standing on the edge of the group.

'Not that I have anything against them personally. For all I know they are fine people,' he said. 'If you like that sort of thing. And of course, there are plenty of people who think they can handle them, who think they understand their natures. But their methods are not the kind that I would want to see practised in England. All that colour bar, and reservations and identity cards business. I have no time for colonials, anyway. Lord Muck riding the range and swopping wives with his neighbour. They give themselves such airs when everybody knows they are not the genuine article. Quite honestly, though, I don't see why we are bothering with these coloured workers. We're only making a rod for our own backs. Haven't we done enough to help them already? Can't we look after ourselves for a change? If it was up to me I'd send them all home tomorrow.' The men around him chuckled, sympathising perhaps but also knowing that such solutions were not possible for Britain. The Germans or the French or other foreigners might do that kind of thing, but the British, bloody-minded though they were, did not chase people out of their country.

Dottie had been on buses with the new conductors, and she had seen them laugh and chat with the passengers as if they had done this all their lives. To see people talking to them so comfortably made Dottie wonder if it was the friendliness of the passengers that was a hoax or if the people she worked with were unusually gloomy and critical. Perhaps the passengers were lulling their guests with conversation in order to laugh at them more fully. She overheard some of the questions the conductors had to answer, and they made her cringe, but they sounded more ignorant than anything else. *Barbados? Do you have houses there?* The conductors laughed and chatted. Did they know what was being said about them?

She did not see where these fears of the black men turning to criminals came from. They were just making a living. Only the other day she had seen in a newspaper that hundreds of thousands of people had left England in the last year to find a better life in America and Australia and South Africa. Hundreds of thousands! In the same year, hundreds of thousands of others had left Italy and Holland and Germany to seek a better life in other people's countries. How was it that a few hundred busmen from the West Indies or some Indian or Pakistani cloth-workers in Bradford or Blackburn was a national catastrophe? This seemed absurd to her. She suspected that if she tried to say this to them, she would not have the words to say it right. She had no education, and if she got something wrong they would only make her feel her ignorance, rub her face in it. What could she say to them? They loved to see themselves as the long-suffering, put-upon victims of her kind of people: heathens and menials who were nothing but trouble from the day Europeans ran across them living in a tree and chucking fruit at each other. After all the sacrifices the English had made for them, all they could think of was to come to England to wring the last drop of blood out of Britannia's withered dugs. No wonder people were emigrating.

3

Sophie's new school was in Wandsworth, and for the first few mornings Dottie took her all the way there. It was a special school for slow people who could not read and write, Brenda Holly had said, hesitating and looking stricken before choosing *slow* out of the range of words available to her. Sophie hated it, but the sisters talked it over between them and decided that it would do her good if she stayed there until she had learned to read and write properly, or, if she got too fed up, until they could get Hudson home. Dottie took Sophie to the library to show her the books she would be able to read once she had mastered the art, and told her of the treasures that lay hidden in them. She thought it would encourage her, and perhaps also she wanted to show off her knowledge.

Dottie herself went to the library regularly, and found comfort and virtue in both the place and the self-discipline of her observances. Sometimes she just looked at the books and got nowhere, looking and looking because she had nothing else to do. She wondered if the women working in the library, who mostly looked as if they had a heavy enough burden to carry, minded people like her, people who wandered aimlessly among the shelves, sheltering from the desert winds. What did they call people like her? Customers? Punters?

Often the old black man was sitting at his usual place, stroking his white beard and poring over the newspaper.

He looked out for her, she knew that now. When he saw her he rose to greet her in his habitual way. One day he lifted up the newspaper and pointed to a headline which read: Army Loses Control in Algeria. His face was radiant with triumph. He pointed to the headline again, grinning and shaking his head. She nodded as if she understood what he meant, and promised herself that she would look up the place in the encyclopaedia when the old man was not around. They saw him in the street sometimes. His eyes always sought out Dottie, even though the two sisters now went everywhere together. He made no attempt to speak to them or to extend their acquaintance in any way. When they passed in the street he paid his homage in the same extravagant way: a small bow and a raised hat. When she was on her own, sometimes, he tilted his neck forward and dropped his head a little, in a gesture that looked painful and penitent.

Dottie wondered what he would have looked like as a young man. He was still tall and upright, although he walked with a stick and took slow, careful steps. It was the joy in his smile and the genial light in his eyes that she found so overwhelming. He was her true fantasy of a grandfather, she thought. She could not imagine what could make a man like him take notice of her.

She mentioned him to Brenda and saw her eyes dart with suspicion. Brenda Holly did not say anything at first, but Dottie could see that it was only with an effort that she prevented herself from doing so. Her face turned queasy with worry, making Dottie laugh. The more she heard, though, the more Mrs Holly became reassured and interested. In the end, she took command of the conversation and asked many questions, and was free with her advice. 'I should think he's an old soldier or a sailor. I wonder where he lives. Did you see which direction he went? There's an old people's home down towards Nightingale Avenue. Do you think he's some kind of a war veteran? You should speak to him next time you see him. He's probably lonely and could do with a bit of company. I wonder why he treats you like that. Oh you must speak to him, Dottie.'

Dottie had no intention of speaking to him. The old man overawed her, and had honoured her with his greeting. She wanted to know nothing more about him. She did not want to find out that he was an old soldier or sailor who had led a wandering life of wretchedness and penury. She did not want to be misunderstood, or to find herself burdened. She wanted him as he was, a grand old man whom she met in the street or the library, and who greeted her with friendship when he saw her. If she sought the meaning of his mystery, she would only discover that he was less than she was able to imagine for him.

Then, in the deep midwinter of 1958, for three consecutive weeks, his chair was empty. She asked one of the women librarians if she knew the old black man who usually sat at the table between fiction and the encyclopaedias reading the paper.

'Dr Murray? He collapsed in here about a month ago,' the librarian whispered. 'Sitting there reading the paper as usual. The ambulance came for him, but it was too late. He died in hospital on the same day.'

Dottie stared at the woman in disbelief. 'Here?' she asked, her senses whirling. Tears filled her eyes, and she felt the strength leaving her body. Without warning or thought, she started to sob for her bereavement. She gritted her teeth and covered her face, muffling the sound of her weeping with her hands. The librarian touched her on the shoulder, whispering urgently beside her, agitated with embarrassment. She took her to an inner office and gave her a glass of water, and apologised for her clumsiness. She told Dottie that Dr Murray had had a practice in Clapham, and lived in a large house overlooking the Common. That was all she knew about him, except that he had had a daughter who was a teacher, and who had been killed during the war-time bombing. If she wanted to know more there was bound to have been an obituary in the local paper for such an eminent man. When they looked they found no obituary, and the librarian knew nothing more. She was very sorry, as if in some way the omission was hers.

Every time Dottie went to the library that winter she thought of the old man. She thought of the daughter as well, and imagined that in some way she had reminded the old doctor of his child. Whenever she went to the library in those months, she felt the absence of the old man's affection in the midwinter cold. Sometimes she thought of that other old man in Cardiff, whose daughter had disappeared to God knew where. She thought of him with guilt and apprehension, as if one day he would find her and scold her for not seeking him out. Perhaps he was dead too, or had forgotten his wayward daughter many years ago. The thought of her ignorance of the old people her mother had left behind tortured her in the weeks after Dr Murray's cruel death, but the time passed and, in the end, the pain left her too. There was little enough she could do about any of it, even if she had wanted to.

Brenda Holly thought she understood something of the way that Dottie felt, and assumed that the old doctor had made her feel her lack of parents and relatives. In truth, she too was intrigued by the thought of a black doctor living on the edges of Clapham Common. Mrs Holly thought of herself as a liberal woman, and would not have been too surprised to find herself accepting a black doctor as her GP, but she found it harder to think that such a GP would have found enough patients for a practice forty or so years before, during England's dark ages. She made some enquiries. First of all, she asked her colleagues and her 'cases.' Had anybody heard anything about a black GP who used to have a practice in the area? None of them knew anything, but they promised to ask. Eventually something turned up at a British Legion gathering, where the mention of Dr Murray's name elicited a surprised response from the president of the women's section. She was the wife of a local banker, and had herself been a teacher when she was younger. Both she and her husband were now retired and living in Lavender Hill, but they remembered the doctor quite well.

Dr Murray had had a practice in Wimbledon, it turned out, although the story about the large house by Clapham Common was also true. The teacher and her banker husband had lived in Bromwood Road. It was a pleasant, leafy street then. The school was at the bottom of the road in Chestnut Grove, and the house was handy for the bank as well, which was on the corner of the High Street and Stonehouse Street. Dr Murray's daughter had been a pupil at the school, a tall slim girl with a pouty mouth which gave her a look of misery and sullenness. She was very well mannered, though, and was a genius with the flute. She could play several instruments but the flute was her best. The teacher remembered the tall, black man who used to come to the school concerts that the girl took part in. He had such a presence that eyes were always drawn to him, but *he* only appeared to have eyes for his daughter, whom he watched with a mixture of concern and pride. He had been a bones doctor, with a clinic of his own. He was very glamorous, and his speech even had a hint of a French accent. The teacher thought his practice must have been quite successful, at least to judge by appearances.

Oh no, the daughter had not been killed, the teacher said. She had become a school teacher too and moved north before the war started. It was the doctor's wife who had died in the bombing. She was a young woman, a second wife. She remembered the doctor had married again in his fifties. It was she who had been killed visiting relatives somewhere near the coast, near Portsmouth or Southampton. The teacher could not be sure, but she thought there was a young child who had also died with the mother.

How odd, the teacher said, to find herself talking about that family again! There was something about them that was touched with sadness. The man, despite his charismatic appearance and the arrogant tilt of his head, had an air about him that the teacher could only remember as a kind of weakness, although she no longer knew why. Perhaps it was because he had a look of pain sometimes, as if his thoughts caused him misery. And there was the young wife who had died with her child, and who herself would not have been more than a child to the doctor. Her death was one of many at that time, but each death was as tragic as if it was the only one.

The teacher felt sorry for the daughter most of all. It may only have been because she knew her best, but it was she who seemed the worst off of that family. She was good natured enough, but she was withdrawn and silent the way a child her age should not have been. Her mother was already dead then. After a long moment of silent thought, the teacher said, 'There was something odd about that girl. You could see it around her mouth, so much seemed to hurt her. Perhaps some of the teasing used to distress her, you know how unfeeling children can be. She was tall and thin, with large eyes and that surly mouth ... and, of course, she was a coloured girl. They used to rib her about that but there was no malice in it.'

Brenda Holly could not believe her luck. She raced to Dottie with the story, as if it was a gift she was taking to her. Dottie must look like the daughter. She must have reminded the old doctor of his child. Perhaps something bad had happened between them, perhaps when Dr Murray married again the daughter had felt rejected. Maybe they were not even in touch, had cut each other off in their pride and hurt. Families often behaved like that. 'Oh, isn't it fascinating!' Mrs Holly cried. 'The daughter probably had no idea that her father was dying. She could be a rich woman and not know it. Just think! She'll feel terrible when she finds out!'

4

In the silence that followed the story, it was Brenda Holly who first mentioned Hudson. She said his name and then wrote down his foster parents' address. When she gave it to Dottie, the latter snatched at it ravenously. 'Perhaps you should get in touch. I'm sorry if it seemed cruel but I thought it would be best for him to forget about you for a while. I thought it would help him settle in his new place ... and give you a chance too. We talked about it at the office and decided that this was the best way. You were so tense and unhappy ... I was afraid for you,' Mrs Holly said, her eyes on the brink of tears. 'You've done wonderfully well since then, you really have! I can see it ... and I can see how much happier Sophie is compared to the way she was when she first came back. Forgive me if I seemed cruel. I did it for the best.'

'You could've let him visit,' Dottie said, dropping her voice because of the misery on Brenda Holly's face. You talked about it at the office, did you? You put your professional heads together and decided to smash up our family, she thought. A part of her was already jumping for joy, and did not mind giving what comfort Brenda desired to receive in her surrender. Another part of her was hardening against Mrs Holly, and wanted to cause pain for the pain she had suffered. 'What right did you have ...?'

'He was lucky to have such foster parents,' Brenda Holly said, plaintive in her defence. 'Their advice was that we should give him time. I suppose ... I was surprised that you wanted him back so much. Most people in your place would have been grateful for the respite. That was what I thought, anyway.' Mrs Holly waited to see if Dottie would say anything, if she would blame her again, but Dottie just shook her head, not trusting herself to speak. 'I still think it was the right thing to do, and I hope you'll agree later,' Mrs Holly said, and when Dottie still made no sign she sighed with defeat. 'I'll get in touch with the foster parents and begin the process of having Hudson returned to you if that is what you would like. It will take a while ... perhaps until the summer. It may be best to wait until the end of the school year.'

Dottie did not want to wait, not for one more day. Had she not been waiting long enough? In the months of silence, she had not been allowed to write, at the request of the foster parents, Brenda Holly said. They thought Dottie's letters might stir him up, and wanted him left to them long enough so he would forget his real family. No, it was not right to expect her to wait even more, not while Hudson was being stolen from them under their very noses. But Mrs Holly had come round so completely that she thought it best not to antagonise her, not to give her cause to become indignant and unhelpful.

'Yes, I think that will be best,' Dottie said. 'Let's aim for the summer. It will give us time to prepare for his arrival. We'll have to get ourselves organised. Sophie'll be delighted.'

Brenda Holly looked at her young charge for a long moment. Dottie expected her to say something affectionate, as she would usually have done, but she did not. In the end she nodded, as if she understood something or had made a decision. Then she smiled, but it was a tired, self-mocking smile. 'I hope I'm doing the right thing,' she said. 'It's not only you I'm worried about. I don't know if it's the right thing for Hudson either.'

'Don't worry about us,' Dottie said, turning away and failing to catch a look of hurt surprise. Brenda Holly opened her mouth to speak, to protest at the abrupt manner in which Dottie had pushed her away, but in the end she said nothing. Dottie would get over it, she thought. Her bitterness was understandable. It could not possibly have been addressed at her. They were good friends and Dottie depended on her.

5

The landlord was sceptical when he first heard about Hudson. 'All of you in one room?' he asked. The problem did not really engage him, although the thought of a brother sharing a room with two grown-up sisters aroused his interest. He suggested they might consider renting another room but was not surprised to find them reluctant. They were not much more than paupers, after all. If it had not been for his warm heart, and his dependence on the good-will of the social worker who could have caused him trouble with other tenants, they would have been out on the streets by now. In any case, he was more intent on paying court to Sophie than in talking about Hudson.

His pursuit of Sophie was casual but insistent. He asked about her, brought her small presents, chocolate or candy, and always managed to hold her hand or stroke her cheek. Dottie had thought of putting a stop to it, but Sophie seemed to enjoy the attention and the landlord was never difficult. He stopped as soon as Dottie told him he had gone far enough, and laughed happily at the warnings that Dottie issued to him. She had taken him out on the landing one day, and told him in no uncertain terms what she would do to him if he tried anything funny with her sister – she'd call the police – but he had laughed at her threats, waving her away. Dottie tried to talk to Sophie, not wanting to be heavy-handed with her but afraid that her sister's innocence would leave her vulnerable to the predatory man. But Sophie smiled with embarrassment. 'Oh Sis,' she said.

'If you need help or something like that when your brother comes, we could arrange something,' the landlord said, making comic faces of lust at Sophie. Sophie laughed at his crude advances, but Dottie only gave him an angry frown, which made the landlord shrug with indifference.

Dottie wrote a letter to Hudson, reading out each sentence to Sophie before moving to the next, in case she wanted to add anything. They were careful not to mention his return, but gave him several large hints. Mrs Holly had insisted that Hudson should be told nothing until a definite decision had been made. She had thought of asking to see the letter before they sent it off, but her nerve had failed her. She was a little afraid of Dottie now, she realised. She did not want the young woman to dislike her or think ill of her. She found herself becoming self-conscious about visiting, deliberately perking up her manner to seem cheerful when before she would have breezed in without a thought. Whenever she said anything, she watched more carefully for Dottie's response. She asked more questions, wanting to find out what Dottie thought, how she felt about things.

Brenda Holly smiled at herself when she reflected on this. She had taken the girl for granted, and assumed that her silences and acquiescence were a kind of deference to her, and perhaps even affection. Once she had learned to see, she could not avoid noticing the way Dottie's eyes glazed over whenever she did not want to listen. She felt the biting rejoinder thrown casually over one shoulder now, when before she would have talked over it, drowned it with the noise of her voice and her sensible advice. It was a small crisis, she thought, and she just needed to keep her wits about her. Her confidence had gone, that was all, and she was being over-sensitive. Everything felt like that, since the news of her husband's illness. It was unprofessional of her to allow her life to interfere but she could not help it. She felt indescribably tired. At times it was hard enough to persuade herself to take any interest at all in her cases, which was a terrible state to be in.

Dottie noticed some change in Brenda Holly's manner, but was not attentive enough to plumb its meaning. She took her friendliness to be a kind of bond that the decision to return Hudson had forged between them, or even a relief that the boy would be returning to his family. Dottie was inclined to prefer Brenda like this, and she was grateful that she cared for them as she did, even if at times in the past she had been hard and unfeeling. 'We could've done much worse than this,' Dottie said to her sister. 'She talks too much sometimes but she's all right. To begin with she used to interfere too much ...'

'She's very strict,' Sophie said in her playfully exaggerated voice of awe. 'I wonder she don't frighten you.'

'Like the matron?' Dottie asked, and smiled to see Sophie's playful look of fear turn to a parody of terror as she rolled her eyes and wobbled her jowls. 'Brenda's bark is worse than her bite. She gave me most of these books, you know, and she helped me in a lot in other ways.'

Dottie looked at her small pile of books with pleasure. Among them were one or two she had bought for herself from the second-hand stall in the market. She had not had much luck with those yet, going more for the size than what was in them. She had acquired a book called *Far Away and Long Ago*, which she had taken at first to be a collection of fairy stories, but which she discovered to be something unreadable about cattle ranching in Argentina. She bought another book called *Officially Dead*, which had tempted her because it told the story of a man who was thought to have been killed by the Japanese in the fighting in Burma but turned out to be alive and in hiding from enemy soldiers. She had read that in great haste, wanting to get to the heart of the matter, to know how the man would have felt when he discovered his own death. But the moment never came, or if it did it passed her without being in any way remarkable. She must have missed it, she realised. Her latest purchase was the *Collected Poetical Works of Sir Walter Scott*. She knew about Sir Walter Scott because she had read an abridged copy of *Ivanhoe* in her children's library period. This was her first poetry book, and she had stood a long time at the stall, wondering if she should get it. She had been seduced in the end by its size, and by the message inside that read: *With love, From Uncle Bryan to Irene, 1893*. At a shilling, it was worth rescuing that affection from the junk barrow in Balham market.

Dottie saw that her sister's eyes had turned glassy with all the talk about books. It was a shock for a moment because it reminded her so powerfully of Sharon, her mother. She had done that whenever she disapproved of something, and Dottie knew that Sophie disliked all the fuss about books. At first Dottie had tried to persuade her, to show her the pleasure she had found in them. Sophie had gone along with it for a while but had silently rebelled in the end by just not reading the books that Dottie spent hours choosing for her in the library. She smiled now as she watched her sister's ostentatious show of indifference. Sharon would have turned round and laughed, she thought, having made her point. Sophie waited, her head turned slightly away, waiting for Dottie to release her.

'She helped me find work too,' Dottie said brightly. 'And she used to come round to cheer me up. She didn't make any fuss, but would turn up some evening, just like that. I remember she came one night when I was feeling low, and she took me out for a walk. Down the road and back, but it helped to lift the misery a little.'

'Will she help *me* get work?' Sophie asked. 'I'm just wasting my time in that school, Sis. Better I go to work and earn something. We'll need things for Hudson soon, you know that.'

'Oh Sophie, you must learn first, otherwise everything is a waste of time,' Dottie pleaded, but saw the distant look return in Sophie's eyes. They had already spoken about this several times, and although on each occasion Dottie had argued Sophie to a standstill she knew that she had not won her over. It made her laugh to herself to see the stubborn way Sophie pressed her lips together. 'But if you really want to leave, then we'll try and find you work.'

Sophie clapped her hands with joy and rushed at her sister, who tried to dodge her powerful embrace but failed. Sophie's birthday was in May, and they decided that that would be the best time for her to leave, so that her departure would endanger the prospect of Hudson's return as little as possible.

'I'll be eighteen in May, Sis,' Sophie said, laughing at the thought. 'And I'll be working in a factory to help you look after Hudson. He'll be so surprised to see how we've changed! Do you think he'll be grown-up?'

'I should think so,' Dottie said, feeling uncomfortable with the authority she was required to display. Sophie was in one of her childish periods, putting on baby voices and pouting over everything. It was disconcerting when it happened, because Dottie was not always sure if Sophie was playing. 'He is fourteen now. He is probably a big, tall boy with a deep voice. You won't be able to cuddle him all the time like you used to.'

'Why not?' Sophie asked, her face stricken with misery.

'Because he won't let you.'

'He will!' Sophie cried.

'And because you've grown too,' Dottie said. Sophie had not lost the weight she had put on at prison-school, but had redistributed it on her body in a way that made her seem decidedly a grown woman. She drew looks wherever they went – admiring glances whose meaning she did not always understand. She took these small gestures of homage men were ready to pay her as disinterested acts of kindness.

The weeks passed and no word came from Hudson. Dottie questioned Brenda Holly, her mind troubled by suspicion and anxiety. Was everything going well? The foster parents weren't making trouble, were they? Brenda smiled and told her that she had received a letter from the foster parents agreeing to the move. Not that there was anything they could do about it, Dottie declared. *Was there?* Brenda smiled at the uncertainty in Dottie's voice, then she shook her head. She did not tell Dottie that the foster parents also said that Hudson did not want to return. They did not want Mrs Holly to misunderstand them, and assume that their letter was a stratagem to hang on to Hudson, but she should know that the boy was violently opposed to leaving Dover.

There was no need to upset Dottie yet, Brenda thought, suppressing her own unease. Such a reaction from Hudson was only to be expected. It showed that his foster parents had treated him well, and being an affectionate boy he was understandably torn by conflicting loyalties. Nearer the time, she would have a long talk with Dottie and prime her for the battles that would surely come, at least in the early days.

Dottie wrote to Hudson again, this time openly talking about the joyful news. She told him about the plans they were making and the school he would be going to. She mentioned that Sophie's eighteenth birthday would be in May, hoping to nudge Hudson into a reply. No word came from Hudson. At last, with only days to go before Sophie's birthday, Dottie wrote again. In her letter she asked Hudson directly if there was a difficulty. Why was he not writing to them? Did he not want to come back? Brenda Holly thought the time had come to intervene.

'They've been good parents to him, and he feels loyalty towards them,' she said to the sisters. 'It's only natural that the boy should be torn. You'll have to be patient with him and not expect him to throw himself into your arms and that sort of stuff. He'll come round. I've been trying to get a school report on him so we can sort all that out this end.

The parents say he was doing well but that recently he has fallen off a little. I'll need a school report, and that may well be awful. So he'll need help to adjust to school as well. The important thing is not to over-react. You'll have to do what you can to welcome him back, and you may have to put up with a little unfriendliness to begin with. I'll be around, obviously, if you need help or advice.'

Dottie took the news in silence, feeling her heart sink. She had been afraid they would steal him, teach him to be a little English boy so that he should despise his real family. They probably told him all the stuff about Sharon and the way she had died. To him she and Sophie must seem like ridiculous and dirty monkeys, the children of an old whore, who were living in a one-room slum in South London. She stopped herself at once, afraid that if she allowed herself to feel bitterness it would turn against Hudson, sooner or later. She must be patient, look to win back Hudson slowly, persuade him that it was with them that he belonged.

Sophie did not believe what the social worker was saying. She glanced at her sister, a small smile hovering round her lips. The woman could not mean it, she thought. Even when she saw that Dottie believed, she still shook her head and grinned with derision. They were trying to keep him there so he would be a servant. What had they done to him to make him say such a thing? It was not true that he had said that about not coming back. It was a lie, Sophie said, dropping her eyes, although every line of her features spoke of obstinate determination. Dottie kept her eyes on Brenda Holly, hoping that she would somehow take it all back and say that Sophie was right. It was all a lie, a trick that jealous foster parents were playing on them.

'I don't think it is a lie, Sophie,' Mrs Holly said after a moment. 'We've had a letter from Hudson himself saying he doesn't want to leave his parents. The social worker who keeps an eye on him in Dover reports the same thing. Of course he must come back to his real family. We're all agreed on that, including the foster parents, as a matter of fact. All except Hudson. I think this is understandable, and perhaps even unavoidable. You all had a very rough time, and the kindness these parents have shown your brother has won his loyalty. What kind of a boy would he have been if it had not? From your point of view, you will have to make him happy to be back. I know you would have done anyway, but you'll have to try harder than you thought, maybe.'

The two sisters sat in silence after Brenda Holly left. Sophie was still inclined to be sceptical, to wait and see, but Dottie had a feeling that what Brenda said was true. It was the worst that Dottie would have expected, therefore it had to be true. She took the blame for it, at least a big share of it. She should never have allowed him to be taken away in the first place. She should have fought tooth and nail to save him from the fate that was being prepared for him. They would make him into a little white boy first then reject him later, and laugh at him because he had no idea who he was. Then he would have nothing but contempt and bitterness for everybody. In the days that followed Dottie waited nervously for further news. She was afraid the council would change its mind and keep Hudson in Dover. At other times she was terrified that they would not be able to make Hudson like being back. Sophie had persuaded herself that everything would turn out right once he was back. She would cook him his favourite sweets and give him lots of cuddles. She cheered Dottie with her optimism, but the effect did not last very long.

On the evening of her birthday Sophie went to the cinema with Andy, the landlord. Dottie did her best to prevent it, but short of quarrelling with Sophie or barring the door to the landlord, she knew there was nothing she could do. Sophie laughed at all the objections that her sister raised, pretending that Dottie was just teasing her. Dottie waited up for her, not knowing what else to do. They came back late. The landlord was strutting in the flush of his conquest, stroking his moustache and smiling. Sophie was glowing with happiness, on her face a look of achievement and contentment. The landlord kissed Sophie's hand as they said goodbye, and Sophie laughed with pleasure before shutting the door on him.

A Picnic on the Cliffs

1

Sophie was in a stew of apprehension for the whole day, bubbling with impatience. Brenda had refused to let them go to Dover with her, and had even refused to let them meet her at Victoria. They had to stay behind and wait. Dottie laughed as she watched her sister worrying, and tried to interest her in the chores that remained to be done, thinking they would help her pass the time. They had put a curtain across one part of the room and made that Hudson's. It made a triangle with the walls, across the corner by the window. The curtain was made of two bed-sheets sewn together, old and worn thin with use. It would do to begin with and would provide some privacy. Thin though it was, it was too heavy for the wire holding it up and sagged badly in the middle, but none of them was tall enough to see over the top so it did not matter. They had also found a bed in one of the second-hand shops near the market for a few shillings, and cleaned it up for him. It was a little too big for the space cut off by the curtain, so that the worn cotton sheets draped over the end of the old divan and revealed its battered and clawed legs.

They laughed until tears poured down their faces, and their chests ached as if they were bursting at the sight of the *room* they had prepared for Hudson. The clawed legs suggested an animal hiding behind the old bed-sheets.

From the position of its feet, it would be facing into the room, waiting for an opportune moment to leap out from its hiding-place. It would only be for a while, they reassured each other, because the landlord had promised them a *flat* in the house. It was not really a flat at all, but Andy liked the sound of the word. As a special favour to his darling Sophie, he had offered them another room upstairs. *A two-bedroom flat*, he said, and suggested an exorbitant rent. The room was barely much more than a cupboard under the eaves, and in any case it was occupied. Dottie haggled furiously over the rent, and in the end a compromise was agreed. Since the *flat* did not yet have a front door of its own, they would pay rent for the separate rooms. Once the landlord had added a front door, the rent would go up.

It was a ridiculous compromise since the rooms were so far apart. The form of words, however, meant that honour was satisfied. Dottie reminded Andy that the room was occupied, but the landlord anticipated no trouble, especially as it was for his Sophie. Its tenant was a young man who looked no more than eighteen or so, and whose pallid expression and evasive eyes made Sophie giggle with incredulity. He seemed the very picture of a sickly and terrified boy. The landlord gave him notice to leave in a week, but the young man burst into tears and begged for an extension, mentioning aged parents and his dependent and dissolute siblings as part of his defence. He was working for a reputable solicitor in Aldersgate Street near Smithfield, and his prospects were good, he hoped. His snivelling appeal touched the landlord, who recognised deviousness when he saw it and was partial to it.

'So I gave him a month's notice. Me and my big heart!' the landlord said, bitterly slapping himself on the chest. Dottie felt a twinge of guilt about the young man. She had greeted him on the stairs, and he had responded with faded and tremulous smiles. After the landlord's notice he gave her a wide berth whenever he passed her on the stairs, and kept his eyes down.

It was late afternoon by the time Brenda Holly arrived with Hudson. Dottie heard their steps on the stairs long before Brenda knocked. Hudson smiled shyly and dropped his eyes, but Sophie brushed Dottie aside and swallowed her brother up. She danced him round the landing, bouncing him up and down as if he was lifeless and without resistance. Dottie laughed hysterically, delighted that her sister had known exactly what to do where she would have stood irresolute and embarrassed.

They did not calm down all evening, and hardly noticed when Brenda silently departed. Hudson sat quietly while his sisters entertained him. He ate jelebis with amazed delight, opening his eyes wide as the memory returned. Sophie told him about how silly he used to make himself with his greed for jelebis, and he laughed with them. He relaxed a little as they talked to him and tried to cheer him. He said very little, but at least they had avoided any awkwardness or a terrible scene. It was when the time came to go to bed that there came the first sign of trouble. He asked where he would be sleeping, and the two sisters fell about with laughter as they showed him. He stood in front of the curtain with a look of amazement on his face, a boy of fourteen in front of that backdrop of thin, grubby sheets, looking humiliated and angry. It suddenly struck Dottie how small he was. On his face was a look of loathing, his eyes looking up at them from underneath lowered brows. His hands were bunched into fists, and he looked tense, ready to leap. Without another word he whipped round and disappeared behind his tent.

Sophie whimpered slightly. Dottie put a hand on her arm to soothe her but Sophie shook it off. No sound came from behind the curtain, and the three of them stood in a tense silence until Hudson suddenly shouted: 'Bitches!' Sophie howled her misery, and Dottie ran to the curtain and pulled it aside. Her first thought was to give the boy a good clout and then slap his stupid face a few times, but Hudson was ready for her, his feet wide apart and his fists raised. He bared his teeth with the unutterable fury of his hate, and shouted the word again, wrapping his lips round it to express his full disgust.

'Bitches!'

Dottie involuntarily took a step back, and was unaware of the small defeated sigh that escaped her a moment later. 'It's only for now, until we get the room upstairs,' she said, the unaccustomed plaintiveness in her voice hinting at the hurt she felt. Hudson lowered his arms very slightly. The shoulder pads of his emblazoned school blazer, which had arched up with his anger, straightened out a little. He did not feel sufficiently mollified to drop his arms altogether, though.

'We'll do the best we can, Hudson,' Sophie said, and a melodramatic snivel escaped her. 'We love you so much, and we are so happy to have you back ...'

Hudson snorted with contempt and lowered his fists. He angrily pulled the curtain back so he was hidden in his tent again. 'I didn't want to come back,' he said bitterly. 'You made me.'

'Oh Hudson!' Sophie cried, and would've rushed for the curtain had Dottie not stopped her. Dottie put her finger across her lips, stopping Sophie from saying any more. She nodded towards the beds, and, when her sister shook her head violently with protest, Dottie put an arm around her shoulder and pushed her. Sophie made a crying face and they exchanged miserable smiles. It will pass, Dottie thought as she made herself ready for bed. He was only a little boy who was selfishly distressed at having to return to the discomforts of their poor lives after having been spoiled by the foster parents. It was what she had been afraid of, but she was sure it would pass. And perhaps it was not so surprising that Hudson was so irate. It had been a difficult day for him. What kind of a boy would he be if he could not feel some loyalty to the people who had looked after him for two years, and may even have treated him with affection? No, Dottie thought, there was no need to exaggerate. They may have looked after him and provided for him, but how could they possibly have found room in their hearts for a black boy who was nothing to them, just someone they had found in a file.

In the morning she would act as if nothing had happened, and soon enough it would be as if the outburst had never taken place. As Brenda had said, they had to expect some grumbling at first. What was required of her was calmness and control, to smooth the surface so that it would look as if it had always been placid and unmarked. She could not help feeling some bitterness, though, that after all the trouble she had gone to, Hudson should come out with that *bitches* business. If he did not like the way they lived, perhaps he should think what it had been like for her. Perhaps he thought he was above it all, now that he was civilised, whereas they were accustomed to living like hogs and did not know enough to mind. Well, he had best get himself used to it, because this was where he was going to find himself sooner or later. It will pass, she reassured herself. She spent an uncomfortable night, first turning this way and then that. Perhaps they should not have made themselves seem so weak, so loving. Should she have clouted him? She should have shown him from the beginning that they would take no nonsense. No, that would not have done any good, she thought. He was so obviously unhappy. What he needed most of all was the love and affection that only his family could give him. Soon enough it would be as if none of the troubles had ever happened.

2

When she saw him in the morning, he was sitting on his bed fully dressed, with the curtain pulled to one side. As soon as Dottie opened her eyes, a torrent of complaints and grumbles poured out of him. He had had no sleep in the horrible bed, which was lumpy and full of bugs. Look at all the bites on his arms and legs. They had both snored all night, keeping him awake. The room was dirty and smelt of grease and garbage and dirty washing. A terrible draught had whistled in from the window, making him stiff. He was not used to draughts. How could they live like this? He had tried the toilet but had been so disgusted that he had come out without doing anything. He had not yet had the courage to try the bathroom, but was resigned to being unable to wash. Why had they forced him to leave Dover to come and live like this? There he had lived in a nice house on the Folkestone Road, and had had a room of his own which looked out to sea. 'You are nothing but a stupid selfish bitch to force me back here,' he spat at Dottie, his eyes watering with misery.

'Only for a while, Hudson. Please don't take it so badly. Until we get the room upstairs,' Dottie said, dropping her voice so as not to excite him any further. 'The landlord has already given the upstairs tenant notice to leave. Only a few days ...'

'I don't care. I hate you! I hate you! You're just stupid and bossy, and you've always been jealous of me. I want to go back to Dover. Why did you force me to come and live here?' he shouted. His face was hot and fierce with loathing, and tears of anger and frustration streamed down his cheeks. The memory of Hudson as he had been before he was taken away came flooding back into Dottie's mind, and made her catch her breath with dread. She prayed they would not have to live through those times again, on the edge of violence and uproar all the time, their days filled with tantrums and screaming, and suffering his constant contempt. Sophie was awake too now, and called Hudson's name with a voice that was on the point of breaking. He dropped his eyes for a moment, then looked up quickly, his glance darting from Dottie to the weeping Sophie. Then, with a look of insolence and cunning, he sneered at them and grinned. A moment later a small snivel escaped him, and he looked shamefaced and confused, frightened by all that had happened to him. Sophie lumbered out of her bed and threw herself on him. The two of them sat silently clinging to each other, with Sophie gently rocking Hudson from side to side as she used to. Dottie went round the corner to buy some fresh bread, so she could get breakfast ready for all of them.

3

Brenda Holly told Dottie not to worry too much about it. 'It's bound to happen at first, my love. I told you. You just keep treating him with affection. You'll have to move him out of here anyway, get him a room of his own. When he's got over things a little bit, he'll be fine. Not everybody is as hardy as you.' Dottie laughed at that. She felt silly and interfering, and a distant part of her was viewing the task ahead with impatience and dislike. She did not feel hardy at all, not in the slightest.

Brenda came round often. She had no choice. There were complaints from Hudson's new school. He did no work at all and did not complete a single assignment that he was set. Not a day went past without him being involved in another fight, in class, in the playground, on the way home. He was unbelievably rude to the teachers, disruptive during lessons and a nuisance to everyone. He showed no signs of self-control, and when he fought he showed a streak of viciousness which the teachers found deplorable. Even against girls! Brenda spoke to him for hours, taking him to one side and speaking urgently and kindly to him. She would not allow Dottie to come near them when they were like this. And although Hudson fought a ferocious rear-guard, battling over every inch in his retreat, he appeared to listen to her and even agreed, at times, to try and improve his behaviour.

He listened to Brenda when he would not listen to Dottie. Dottie lectured him on the benefits of education, pointing to herself as someone who had missed out on all of them. She tried to persuade him to visit the library where she herself had found so much to please and educate her. He sneered at her while his eyes glazed with a deliberate show of inattention. Invariably, Dottie's attempts at inspirational heart-to-hearts with him ended in furious rows. After every confrontation she made herself swear not to lose her temper, not to mention the library, but when it came to it and she saw Hudson's lip curl up with disdain, her resolutions came to nothing and her bitterness flowed out. How had he earned the right to hold her in that kind of contempt? Hudson would laugh tauntingly, and within moments would begin his own reply. Dottie was always quickly silenced, because she could not achieve the depths of cruelty that Hudson so effortlessly could. It revolted her to watch him turn poisonous, and she would feel herself growing smaller, gathering herself in like a small animal that had no defences and was rolling itself up for safety.

Often Dottie looked away when Hudson was doing something that she had asked him not to do. There were times when the thought of returning to the house was unbearable, when the thought of being faced with the boy's hate was too much. She stayed at work later whenever she could, but this was not something she could do often. She had to get back in time to get food ready. Sophie was now working in a British Rail cafeteria in Victoria Station, and by the time she came home her feet were killing her. Dottie sometimes came home to find Sophie asleep on her bed and Hudson out on the streets somewhere. She pretended not to see when Sophie held Hudson for too long, fondling him until he fell silent with a peculiar stillness. It was Sophie's gift, she thought. She had a way of giving comfort, a warmth that drew people to her. Dottie made herself look away rather than say anything. It comforted both of them, and she knew there could be no harm in it.

They had a celebration for his fifteenth birthday. That was one of their happiest moments: gifts and a birthday cake with fifteen beautiful and dainty candles. The little flames shone with a steady, held-in strength, ready if required to burn until the end of time. Hudson hesitated before blowing the candles out, as if he was thinking of saying something. Then he smiled and took a huge breath which spluttered out prematurely as he was overcome by suppressed laughter. His sisters prevented the bad luck that attends two attempts at blowing out birthday candles by joining in mightily and the three of them blew out the fragile lights together.

When their festivities had passed beyond the stage of raucous excitement, and they were laughing and talking quietly, he told them about his time in Dover. He spoke tentatively and reluctantly. If they asked any questions he became difficult and abusive. They learnt to listen with ready smiles while his eyes darted suspiciously from one to the other, watchful for mockery or censure. He had gone to a really good school, he told them. Not like the dump he was attending now. 'My dad got me into a public school for nothing, because he knew some people there. Sometimes he taught there. The boys were all right. They called me Sunny and I didn't have any of this racial shit I get here. Sometimes they called me Chalky because I wasn't, like Little John. You know, like in Robin Hood. Little John because he was so big. The teachers were brilliant and everybody was really all right. I got into the Rugby fifth. Do you know what that is? There were five rugby sides and I was picked for the lowest one, but the captain said he thought I would make a good scrum-half one day.'

'Don't they play rugby at your school here?' Dottie asked. She had no idea what rugby was, or whether it was a good thing to do, but the look of pride in Hudson's face was enough to prompt her question even though she knew he did not like to be interrupted.

'Don't be so thick!' Hudson said and shook his head at her imbecility. 'My dad was good at rugby when he was younger. He showed me photos of when he was at school. During the war he was in the Royal Navy and travelled all over the place. Once he played rugby for the Navy against Hong Kong Colony in the Far East. He was always making jokes and taking us places, my brother and I. At Christmas we went to a carol service in Dover Church. All the schools came and the church was really crowded. The church had huge pillars, really fat, stone pillars. I was standing behind one of them so I couldn't see all the people singing. It was as if the songs were coming from behind me and all around. I had never been to a carol service before. It was beautiful. The light was like in the caves under the cliffs, soft and hazy. My dad took us there too, but it was dangerous. You could hear the pebbles rattling down, and you had to be careful that the tide did not catch you out. Afterwards we had a donkey ride on the cliffs. On a really clear day you can see France, you know.'

'It sounds lovely!' Sophie said.

'He was going to teach me to swim this summer. I started to learn last year, and I did a little bit at school, but he said that by the end of the summer I would swim by hook or by crook. My brother could swim from when he was four.'

'What's your brother's name?' Dottie asked.

'Frank,' Hudson said, and started to sob. Both sisters made a movement towards him but he leapt up and screamed at them, telling them to keep their filthy hands off him.

'What does your ... dad teach?' Dottie asked after a moment, after Hudson had sat down again. She was hoping to persuade him to continue talking. It made him sad to do so, but she could not doubt that it was better for him to speak about his loss than to hug it to himself as if it were something much more precious than an intimate and prized pain. They needed to sit together and talk about these things, because it was about all their lives, she thought. Perhaps she had been wrong to take him away from so much happiness, but she had only sought to repair what had always been there before, to make life whole again.

Not just for herself, but for all of them. 'What does your dad teach?' Dottie asked again, passing more confidently over the *dad* that had made her stumble before.

'He doesn't teach,' Hudson said after a moment. His face had knotted and unknotted itself in the time it took him to make a reply. The muscles on his face had contracted with anger, and his mouth had sharpened to a tight pucker as he sought to control himself. 'He's a headmaster,' he said, and ran out of the room.

4

Brenda urged Dottie not to give up. 'He'll come through. Don't blame yourself. You've got to keep trying. I'm sorry, my darling, but I've got some more bad news. He threw a stone at a teacher's car yesterday … smashed the windscreen and hit the teacher's daughter. Did he say anything?'

Dottie shook her head, but did not find it difficult to believe that Hudson could have done that. At least, part of her understood that he could have done such a thing even as another part wanted to protest and argue a case for him. Brenda smiled wearily, and sighed at the complications that lay before them, indulging a moment of self-pity. 'The police have been called in,' she said. 'They picked him up from school, and apparently he claims that it was an accident. The teacher didn't see who had thrown the stone, but several of the schoolchildren did. He denied it at first, but then he said it was an accident. The school rang me to tell me about it, in case I wanted to go to him. Hudson asked for me to be sent for. Do you want to come?'

They got him home late in the evening. He sat silently through all the questions, sullen and angry, glaring at the floor. At first he had looked at Dottie with incredulity, as if surprised to see her there. Then he had looked away from both the women and refused to say a word to them. The police sergeant kept in the background but it was obvious he expected little to come out of the conversation. They asked him what was likely to be the outcome. 'Juvenile Court,' he said with a shrug, and offered them another cup of tea. At about nine o'clock in the evening, the teacher rang the station to ask if he could withdraw his complaint. The sergeant was doubtful but bowed in the end to the teacher's insistence. They had to wait for the teacher to come to the station and make his withdrawal in person before they were able to go home.

Sophie was still not home when they got back. She stayed out late sometimes with her friends, some women she had got to know at the cafeteria. Dottie knew that sometimes she went with men. She could tell it on her when she came in, but she did not feel she could say anything to her about it. What was there to say? What did she know, to say anything? She was having to learn to leave people alone, she thought. This was what Hudson was teaching her. If she had minded her own business, instead of allowing her nostalgia for times that had never been to direct her, Hudson would have been spared the terrors he was living through. If she had thought less about being right, and tried to find out from him what he wanted to do ...

'Come here, you horrible boy,' Brenda said when they were home. 'I've a good mind to wring your neck. When are you going to stop being a nuisance to everyone and straighten yourself out?'

'Fuck off, you stupid cow!' Hudson shouted. 'Mind your own business. I don't want anything to do with you. I didn't even want to come here.'

'Well, you are here, and you might as well get used to it and stop making such a pathetic display of yourself,' Brenda said, her face red with anger.

Suddenly Hudson started to laugh, pointing at Brenda Holly's red face. 'You look like a boiled crab,' he said. 'Ugly bitch!'

Brenda Holly slapped him as hard as she had the strength to. She saw him stagger backwards and almost fall. Dottie rushed towards him and took hold of his elbow. She looked round at Brenda, her eyes flashing. Hudson shook her off and ran out, shouting obscenities over his shoulder. 'I'm sorry, I should have known better,' Brenda said, looking tired. 'I had no right to do that … I don't know how you can stand it. Why do you let him terrorise you? You poor love, after all that you've done for yourself! You shouldn't have had to put up with this misery for all these months.' Brenda sighed, then lifted her head to look Dottie in the eyes. She smiled and raised her eyebrows to acknowledge the difficulties they were in. 'He'll come through,' she said, nodding firmly. 'Don't give up on him. Tell him I'm sorry. I'll come back tomorrow and see him. I'm sorry, my love. I'd better go …'

'He won't have anyone to talk to if you don't come,' Dottie said. 'He won't talk to me.'

Brenda shrugged, then shook her head wearily. 'I can't take any more now. I'll see you tomorrow,' she said.

Hudson must have been watching, for he came back moments after Brenda left. 'If you let that white woman come back here, I'm leaving,' he said. 'I don't want to see her again. Do you understand? You've been letting her come into our lives and mess everything up. You don't understand what these white people are like. It was her fault. She messed things up for us from the start.' *It was her fault, it was her fault*, and more and much more along those lines. Dottie listened without saying a word, which gradually drove Hudson to greater excesses and wilder accusations. 'If that woman ever comes here again I'll beat her up. I'll slash her tyres. White people hate us. They'll do anything to keep us down, unless we fight back and protect ourselves. I should've hit her with something when she touched me then, but she'd have just taken me back to the station … and … and made something else up. Like I was trying to rape her or something like that. Well, that's what will happen if she comes back here. One of my mates at school, his brother did that. He got a few friends together and they did that because this council woman was always interfering.'

'Your pants are still smelling of piss and you can talk about doing things like that to people!' Dottie said quietly, describing her own incredulity rather than expecting Hudson to take notice of her.

'So you'd better tell her not to come back here. I'm warning you, that's all,' he shouted, pretending he had not heard her.

She wished they had the mythical two-roomed flat that the landlord had promised them, so she could get away from him. The promises had come to nothing because Sophie had fallen out with the landlord, and the little room under the eaves remained occupied. The sallow young man proved more resourceful than appearances suggested, manufacturing ingenious excuses and launching cringing pleas for time when all else failed. The landlord lost interest in harrying him, but perhaps he was also punishing Sophie for whatever offence it was she had caused him. Now when he came for the rent, instead of warbling his crooked love-song at the door, or even taking a step or two into the room, the landlord glared into the corridor until Dottie had finished checking the cash and was ready to hand it over.

As she listened to Hudson's cruelties, she wanted, more than anything, to be by herself, to think about what had happened. But she did not want to shut him up. She was afraid that he would become even wilder, and would do something terrible. In the end, she sensed him winding down, running out of steam. His voice became more whining, asking for sympathy. Dottie still kept quiet, resisting his appeal, wanting him to go to bed. 'Where's Sophie?' he asked. 'She's playing about with some man, isn't she? I can't understand who'd want a fatty like her. Do you know what she promised me for Christmas? She said she'd buy me football boots. What are you going to get for me?'

Dottie tried not to say anything, but Hudson waited. In his eyes was a blank look, as if he had not really said anything, and was not waiting for an answer from her. She felt his edginess and it made her anxious. She knew that she was expecting him to do something unpredictable, and she understood that she no longer fathomed him. It frightened her, and made her realise the extent of his ascendancy. 'I don't know yet,' she said. For the first time since his return, she wondered if there was something wrong with him, something wrong in his head. She hurriedly dispersed the thought before it had had time to take root. 'I've got some ideas, but I'm not telling you yet,' she said with a smile.

Without another word, he went to get ready for bed. She heard his preparations and saw the curtain bumping up here and there as he manoeuvred himself around the triangle of space. When she came back from the bathroom all was silent. As she undressed, she had a powerful feeling of being watched. She suspected that he often watched them when they undressed, but there was nothing she could do about that. The position of his corner meant there was nowhere to hide in the room. The sheets were so thin that the holes that kept appearing in the curtain could easily be no more than accidents and ordinary wear. She had stitched some of the tiny holes, but they kept reappearing. She was afraid that if she persisted with the repairs it would seem as if she was prudish about such things. She might even drive herself into a state over it all. Once or twice she had switched the light off before changing, but Sophie had laughed at her and told her not to be such an old maid. Her fears would look too obvious if she switched the light off to change and then switched it on again moments later to wait for Sophie. She could not bear the thought of Hudson jumping out of his tent with even more abuse.

5

Brenda laughed when Dottie told her about what Hudson had said, but she never got another word out of him. However much she teased or cajoled him, he either completely ignored her or left the room. She bought him a large reference book for Christmas, but he refused to accept it, and in the end she was forced to leave it on the chest of drawers and go. As the months passed her visits became less frequent, and tended to become more formal. If she found Dottie alone, then she became her old self, full of advice and self-importance, and unstinting in her affection for her young friend. She tried to encourage Dottie to call her at the office sometimes for a chat, but Dottie hated the phone, and the only time she had gone to the office the clerk at the main desk had refused to let her through without an appointment.

She could have done with a friend. Sophie was out most of the time, running with a crowd of women who always seemed to be going to drinking parties and dances. We put up with hardships from our first day out of the womb, Dottie thought. Until one day we can choose our lives for ourselves. And then we can make nothing more of it than to drink and dance like an advanced kind of monkey. She had hoped that with Sophie working they could afford somewhere better to live, but that had come to nothing. She saw as little of Sophie's money as of Sophie herself, and she was not interested in fighting things out with her. It was all she could do to keep her mouth shut when Sophie was setting forth for her parties, with her bright shiny dresses and tarty make-up. It had happened slowly, and with each advance Sophie's manner became stiffer and more stubborn, as if she was expecting to be criticised. Dottie wished she had said something earlier, but she was then educating herself to be less interfering. She could not think what she could say now that would make the situation better.

It made everything seem worse for her that she had no one to talk to, she thought. Hudson was driving her crazy and there was no one she could go to for a good grumble and moan, or for words of comfort or advice. He had become answerable to no one. He came and went as he pleased, especially after the New Year, when the landlord relented and let him have the little room upstairs. It was only big enough for a bed and a couple of sticks of furniture, a chest of drawers and a rickety table Dottie had bought for him to do his homework on. He was to come down to their room to eat or sit and talk, but it became impossible to keep track of him. He went to school when he felt like it and sometimes did not come home for days.

The school did not bother to complain any more. He was already over the age when he could be forced to attend, and no doubt the school was only too pleased when he did not turn up. Once he disappeared for two weeks, and Dottie began to fear that something terrible had happened to him. She would have gone to the police, except she suspected that that would only add to Hudson's troubles.

She tried to talk to him, to persuade him that there was more to do and take pleasure in than wandering the streets. She did not dare mention to him the other things she was afraid he might be doing when he was not at home. Where had he gone for two weeks? She described the rich possibilities of his life, if only he would put his mind to making them amount to something. She heard the insincerity in her voice, the strident insistence on fantasies of achievement and fulfilment. *You could be anything you like*, she told him, clutching wildly at old lies. Whenever she appealed to him in this way, he turned his face away from her with a pained expression. In some desperation, she once suggested that he write a letter to his old foster parents and his brother Frank. His face set into a look of anger at the mention of his brother's name, but only for a moment. Perhaps they could all take a trip down to Dover for the day, Dottie continued, encouraged that the memories were still potent for him and could still rouse a show of protest. To say hello to them and thank them for having been so kind, she said. At that he had laughed with raucous mockery, his growing body shaking with exaggerated mirth. It was the laughter of a hooligan, deliberately jeering and uncouth. It was intended to be as much a challenge and an insult to her as it was a response to her over-eager optimism. 'Don't be pathetic,' he said. 'What do you want to go and see those white creeps for?'

Hudson was more or less living in the streets, and never asked for money from her any more. When she asked where he stayed during his absences from home, he refused to say more than that it was with some friends. Most of his friends were young black men who seemed older than him. They swaggered and strolled the streets, and indicated with every gesture and act that they wanted to be thought of as violent, cruel men. They called for Hudson sometimes, and filled Dottie's heart with dread. They spoke to her in the streets, and were always friendly and polite, calling her by her name and asking after Sophie. Then after they had passed her she would see them turn their jeering attention to a stall-holder in the market, or someone else whose appearance or misfortune had attracted their attention.

It is such a stupid waste, Dottie thought. Whatever has happened to us, to Hudson and Sophie and those young men, has made us believe that we came into this world as if we were beggars, squalling and throwing tantrums, expecting those who summoned us to be dissatisfied and to give up on us. Then when this happens we say how right we were all along. You made me like this. Look at me. This is your work, and now I'll make you pay for having been foolish enough to want me here in the first place. It was themselves they tortured most of all, she thought, then their loved ones, and all the time, while they ranted and strutted, their enemies waited at the rise of the hill to mow them down. They looked strong and healthy, with sharp, flashing smiles, and a mischievous glint in the eye. It seemed a terrible disaster to her that all the use such natural skills were put to was display and gesture.

Hudson was growing tall, and was much stronger than he had been the year before. Everything about him had changed, she thought. Even his skin had a darker, richer glow. He was more self-conscious, and very deliberate about how he did things. He refused to hurry with anything. When he turned to look at her, it was always after a moment or so, and then with an abrupt, mannered swivel of his head. He was less inclined to abusive outbursts and never dashed out of the room. It was maturity, perhaps, but she wondered if it was the new image of himself that he was creating for the street. She had seen him cleaning and admiring a new flick knife he had acquired, had seen him practise stabbing with it, although that need not be much more than play-acting, she reassured herself, barely suppressing her disgust. She talked to Sophie about what was happening to their brother, but Sophie dropped her eyes guiltily, ashamed of her lack of interest and too involved in her own dramas to spare any of her strength for anyone else.

Dottie could not stop herself from saying things to him. She tried to teach herself to keep quiet, to avoid being critical of his street-life, of his selfishness, but she could not. Sooner or later, when he was around, she said something that would start them squabbling and fighting over the same issues, again and again. Once he lost his temper with her nagging, as he called it. He screwed up the front of her jumper in one hand and told her to leave him alone. She had felt his strength then and, although she struggled and threw a punch and a kick, she felt the contemptuous ease with which he flung her away. The far wall and the stone sink by the window put an end to her headlong rush, but the shudder which shook her slight frame testified to the power with which she had been despatched. 'What would our mother say if she could see us? What would Sharon say?' she asked him.

He thought for a long time before replying. 'She was no better than us,' he said at last. 'She got us into this, the smelly old cow.'

She was on her own with him, she thought. She was a little afraid of him and she guessed that he was beginning to suspect it. He looked oddly at her sometimes, a distant, speculative look. Whenever she caught him doing this, she moved away and bustled around the room, shifting or cleaning something. She had resisted admitting it to herself, but she knew that he was taking something. The long, brooding stares and the hooded eyes were not mere style. When she caught this look turned on her, then she feared violence. There! She had said it! She feared her own brother would hurt her. She knew that the boy whose life she had ruined would one day pay her back. She began to find relief in his absence. The loneliness was bearable, she thought. Better that than the anger and resentment she felt when her brother and sister were around and expecting her to skivvy for them. It was time she stopped behaving like a mother-hen and put some order in her own life.

Sophie had been moving her things out slowly, so that she only came to the room for the odd night. She told Dottie she had moved into a flat in Stepney with three other girls who also worked in the cafeteria at Victoria Station. Dottie shrugged, meaning that it was Sophie's business. She was sceptical about the move but neither her agreement nor her advice was being sought so there was no point in offering an opinion. Sophie had put on more weight, but she now wore dresses that were tight on her and low in the cleavage. The make-up on her face was cleverly done, but it was too much. It made her look like a street tart. Perhaps such things did run in the blood, Dottie thought as she watched her sister walk away, waving as if she was leaving for a long journey. Sharon must have taken the same pleasure in things like that, at one time anyway. Dottie had no doubt that the flat in Stepney would be like one of those rooms she remembered as a child, full of noise and drinking men. She took no pleasure in the memory, and felt no desire to revisit that old territory.

The silence in her room was menacing at first, but she waited it out, feeling her heart find its beat. As before, when she had lived on her own for the first time, she heard the desperate gurglings in the water-pipes when the silence was deep enough, and felt the stealthy movements of the house in the dead of night. She was more ready this time, and stilled her anxiety with thoughts of the gains she had made. It was *her* room again, and she would look for things to make it better, more cheerful. The landlord had muttered about changing the sink, and she could paint the door a bright colour. Perhaps it was something in the blood, she thought, that made Sophie as she was, and as Sharon had been. When she thought of herself that way, with a man, Dottie felt only a kind of terror. There were times when she wished she could have a man so that she could have that business over with, and have someone to talk to late into the night.

The Image of an Idea

1

Dottie was a veteran in the food-packing factory where she worked. Most of the people employed there were casuals, on a week's notice and at a different rate of pay from the regular workers. They were part of the city's shifting and restless crowd of unskilled labour. They came from everywhere, out of every nook and cranny, and drifted in and out of the factory without questions or explanations. Among them were Ukranians and Romanians who had fought with Hitler's armies; Czechs and Hungarians who had fled Stalin's cohorts; Iranians, West Indians and Arabs who had come for learning or for work and soon found themselves adrift; Ghanaians and Chileans, who came to seek safety from the child-devouring Molochs who ruled their lands. The world was seething with endless turmoils and industry. The factory was like the metropolitan heart of an empire, drawing to it, as all empires had done, its share of fantasists and fugitives.

Some were bursting with impractical ambitions, which they pursued with the single-mindedness of self-mistrust. Others nursed deep, unassuagable wounds. Even the best among them were overshadowed and made insignificant by the events which had swept them to the banks of this ancient river. They did not yet credit the grandeur of the transformations they were living through, could not yet believe that the short-lived empires which had loomed over their world were being swept away in front of their eyes. Later they would learn to shrug off their exclusion from the higher affairs of men, and stop believing the old lies about the treachery and corruption that pounded through their veins. All they could feel at the start of the new decade was their insignificance to real events, their inability to achieve what they had suffered and sacrificed for. Their lives were filled with bitterness, and were poisoned by a sense of their inadequacy and failure.

There were others among them who liked to act as if they were lovers of life, free-spirits who were not going to allow themselves to be shackled by the mean ambitions of the people around them. They laughed at everybody and made disgusted remarks about the food in the canteen. When they found the time, they tried to bed as many of the women as they could. Something in their manner made them irresistible, and crowds of young women, themselves fugitive and anguished, sacrificed themselves at their feet. They made it known, these untrammelled souls who could sound the blackest gorges and soar out again, that money was no object to them, despite the temporary discomforts under which they lived. Rich parents of exotic and ancient glamour hovered not far in the wings, and could be conjured with nothing much more than a desperate telegram or two. It was a desire to prove themselves that prevented these heroes from taking the easy course and catching the next plane back to Santiago or Teheran or wherever.

A few of the labourers were students, who looked frightened and depressed but none the less held themselves with the self-conscious stiffness of martyrs. They rested large books on machinery and pretended to read them, and looked delighted and a little agitated when one of the regular factory workers spoke to them.

Dottie was one of the permanent workers. There was so much work available that no one had been laid off in the whole period that she had been there. They thought of themselves as the people who really ran the factory, even though many of them were nothing more than line workers, and did nothing much different from the casuals. It was the fitters and the electricians who were the true aristocrats. They took their time when they were called to a job and arrived looking sleek and put out that the more important things they would normally have been engaged in had had to be abandoned to deal with a troublesome conveyor belt or an ancient pastry mixer. The charge-hand would hover for a few moments, to get an idea of the damage before deciding how to redeploy his staff of line workers, almost all of whom were women or casuals. He could not redeploy the pastry mixer, who at the first sign of trouble from his machine would wash his hands and wander to the coffee room. But the line workers were technically unskilled, and could be shifted and moved without damaging the smooth working of this social machinery.

Because the machines broke frequently, and the fitters and engineers were incompetent, no one had to work very hard. As stocks dwindled and delivery deadlines loomed, there would be plenty of over-time. This was in the gift of the charge-hands, who would have a word with their favourites and friends first before inviting any of the other, selected regulars that they thought deserved the opportunity to make more money. After two years at the factory, Dottie was an old hand and could take as much over-time as the law allowed.

Her charge-hand was a talkative and genial man called Mike Butler. When he was not talking, Mike Butler was striding self-importantly from one place to another, in the midst of pressing business. He was a man in his late fifties, of medium height with a head of lush, silvery hair that he was very vain about. For all his clownish airs, like a busybody village functionary with too many stories to tell, he was unusually strong and very few people dared to make fun of him.

He seemed to have been present at every important event in recent years, perhaps at every notable happening in the entire twentieth century. He remembered the moment Chamberlain declared war on Germany, almost literally picked the words off his tongue. He had seen the Americans land the first troops in East Anglia, when he himself was serving as ground crew with the RAF. He had been present when Winston Churchill, *that war-monger*, moved out of Downing Street after losing the election in 1945. He claimed to have been in Korea, China, Japan, and Suez at one time or another, and to have seen enough from his visits to predict the various outcomes that befell those far-flung places. Despite this busy schedule, he still managed to spend much of his youth working for the Ford Car Company, and he did what he could to help the company develop its Popular model. The men tended to find him tiresome, groaning audibly when he appeared. The women enjoyed him more, playing on his egotism for laughs, asking his advice about the best way of roasting a shoulder of lamb or of propagating honeysuckle or whatever. Mike Butler was never defeated by anything, and did not worry unduly about the merits of the questions he was asked. The women took liberties because they could rely on him keeping his hands to himself, which was more than could be said for most of the other men.

He had ignored Dottie at first, if Mike Butler was able to ignore anyone who had the potential to be dazzled and awestruck by his tireless achievements. Just after the race violence in Notting Hill during the winter of 1959, when gangs of Londoners scoured the streets for black victims, he spoke to her. The newspapers were full of outrage at the disturbances that had been going on for months in that part of London. They quoted furious citizens demanding retribution and redress, and tight-lipped officials whose patience was beginning to run out. Their reports put the blame on the tolerant and democratic British way of life for landing the country in another difficult mess. They had been too generous in allowing foreigners to come and live among them. The analyses of the causes of the disturbances lacked neither clarity nor courage. The blacks had been unable to keep their lustful and tormented eyes off the women, and had failed to prevent their turbulent and unruly urges from dictating their behaviour once again. The enraged citizens of West London, and Nottingham and Liverpool, were provoked to the point where they could no longer bear this insolence and took measures to end it. That was what was really at the heart of it all! To make matters worse, the blacks had insisted on moving into areas where English people lived, taking their jobs, walking the same streets as they did and eating in the same restaurants and cafes. And although the newspapers did not praise or condone the thuggish behaviour of the white mobs, there was no question that they had been sorely provoked. Was there ever any hope of solving the colour question? Who would now dare to predict the integration of coloured peoples into our society? Should we begin to think the unthinkable, and expel the miscreants even though such recourse is against all the liberal traditions of this nation?

Some people at the factory made remarks at Dottie in the days that followed the violence. There was talk of jungle bunnies and nig-nogs running amok, living ten to a room and breeding like rabbits. In the changing room she had to put up with the usual insults about bad smells. When she went to the toilet, someone reached over the wall and flushed the cistern while she was still sitting on the toilet seat. There were grumbles about niggers ruining the country and contaminating the culture of the English with ju-ju drums and uncouth dances. The other charge-hand, William Hampshire, who had spoken of sending the bus conductors back to wherever they came from, turned his face away whenever Dottie appeared, only his heavy breathing through pinched nostrils betraying the emotion he was keeping in check. By the middle of the afternoon, his passion overflowed its banks, and he looked meaningfully at Dottie, his mouth prim with disdain while his eyes burned and his mild, pasty face flushed with anger.

To these outraged citizens at the factory, Mike Butler recounted how the present troubles reminded him of the riots in Stepney in 1919, which of course he had witnessed as a young lad of twelve or thirteen. He spoke to whoever was willing to listen, and described the black men and *women* he had seen being chased in the streets. The newspapers were full of stories then too, although the violence was much worse. There were killings in Cardiff and Port Talbot, Liverpool and South Shields. Houses were ransacked and dens of blacks and Chinese were found lurking everywhere and put to the torch. Hundreds were sent packing, back to their own barbarous lands.

Some people were killed in Stepney too, Mike Butler told them, and he himself saw a black boy in a butcher's apron being stoned at the corner of Jamaica Street and Stepney Way. The boy was still hanging on to his delivery bicycle as the stones rained around him, worrying perhaps about losing his job, or maybe unable to make himself run for his life without completing his rounds first. 'This was the period between the wars,' Mike Butler said. 'England was an earthly paradise then, my friends. The summers were dry and warm, and the winters were mild. Everybody knew his or her responsibility, not like now with this dog-eat-dog competition and greed. You've never had it so good, Macmillan tells us, but it ain't like it was. There was the butcher and the baker down the street, and always a policeman strolling quietly on his beat. You couldn't imagine anything horrible happening in England. None of this rioting and rape and strikes like we have now. That's why that boy wouldn't let go of his bike! He wanted to be sure to finish his rounds after they'd done stoning him.'

The older people, especially the men, made faces at what Mike Butler was saying and moved away. The younger ones listened, but with an incredulous look, as if inclined to take this as another tall story.

'What happened to the boy?' Dottie asked, as comments and questions were flying around Mike Butler. He raised his arms in mock surrender, and said that he would take one question at a time. It was an opportunity to talk, and it was clear that he intended to make the most of it. As he moved into his stride, embellishing his story with asides and convoluted interconnections, his audience began to drift away. Soon his eyes were moving around with the manic hunger of the egotist, looking for the listener who would not desert him in mid-sentence. Dottie made her escape before her vulnerability revealed itself.

Later, he caught up with her as she was going to lunch and walked alongside her for a while. 'Don't take any notice of this shower, my dear. You wanted to know what happened to the boy didn't you? I heard you,' he said and smiled, pleased with himself. 'Well, he chucked his bike on the ground and ran, didn't he? You should've seen his little nigger legs pumping like pistons. He just legged it out of there for all he was worth, and good luck to him.'

'Did he?' Dottie asked, grinning. 'Was he hurt badly?'

'I wouldn't know about that,' Mike Butler said. 'He didn't hang around long enough for me to ask him. Once he realised that the gentlemen chucking stones at him weren't joking, he just dumped the bike and scarpered. Like a streak of greased black lightning he was.'

'That's good!' she said, wanting to clap her hands with glee.

'Just like that, phew!' Mike Butler said, clapping his hands to demonstrate the suddenness of his departure. 'Like a bat out of hell. You couldn't see him for dust!' Mike Butler said, with an air of someone delivering a definitive account.

'What were you doing in Stepney anyway? You seem to have been everywhere,' Dottie said, unable to resist the mischief.

Mike Butler grinned too. 'My dad used to live in Stepney, before he move out to Norwich. My grandad was a cobbler just by Mile End Road, and every summer we used to stay with my dad's family for a few weeks. They were all there, his brothers and sisters, and his mum and dad. There were no uncles and aunts yet, because my grandad emigrated from Russia on his own. Well, with just my grandma and their three children. Grandma's family was scattered God knew where in Siberia and everywhere, but Grandad's family still lived in a town south of Minsk. They left all his family behind there, you see. They never got out, none of them. By the time I'm talking, of course, they couldn't have got out even if they wanted to. The Revolution had caught up with them and that was that.

'My grandad used to talk about that time and the things they did to them, and tell us about how we must always stick together. But my dad wouldn't have none of that, and he left. He was the only one to leave Stepney, and he changed his name to Butler and went to work for a bookbinder. Me and my brothers and sisters were all baptised Christian Englishmen and Englishwomen. When the war came, all his family was killed in the bombing, although Grandad had already gone by then. So that's what I'm saying, love. Don't take any notice. You just get on with it, and make the best job of it you can. Some of these people think they are characters in Tarzan or something like that.

'I know what you're dying to ask me,' Mike Butler continued, for he was never one to under-work a captive audience when he had one. 'How come Grandma's family were scattered all over Siberia or wherever? Well I'll tell you. They were Jews, weren't they? In Russia that meant they could be taken from pillar to post and accused of everything, from drinking bat blood to overthrowing the Tsar. They were banished and exiled and all kinds of things, pogroms, special taxes, you name it. On top of all that, Grandma's family was accused of being unpatriotic and packed off to somewhere. When my Grandad met her, she was the only one of her family that the authorities had overlooked, so he married her. You can't pass up that kind of luck every day, and he always had a superstitious streak in him.'

'I didn't know that,' Dottie said, thinking about the scattered people that Mike Butler was describing. They were standing outside the canteen by this time, and people walking past glanced at them. 'Why does everyone hate the Jews so much? The killings and the expulsions ... and all the terrible names they give them.'

'I don't know, my dear, but I'm glad you've asked,' Mike Butler said, smiling at her and stroking his silvery mane of hair. 'Perhaps they're envious of them. The names aren't nothing, everybody's got names for everybody else. It's the chains and the whips and the ovens that stagger you. Jews aren't the only ones, you know that. Look what we've done to other people too, to your lot. This is how we are, all of us, a degraded and degenerate lot, if you don't mind my saying. The history of man consists mostly of plunder and looting and murder. That's how human beings have been, whether in China or Rome or America or Timbuktoo, and they'd be the same even if you put them on the sea-bed. Don't believe all that stuff about glorious victories and great men. Wherever human beings find themselves, no matter how much food or prosperity there is for everyone, they loot the place first and kill what they can. It's only when the easy pickings have run out that they think about what they've done. Or when they've killed everybody off or reduced them to beggars and drunks. Then they put what's left in ghettoes and reservations and bantustans and game parks and what have you. We're a despicable lot however you look at us.'

2

After that she began to be offered over-time. She gladly accepted when she could. The worse everything was becoming at home, the more time she spent at work. After Sophie left, she stayed on almost every day, especially as summer was round again and the days were light until late in the evening. On her journey home, she would work herself into a state, ready to take on anything, determined to begin to do something about her life. The late journeys home frightened her and made it easier to get herself worked up in this way. Although she did not know anyone who had suffered such a fate, the newspapers were full of stories of solitary black people being set upon in the streets, sometimes in broad daylight. She stirred herself up to hide from the terror of being abused or beaten by teddy boys and young thugs. On weekend afternoons she had seen them strutting down the High Road, laughing raucously and jostling people off the pavements. She turned another way whenever she saw them, although this made her feel cowardly. By late afternoon the teddy boys became bored with seedy Balham and went to more interesting pastures in Clapham or Chelsea. The black youths that they had driven off the High Road would then return from the side streets, strolling into shops and leaning against street corners.

The afternoon crowds were a reassurance. It did not seem likely that anything very bad could happen with so many people around. In the evenings, Dottie felt more exposed. She hurried through the warren of quiet side-streets that took her from the bus stop on the High Road to Segovia Street, keeping her eyes down and focusing on the things she would do when she got in. The room was often empty, but there were usually signs that Hudson had been in: dirty dishes, a hunk pulled out of the loaf of bread, a tin of baked beans that had been opened and consumed cold. He never did anything helpful. Either he stayed out of the way, or he made his presence felt by leaving a disgusting mark of his passage. She cleared up, cooked herself something on the grimy Baby Belling, and ate the food that tasted good despite everything else.

The room had become her prison, she thought. She could feel it draining the hope and the energy she came home with, leaving her with doubts and feelings of self-contempt. She did what she could: cleaned, read a book. She found recipes in newspapers, impractical exotic-sounding hors d'œuvres or magnificently evocative desserts that she promised herself she would try one day. She had bought herself a small radio with the over-time money, a Pye in maroon plastic casing with a cream-coloured grille. The smug voices that came out of it irritated her, but the music helped to pass the time.

She found that she was earning enough money to have some left over every week. She hid the money in a jewel box that Brenda had given her for her birthday the previous year. It had a tiny padlock on it, and she thought it was better not to leave the money unsecured. The box reminded her of Brenda. Dottie smiled at the thought of her old friend, and felt pangs of guilt that she did not try harder to see her. She could just imagine Brenda Holly getting annoyed with her, and lecturing her for the way she had allowed events to overwhelm her, but really she was too exhausted to do anything about any of it.

She kept out of Hudson's way when she could, and he showed no inclination to seek her out. He was too much for her, she had conceded that. There was nothing she could do to stop or persuade him from whatever he wanted to do. The landlord had tried to interest himself in Hudson's affairs too, and had been rebuffed. He had banged on Hudson's door because he could smell the hashish he was smoking. 'Hey you, open up! None of that in my house,' he shouted. When Hudson opened the door, Andy threatened him with eviction if he caught him again. Hudson pulled a knife with one hand while with the other he took hold of the landlord's trousers-front, squeezing his genitals through the cloth. The landlord yelped with terror and ran down to Dottie as soon as he was released, close to tears and clutching his mortified gonads.

Sometimes she heard Hudson with his friends upstairs, and heard laughter cutting through the rumble of conversation. He had become pleasant enough with her, but only because she left him alone. She knew it was because of that that he had stopped defying her at every turn, and she felt that she was failing in a responsibility bequeathed to her. She was ashamed to think what Sharon would have said to her if she knew, or what Sharon would have said if she had not herself been such a ruin. At one time, Dottie would have risked her life for the boy and Sophie, but they had not required it of her, and now they no longer wanted anything from her.

3

After an absence of several weeks, she thought it was time she went to the library again. She would remake her life, as she had done once before. The idea gave her strength, and new energy. She was eager to take it up before it dissipated itself in her habitual uncertainties. She wanted to read about the riots in Stepney, and about the Jews in Russia, and she wanted to find out about thousands of other things that she had once begun to develop an appetite for. She always glanced at Dr Murray's chair whenever she went there, not because she expected to see anything extraordinary, but because she thought of him every time she entered the reading hall. Once, the woman who had told her about him intercepted her look and smiled at her.

On the day she returned to the library, she saw a black man sitting in Dr Murray's chair reading a magazine. He was turning the pages idly, glancing up frequently as if he was on the look-out for someone. He noticed Dottie browsing through the encyclopaedia shelves and gave her a couple of speculative glances. When she made no response he did not pay any further attention to her. He was a tall, slim man with a very thin moustache. His jacket and tie hung badly on him, as if he was not used to them. He looked like someone from the country, she thought. Right down to his yellow shirt. She wondered if he was new in England, and had turned up for a rendezvous arranged months ago across thousands of miles. If she went near enough she would smell hot earth on him, she thought.

At last, the man he was waiting for turned up. The new arrival was another black man but seemed much more at ease. He was wearing a checked blazer and an open collar. His brown felt hat was tilted forward at a rakish angle, and his knees wobbled stylishly as he strolled into the library. The man who had been waiting rose to greet his friend, whooping with delight, his face wreathed in smiles. The dude who had just arrived in the library raised a finger in greeting, making as if to touch his hat but not quite doing so. The country cousin, as Dottie took him to be, clapped his hands together without making a noise, and then convulsed with silent laughter to show appreciation of his friend's city-slicker elegance. They lunged for each other's hands, grinning in a dumb-show of welcome and waving each other down, concerned to act with restraint and decorum in such a public place. She was smiling too as she watched them go, infected a little by their mutual joy at meeting again.

Dottie had not got anywhere with the encyclopaedia. She did not know how to look up Riots in Stepney in 1919. *Riots* told her nothing about Stepney, and *Stepney* told her about the Tower of London and Petticoat Lane and paragraph after paragraph about Roman remains. She read several other entries that her eye lit on: Prometheus, the Ruhr,

Rabindranath Tagore, but could find nothing on the riots in 1919. Saskatchewan, Smuts, Stone Age: after a while she knew that her mind was no longer taking in what she was reading. So she went to fiction and borrowed a copy of *King Solomon's Mines* instead, because Mike Butler had mentioned that too and told her to look out for it.

4

In the summer months, the work increased several-fold at the factory. Scores of students were taken on for the holidays. It was the busiest time of the year, and Dottie worked herself to her limit, going home exhausted every night. She worked so hard because she found the long evenings unbearably lonely. Hudson disappeared again but she did not think she really cared, just as long as he did not get into terrible trouble. She took armfuls of books out of the library every weekend, and read furiously. Romances and detective thrillers she devoured with growing ease, but she struggled unavailingly with more difficult things. She tried to read *David Copperfield* again, but could not manage it any more. She could not keep her mind on it, and could not be bothered with the labour of trying.

Every night she lay alone, listening to the noises of the house. Above her, she could hear the mad Polish woman talking to herself. Her cats roamed the dark house, their eyes glittering with malice. The woman on the same landing as Dottie sometimes shifted furniture late at night. She never spoke and rarely went out of her room once she came in from work.

In the long, gloomy evenings, Dottie sometimes stood at the window looking down on the garden. It was the middle of August, and the garden was overgrown with bushes and long grass. The brambles had twisted and wriggled their way into every corner. The rank fumes of rampant nettles mingled with the sappy smell of cow-parsley, which despite the brambles grew to enormous sizes. Here and there in the primordial chaos, a little flower appeared. Pale and undersized, it was a feeble descendant of a more pampered and luscious ancestor: a tiny rose that had lost all pretensions, and now displayed itself deferentially, scraggy daisies that had learned to grub around for space and light.

The huge elm tree at the back of the house no longer put forth any leaves. It was blighted with the beetle and was going to be cut down, but some stubborn, russet leaves still hung on to the bare branches, dried and misshapened, tossing and rattling fruitlessly in the breeze. That was how she was, she thought, dried up and terrified, like something that had already died and now could only contemplate its extinction.

It was a relief to escape the room, even if only to go to work and suffer the boredom of mindless labour and stupid conversation. One of the new people at the factory was taking an interest in her. Sooner or later, the summer workers paired off with someone, usually another summer worker like themselves, a student, or a flashy young man with an exotic story to tell. Dottie received her share of casual invitations to go out for a drink with them, which she casually declined. She thought of them as people with places to go. Unlike her, they were not staying on at the factory, just doing a job in passing, on the way to somewhere else. To these men she would only be something to pass a few hours with, to torture and dismember for the violent thrill of asserting dominance and inflicting pain. It was not something she had thought out thoroughly, and sometimes she suffered unexpected pangs of guilt and shame for it, as if she was refusing to accept some kind of obligation. But when she pictured herself with men, she saw herself being fearful of their violence.

There was a dream of a little girl that sometimes came to her. The girl was walking or playing on a large green, strolling in the wistfully self-absorbed manner of little children. At other times she would be skipping and trotting joyfully towards the canal and the line of trees beyond that, the very picture of innocence. Later she was howling with fear while a man whose lips were smeared with slime tried to drag her by her arm. Another little girl was sitting on the grass, crying and holding out her arms. She thought of it as her own nightmare, the fear of abuse that she had lived with, that Sharon had taught her to beware of. The dream was so real at times that she woke up with the conviction that it had really happened, although she knew very well, she thought, that nothing like that had ever happened to her.

So she did not require much reflection to turn down the invitations from the restless men at the factory. She understood enough to know that if she went with one of them she would be entertained with a couple of glasses of vodka and orange, and would then be expected to submit to a fierce grope in a dark stairway or in a dirty hall. If she was unwise enough to agree to enter a room, she might find herself having to submit further than this. Some of the students from less worldly-wise backgrounds, or the young girls who could not resist the cynical flattery of the predatory men, had given a hint of their experiences. The eyes of these men truly roved, moving from one victim to another with egotistical hunger, oblivious of how they seemed to others.

The man she had seen looking at her, and smiling at her whenever he caught her eye, was not one of these. He walked with his head slightly lowered, as if he was deliberately avoiding people. Even when she caught him with his eyes on her, he smiled quickly and looked away. She liked the attention, but did not think anything would come out of it. She did not really want anything to come out of it, she thought. It was better that she caught his eye now and then and felt a thrill of excitement run through her, and felt a trickle of sweat begin to run from under her armpits. His name was Ken. He told her shyly one day after he had sat down next to her on the bus. He was fair-haired, with bright, cheerful eyes. His small, red lips were pulled back in a smile, but at the corner of them she saw a kind of tightening, as if he was anxious about something. He grew a small beard and moustache, like a Frenchman or a painter, she thought, although she did not know anyone who remotely fitted those descriptions. He was dressed in a shirt and trousers, and seemed very casual and comfortable despite the mildly uneasy smile on his face. He glanced at the book she was reading, then raised surprised brows.

'You're reading Jane Austen,' he said, delighted.

'I got it from the library,' Dottie said after a moment, disliking the tone of surprise in his voice. Why shouldn't she read what she liked? At first she was inclined not to reply. When he sat down and spoke, she had found herself tensing, preparing for withdrawal.

'Do you like her?' he asked, half-turning on the seat to face her.

'Yes, I like reading historical books … romances and things like that. I only found out about her last week, but I've read two of her novels since then,' she said quickly, and then stopped suddenly, thinking she was talking too fast. He nodded for her to continue, an expectant smile on his face. She shook her head slightly and looked away.

'Jane Austen a writer of romances!' he said, a hint of suppressed laughter in his voice.

She assumed he was mocking her. 'Yes,' she said defiantly, leaning back a little to get a good look at him. She saw that his lower lip trembled, and that a flicker of misery appeared behind the brightness of his eyes. It was a shock to see at once into a man's face like that, and she looked away again, surprised by his vulnerability.

'I'm sorry. I meant ... I should've thought of that myself,' he said, explaining himself. 'I like her too, but I was always put off by the seriousness with which the teachers spoke about her. That's what I meant when I said that ... I should've learned to think of her like you say, then perhaps I would've enjoyed her more. Although I do get fed up with all that dreary drawing-room conversation sometimes. I haven't read her for a long time ... perhaps I should.'

'She is so funny,' Dottie said, smiling, losing some of her own fear as she heard him stumbling and feeling for the right things to say. This time she forced herself to speak calmly. 'And she does it so cleverly. Those pompous women! They would be frightening in real life, but she makes them seem ridiculous,' she said, thinking in her own mind of the matron of the school where they had kept Sophie. It was with a glow of self-satisfaction that she remembered how she had dealt with that fierce woman. 'The men are all so English,' she said.

'So *what?*' he asked, laughing and pretending to look offended at the same time.

Dottie smiled too. 'So dignified ... but you feel she is laughing at them too. I've been thinking, while I've been reading this,' she said, holding up a copy of *Mansfield Park*, 'She would've been a nice person to know. Don't you think?

'I'm not sure,' he said looking dubious, but his smile none the less broadened as he talked. 'You've almost convinced me, but I suspect she might turn out to be too much for me if I actually met her. There was something I remember disliking about her. I think it was that I had no feeling that she thought there was anything amiss in her taboo-ridden world. Perhaps I'd better start reading her again as soon as possible before I say something really foolish. Do you think she gives the men the same treatment as the women? You know, pompous old jokers? I seem to remember them being undeservedly rich and constantly moralising.'

She liked the way he said that. 'The men she writes about are all so ignorant!' she said, making him laugh.

Dottie found herself thinking about Ken that evening. He had spoken in such an easy, pleasant way that she regretted his going when he changed buses at Clapham Common. The look of pain had surprised her, made her feel for him. There had been such little time, but she liked the comfortable way he had of leaning forward to talk, as if he was unaware of himself. She guessed that he was more knowledgeable than he made himself seem, and she was slightly ashamed for having shown off, but that had pleased her too. If he had challenged her, she would have taken everything back, but he did not. Perhaps that was what people did, she thought. They talked as if they knew what they were saying.

The next morning she looked out for him but he was not on the bus. She made a face at herself. As the bus travelled the short journey to Stockwell, she began to shake herself out of the fantasy she had allowed herself to fall into during the lonely hours in her room. He had only spoken to her out of vanity, unable to resist the flirtation which he assumed she had signalled with all those intercepted looks. Above all else, he was an Englishman, and probably thought of her as a dusky bit of stuff that he could use and discard. She had seen the look in his eyes, and it was no different from the cruel light she had seen in men's eyes ever since she was a child. The thought made her smile, for it made her think of Ken's face and the laughter she had seen in it. She was trying too hard, she told herself, because she didn't really mean it. She was just pretending to be fighting him off.

When it was time for a coffee-break, she saw him hanging around near her line, sweeping behind the machines and keeping an eye on her. He gave her a small, surreptitious wave, and she grinned. The women in her line noticed and nudged and winked at each other. 'Look what I bought on the way to work,' Ken said, after they had got their coffee and were standing outside to escape the crush of people in the absurdly tiny pre-fab that served as the coffee bar. Out of the deep back pocket of the factory overall, he pulled out a copy of *Emma*. 'I started to read it on the bus,' he said with a laugh.

She noticed that the skin on his face was weathered. Perhaps he had had a strong tan which had faded. The creases in his cheeks were sharply etched, as if newly-made on an otherwise unblemished surface. A sign of some recent troubles, she thought, that time had not yet kneaded and pounded into the contours of the face. In his laughter she felt the anxiety she had sensed before, but it did not seem now like a sudden glimpse of something raw. It was more an attitude, a kind of uncertainty. Perhaps he was simply miserable underneath the smiles, she guessed, and was doing his best to hide his unhappiness.

'Have you been working here long?' he asked.

She nodded, disappointed that he had not taken her for one of the students. He had only been working there for about three weeks, he told her. They offered him a permanent job but he had preferred a weekly contract. 'I don't know whether I want to stay in London. Maybe I'm just passing through. I don't really like the big, dirty city. I was born in Dorset, you see, and I was brought up on a farm. Anyway, I don't know why they offered me a permanent job. There must have been about half a dozen of us turned up that morning.' He glanced at Dottie, then smiled when he saw the accusation on her face. 'I suppose the personnel woman did not want to offer Pakis and wogs a permanent job unless she had to.'

The women teased her when she got back, asking for his name so they could make their own approaches to him. Whenever he walked past they called out to him, and he walked past often as the day approached six o'clock. On the bus he told her that his other name was Dawes. 'I've just come back from Australia,' he said. 'I went to work on a farm there too. I love farms. That's my ambition, you know, to live on a farm; and paint and write poems and go fishing. Not that I'm doing anything to make that ambition come true.'

'Didn't you think Australia would make it come true?' she asked.

He shrugged. 'Maybe, but it didn't work out. I think I've just got into the habit. I travel around a lot, bumming around. And when things don't work out I travel some more.'

She saw that he looked shame-faced as he said this, that it was something he disliked himself for. He took a sudden deep breath, as if he would change the subject.

'What was Australia like?' she asked, intending to help him. 'I've always liked the sound of it. Starting again, making a fortune ...'

'I'm not sure you'd like it,' he said, looking uncomfortable. 'Not that I really know anything about the place. I said that I went there to work on a farm but I never made it out of Sydney. All my time in Australia I washed up dishes and waited at tables in an Italian restaurant. I don't think it's an easy place to start again and make a fortune. Not any more, anyway, and certainly not for a woman.'

'They wouldn't even let me in,' Dottie said. 'White Australia and all that. I was just saying I liked the idea of starting again, wiping everything off and writing a completely new story. I expect if I was given the chance I'd find myself doing the same thing again, working in an Australian factory rather than an English one.'

He smiled. 'I don't think so,' he said. 'I suspect you'd turn the place inside out.' She saw that he did not get off at Clapham Common, and glanced at him for an explanation.

'Can't I catch a Streatham bus from your stop?' he asked.

'Yes,' she said.

There was a look in his eyes, as if he was expecting her to say more, perhaps extend an invitation. She looked away towards the darkening Common, and saw the usual crowds outside the pub by the pond. The late evening light had lost its lustre, and the trees and lawns it illuminated looked flat and leaden-coloured. Children were running on the grass, chasing each other and tumbling over their frantically excited dogs. A handful of fishermen were still sitting patiently by the edge of the pond, as absurd and still as garden gnomes.

'The United States was much more interesting,' Ken said after a moment. 'I came back from Australia through there. From West to East ... and a bit of North and South as well. I even got as far as Canada. It was my first time in America. There's so much happening there. You can feel the place moving, and nothing seems impossible. This new man, I hope he wins, John Kennedy. Can you imagine anyone more different from old Eisenhower? I saw a Civil Rights march in Tennessee. Those people are brave, you know. The marchers and the freedom-riders, I mean. You should've seen the Gospel-spouting barbarians who were opposing them with their whips and dogs. If I could've I would have stayed in America.'

'How could you afford all that wandering?' she asked. 'It must cost a lot to travel like that.'

'I saved some money in Australia, and worked my passage to California,' he said, smiling easily. 'Then I worked across the Atlantic as well. It's not that hard when you know how to bum around.'

'Where else have you been?' she asked.

'India, Argentina, Indonesia. For one year I worked on a tanker. The Suez Canal and the Middle East.'

'You've done so much! I haven't been anywhere,' she said, her voice soft with self-pity. 'And you can't be much older than me.'

He got off the bus at her stop as well, but he stood still beside the road, making no effort to accompany her further. 'I'm not as young as you think,' he said. 'I'll see you tomorrow. Shall I wait here for the Streatham bus?'

They travelled home together every evening of that week, and on Friday they stopped off for a drink at the pub on the Common. It was too crowded to stay inside, so they took their drinks outside and strolled slowly in the evening gloom. Dottie did not say anything very much, relishing Ken's effortless conversation. She did not tell him that it was her first time in a pub, and that pubs were places she had always taken long detours to avoid walking past, let alone going into. It was something to do with Sharon, she supposed, and the people who used to come round to see her. She had always associated drinking with their harshness and unpredictability. No wonder Hudson and

Sophie had found her unbearable to live with. No wonder they had left as soon as they could!

She was glad Sophie and Hudson were not there, though. In her mind she had all but agreed to the suggestion that she was certain Ken was going to make. She hoped he would not say anything yet, would not make it seem that he was in a hurry, but she would agree whenever he did. She thought that what was happening to her must be falling in love. Whenever he was not with her, she thought about him. At night she imagined him with her, and lay awake rehearsing every stroke of her hand on his body. As they walked, she deliberately nudged into him now and then, to feel his warmth along her arm while she listened to him talk about the things he had done.

'You said you grew up on a farm,' she said after a long and friendly silence. 'Were your parents farm workers?'

'No, no, they own the place,' he said.

'Why don't you go back there then, and fish and paint and all those other things you said?' Dottie asked, amazed that anyone should choose a rootless life when they had some land to which they belonged.

Ken smiled at her and shrugged. 'Maybe I will,' he said.

Later, he kissed her before he left her at the bottom of Segovia Street to go and catch his bus. 'I feel like a teen-ager,' he said, before turning to hurry away.

The following night they went to the cinema. On the way home she took Ken's arm, sliding her hand into the crook of his elbow, and she felt him turn to glance at her. She invited him in, hoping that her inexperience in such matters would not show. She had debated if she should say anything and was still irresolute when they reached her room. The house was silent but she could hear music and laughter through the open window. When she turned to

Ken after drawing the curtains and putting her things on the chest of drawers, all thought of what she should do or say left her. She went to him eagerly, and he held her in his arms for a moment before he kissed her. In the terror and wonder of being with a man, there was also some feeling of dread. The pain mingled sweetly enough, though, with all the other unexpectedly gentle pains that her body suffered, and she was swept along by the happiness of her first love.

First Love

1

It was a lovely September, with a mellow warmth that is impossible to imagine later in the year. To Dottie it seemed that there was a hush in the air, as if all the urgent and irresistible forces of creation were at rest, gathering strength for the next long haul. The skies were clear and bright, and gentle breezes blew from the south, making tree-tops rustle and whisper in the lavender light. The crash of metal on fatigued bones, the silent howls of doomed crowds, the growls and lurches of runaway machines and other elegies of urban life, made way for gentle, benign sounds uncommon to Dottie's ear. Nine bean-rows of growing things and hives for the honey-bees.

She knew that it was not really like this, and that the gently swaying trees, leaning towards each other in the warm breeze, were pushing armour-tipped roots deeper into the earth in a frenzied search for food, and that behind the most banal or tranquil exteriors seethed hives of corruption and violence and waste. Yet even though she knew all this, she still liked to think that everything was becalmed before a transformation. She laughed, thinking that all the romantic novels she had been reading had gone to her head, but she could not resist the picture of herself as someone between lives, about to discard a useless, dried-up self for a healthier, hardier one. All else around her seemed to be silent with similar resolve, waiting to move itself into the next journey. It was not even spring, a traditional time for such delusions, but the height of the growing season when ahead lay only the frantic weeks of accumulation against the biting cruelties of winter. On reflection, she liked this idea better. Like a giant tree, or a thrifty rose, she was already planning a regenerated self in the spring.

It was tempting to think that her life, or whatever it was inside her that was noble and capable of sure deeds of imagination, was no longer indifferent to the fate she was to suffer. Of course it could not be like that, but she felt that the world itself was aware of her at last and was pausing in its business to take another look. My, Dottie has found a little happiness! For the first time she was not running in fear from what was around her, and had learnt how unnerved she had been. Now she knew the meaning of her life, she thought, when before she had known nothing but a cringing expectation of pain and suffering, a victim's genuflection. She had shut her eyes, drawn a deep breath and plunged in. When she came up again she was laughing, joyful for the sheer majesty of her deliverance. That was the meaning of her life, she thought, to make sense of all the enchantments that the world was full of. Not just because she had known a man, but because he had lifted the fear and oppression she had lived with all her time. She would once have tossed that kind of declaration off as worth nothing more than a lot of hot air. But she had been allowed a glimpse of the mysteries of the world, no less, and had a sense of having found a place for herself in them. That sense had swept away the numbness that had dulled the quickness in her, and she now felt alive and full of zest. No longer would she be gainsaid by the clutter that had penned her in for so many years.

She thought all this secretly, with embarrassment, because there was enough scepticism in her nature to make her hold back, to make her stand off with a sneering expression, while another side of her threw itself into the flood. Her birthday fell within the first week of being with Ken, and she had had to wait until she was twenty-one, she thought, before she could gain such simple knowledge.

They spent all their time together. After work they caught the bus and went back to Balham. It was obvious from the start that he was not bothered about rushing back to his room, and he was happy to spend all his nights with her. Dottie had to overcome an anxiety that came easily to her, and stop herself from asking him to go home at night, at least. Could they not do this casually? Gently? Did they have to behave quite as recklessly as they did? The part of her that urged caution was routed and despatched, and she surrendered herself to new pleasures with a kind of relief. She had heard the voice that advised her to take care, but that voice wanted to ask about how long she and Ken would last. Whether he had someone else and was only using her, violating her. She did not know the answers to these questions. If her feelings were not much more than the gushing immaturity of an emotional adolescent, she knew there was something finer in entertaining them than in allowing herself to turn sour and deformed with loneliness. Perhaps she was overawed by the pleasures her first love released, or perhaps she would have done better to make herself difficult and force Ken to value her more. But she knew that she had never lived through a time like it, and that was enough to begin with.

He found ways of being near her at work. When he had a trolley-load to take anywhere, he managed to include her line in his route. If he had a message or an errand, he would stroll past her on the way, a triumphant smile on his face, stroking his little golden beard with self-satisfaction. She saw his proprietary airs and found a kind of pride in them. I belong to him, she said to herself, and thought she sensed the envy of the other women. Whenever he had time to kill, or whenever his charge-hand was taking too long over his coffee break, he would be sure to find a broom somewhere and give the floor around them another sweep. The women had laughed at first. *Gordon Bennett, what are you giving that poor man? Give us a clue, Dottie love! I wouldn't mind trying it out myself.* Their mockery quickly turned to indifference when they saw how persistent he was. *He must be in love*, they said, which made Dottie thrill with the memory of his whispered vows while they lay in bed in the dark.

Mike Butler was consulted by the women, and he felt that something definitive was required from him. He gave Ken several long, thoughtful looks before he agreed with the women. There was no question that they were too far gone for anyone to be able to do anything for them, he said, shaking his head sagely. Best thing under the circumstances, if anybody was to ask him, was just to let them get on with it. For a few days, men and women became the subject of his sermons and disquisitions. It was clear that Mike Butler found men and women puzzling. They negotiated quite unpredictable attachments and entertained inordinately disproportionate obsessions about each other, he said. It was too much for a simple, hard-working man like him to work out. *To be or not to be*, he declaimed, and winked at Dottie when no one was looking.

In the evenings they went out, and Ken showed her the city she had been living in for nearly eight years but from which she had cowered in terror. Her round consisted of Balham and Tooting and the bus to Kennington. She recalled rare outings to other places, but they were faded, part of the memory of Sharon. That was all she knew. The rest was a maze of streets and numbers on a map, and legendary sites that were part of the shadowy myths of the city. Ken took her to many of them, the parks and the waters, the arches and the squares. He took his cue from her, laughing with disbelief as she named one place after another. Hyde Park, Tottenham Court Road, Chancery Lane, Kew Gardens. They strolled along the banks of the Serpentine on a sunny, glittering day, and Dottie could hardly credit that such scenes existed in the great, dirty city that she knew. In Richmond Park they slipped into a grove of rhododendrons that was as huge and roomy as a church. In this gloomy bower they lay silently for a long while, drifting in enchanted daydreams. From where they lay they could see the path, and saw people walking past to whom they were invisible.

She wanted to see City Road where the Micawbers lived when David Copperfield first met them, and go to Highgate where David and Dora spent their brief marriage, and where Steerforth's mother lived. He took her to concerts and to the theatre, showed her the famous shops and even made her try clothes on that the assistants knew she could not afford. They went to Parliament, the most boring theatre in town, he said. The Members were in recess but she thought the building was magnificent enough. On the evening of her birthday, they had a meal in an Armenian restaurant, and Ken entertained her with tales of his experiences as a waiter in the Italian restaurant in Sydney, the Romantica. The manager was called Giuseppe, he told her, and his wife was called Carlotta. He had a huge handle-bar moustache, which he loved to twirl between forefinger and thumb at the women customers, like an old-fashioned lecher. She laughed at his description, but told him she did not believe him. In the end he confessed that he had made up Giuseppe and Carlotta. The real manager was a lean young man with a cold eye and a short temper, who neither drank nor leered at women, and was not a fit subject for conversation between civilised people.

When their money ran out, they took long walks on the Embankment and across Westminster Bridge. It was the companionship that gave Dottie the most joy. She talked to him about how Sophie and Hudson had left, and she found release and support in what he said to her. She did not speak freely, although this was not a decision that she had consciously made. His experiences seemed to her so full of adventure and courage, so varied and wholesome, that her own life sounded sordid and mean in comparison. She was not at all tempted to talk about all that. She told him about Sophie and Hudson because it made her feel that she too had a complicated life, and suffered the disappointments that everyone did from undeserving brothers and sisters. She had heard the women at work talking like that, describing the misdemeanours of their loved ones with unmistakable relish. How this one had cheated a grandmother out of gold trinkets that were a gift from a China trip her husband had made way back when! And that one had tried to get rid of a pregnancy without asking for help, and nearly died with the terrible things she did to herself ... and still never managed to get rid of the little goblin, which would probably arrive with addled brains after being messed around like that and torment her life for years to come. There were tales of parents abandoned by neglectful offspring, lovers jilted by philandering suitors, and husbands who freely swung between adultery and beatings.

So Dottie told Ken her story as a way of laying claim to her normal share of misuse and family tragedy. Ken listened with interest and asked her questions which gradually began to alarm her with their intensity. They drew her attention to the gravity of the crimes she was accusing her sister and brother of, and she found herself guiltily taking much of what she had said back. Ken said they should go and see Sophie, if it had been that long since Dottie had last heard from her. He admonished her, for God's sake, not to let her family drift apart. It was not as if she lived very far. Yes, they should go and look her up, Dottie agreed, but neither of them proposed a time when they could do so. They would deal with that when the more urgent pleasures they were engaged in had become less insistent.

He teased her about her name, using it in conversation to mean that she was scatterbrained. 'What a dotty thing to do,' he said, laughing and ignoring her glaring look. 'Couldn't you have found a better way to shorten your name?'

'That's my name,' she said defiantly. 'It's how I was christened, Dottie Badoura Balfour.'

He tilted his head to one side, the way a bird does when it wants to give a worm a good look. 'Say it again,' he said. 'What was that name? The whole thing.'

'Dottie Badoura Balfour,' she said, still defiant and resenting the broad grin on his face as he asked his question.

'What does it mean? That middle bit,' he asked, chuckling. 'Where does the name come from?'

'I don't know,' she said sharply, just as annoyed with the question as with the fact that she could not give him an answer. 'What does Ken Dawes mean?'

'Hey, don't get annoyed,' he said, reaching for her and pulling her towards him. 'I think foreigners have much more interesting names than we do, anyway. Imagine being called Ken Dawes! I suppose its one advantage is that I know that it comes from no further away than Dorset.'

I'm not a foreigner, she thought, but she did not say anything. The moment after she had thought that and kept her thoughts to herself, she knew that she had left out the Fatma in her name deliberately, because it sounded so obviously and familiarly foreign, like a cliché. Suleiyman the Magnificent, Paddy the Navvy, Sindbad the Sailor, Cohen the Money-lender, Fatma the Belly-dancer. In her preoccupation with the guilt she felt for having so lightly discarded one of her beloved names, she did not realise how plain on her face the grimace of remorse and misery was. A small frown of impatience passed across Ken's face.

Dottie was tempted to say something, but then let the moment pass with a defeated sigh. There was no point getting annoyed about such things, not when you knew who was saying them. She would only look a fool. So she let him pull her into his arms and felt the ridge of anger down her back melting under his touch. Later she found herself talking about Leeds, in the most general terms. There was a sweet-shop on a corner which was run by an old woman, and she used to go there with one of her mother's friends. She gave up in confusion as she realised how much she would have to reveal to finish her story. She would have to tell him about the Church of Our Lady of Miracles, and the silent well that stood in the church-yard. And explain that her mother's friend was the same man who had taken them to the church to be christened. She remembered almost nothing of him, only what Sharon had told her, but sometimes on her own, late at night, there flashed through her mind bright pictures of a tall slim man with a wide smile. Sometimes she saw him with a large dog, walking across a common. She did not strain for the memories, did not conjure them, but when they came she felt them tenderly and hoarded all the small details that the passing of time seemed to throw up. It was strange how clear such pictures became as she grew away from them.

2

Ken too talked about the way life had turned out for him, but he spoke more guardedly, looking to find the right emphasis in his narration, ready with a self-deprecating joke if he felt himself becoming too earnest. He had been sent to a public school in Somerset, he told her. It was a famous place, which cost his parents a handsome pile of money, but he hoped its name would mean nothing to her. That was quite soon after the war, for he was five years older than Dottie and was nearly eleven when the war ended. His parents were reluctant to send him away. They both detested the thought of boarding school, especially his father, who had spent some of the most miserable years of his childhood in one. But they thought it would be best for him not to be on the farm.

His elder brother had been brought back home from the hospital, and he needed to be looked after in every conceivable way. He had been badly injured in an air crash, after the war was over, of all things, when he was being flown to his first posting in northern Germany. It was a terrible blow to his parents, whom he had persuaded against their wishes to let him volunteer instead of taking the university place he had already been offered. Ken was sent away because his parents wanted to save him the distress of living with a beloved brother who had been diminished beyond recognition by the accident.

'He had forgotten everything, a complete vegetable. He could no longer speak or walk, or even understand what was said to him.' Ken said, then he smiled involuntarily at the memory. 'The only thing he seemed to take pleasure in was eating as messily as possible, both hands in the plate and food plastered all over his face, like a baby. He loved performing huge defecations in his trousers, preferably while he was eating. He'd have this manic grin on his face while blasting noises were coming out from under him and the room filled with his stink. I swear sometimes I used to think he was doing it deliberately, red-faced from the straining but spluttering with joy. My mother used to be furious if we laughed. She said it would only encourage him.'

The school Ken was sent to was not too far away, and at first his parents brought him home most weekends. They thought he would be miserable there but boarding did not bother him at all, did not make him unhappy or cause him any of the vaunted traumas. On the contrary, he loved it there, and loved his holidays on the farm. It was during his time at the school that he decided he would become an artist, a painter. His art teacher was very keen that he should go to art college, and encouraged him to behave like an artist-in-embryo, supercilious about his intelligence and vain about his appearance. He even affected a dark cape and cane, and went through a period of starving himself, eating only breakfast cereals in the middle of the night. He told his teacher that he was trying to purify his soul because he could feel the birth of a great work in him, and wanted to be worthy of its execution. The school doctor sent him home as soon as he found out. Later, after he had returned to school, he took a vow of silence and did not speak to anyone for two weeks, and only broke his vow when the headmaster threatened him with expulsion if he did not answer his questions. Even then, all he said to the headmaster was that sensuality disgusted him because it was inimical to the passion of Art. The headmaster smiled and invited him to tea with his family on Sunday. Ken politely declined, saying he hated his own company too much to impose it on anyone else.

All these adventures and crises confirmed to Ken that going to art college was the proper decision for him. His parents preferred that he should go to university, and blamed themselves and the boarding school for his craziness. 'What they really preferred was that I stop being silly about being a painter and do something about educating myself, or at least acquiring a useful skill,' Ken said with a laugh. 'I told them that what I really wanted was to live on the farm and paint, and indulge the capacity for tragic feeling that I had discovered in myself, but Dad said the farm was no good any more and would not provide a living for all of us. They were quite insistent, my parents, so I thought I would go to university first and become a painter later.'

It did not work out like that. His examination results were terrible. Repeated attempts to retake them came to nothing. He had played around too much and now could not get himself out of the habit of loafing away the hours he was required to spend on study. He was so poorly prepared that he need not have bothered to turn up for some of the examinations. Comparisons were made with his brother, who at the same age had shown remarkable talent and self-discipline. By this time the brother had been moved to a little annex at the back of the house which he shared with a wretched-looking woman who was his nurse. Ken had no fear of comparisons with him. In the end, he was persuaded to try a crammer college in London. 'In Kensington. It cost a fortune, another fortune. I stayed with some relatives of my mother in Kilburn ... but that didn't work out either. So a little while later I signed on for my first voyage.'

'Perhaps you'll still be a painter one day,' Dottie said, filled with admiration. She could not imagine herself with such an ambition, and certainly could not see herself treating life with such cavalier disregard. 'When you've found your farm ...'

'Never mind all that crap,' he said, laughing with a careless toss of his head and then turning away with a pained expression. 'It's the things that we do that matter. All the stuff we have in our heads is just confusion, striving to make permanent the things that we see in our fantasies. Instead of all that we should live our lives to the full, live them as they come. This hankering after what is beyond us misses the point.'

Dottie was thoughtful, seduced by the light-hearted disdain Ken advocated but also made uneasy by it. As if it was that simple to toss the burdens off! She was certain that it was possible to live a better life than the one she had lived, dead certain. She knew she wanted to do much more than she had done. If life was to be lived to the full, did that mean that she should no longer aspire to what would make her happier, or freer or more knowledgeable about what was around her? It seemed like a concession to defeat, as if one was unwilling to keep on because the rules did not suit. She was not always with Ken when her unease came to her with such clarity, and her few attempts at explaining to him her worries sounded confused and laughable. The last time she tried, he did actually laugh at her, then pulled her into his arms and gently slapped her behind. She did not dare say to him, since he took her so lightly, that she sensed in his words and in his voice feelings of pain and despair.

'They're still there on the farm, the lot of them,' he said to her, chuckling with derision. 'Still living their vegetable lives, making manure for the land.' Dottie heard the hollowness of that mockery but did not dare press for explanations, and she felt the tone of self-pity running like an undercurrent beneath his cynicism. She was silent beside him, wanting to say something that would disperse his gloom but not knowing what she could say. She wanted to stop him from saying more, before he began to poison the feelings in her that he had stirred into life.

'Never mind that crap,' he said.

3

The following evening he stayed in while she went to the launderette. When she came back he was already in bed, listening to the radio. They made love in the dark, hurriedly and in silence. Afterwards she heard him sit up. She lay quietly, not speaking, waiting for what she knew he had to say. He sighed heavily, ending with a catch in his throat that was something between a groan and a laugh. She wished then that she had not resisted the temptation to interrupt him with a cheerful generality that would have prevented him from speaking. A long silence came between them, and again and again Dottie thought she should speak and prevent the explanations she could feel trembling on his lips. She had wondered at that tremulous quiver of the lips, and she knew she was about to have an inkling of its meaning. What she feared was that it would make him realise his distance from her, would return him to whatever he had fled from.

'There's more,' he said gently, when the silence was no longer bearable. 'I stayed in Kilburn for two years, working for an estate agent and living with my mother's cousin and her family. She had a son about my age and two daughters. They treated me like one of them, and included me in everything they did. I was one of the family, they told me, and their home was mine too. The father was a civil servant in the Ministry of Defence, and he often came home late. After I'd been there for two years I married one of the daughters. We'd been sleeping together secretly for over a year, whenever we could, whenever the house was empty. We hardly ever talked about it, even when we were on our own. It was stupid ... She became pregnant. They would've killed me if they could. They would've loved to punish me in some way. Her family.'

Dottie did not want to hear any more, because she knew that after telling her all this he would go. She did not think she needed to hear more. She did not want him to go. It was not difficult to guess the rest, she thought, and she was not curious about the details. 'Ken,' she said, thinking to stop him, but she could not say the words.

After a long silence, he started again. 'She was the youngest, just eighteen. Only just out of school ... She had been spoilt by everybody because she was good-natured and affectionate. It was only a game at first, pretending to be fighting, wrestling on the floor. The kind of thing we used to do at school ... Then her parents went away for a few days' holiday, leaving their grown-up children to look after the house. That was the first time. I took a day off sick from work. She was always the last to leave, but this day she decided at the last minute not to go to school. We hadn't planned it. We had not arranged it or anything, but we did after that, whenever the rare opportunity presented itself. There was nothing reckless about it, no vows or passionate declarations. We did it like it was dirty, hurriedly and silently ...'

'Ken!' Dottie said, pained and made jealous by these descriptions despite herself. 'I don't think you should tell me more. Not if it makes you feel so bad.' She did not say that she did not want to hear more, although she was glad he had told her as much as he had. The hurt she had seen on his face had a little more meaning now. She had taken the quivering of his lips, the long, terrified silences, to be signs of some ancient instability and fear. Why else would he be with her, unless he was frightened of normal people? Without thinking of it clearly, she had taken him to be damaged goods, deformed in some deep-seated region that was no longer visible. The thought brought a bitter smile to her face as she acknowledged the extent of her self-contempt. Really there were no depths she was not prepared to sink to, to persuade the world to despise her, she thought, filled with self-pity. She looked at Ken sitting up beside her in the dark, his shape upright and tense, and felt the first stirrings of revulsion for him. She was not sure whom she felt more sorry for, the man demoralised with shame, or the young girl he had injured, and who thought she was only playing.

Eventually he laughed. It was a sudden, strained, wheezing laughter, false with melodrama. 'I suppose she thought she would get away with it, as she'd always done with everything. She used to say that nothing bad had ever happened to her. Everything always worked out ... She would apologise nicely and give someone a warm hug, and everything would be all right again. She was like that, very loving,' he said. In the dark, Dottie imagined him looking sad and wistful as he recalled the girl and her affectionate nature. She smiled wryly to herself, and wished that she was not the lucky recipient of these confidences. 'No, not thought! Thought is too strong a word for what either of us did,' he continued after a moment. 'Perhaps she hoped ... It's always the woman who has to pay, though. She must have known that ... you'd have thought. When she told me, she did not cry or beg or anything like that. She just told me, and waited.'

He laughed again, this time a note of real mirth bubbling underneath the surface of his mockery. 'She waited while I uttered my exclamations of horror and my reassurances ... until I had run out of the easy things to say. And she still waited. I don't know where she could've learned such cunning. I could feel the words being dragged out of me, being hauled out like ... like ... like they were life itself. I said something, you know, a vague mumble in the midst of which came *marriage*. Even then she did not say anything, did not even look up, but I heard her sigh. My mother insisted I should marry her. We're Catholics, did I tell you? What are you? She was frightened by all the fuss, all the troubles she had caused. Diana, that was her name. Diana. She was plump and slovenly but ... I should not have done what I did. It shames me to think of that time, and the way I was. Her parents were devastated, but that was only at first. They came round. After the wedding we were to go and live on the farm. I ran away rather than go back there.'

'But you liked it on the farm,' Dottie said at last, when it seemed that by his tense silence Ken was waiting for her to say something before he continued. She said this gently, asking for the explanation that she thought he wanted to give rather than making an accusation, but that was not how he took it. He moved suddenly, punching out at her in the dark.

'You want me to go back there like another cripple? What the fuck do you take me for, you stupid bitch!' he shouted, landing blows on the arms she had thrown up to protect her head. She waited until he had calmed down and had turned away from her, breathing heavily in indignation. Then she moved nearer and touched him on the shoulder. He sighed and turned to her with tearful apologies, kissing her arms where he had hit her, making her better.

Later, in the silence that made Dottie think that he had gone to sleep, he started again. 'I was a complete bastard. I left her in the hotel where we were spending our ridiculous honeymoon. On the third morning, while she was still sleeping, I walked away from her. I ran away.'

'Is that where you're going now? Back to the farm?'

She did not care whether he answered or not. In her mind, it was as if he had already told her that he was going, leaving her. And although she was sorry, and guessed that the pain would get worse when he was no longer there, she wished he would stop talking and just leave.

'You don't know what such pain is like,' he said. 'You're such an innocent. I've been wandering the world for four years, carrying that kind of burden, not even knowing how my parents are ... whether they are alive or dead. I felt completely alone. Not that I didn't get to know people, but that was just in passing. None of it could last. How could it when I was being torn apart inside? When I met you, you seemed so good, so gentle and pure that I thought perhaps the innocent pleasure you took in things would rub off on me. It seemed like that for a while, didn't it? I don't know whether you can understand the kind of loneliness I'm describing, the kind of guilt. That's what makes me so restless.'

Dottie started to say that he should not worry, that he should do whatever he thought was right, but he interrupted before she had got more than a few words out. 'No, please don't insist. Don't cling! I can't stand that,' he said, softening his voice but obviously speaking through gritted teeth. 'I would stay if I could, but I just can't make those kinds of promises. Don't make it any harder than it is already. It may seem mad to you ... Oh I wish I could make somebody understand! This life is driving me crazy.'

He suddenly turned away from her and curled himself up as if he was going to sleep. She resisted the urge to protest that she was not clinging, was not a pathetic little innocent that he could talk to as if she could not feel pain. Let him go to sleep, she thought bitterly, and she felt a sneer crossing her face. She had not forced him into this, had not pursued him into her bed. She would not have known how to. He had appeared to her in that gloomy cave where she spent her daylight hours, like an angel with his golden hair and fragrant breath, and touched her with his warmth and his maleness. She had felt herself shrivelling into a shape that would announce her deformity to the world, abandoned even by those she would have sacrificed life for. He had come and breathed life into her, held her and warmed her and made her feel whole and ordinary. But she knew from what he had told her that she could offer him little that would assuage the pain that he felt. She felt her own lack too much to be able to do much for him. It was almost, she thought, as if he relished the agony. And in the end, she suspected, he had already made up his mind to return to his parents' farm, and was only delaying the prodigal's return with anguish-ridden dalliances on the road. She smiled grimly as she made herself ready for sleep, and thought she should kick the backside he had stuck out at her, just to show him that she had seen through him and was not going to be made an idiot of.

In the morning, she left for work while he was still sleeping. She stood at the door for a long moment, wondering if she should wake him, but the anger she had felt in the night returned and made her shut the door decisively behind her. The women asked after Ken, as did Mike Butler, coming round with a message from Ken's charge-hand that he was getting fed up of the absences. Dottie shrugged, and saw Mike Butler smile sadly.

'I'll tell him,' she said, disliking the presumption of that pitying smile.

She did not know what to expect as she hurried home. Many times during the long day she regretted that she had closed the door behind her without a word. Instead of leaving him asleep, she thought, she should have repeated his own words to him: live life as it comes. But he had not really meant that, and she did not believe in it anyway. They were only words, a manner of speaking, to show himself that he lived a full life because he had been elected to bear pain. She suspected that he would have gathered his things and gone, and as she sat on the bus she made herself ready for the emptiness she would find in that room.

He opened the door for her and held her in his arms for a long time. *Sorry*, he whispered, again and again, while she clung to him with joy. Please don't hate me, he said. He had been to the market and bought her flowers, lilies and fat, white daisies, which now stood resplendent in an old Blue Band margarine tin. He had cleaned the room, and had tidied everything away, had found an old bed-sheet in one of the boxes and used it as a rag to clean the window-panes. Hudson, she thought, suddenly seared with guilt. Where was that poor boy? They really came out filthy, he said. The windows. He suggested they go out, to escape the room which was beginning to make him feel cramped and hemmed-in.

They walked all the way to the river that evening, down Clapham Road, past the Oval, and along the Embankment to Lambeth Palace Road, walking slowly for hours until they crossed the river at Westminster Bridge. They stopped for bangers and chips in one of the grimy cafés on the other side of Waterloo Bridge. The nights were getting chillier and they decided to take a bus back to Balham, laughing at everything they saw, as they once had done. He wanted to stop at the Common and take a walk by the pond, buy a beer in the pub and take a stroll across the rimy green, where mist was rising like passion in the moist air. But she was too tired and begged him to come home. The next day he came to work with her but there was a swagger in his manner which suggested that he was doing this satirically, and did not hope to continue for long in this indenture.

4

It was as if he was only playing for time. She did not believe his smiles any more, and thought of his love-making as something crude, which he disguised with excess. There were longer silences between them, unless Ken wanted to talk about an event in his past. Usually their conversations were about the petty details of their lives. In the evenings they went out rather than sit in the room, skirting their misery.

'There was a painting I was trying to do once,' he said one evening as they sat in the pub. 'I was staying with some people in the country. I didn't really know them. They were just people I met while I was wandering around England in those first weeks after I ran away from Diana. The man was an electrician and the woman was not quite right in the head, I remember that. They offered me a room in their cottage. It was two cottages knocked into one, full of rooms that were half-decorated and half-gutted, with bare floorboards and sometimes no floorboards at all. There were naked wires hanging down from the ceiling and thrusting out of the crumbling, buckled walls. It was as if there had been a blast near by, and they had not yet got round to clearing up properly. Like some of the towns I had been in, still with their bomb craters and crumbling houses, derelict sites with water-filled pits and piles of rubble. I don't know why they offered me a place to stay, I don't remember now. I must've met them at a party or in a pub. These things happen to you when you're young.'

Dottie wanted to ask about the people: couldn't he try to remember how he had met them, how the woman was not right in the head? But she guessed he would not want to talk about that. He was looking into his glass of beer with singular concentration, and he winced slightly as if he was seeing things in there that were causing him pain. She kept her eyes on Ken, but she had seen out of the corner of her eye that a group of men at the bar were glancing at them every so often. It was not so unusual for that to happen, and it always made her a little anxious. She saw that one of them was very drunk, wobbling as he rolled against the bar.

'When they found out that I painted, they were very pleased. Very protective. They got me an easel from somewhere, and some canvas and frames,' Ken said, looking up with a grin on his face. 'They were incredible. He was like a great, soft animal. Everything made him laugh and he performed the most wonderful kindnesses as if he had never given them a thought. I'd say silly things and he'd just go and do them. I fancy a beer. How about a picnic tomorrow? I would say that kind of thing ... and he'd act as if it was the best idea he'd heard in ages. They set me up in one of the rooms, overlooking the fields at the back of the house. Perhaps they thought I'd like to paint that landscape, and perhaps I would have done, but only one picture kept appearing whenever I tried to work.'

Dottie must have looked sceptical, because Ken smiled wryly. 'I know, it sounds all arty-farty. However hard I tried, only one picture came out any good,' he said. 'I did paint other things, but they were rubbish. I wasn't interested in them, only this one … It was a picture of a deformed man writhing in some kind of a struggle, squatting on bent knees and glancing upwards as if he was about to be crushed by something he expected to fall on him. There were sores and wounds on his back and shoulders. He was a short, ugly creature with a flattened head and a powerful-looking body, but he was bunched-up like an overdeveloped muscle. He looked very frightened, terrified. It made me desperate to work out what the picture meant. I didn't realise it at the time, but it was obviously something to do with my brother, something to do with his squalid, truncated life. He used to look like that sometimes, as if he understood what had happened to him. I was thinking about that painting last night, and even when I slept it came to me in nightmares. I think that is how I have become, wounded and terrified.'

'No!' Dottie said, smiling at him and reaching out to touch him on the cheek. 'You are beautiful, nothing like that.'

'No, you don't understand,' he said, shaking his head violently, shaking her off, and suddenly frowning. 'I feel like that. Deformed and crippled! Dying! I have nothing good left in me.'

She wished they were not in such a public place so she could hold him and make him better. She looked round her in the pub, and saw that the drunk was making his way in their direction. The other men were looking at him and laughing, glancing at Dottie and Ken as well. 'Oh God,' she said, torn in confusion between the man in front of her and the humiliation that she could see approaching them.

'I don't think you can imagine what it's like,' Ken said, looking down at the table.

The drunk slid into a chair at a nearby table and leaned towards Ken. 'Excuse the interruption, guv,' he said, his head reeling a little but his face breaking into a large, delighted grin. He pointed an unsteady finger at Dottie and slowly swivelled his head towards her. 'Can I have a talk with the woman when you've finished with her?' he asked.

Ken smiled vaguely and shook his head. 'I don't think so,' he said.

'No rush! When you've finished,' the man said, leaning back as if he intended to wait beside them like that.

'I don't think she's interested,' Ken said, frowning.

A long, stertorous and dramatic sigh escaped the drunk. 'You lucky bastard ...' the man said, croaking with laughter and clutching his loins.

Without a thought, Dottie rose and tipped the drunken man out of the chair. He crashed into the table and slid to the floor, swearing with anger and surprise. She glanced towards the men at the bar, frightened of what would now follow, but she saw that they were rolling with laughter, holding on to each other as they bellowed their cruel and noisy mockery. Ken took her arm at the elbow: 'Let's go,' he said. She shook him off and went back to her chair, shaking with righteous and frightened fury. The landlord came round and helped the drunk to his feet. Ken spoke softly to him, and Dottie thought she saw some money change hands. In the end, the landlord nodded silently and gave Dottie a long, cold glance.

'There was no need for that,' Ken said as they walked home.

'You heard him!' Dottie said.

'I said there was no need for that,' he said sharply. 'He had just had too much and was behaving obnoxiously. You should've left it to me. Instead you demean yourself by behaving at his level. Couldn't you see that he was not worth the trouble? You've got to learn … For your own sake as well as for others like you. I've told you before, if you react like that you'll go on receiving that kind of treatment.'

'When did you tell me?' she asked, playing for time, not liking what she thought he could mean. She had never done anything like that before.

'Well, all right! I should've told you then,' he said, and then sighed. 'There's no point getting annoyed with people like that. You've got to show yourself superior to them. That's the only way you'll be accepted in England.'

She knew what he was trying to say to her, but she did not want to hear him say it. She made no reply, and walked silently beside him while he talked. Perhaps if she offered no challenge, he would stop, and would restrict his homily to advice about how she should conduct herself in the land of the Romans. But he circled nearer, unable to resist the temptation to spell out her ignorance. 'That squabbling fishwife kind of indignation will only expose you to further prejudice,' he said in a pained voice, hinting at the discomfort her silence was causing him. 'You may think I'm just being tiresome, but I assure you I'm on your side. And there are many who aren't, just remember that! It isn't only yourself you've got to think of but other coloured immigrants as well.'

Faces glanced out of car windows, looking Dottie up and down. Strollers in the late September twilight also looked at her. This was street-walker country, and most of the oglers were punters looking for a woman. 'Anyway, I was trying to tell you something important,' Ken continued in the uncomfortable silence, his voice sounding wounded again. 'About how I felt. Instead you get involved in a bar-room brawl.'

Dottie felt the pressure of his disapproval, and as they walked home without talking she sensed the words of apology beginning to rise in her. She muttered 'Sorry' as they entered the poorly-lit Segovia Street, and in the gloom she heard him sigh softly. He pressed her to him, and she felt the tenseness leave her and a smile grow on her face. He talked late into the night when they got back, describing to her the misery of the life he had lived. She lay close beside him, running her hand over his body and stroking his golden hair. In the end, he caught her nodding off, and laughingly smacked her before letting her go to sleep.

The next morning she woke him, but he shook his head and turned over. He did this again the morning after that, and she came home to find him sitting in a second-hand chair he had bought in one of the junk-shops by the market. He was listening to the radio and reading the evening paper. 'It's Nigeria's independence today,' he said, moving his feet to let her pass. 'Perhaps we should emigrate to there. It can't be worse than this dump. They might make me the big white chief or something.'

'Mike Butler told me today that they don't want you back,' Dottie said, irritated by the look of amusement on his face. 'There's some money owing to you, and they want you to go and collect it. Did you do any shopping? I haven't got any dinner. Are you going to look for another job? I can't support you, you know. I don't have any money.' She blurted out one thing after another, restraining herself from storming up to him and hitting him. He was smiling at her, and then he pursed his lips and gently blew her a kiss, soothing her. She saw his lips tremble, as if he was frightened of what he was doing.

'You don't have any money! That's not true, is it?' he said, and pointed to the little jewellery box on the chest of drawers. 'I ran into your little piggy-bank today. An impressive hoard of sixty-five pounds, to be exact. We can go and have a feast on that. What a miser you are!'

She glanced at the box and looked angrily back at him. 'That's my money. You keep your hands off it,' she said.

'It's all there,' he said, laughing and rising to go to her. 'You see what a materialist you are. You pass yourself off as this tragic little heroine when you're nothing more than a greedy little housewife. You thought I'd pinch it and go bet on the horses or something, didn't you? How crass you must think I am! What are you saving up for? Your wedding? Where did you get that jewellery box anyway? It looks valuable.'

'From Brenda,' she said after a moment, disliking his question, disliking everything that was happening. She did not want to react angrily, or make a fuss. She was too tired. 'She gave it to me last Christmas.'

'Who's Brenda?' he asked, taking her handbag from her and putting it down on the chest of drawers. He helped her take her jacket off and slid it over the back of the chair, gently brushing dust off the shoulder seams.

'A friend. She was our social worker, but she became a friend. A kind of friend ... she helped us out,' Dottie said, feeling a little guilty about Brenda.

Ken picked up her hand and kissed it as he talked. 'Social worker! Your own tame white liberal,' he said. 'I must say I'm surprised. I wouldn't have thought you would tolerate one of those. Don't tell me, she found you that slave-job you're doing, and helped you find this slum you live in. And at Christmas she gave you an expensive present that she could easily afford. I don't suppose you realise how dangerous she is.'

'No,' she said, trying to stop him kissing her hand.

'No?' he asked, misunderstanding her. 'Why do you think you're doing that work and living here? This is where she wants to keep you, a docile little nigger girl doing her bit for the great white race. That's the white liberal for you, no different from anyone else. As racist as they come, just like all of us, but pretending to be so full of concern.'

'No, no, no,' she said, snatching her hand away. 'Stop doing that. Please, I'm tired.'

Ken dropped her hand as if he had been stung. His face flushed and swelled with anger, and his eyes seemed to light with affront. He looked away quickly and went back to his chair. For a long time he said nothing, looking down at the floor while he stoked his rage. Dottie stood just inside the door where he had left her, not knowing what had made her repel him. She wanted him to go, back to his Diana and his tragic life. But she did not want him to go, despite the way he tormented her.

'You're tired of me,' he said at last, his voice small with regret. For a long time after that he said nothing more, and Dottie did not dare speak, waiting to see which way the tide would go. 'I haven't been fair to you, have I? Is that what you're thinking? I should've told you that I was going back, that I was on my way back when I met you ... Don't you think that's pathetic? To give in to all that crap about guilt and duty. After all the things I've been saying? It was all right to begin with, wasn't it? I know you liked being with me, didn't you? Dottie!'

She saw him smile to himself as he said her name, and a small look of triumph crossed his features. It surprised her, but also gave her the strength not to say something abject, or rush to him with her regrets. He looked at her and grinned. 'It was all right, wasn't it? We can part like friends, can't we?'

Something Broken in Her Whole Life

1

It rained for thirteen days without stopping. In the mornings a pall of fog and mist shrouded the streets and the trees. It hovered on derelict sites and clung to the sides of buildings. Spars and scaffolding rose out of it, parts of a ghostly craft lost in an endless ocean. When evenings drew in, which they did suddenly earlier in October because of the change from summer time, darkness muffled all noise except that of dripping water. The rain made a ceaseless patter on the roofs and window panes. Pavements glistened in the gloomy streets, and the skies glowed with a grey refracted light. Dottie sat by her window in the evenings, the casement open in the unseasonally warm weather.

Sometimes she heard the sound of a flute coming from the house at the back of them, many yards across the tangled and overgrown gardens. She saw lights there in the early evening, and a door usually opened to eject a large dog. It was some kind of setter, and in the light that shone on it through the glass door she saw that its colour had some russet or red in it. The dog would stand attentively in the patch of light, its head lowered eagerly and its muzzle extended in submission. Even from such a long way Dottie could see fear in the way the dog stood. She imagined that if she was nearer she would see small ripples of terror run quivering through its body. Instead of bounding joyously across the back gardens, leaping the derelict fences, and making a bid for freedom, the dog whined gently, piteously begging to be allowed back inside.

Dottie wondered if it was love for the person with the melancholy flute that made the dog so selflessly devoted, or if it was knowledge of some later retribution that habitually followed unavoidable wrong-doings that made it so abject. She never saw the person who lived there, could not even tell if it was a man or a woman. The elm tree at the back of the garden, depite losing all its leaves, still obscured a full view of the doorway. Dottie was left to imagine the look of triumph and satisfaction that would cross the face of the dog's beloved as the animal cringed with restrained joy at being re-admitted.

At first, in the early days of Ken's departure, she was tempted to think herself similar to the cringing animal, and she wondered if the look of triumph would be at all like the one on Ken's face. She had seen a dart of pleasure in his eyes when he spoke of leaving, and when he finally left the following day he was struggling to suppress his smiles. He was eager to go in the end. Was it relief that it was over that made him act like that?

She was surprised that he expressed no regrets, did not even tell her a lie about how much he would miss her. He seemed cheerful, treating her like a friend he had enjoyed meeting and would be bound to meet again sooner or later. Perhaps this was how he had planned everything all along. When he became bored with her, he brought the story of Diana out of his kit-bag, and then made himself disagreeable enough so that separation was the only sensible thing. That was what his look of triumph meant, she thought, that he had made his escape, had made his plan work. She knew nothing about such things. She was a complete beginner, naive to the point of embarrassment, a proper baby, and she must have seemed a very simple game to him.

She hated herself for her persistence in searching for motives and explanations that would condemn her ignorance, and make her gullibility and gratitude for his affection seem part of his plan. The more she thought about how they were, the more she turned the matter over, the more sordid seemed the time they had spent together. She had been a fool. Sometimes she was filled with disgust at her inability to stop worrying at the small humiliations she had accepted at his hands. She told herself not to get carried away with her stories, not to worry everything into squalor.

She allowed herself to get into a daze, giving in to the drama of her isolation. Her days passed in a blur while she repeated her grievances to herself with unflagging insistence. Some of the people at the factory tried to talk to her, avoiding the mention of *his* name, but waxing philosophical on the ephemeral nature of youthful love. Reminiscences of unsuccessful affairs were unfurled in her hearing, and the faith in Mr Right turning up in his sweet good time was emphatically re-affirmed, and casually held out to her as a life-line. Only one woman mentioned Ken by name. She was the unofficial leader of the section they worked in, a tall, fair-haired woman of heroic proportions. She seemed to know everyone and was always laughing and back-slapping with the men. She had hardly ever spoken to Dottie before, and Dottie would not have dreamed of seeking her out. Not only was her appearance and the clatter that accompanied her intimidating, but Dottie had seen the pained look she always assumed when ordering the foreign workers to a task. She had no authority to do this, but none of the workers challenged her, overawed by her imperious ways. It was obvious from her superciliousness that she took some satisfaction in her presumed pre-eminence over them.

'I hear that shyster Ken has left you high and dry. Good riddance, I say,' she came to tell Dottie, and looked at the rest of the line as if she expected the people there to burst out with applause. 'He weren't any good for you. Blimey, anybody could see that!' After that, Dottie deflected the rest of the women with scowling looks.

Mike Butler spent three long lunch-times with her. Dottie understood that he was trying to be kind, to show sympathy, but while his face indicated the discomfort he felt at her unhappiness his tongue lived an independent existence. When it came to it, she was an audience and it would be to offend against all natural laws not to accept such juicy morsels of fortune with gratitude. So he told her more about Stepney between the wars, and the journey his grandfather had made from Russia in the 1890s. He described the life of great poverty that his grandparents were forced to live in the slums of East London, and the persecution they suffered for being Jews: riots, beatings, and later Moseley's dreadful blackshirts.

'They lived through all that, pogroms in Russia, the long journey across Europe and then stretched out and downtrodden in Stepney. But if you saw them, you would never guess that they had seen anything resembling those horrors. They just looked like a couple of old Yids in a gloomy tailor's shop. It inspires you when you think people can be good like that, doesn't it?' The next day he brought a picture of the old people, taken in London in 1936. The grandfather was sitting in a chair, older and more ill than Dottie expected. His wife stood beside him, a smile hovering at the corners of her face. Mike Butler said nothing about the photograph but he smiled too as he watched Dottie studying it.

When they tired of the photograph, Mike Butler launched into an unstoppable discussion on the best kind of wool for knitting cardigans, a project he was considering taking up. He had learnt to knit in the RAF, he said, but had been out of practice for a few years. It wouldn't do to let a skill like that go to waste, would it? Dottie listened to him with polite wonder, grateful for his eccentric kindnesses.

In moments of clarity, sitting alone in her room, listening to the sounds of the house, she was amused at the relish she took in her rejection. There was an acuteness, a wholeness about the pain she felt at her loneliness which was different from the miseries she had known before. She wondered if it was simply a kind of indulgence, something she knew she need not suffer to such an extent but was doing so out of choice. When she went to bed, she could not resist thinking of Ken lying beside her. She sifted through the memories of those few weeks they spent together, and lived again through the ones she relished. And then she wept for his loss.

Her inclination was to crush the memory of the time with him, pulverise and disperse it to the four corners. She scoffed at his airs and his affectations. *You have no idea how hard it has been for me*, she mimicked, shutting her eyes to simulate the agony of such recall. *How I have wandered the seven seas, racked by guilt and remorse! My life in ruins and my art unfulfilled! Some people were kind to me, but I don't remember their names because they were soft in the head. They were like big soft animals that whimpered in the dark*. If she allowed herself to, she could spend all evening digging out examples of his self-importance, little hard nuggets of his ridiculous selfishness. Then she would tramp and stomp across the floor of her room, snorting with contempt and consigning small, excruciating tortures on him and his farm animals. But she did not often allow herself to go that far. It seemed such a waste, of her strength and of whatever there had been between them that was good. She would just have to learn to keep what she wanted of him, to recall the memories of the comfort and reassurance she had found with him. And trash the rest.

She sensed, rather than fully grasped, the intimations of cynicism in the lesson she was attempting to force on herself. He had hurt her, so she would not allow herself to think about him. The thought made her shudder with guilt, and brought an irresistible flood of regrets. If she could have learnt to chase away the thoughts that caused her pain, would she not have begun by despatching Sharon? And then Sophie and Hudson? Was that what she had done? In her obsession with finding pleasure for herself she had given no thought to anyone else. She had not bothered to check on Sophie and had not even worried about Hudson for days. And now she was learning the full selfishness of denying the meaning of what had happened to her with Ken.

She went back to the library, and smiled with pleasure when the librarian who had been kind to her before welcomed her with a delighted grin. She browsed through fiction, and wandered into encyclopaedias for old times' sake. The thought of Dr Murray brought Brenda Holly back to mind, and made Dottie remember the little kindnesses that she had wrung out of her. She could not have got Hudson back without Brenda's help. She took out a book called *Living*, because the title appealed to her. On the way home, she went into the Post Office and rang up Brenda's office number. They told her that she had moved to Wales. After a long silence, which made the man at the end of the line ask anxiously if she was still there, Dottie asked for an address.

'Are you a friend?' the man asked. Dottie hesitated, she was not sure if she could call herself that.

'She helped me,' she said. When the man answered her with a long silence of his own, she did not know what else to say. At last, he sighed and told her to wait while he went to look. She had to put in another coin, and then another, but at last he came back.

'Look, I hope you're not going to bother her,' he said. 'She's having a bad enough time already. You know she's retired. She doesn't work here any more.'

'I'm sorry,' Dottie said, wishing he would just give her the address.

'Is it about work? Have you got a problem?'

'No, it's not about work. What's happened to her?' Dottie asked.

The man came back after a brief silence. 'Her husband's dying. She gave up her job so she could look after him. So they could have some time together. I hope you're not going to be a nuisance or anything.'

'I was only going to greet her, to say hello.'

'I shouldn't really do this,' the man said. 'But if you're a friend ...'

She realised as she walked home that she had not thought of Brenda as having a husband who could die, of having a family that could suffer just as much as she could. Who comforted her when her turn on the rack came? There were times when she had hated the smugness with which Brenda had quoted official rulings to her. *This can't be done because regulations utterly forbid it, but out of the goodness of my kind, long-suffering heart, I will allow you to do such and such. It bears no relation to what you really wanted, but it's the best I can do, my love.* Dottie had thought to herself at such moments that a woman like Brenda Holly could not possibly have any understanding of what it was like to live with any of the things that burdened her. The friendship that grew up between them was only a stunted and accidental one, quickly crushed by Hudson's tantrums. But as she pored over the remains, and followed the vestigial lifelines on the rock, she knew that perhaps that was another opportunity missed. So sure had she been that everything sought to wound her that she had taken no care how she herself lashed out.

She tried to express some of this in her letter, to give an inkling of her regrets and to tell Brenda that she understood more now of what help she had tried to offer her, but in the mood she was in her effort came out as abjectly miserable and self-pitying. In the end she wrote only a few lines of greeting, saying that she had only just heard about her move.

2

The next day Sophie came. It was late on Sunday morning, and Dottie was lying on her bed reading and listening to the sounds of the house. Someone downstairs had acquired a sewing machine, and she guessed it was the Indian woman on the ground floor. The family had moved in only recently. At first Dottie thought that the older man was the woman's father, but later she found out that they were husband and wife. Andy, the landlord, had told her on one of the few occasions he still came round for rent. More usually he sent a young cousin of his to collect what he could. Times had changed for Andy and fortune no longer smiled on him. His wife was divorcing him, he told Dottie, put up to it by her brothers, who were envious of him. Well, she couldn't really divorce him, he explained, but she wanted a settlement so she could set up on her own in Cyprus. Business was bad and money was short, and all they could think of was how to steal everything they could out of him. So hard had life become that Andy could no longer afford to dress like a dandy. His clothes had a ragged look and were not always as clean as they used to be. Sometimes he had a stubble of a beard on his chin and his breath smelled stale.

'They should lock up the dirty old man,' he said about his newest tenants. 'You don't know these Indian people, but I'm telling you they sell their own children. They are so poor … That's how an old man buys himself a young girl like that. But tell me darling, what are you doing with yourself these days? You want to come to the pictures? When is your sister coming back?'

On that Sunday morning, Dottie heard the tread of Sophie's step on the stairs and recognised it. Her knock on the door came seconds after Dottie had started to rise, smiling with incredulous expectation. As they hugged and kissed with joy, Dottie saw that Sophie had put on more weight. Her face was brightly made up, and she was wearing a tight satiny dress. She had brought her bags with her. Dottie registered all these things without pausing in her questions or her joyful welcome. Later, as they sat talking in the early evening, Dottie saw the marks that the good-time life had left on her sister. She saw the brash smile and the knowing, cynical look that Sophie gave her, and she heard the forced insincere laughter. But she was still the same Sophie, and before too long was curled comfortably in a corner of her old bed, smiling languorously as she listened to her sister. Dottie told her about the new tenants, and the story Andy had told her about them. Sophie made a face of disgust. Dottie teased her by telling her that Andy was always asking after her, which made Sophie smile. Before she went to sleep, as they lay with the lights out, Sophie told her about a man she had met. His name was Jimmy and he would probably come by for her sometime.

Sophie's presence lifted Dottie's spirits immeasurably. She started cooking again, and realised she had been living too much out of packets and tins. The little stove in their room did not allow anything ambitious, but, with Sophie there, Dottie found herself thinking and managing again instead of just consuming whatever was easy or near to hand. They talked for hours in the evenings, finding pleasure in the things they learned from each other. Dottie proudly recounted her time with Ken, holding back many important details, and opting for simplicity as a way of heightening the dramatic impact of her story. She made one or two small changes as well, and felt only a twinge of guilt for doing so. Thus it was she who asked Ken to go in the end because she could not bear his indecisiveness any longer. Sophie sympathised, and quoted Jimmy on the matter. Jimmy's general advice was simply not to trust a white man.

He was equally adamant on a number of other issues, Dottie discovered from what Sophie told her. But it was on white men that he was most authoritative. He could smell a white man at twenty paces, even in the dark, through sweat, urine, manure, perfume, you name it. No disguise could fool him. He described this white man's smell vividly. It was the smell a chicken gave off when it had been drenched by tropical rain, a mixture of steaming feathers, chicken dirt and wet fleas. Being close to Englishmen always made him homesick, reminded him of the rainy season in Trinidad, where he came from. But that smell was nothing compared to the odour an Englishman gave off when he was wet. Sophie could not get the words out for laughing, so Dottie never got to find out for certain what this smell was. She could not be bothered to ask afterwards, but she thought she caught snatches of the word 'corpse'. Jimmy had views on the smells of English women as well, and on the other qualities they possessed, but Sophie did not pass these on, saying they were too disgusting.

It was Jimmy who had told Sophie that she was too good to be associating with the low-class women who were her friends, and that she should go back to live with her sister. Low-class people are too envious, he told her. He had been seeing her for several weeks, and had promised to come and call on her in Balham after she moved back. He himself lived in Camberwell, sometimes.

'What do you mean sometimes?' Dottie asked.

'He has to move around for his work. There's no point him having a place when he's not settled,' Sophie said, sounding defensive, but smiling with a kind of pride for Jimmy's free life. 'He's a welder.'

'Why can't a welder have a place to live?'

'Oh Sis, because there's no point,' Sophie cried, becoming exasperated with the questions.

In any case, Sophie was only too happy to take Jimmy's advice and move back in with Dottie. She had been getting tired of the nightly carousing, although she had had some good times too. She said this with a hard-edged laugh that rocked her large body and brought a sudden glint of mockery to her eyes. Some of those friends who came round were mean people anyway, thinking they could live off the little money that others earned from the sweat of their brow. She was still working in the cafeteria in Victoria Station, wiping tables and cleaning floors, and she was not doing all that to have some useless man drink it all away. Why are we black people so useless? she asked. Dottie was taken aback by the question. Are we? she thought.

'Only it wasn't all like that,' Sophie said, smiling again at the look of disapproval on Dottie's face. 'We had laughs, lots of laughs. And some of the men were really fine. It was just my luck, Sis. I always used to get the funny ones. Until Jimmy came, and he is funny in the best way. He just makes me laugh all the time. He's fair too, did I tell you that?' So when he said to her that she was too good for the company she kept, Sophie decided that the time had come to pack in the bacchanal and go back home. The weather was turning cold anyway, and winter in those rooms they had rented in Stepney was not going to be a joke.

'Well, the sister's here but the brother's disappeared to God knows where,' Dottie said, shocked by all the stories but determined not to annoy Sophie with her disapproval. 'I haven't heard from him since he left, have you? A couple of months, maybe. I suppose he'll turn up when it gets cold enough.'

'Oh I'm sure he's all right, and he'll have lots of stories to tell us when he comes back,' Sophie said. 'I had a dream that he was travelling in other countries. You remember how he always used to go on about America? Only I don't think it was America I dreamed about. I think it was France. I don't know why ... He was in a crowd and he was laughing and having fun.'

'He's not even sixteen, and no one knows whether he comes or he goes, or what he lives on. He doesn't go to school, he doesn't do any regular work. You tell me, how is he going to end up? Even talking to him is impossible.'

'You worry too much, Sis,' Sophie said, looking unhappy. 'He'll be all right. He's just a bit rough now but he'll grow up. Maybe this trip will do it for him. You just got to give him the room to make his own mistakes.'

Dottie said no more, because whenever she did she heard herself sounding like a tired and disappointed old harridan who was getting in the way of other people's youthful adventures. It did not seem right that Hudson and Sophie between them should have silenced her so unfairly, and should have made her anxieties into something interfering and annoying. When she thought of Hudson on his travels, she did not imagine fun-filled adventures in gay Paree, or in whatever part of France Sophie's dreams had deposited him, but violence and danger. In her mind she saw him with those other young men, the ones with whom he had languidly strolled the High Road, frightening shoppers off the pavement with their swagger and their noisy mockery. Only now they were desperados, relishing their cruelty, picking fights and pulling knives on people whom they sought to rob and terrify. It made her weak with worry when she tried to guess how Hudson would find money for food, or where he might be sleeping. Sophie considered herself worldly and knowing, and liked to think of Dottie as the innocent one, but all she saw for Hudson were laughing escapades in France.

In the weeks that followed, the two sisters picked up their lives together with consummate accommodation, making room for each other and taking pleasure in the company. Sophie's stories were always full of Jimmy, and of the hectic dramas of her friends at the cafeteria. Dottie talked about the things she had learned from the books she read, and from the newspapers and the radio. It was Sophie herself who asked Dottie to talk about these things, making flattering comments about all that her sister knew. Dottie tried to be careful, telling herself not to get carried away by Sophie's ignorance, nor to pretend that she knew more than she did. She admonished herself not to show off, but she could not resist the opportunity when it unfailingly presented itself. When the gaps in her knowledge loomed unavoidably, she had no choice but to invent, although she tried to keep her inventions modest and discreet. It did not matter too much in the end, for Sophie took in very little of what was said to her, listening with open-mouthed incredulity to all the varieties of bits and pieces that her sister was full of. Sometimes she laughed with appreciation, admiring Dottie's zeal in acquiring this knowledge. What is it all for? she exclaimed, impressed by the very purity of what she took to be useless learning. She had no cynicism in her admiration, and could answer with honesty all of Dottie's repeated pleas for reassurance that she was not being boring.

Early in November, John Kennedy was elected to the presidency of the United States of America. It was a close-run contest, and the final counting in Illinois gave off a strong whiff of skulduggery and corruption, but none of this diminished Dottie's pleasure at the young senator's triumph. She explained to Sophie the significance of this joyous news. She could not avoid linking the new president with stories of race riots and protests that Ken had witnessed and described to her, and that she herself had heard about on the radio. In some way, she connected Ken with the president, she realised, even though she understood clearly that there was no conceivable comparison between them.

'This is the man who will put an end to the suffering of black people in America,' she said to Sophie. 'At last they have found someone who will listen to them, and who will help them lift the burden of oppression from their necks. For hundreds of years they have borne this yoke.'

Dottie's description of the new president touched something in Sophie, and from then on she venerated him. In

Stepney Sophie had rediscovered religion, and she relished its ceremonies and certitudes as she once had during the months she spent in the school in Hastings. The women she had lived with, her goodtime friends, went to church every Sunday morning, dressing up in tight flimsy dresses and large pale-coloured hats. Sophie had been tentative about the style of worship at first. The noise and exuberance, the yelling and hand-clapping in church were embarrassing and nothing like the services she had gone to in Hastings. The words of the songs were familiar, though, and as they started to come back to her she joined in lustily, and before long found herself calling for the Lord's Mercy as loudly as anyone else, and streaming with perspiration and sin as the pastor lamented the world's errent state. John Kennedy happened to Sophie while she was still in the after-glow of this bliss, and the language Dottie used to describe him meant that Sophie was able to admit him effortlessly into her gallery of saints.

Dottie tried to tell her about the Congo as well, and the troubles they were having there. She told her about the man Tshombe, a shameful braggart who was selling his people to the Belgians all over again, just so he could swell himself up with booty and blood. Sophie looked at the photograph of Moise Tshombe which Dottie showed her and made a face at it. 'He looks so cruel,' she said. 'Is this the man who is causing all the trouble in Africa?' The Congo and Tshombe did not have the appeal for her that Kennedy did, even as a demon to Kennedy's saint, and she sucked her teeth with emphatic disdain before giving the newspaper back to Dottie.

In any case, there was something shameful about all the killing and chaos that was going on in Africa. She had to admit the people there sounded completely primitive. Some of the stories she had heard, and the bits and pieces she had seen on newsreels, or the newspaper reports that some of the people at work had told her about were disgusting. She thought of them with a shudder. Nuns being raped in the middle of the jungle. Rebels wearing skins and doing crazy dances, eating their own dirt and swearing to kill white people. All the progress that had been made was being completely squandered: churches burned, plantations looted and neglected. And the picture of the man that Dottie showed her confirmed everything. He was an ugly man with a pointed face, as if he had been hacked out of one of those jungle trees.

Dottie understood her sister's superior aversion to her stories about the Congo, and Nigeria and India. She guessed that Sophie's apparent lack of interest was a deliberate rejection of the places her sister was talking about. Not boredom or ignorance, but a refusal to be put in the same camp as those foreigners with their primitive ways. This did not surprise her, for she too had felt that kind of disassociation at first. She had taken up the country's prejudices about those places and held them defensively to herself, not wanting to be taken for one of those ridiculous foreigners. The memory embarrassed her – how ridiculous she would have seemed to anyone who understood what she was doing. Later, her own discovery of how complex the reality of *those places* was had given her more strength. She had found pleasure in learning an abundance of new things about people and times she thought she had already grasped.

She discovered that her sketch of the world was little more than a tenuous and unstable metaphor, patchily blank and shimmery in the oddest places. What she learned made her more able to resist the feeling of unworthiness that her exposure to the English way of viewing the world had forced on her. She remembered Hudson's angry tears when she had tried to get him to understand that the *natives* in those Tarzan movies were not intended to be any different from them. She herself had not understood the meaning of what she was saying, not clearly, and had simply been angered by his boastfulness about his American father. Sharon was dying of something vile, which for all they knew, was acquired from the same shameless American who had used and discarded her, and Hudson was singing of him as if he was a flawless knight out of an antique legend.

Despite knowing that Sophie was quite satisfied with her picture of the world, Dottie could not resist turning the polite questions she asked her into opportunities for subverting her blissful ignorance. She knew that Sophie was only asking them to make conversation. It all went in one ear and out of the other, she told herself, but she could not curb her tongue. She knew that Sophie was listening really, but more often just did not remember the meaning of whatever it was that Dottie had told her. All attempts to make Sophie find out things for herself, take up reading or listen to the news, came to nothing. She dropped her head with a mixture of guilt and stubbornness whenever Dottie started. She could not read very well as it was, Dottie argued with her. If she did not try and improve … Sophie lowered her head and took her sister's chiding with submission, but she did not read anything and the news was boring. She went to the library whenever Dottie went, to keep her company and because they went almost everywhere together, but she only browsed desultorily through the books. She liked going to the library because it was full of people bent silently over books and papers. She admired that, and thought of it as something wholesome and valuable, quite unlike what she did most of the time.

In the street, one turning down from the library, there was a church. Sophie looked at it longingly whenever they went past, but Dottie was not interested. It was in a terrace of large Victorian houses, with steps and a balustrade leading to the front door. The downstairs windows had been extended so that almost the entire frontage of the house was glass, which made it look like a shop. Net curtains of impenetrable opacity draped the windows, giving the building a look of an undertakers or a disreputable medical practice. Between the upstairs windows hung a wooden cross, painted white and pinned to the wall by four nails which were weathered with rust. Above the front door was a painted board that declared the building to be The Sacred Church of the True Christ.

The house to the left of the church had no curtains of any kind on the downstairs windows. At these windows, one on either side of the front door, sat two dark-haired young women. They paid no attention to the street although they were clearly intended to be visible to anyone who might have been strolling past on the pavement. Both women wore dressing gowns or house coats which were only loosely gathered together and inevitably slid open as they saw to their knitting or sewing or whatever they were engaged in which was not visible below the sill. The house had a Bed and Breakfast sign on the steps. In warm weather Dottie had seen a fat, unshaven man in a singlet sitting on the steps, while his slatternly daughters or accomplices dangled their bruised wares out of the open windows. It was now late November, and the air was chilly and damp enough to dispirit more resourceful men than the sweaty brothel-master from unnecessary exposure, but not the scantily-dressed young women from their usual informality.

Dottie barely glanced at them. On an earlier occasion, she had fastened indignant glares at them, and one of the women had pushed up the sash window and lashed Dottie with abuse for her insolence. She had not understood what the woman was saying because she was unfamiliar with the language she spoke, but she took in the look of fury. Her face had been dark with anger, shining with sweat as she shouted across the street at her. So now she kept her eyes away, but in her mind she pictured their shameless display and their gleaming faces.

'In this weather, it can't be much fun having to sit around like that,' Dottie said, but Sophie barely glanced at her, her eyes still longingly fastened on the Church of the True Christ. Talking of the unpleasant weather made Dottie think of Hudson. She had hoped that November would bring him back. She had set great store on the cold, and even more store on his sixteenth birthday. She had not thought he would be able to resist coming back, just to see what fuss they would make of him. But he had! He had not even sent a postcard, or a note. On the day of his birthday, Dottie had been left at home on her own, waiting without hope for his return. Happy birthday sweet sixteen! Sophie went to spend the night with Jimmy, which she did at least once a week.

Dottie had met him only once, when he brought Sophie home late one evening. It was clear that he was not at his best, his eyes watery and blood-shot, and his movements a little wayward and out of control. He was a shortish man of about thirty or so, just beginning to turn plump and carrying a hint of a stoop. He wore a thin, clipped moustache which gave him the look of a dandified movie villain. His appearance suggested something just about to go bad, just on the point of slowly turning sour or running down. Dottie knew her glimpse of him not only caught him at a disadvantage, but that it had only been brief. None the less, the sight of him made her feel concerned for Sophie. That was the only time he had come to their room. Usually it was Sophie who went to him, sometimes in Camberwell or New Cross, occasionally in Catford where he had friends.

'Where does that man *live?*' Dottie asked, exasperated for Sophie's sake, but Sophie laughed, enjoying Jimmy's unpredictable ways. Men want to be free, Sophie said. That's the way men are.

Once Jimmy took her to Leeds for the weekend, to go to a party there. When Dottie laughed at the thought of going that far for a party, her sister looked hurt. You're just jealous, she said. Afterwards Dottie admitted to herself that she had felt a pang of envy and a kind of homesickness. She thought of Sharon and the man she had told her about, who had loved her and had her children christened. Dottie Badoura Fatma Balfour! Sometimes she thought she remembered him. She must have been nearly five when they left Leeds, and sometimes when she was alone she saw him walking a dog and smiling down at the child beside him. But that could only be her own day-dreaming, she thought. She did not remember anything, only Sharon going from one bad man to another, surrounded by creatures who misused her and fed her diseases and alcohol. And she was afraid of Sophie travelling down the same road, and of Hudson going bad and turning into one of those scavengers.

3

Then one day, when the gloom of winter had thoroughly set in, and the nights had drawn in so that light turned into darkness and night into day without drama or demarcation, Hudson came back. The house had fallen silent at that late hour, only the gurgle and slosh of winter drains breaking its muffled stillness. Sophie was out, as she usually was on Saturday nights, and Dottie was already in bed. When the noise of his footsteps first reached her, although she did not know that they were Hudson's, she remembered a story she had read about an old man who falls asleep while reading in front of a fire. The man lives alone, surrounded by the few objects he has gathered together over the years. He is suddenly woken by the noise of knocking. A storm rages without and at first he does not hear the knocking. Something taps on his window, and the knocking resumes with an insistence that cannot be denied. He opens the door to find that Death has come for him, but that first Death wants to have a chat about mortal coils and various undoings that the old man had been party to. Dottie had enjoyed most the moment of Death's arrival. She was terrified as she read but was impressed beyond belief at the audacity of making Death speak to the victim in such a reasonable way. She lost interest before the end of the story, put off by the high-flown poetic excesses that Death was credited with, but she had no doubt that the visitor had everything his own way after all was said and done.

The steps on the stairs paused dramatically on the landing and then continued upwards to the next landing. She heard the ceaseless chatter of the Polish woman who lived above them, and talked to herself, suddenly stop. She must have heard the steps on the stairs, and perhaps shivered at the thought of the solitary reaper calling on her. After a few moments the steps came down again, and Hudson knocked on his sister's door.

He looked haggard and ill. His face was gaunt with pain, and his eyes dark with fatigue. 'Come in,' Dottie said, after a moment. Her initial impulse, to move forward and hold him, had made him start back nervously. She touched him as he walked past her, laying a hand on his shoulder and feeling him twitch as if he would shake her off. He sat in the old arm-chair that Ken had bought, his head drooping and his shoulders hunched. 'Are you all right Hudson?' she asked.

His head was nodding jerkily as if he was dropping off to sleep, so she repeated her question loudly, with a note of panic in it. He looked up after a moment and smiled. Gently he lowered his head on his chest and closed his eyes.

A River Journey

1

He would not tell her what had gone wrong and she was worried about being too insistent, in case he took himself off again. There was no doubt that his adventures had wounded him and worn him down. He had lost weight, and lost strength, and no longer showed any signs of the youthful zest for cruelty that had been his unpleasing characteristic. Sitting by himself, he flicked his left hand across his face, as if irritably brushing away a fly that was hovering near it. He rubbed at imaginary marks on his body, frowning and frantic with effort. His jaw went rigid and locked into a grimace of distress – teeth bared and eyes bulging out of their sockets. Once she heard banging on the stairs which sounded like a soft, bouncing ball. When she went to look, she found Hudson on his knees, hitting the step with his forehead. Such gestures seemed the classic symptoms of disorder to Dottie, so obvious and predictable that she wondered if Hudson was playing a cruel joke on them, the prodigal nut come home to roost. At times it was as if he found his whole performance funny, and he grinned and chuckled with mad intensity.

The next thing would be for him to start talking to himself, she thought, like the public madman who held court outside Stockwell tube station and performed antics on request, making a living out of the hand-outs amused passers-by donated. *His* favourite trick was to warble an incomprehensible verse, if that was what it was, and then claim it was a praise song in Fula, his mother tongue, which he had especially composed for the worthy whom he hoped would reward him with a piece of silver. Failure to do so usually released a torrent of abuse from the madman, to the delight of passers-by, who then happily donated a few coppers. But Hudson did not sing or talk to himself. He did not talk to anyone. If left to decide for himself, he retreated to his little room upstairs and kept out of the way.

When Dottie went to get him, which she did every evening, he came and merely sat in the room with her, as if he was sacrificing himself. When the evening had worn on, he rose and left without a word. His silence scared her. There was a violent, cruel undertone in it, and it confirmed all her most lurid fears. Whenever she spoke to him or asked him a question, which she did softly and with exaggerated care, his head dropped a little and his shoulders hunched, as if he was hiding himself from her. He did this with resignation, with submission, sometimes smilingly accepting the shame of his silence but none the less refusing to break it. She knew there was a strain of defiance in his wretchedness, an obstinate refusal to be cajoled out of it.

'What happened? Have you got yourself into trouble?' she asked again and again. At first she would be gentle and cajoling, determined to reach him with kindness and sympathy, but finally she would become impatient with what to her seemed like childish obstinacy. If he was mad, then it was out of simple wilfulness. When was he going to stop thinking only of himself? He was nothing more than a selfish little sod. All she earned for her outbursts were small, pitying smiles, or once a loud howl of derision. In his eyes she was the ranting lulu who would not leave him in peace. She wished she could, but he was there for the whole world to see, a sixteen-year-old wreck. How could she just smile at that and wave it past? At least he was back, she consoled herself, out of whatever horror it was that had reduced him to such an abject silence. And if he stayed locked away in his room, he was also getting some sleep and recovering his strength.

She tried other methods. For a whole evening she ignored him. She thought if she ignored him long enough he was bound to get hungry, and then he would have to come and seek her out for food, which would be a start. Dottie held out for as long as she could, but half-way through the evening, shivering in the unusual cold of that cruel winter and imagining that his little room would be like a freezing cave, she was forced to go and fetch him. She could not leave him to freeze to death or starve in his cramped cell. She tried feeding him suggestions, to which he only needed to nod or shake his head to confirm their truthfulness. Was he ill? Had he done something criminal? Was he hiding from the police? Had somebody hurt him? Whatever it was that had happened would not make her love him any less. He knew that, didn't he? Why couldn't he understand? Why could he not speak? What was the matter with him? Why was he so incredibly stupid? He lowered his head with the look of submission that reminded her of the beaten dog in the garden. His soft, sniggering laughter, which before had had the sound of water tumbling over smooth slippery rocks, now contained the beginnings of a whine, she thought.

Even Sophie's powerful embraces, which Hudson had often found irresistible before, failed to move him. He suffered them without protest, deflating himself and going limp in her arms. Sophie had wept bitterly when she first saw her brother in this state, and she too made suggestions, tried to probe without being too insistent. She cooked dainty little sweets for him, as she had done before, and tried to tempt him into indulgence. At least that would show that he still took pleasure in something. When these subtleties failed as well, she knelt at his feet and begged him to speak. Hudson laughed at her and called her *Fatty*. That was his first word.

Tearfully, she turned on Dottie, on the brink of accusing her, of blaming her for what had happened. Dottie saw the blame, and saw the words tremble on Sophie's lips. Yes, have a go, she thought. Let's have a proper family carnival. The words did not come in the end. Sophie sucked in a large snivel, and swallowed her phlegm, allowing her eyes to make the accusation. Dottie knew the words would come one day, and she thought she knew what Sophie had almost said. That it was her fault Hudson was as he was, because she had brought him back from Dover to their life of misery. It was she who had taken him away from that picnic on the wonderful cliffs bathed with sunshine.

Perhaps Sophie blamed her for the way her own life had turned out as well. She wondered what her crime against Sophie was. Who else could they blame but her? As for Dottie herself, she could blame the stars or the fates that her life was as it was. She should have been born the daughter of a lord who was master of large estates in the garden of England, who could feed her strawberries out of season and whisk her south out of the winter cold. Better still, she thought, she could have been born the *son* of such a nabob ... Sophie threw herself on Hudson again, rocking him in her arms as she sobbed. Between the confusion of arms and shoulders, Dottie saw a smile on Hudson's face. It seemed a fully wicked smile at that moment and she was filled with disgust. When he caught Dottie's eye, there was brief spark of shock before he looked away.

His dejection slowly lessened with passing days, and he began to lose his look of abject submission. Slowly, he began to speak. He said bizarre unconnected things at first, hesitantly positioning the words in a difficult symmetry that required thought and labour: the price of dung in a bottle, the tall blue ceiling on the canal tow-path, dirty nail varnish. When they applauded his efforts, he laughed with manic abandon, grunting and hopping like an excited monkey. Dottie could not get over the feeling that he knew what he was doing, that he was manipulating them. Occasionally he would be lucid, stringing several sentences together and smiling because he was making complete sense. One day, she found him in an animated conversation with the old Polish woman who lived upstairs and talked to herself. She was undoubtedly mad, living with uncountable cats and emptying her chamberpot out of the window. Usually she ran away as soon as she caught sight of anyone, which was just as well because she smelled so bad, but Hudson stood talking to her on the stairs while she smiled and talked back at the same time. She spoke Polish while he spoke English, yet they were both grinning delightedly. A couple of nuts, Dottie thought, wishing she had not witnessed the scene.

When she managed to catch a steady sight of them, his eyes told her that something terrible had happened to him. When she looked in on him in the morning, he was always sleeping, curled up like a sick old man. He looked hot and feverish, and his skin glistened with stale sweat. She left money for him before she went to work, but dared not touch him. He looked so ragged, like something discarded. Once she called his name because she thought she heard him muttering, but he groaned without waking. He stayed in his cramped room for long hours of the day, lying in bed with his face turned to the wall. In the evenings he disappeared, and on some nights did not return.

One night, returning late from his nocturnal wanderings, he came to announce his recovery. He banged on their door until they woke up and talked at them with abounding merriment for over an hour. He would not leave, going on at them with flashing smiles and darting eyes. Long after either of the sisters could disguise their exhaustion, Hudson stood between them, performing his high jinks.

Dottie was not so innocent and ignorant that she did not begin to suspect the meaning of what was happening. It took her a long time to think openly that what Hudson was doing was *evil*. At first she thought that he used the money she gave him for drink, but she soon saw that that could not be right. The amount of money she could spare for him was not enough to get him into the fearful state of abandonment he was in. Where did he get the money for that? His soiled crumpled appearance in the mornings made her fear that something truly horrible was happening to him. Anyone could see that he had been places, that he had done things. He gave off a smell which was familiar but which she could not quite identify, and which made her think of a body that was turning putrid. His clothes were soiled with what looked like mud, or the dried slime of decomposing winter streets.

She tried to talk to Sophie about her suspicions but could not interest her. Sophie spent more and more time with Jimmy now, and was inclined to distance herself from Hudson and his dramas. When by chance she saw him, she was sarcastic and cold, and only spoke to him with sneering, disapproving quips. She made her eyes glaze over whenever Dottie started to talk to her about him, or offered peremptory advice that was intended to halt the conversation in its tracks. *Just ignore him, Sis. You should go back to your reading. When was the last time you went to the library? Tell me that. You'll lose all that book you know already if you don't keep practising*. At other times she quoted Jimmy, who was as authoritative on loafing younger brothers as he was on everything else on which he pronounced. Dottie was pleased that Sophie was so obviously devoted to Jimmy, though. She must've misjudged the man that one time she met him, she thought.

2

In the late days of winter in the new year, mobs of white citizens of the United States of America were attacking black schoolchildren in the streets of New Orleans and Baton Rouge, Louisiana, for wanting to attend the same schools as their children. The terrified children ran down charming and odorous alleys of these French-built towns to escape the wrath of their oppressors, while their fathers and mothers massed like zealots in their gloomy catacombs, fomenting the uprising. And while this was happening, Frenchmen were throwing bombs at Algerians in their own capital city for daring to defy the settled order of things. In late February of that same year, Patrice Lumumba, the deposed Prime Minister of the Congo Republic, was murdered in Elisabethville, the capital city of Tshombe's breakaway Katanga. Lumumba had been captured on his way to Stanleyville, his power-base. The new tsar of the Congo at that time was Joseph Mobutu, but he did not want Lumumba's blood on his hands, so he had him flown to Elisabethville, the city of his arch-enemy, for disposal. Lumumba was tortured on the plane. A young American diplomat had struck up a friendship with him and may even have been one of the many who persuaded him to give himself up. He was later to become a US Secretary of Defence but at that time he was only a friend. The announcement of Lumumba's violent death was made by Godefroid Munongo, Minister of the Interior of Katanga, in whose custody Lumumba had been for six weeks. Lumumba's Katangese murderers danced in the streets while their paymasters toasted each other from the torrents of blood they had released by their greed and desire for power.

On this dark night in winter, Dottie was on her own in her room in Balham feeling the lethargy and depression that had overtaken her days and nights. She sat by her open window, watching the yellow glow that hovered like a thickening cloud over the dirty city. The world was growing smaller, she thought, the rain slanting in even as she hid her face from the driving wind.

When it was close to midnight, Hudson came banging on the door for one of his maniac chats. He talked at her like a fury, laughing and jigging with high spirits, and bringing her close to tears with his mockery. He was dressed for the streets, in his tight trousers and studded leather jacket, and both his voice and the poses that he assumed reminded her of his friends and their intimidating ways.

He went on into the small hours, talking about everything, his school days and what his friends had said and done. He even talked about love, his words taking flight when he tried to describe the strength of the emotions that beat in his breast. Sometimes he came up to her as he made accusations or sought to drive a jibe home. He hovered and wheeled over her, prodding and clawing with malice. He ate everything Dottie had in the room, spooning cold tinned vegetables out of the tin, and tearing at hunks of bread with his teeth. Biscuits, milk and what was left in a jar of plum jam. She watched his hysteria as he replenished the energy he had used up, and groaned at the thought of the torture that was still to come. She watched him with an anguish she had not felt before, for she knew at that moment that his life would not be long. In the end she saw him beginning to wilt and became tempted by the thought of confronting him as he weakened. It was not so much calculation as opportunism. She had tried everything else. When the signs of his exhaustion were coming thick and fast, his eyes sliding out of focus, legs wobbling out of control, and long stertorous yawns escaping him, she guessed the moment was right. In any case, she thought, it was worth a try. She saw the look of agony on his face when she asked him the question, and she repeated it, demanding a reply.

'What has happened to you? I want you to tell me. You have to tell me the truth,' she insisted.

For a long moment he looked at her, his eyes still at last but fixed on her with panic. He looked as if he would get angry, his face gathering into a scowl, but then he sighed and spoke. He did not speak at once, and not fluently. Between long silences and sighs, he circled and came back to explain something, to add an important detail or offer a justification, but once he started he offered his confession willingly enough. The story he told her was worse than anything that Dottie had imagined. He had been using drugs for nearly two years, she must've known that, he said. He didn't use anything too expensive and always with his friends. They paid for their pleasures by selling in the streets, and by a little petty crime.

'Selling what? What do you mean a little petty crime?' she asked, her voice low, careful not to frighten him. 'I don't know about these things. You have to be patient and explain.'

His eyes looked away from her. For a moment she was afraid he would say no more but would laugh at her clumsiness and leave. They sold drugs, he told her. The suppliers sometimes gave them some to sell, and gave them a cut. They stole from shops, and sometimes from people in the streets. He looked at her to see if the answer satisfied her and quickly looked away. In the summer he had met a man who had offered him a small cut in an operation in the Midlands. Hudson travelled with this man and helped him run his business, which was selling drugs for other operators. Hudson made deliveries, acted as a messenger or a decoy as he was required. It was dangerous work, and he was learning, getting better all the time. They had some hilarious times as well, jokes and some fantastic parties. His boss told him he was tough and had a talent for the business, and promised to take him to the south of France with him during the winter if he was still around. He was also earning a lot of money, and drugs were easy, because that was their business. Inevitably, he took more and his boss did not seem to mind. It never even occurred to Hudson to resist or anything. Why should he? How could he?

'You're only sixteen,' Dottie cried, and saw Hudson wince with panic-stricken surprise. 'He was a wicked man to do that. Oh Hudson . . .!'

He stood up slowly, poised to leave and looking very tired. His eyes looked smaller, she thought, as if they were already shut. The pupils were contracting and turning opaque. She called him back, tried to get nearer, but he turned away, shaking his head and waving her back. There was no need for all that fuss, he told her. He was getting himself under control, getting his head together. Getting his head together. It was just that it had been difficult, but it would turn out right. Could she keep it to herself?

'Not tell Sophie?'

Not yet, anyway, he said. He was getting himself under control, so he could go back to being himself. That was all.

But it wasn't. Dottie thought that she had managed the matter wrongly, had made him run away from her again, but now he began to look out for her. There you are, Sophie told her, her faith in Hudson vindicated, although he never stopped or said anything when Sophie was around. Despite his brusqueness with both of them, Sophie was happy enough with the new situation. Families were like that, she said. Always having a fight and a barney. It didn't mean they didn't love each other.

In bits and pieces, Hudson's story came out. He did not understand that his life was in danger, not until it was too late. The drugs made him reckless. He did wild things, became involved with people he should have known to avoid. Eventually he was completely in the hands of his boss. He depended on him for everything, drugs, food. He did not even know the time of day unless his boss told him. And he was too much in debt to be able to resist him. It took Hudson a long time to say so, pausing for several minutes with his head in his hands. His boss used him for sex. It was not the sex, he said, weeping with his neck bent away from her. He had already done that, and other even more terrible things. He had screwed every which way, he said, laughing with bitterness and self-pity. It was that he had no choice but to submit. And that was only the beginning. The boss permitted other people to use him as well, and made them pay. In the end he had run away from him, and sold his body in the streets to get money for drugs. He could not say all this by himself, but as the extent of the boy's tragedy began to reveal itself Dottie lost her squeamishness in asking the questions that would let him tell his story. The more he told her, the more dejected and defeated he became. She knew there was a great deal he was keeping back, and she was overwhelmed by the thought of the unutterable squalor that her poor brother had had to live through.

She tried to talk him into going to see a doctor, but he told her, and she knew no better to contradict him, that the doctor would call in the police. He was so distraught about his circumstances that she was persuaded when he said that if he had enough help he could overcome his addiction himself. At first, as the tale of his corruption and licence unfolded, she had felt revulsion. In her mind, she began to draw away from him. No one did that kind of thing unless something was rotten inside them, she thought. That was the smell he gave off. The more she heard, though, the more she felt his misfortune, and wanted to do everything she could to help him. Dottie insisted that they should tell Sophie, if only about his addiction to drugs. Then they would all be able to pull together …

Sophie was not as surprised as Dottie had expected. She nodded, then listened silently as Dottie told her the story. 'Where does he get money now?' Sophie asked. Dottie did not reply, and after a few moments Sophie asked the question again.

'He steals. He sells drugs,' Dottie said. 'Whatever he can … but he wants to stop. He will stop. He swears he will stop.'

The sisters did what they could, but with each week they realised the ferocity of the adversary they had undertaken to defeat. Hudson lied to them, stole their savings. He wiped them out. Everything of value that they possessed he took from them. When they remonstrated with him, and he was feeling low, he wept with remorse. When he was high, he threatened to leave and go to New York to find his father. Sophie brought stories home from Jimmy, warning the two sisters that Hudson was capable of anything, would do any evil when the need was on him. He warned them to get rid of him ... How could they ask Hudson to go? He was their brother. Sophie threatened to move out herself, but was restrained by the thought of leaving Dottie alone.

In the spring, Hudson was arrested. He was charged with robbery with violence. Three of them had burgled a house in Clapham, and found themselves confronted by an old man with a horn-handled carving knife. They dispossessed him of the blunt, old weapon and beat him to a pulp. The sergeant at Clapham Police Station told Dottie that a neighbour identified one of the boys, and he had confessed and implicated the other two. All three, the sergeant said, were addicts and street-boys. Male prostitutes, he said, making sure that his euphemism was not misunderstood. They always go vicious with that combination, and certainly deserve a lot worse than the few months in the nick that they'll get, he said.

To the bitter end, Hudson swore that he was wrongly accused, and the boy on whose confession the charges were based claimed he had been beaten. They had *tortured* him in the station, he said in court, saying the word with all appearance of aggrieved pride, showing off wounds acquired in the gallant defence of his self-hood. Neither the bench nor the counsels seemed at all impressed or disturbed, and seemed quite uninterested when the third boy brought a factory manager to speak for him as a character witness. The old man identified the three black boys as his assailants, and that was more than half-way there. Hudson was sent to reform school for fourteen months. Dottie stood up in court and yelled at the magistrate, outraged by the cruelty of the smug man sitting on the bench and despatching Hudson to a life of misery. When the magistrate became angry and instructed for her to be removed, she fell down on her knees and begged him to show mercy to the poor confused boy. None of it made any difference, and she was driven from the court-room with a cuff round the ear.

Although neither sister would have liked to say it, it was a relief to be without him. Perhaps it would do him good, in some way, they consoled each other. If nothing else it would remove him from the corrupt ways that had almost destroyed his life, and give him the chance to redeem something from it. God willing, Amen! Sophie cried in a fervent whisper, then shut her eyes for a long minute of silent prayer. She had secretly taken to going to church again on Sundays, with some of the friends she had made through Jimmy. She spent almost every Saturday with him, and could conveniently slip to church the following morning without Dottie knowing. Dottie would not have cared, so long as *she* was not expected to turn up every week to listen to the harangues of a loud-mouthed preacher, but Sophie did not know that. When she sensed Dottie's disapproval of her church-going, she did not bother to enquire for the reasons, but quietly went underground.

She was still with Jimmy, much to Dottie's surprise. Dottie was forced to concede that she had misjudged the man. As soon as she felt less pressed by recent events, she promised herself, she would encourage him to come round more. She wrote to Hudson when she was sent an address. She told him about Jimmy and Sophie, and how happy they seemed to be. Then she wrote an enthusiastic paragraph about Yuri Gagarin going into orbit around the planet Earth. *You must have seen a picture of him in the newspaper. He has such a round cheerful face that you have no choice but to believe he is real. Not even the Russians could've made him up. The space suit he wears looks too big for him, I think. It looks like they'll soon have a man on the moon. Who would have thought that that would really happen one day.*

Hudson was sent to Dover Borstal, and she appreciated the irony at the same time as she felt a familiar twinge of guilt. Perhaps none of this would have happened if she had left him alone in Dover in the first place. During the year that he spent there, Dottie visited him four times, although it was four months before they let her go there for the first time. They told her Hudson was in hospital, and was best left without visitors for the time being. When she saw him he was gaunt and vacant, as if the stuffing had been taken out of him. As he got better, he was more animated, but in a furtive way, watching her movements and smiling without explanations. His manner made her think of someone who was scheming something. He talked about becoming a sailor, travelling the world and visiting America. I'll go and see my dad, he said, with a self-mocking smile.

3

'Have you ever stopped to think how pointless we are in this place?' he asked her on one of her visits. He did not bother to explain what he meant by *we*. She had been telling him about the Christmas festivities, although she did not tell him that she had been forced to spend the holiday on her own. Sophie and Jimmy had invited her to join them, but she could not bear to contemplate the revelry that they so keenly anticipated, and she had refused.

Despite being alone, she had had a pleasant enough time, reading a very funny book and going for long, long walks. She told Hudson the story of a Jamaican man who had been murdered on his way home from a New Year's party in Brixton, and it was that that had provoked his question. 'They don't want us in their country. They don't need us for anything apart from dirty jobs that no one else will do. And look at all these thousands of people, these *immigrants*, pouring in before the law changes and denies them entry to this paradise. What use can people like us have here?'

'Use? Do you mean a purpose for living? You have to make a purpose,' Dottie said, dropping her voice and glancing around her, afraid of being overheard. 'This is where we live. We belong here. Where else are you going to go? A place doesn't give you the reasons for living, you have to find them in yourself.'

Hudson threw his eyes to heaven, baring his teeth with derision. He's so young, she thought, and he can dismiss everything that is said to him with such disdain. Perhaps because he's so young …

'Oh very brave! Don't give me that holy roller stuff, that slave talk,' he said. 'How can you find any reason for living in a place where they treat you like an animal? All the time they show you that you are something they hate. Something below them … inferior to them. All the time! If you object, if you fight, they tell you you're obsessed with the colour of your skin. You become a dangerous man, a trouble-maker, and they beat you to bring you in line. If I could, I would destroy this place, wipe it off the face of the earth. Start again somewhere else.'

'Where? Where is it going to be any different?' she asked, not because she wanted to fight him, or because she did not believe that life could be better than the version of it they were saddled with, but because she sensed that such schemes of escape were beyond them. And she disliked the intensity with which he expressed his anger. She thought she understood what he was saying. The prison made it possible, made it necessary, maybe, but she did not want to hear him talking with such bitterness. No, the prison made it unavoidable, but anger of that kind could only destroy a person's mind, and eat away at the parts of it that made people understand what was around them. They did not even know who they were, she and Sophie and Hudson, or what people they belonged to. They knew this place, and this was all they had. There was no choice but to hang on here, and make room for themselves. What choice did they have?

After she left him, and returned to the mind-numbing drudgery of her work at the factory, and the squalor and loneliness of her room in Balham, she thought that perhaps she had been too hasty. It was she who felt overwhelmed by her circumstances, who felt that there was no escape. Hudson had miraculously survived the wretchedness of those months on the streets, and now wanted to make a fresh start with his life. She should encourage the talk of becoming a sailor, instead of telling him how they were saddled with the lives they had. A sailor! It made her think of Ken and the life he had led. Hudson would be a better person for doing all that too, no doubt. He would be able to get out from under the burdens that were crushing him here. Becoming a sailor was better than becoming nothing, and would get him to America, at the very least.

A man could think like that, she thought. He could get up and leave with a sense of doing something noble, preferable to conceding to superior events. She could not see herself doing that. She would worry about Sophie, about

Hudson, about keeping all of them together. Or was that a lie? Maybe she was simply afraid, or did not have the strength to take the risks. What would the big wide world make of a woman travelling alone, poor little Dottie trying to make a new life for herself? Look what happened to Sharon. They turned her into something they could use, and after they had finished with her they left her to die a death of unbelievable meanness. Let Hudson be as selfish as he liked, she thought. That was his chance. One day, she too would see the places she hankered for, although first she would have to do something about the small, mean burdens that constantly seemed on the point of crushing her.

She started saving again, thinking that when Hudson came out the money would be useful to help fit him out as a sailor. She had no idea what he would have to do to become one, but she imagined it would cost money. Sophie was enthusiastic, and lapped up Dottie's account of Hudson's recovery. She could not bring herself to make the trip to Dover, she said. It would make her too miserable. But Dottie guessed that she was really too embroiled in her own affairs to be able to leave them unattended for a whole afternoon. She had her own life to secure too. She had more or less moved out again, coming back for the odd evening to talk and help out. She was putting on weight again, and sometimes she was too easily out of breath. Sophie laughed and shrugged. She would cut down, but otherwise life was good for her and Jimmy was fine. Twice he came with her to say hello and pay his respects, but he never stayed for long. It was obvious that he was uncomfortable with Dottie. His jokes did not quite come off, and his merry manner seemed forced and insincere. Perhaps he was also slightly resentful that a younger woman should make him feel like that. That was Dottie's guess, in any case, from the number of comments he made about her age. Jimmy thought a sailor's life would do Hudson good, and he whistled with appreciation when he heard about the little fund they had started in preparation for Hudson's new career. He's a lucky boy, he said.

The two sisters saved their pennies. In that same long year, the post-war boom in Britain was beginning to fizzle out, and the migrant workers from the old Empire who had come in their thousands in the good years were now no longer required. No one could persuade these pesky creatures that they were not welcome any more, and that the natives were beginning to get restless and irate. *No more work, kapish, basi, imshi*, but they still came. So, for the sake of civil peace, the British government under Macmillan passed the first of its anti-immigration laws, panicked into pusillanimous retreat by the presence of a few thousand of the silent sullen peoples over whom it had been lording it for centuries. The new law immediately fuelled a frantic attempt by migrants from South Asia and the West Indies to bring their families in before the shutters came down, turning migrant workers into settlers.

While these great events were taking place, the sisters put away whatever money could be spared. It was bound to come in useful, even if Hudson changed his mind about turning sailor. He could always use the money towards a passage to New York, for example. His interest in New York was turning into obsession, and was now mixed with his admiration for the defiance of the black movements that were sweeping across the United States: the Black Muslims, Martin Luther King, NAACP. They all filled him with pride and envy, and made him wish he was part of them. In a way he was, he said, because of his father, so it was as well he went and saw the place for himself.

For Dottie the months of that long winter passed slowly, not because of Hudson but because her own life seemed to be going nowhere. She thought she should leave and find herself a different kind of job, but could not get herself to make the first moves. The idea of going back to school tempted her more and more as she learnt her ignorance. She wished for a man, a companion and a lover, or one or the other. She did nothing about any of these things but look on and lament as events passed her by.

4

Hudson seemed better when he came out. Andy, the landlord, had allowed them to keep the room at half-rent, shrugging miserably as Dottie out-manoeuvred him into submission. He could not understand why she bothered with a boy as wild as that. Hudson had been released four months early because of the transformation he had undergone in the later months of his term at Borstal. During the first few weeks of freedom, he was full of optimism and grand plans. The most important lesson he had learned in Borstal, he said, was that he never wanted to go back there. So far as he was concerned, the lesson was well-learned. He had taken an examination during the year in prison, a City and Guilds, and the teacher had told him that he had a real gift for Maths. Next year he intended to take some O levels, but for now he would go to college and try to improve his qualifications. He said O *levels* as if it were an unusual ritual, a secret rite for which special qualities were required. Later, he would go into electronics, he said.

In those early weeks after his release, he talked a lot about the Maths teacher who had helped him so much, Mr Viney. The man reminded him of his foster father in some way. He said this carefully, looking away casually to make light of the subject. He was a bit common, not as refined as his foster father, more of a loud-mouth but really only pretending ... Perhaps the comparison only came up in his mind because he was in Dover, and he had all the time to think about what had happened over the years. The time had come, though, to think about the future, he said, and he was determined he would not end up on a junk heap somewhere. Electronics, that was going to be his thing.

Then, in no time at all, he was back with his old friends and flush with money. Almost without warning he was his old self again. He went out one morning still talking of going to college and getting a part-time job, and returned with a swagger and the old drawl in his voice. Everything happened quickly after that, because they were all familiar with the routine now. Hudson came and went as he pleased, and sometimes brought a friend round. Whenever he caught sight of the dirty Polish woman whose cats roamed the house, and with whom he shared the top landing, he chased her with raucous yells and laughter. When he caught her he tickled and felt her up crudely, spitting with disgust afterwards because of her smell. He was again the dangerous man who swerved violently between antic joy and deepest gloom. When Dottie tried to talk to him, he became angry and threatened to leave and find a place of his own. He waved his bundle of notes in her face, and boasted about how good the times were for him. If Sophie looked like approaching him with her tearful embraces or her sneering rebukes, he shouted at her, abusing her without mercy. He made a habit of pulling a knife on them as he harangued them on one grievance or another. In the end Sophie moved out completely, because she said that Jimmy had sworn that he would come round and deal with Hudson himself if he ever threatened or abused *his woman* again, and she did not want her own brother's blood on her head.

One day he announced that he was ready to go to New York. He had been out of Borstal for two months and was not yet eighteen, so he still needed someone to sign his forms for him. Dottie hunted through Sharon's old papers for his birth certificate, and filled in the forms for his passport application. She put her name down as guardian and next of kin. He took the money that his sisters had saved for him, although he seemed to have enough of his own, and within four weeks had left, saying he would return as a millionaire. That was the last they had seen of him. Some days after he left, the police came round saying that Hudson had killed a man while drunk and driving. They had been on the case for some weeks and had just traced the incident to him. The policemen, young and fair haired, with wide red mouths that grinned with the pleasure they took in their work, reminded Dottie that the terms of Hudson's release were a kind of parole. *That lad's going to spend the rest of his fucking life in the nick. I thought you'd like to know that, love. I don't understand why you people didn't stay in your own country and do your stuff there. We got enough wankers of our own, right here.*

Several weeks later, word came from a government office in London to say that Hudson was dead, drowned in the Hudson River in up-state New York. Dottie somehow found the courage to ring the number on the letter-head but was simply kept waiting in the telephone kiosk until her money ran out. She went to the office in the Mall but nobody would see her. The porter was very polite, but he insisted that she wait in the entrance hall or leave. Eventually, a silver-haired man with a flushed, distraught face came out and told her that it was impossible to offer her an interview. He advised her to write a letter, requesting the details of her brother's death.

The two sisters went to see Reverend Mosiah of the Sacred Church of the True Christ in Balham, the terraced-house tabernacle that Dottie had so often passed. One of the black women at Dottie's work had told her about him, and told her that he had helped other black people with the authorities. He was a big, handsome man who spoke softly to them, as if he was afraid of scaring them away. He tried to persuade Sophie to speak to him as well, but she kept her eyes on Dottie, or, when the Pastor became insistent, dropped her eyes to the ground and waited. In the end, Reverend Mosiah turned his full attention on Dottie, observing her scrawny form with clearer eyes and seeing the checked intensity of her stillness. As she spoke of the office that had turned her away without word of the circumstances of Hudson's death, his face became harder and angrier. He clenched his fists and visibly gnashed his teeth.

'What do these people take us for?' he asked. 'They think because we're black we can put up with this kind of mistreatment? My dears, we will go there tomorrow morning and demand our rights. Accept my condolences on your brother's passing away. He has gone to a better world.'

'Amen,' Sophie cried. Her eyes were shut but her face was rapt with joy.

The Pastor accompanied them the next day to the office in the Mall. At the office, the same man who had spoken to Dottie came out to see them. He looked angry again, but after listening to Reverend Mosiah quietly for a few moments he invited them to another room. There, briefly and properly, reading from a piece of paper in a file, he told them what he knew of Hudson's death. He had been pulled out of the river by the police, who had found on him the papers that had enabled his identification. The autopsy revealed that he was unconscious when he fell in the water, and so it was likely that he had been attacked. The man put his piece of paper back in the file and looked up with the air of having completed his task, of having done all that was possible under the circumstances. The Pastor said they wanted to hear more. 'The details of the autopsy are not available to us,' the official said. 'But you can obtain that information from the proper authorities in New York. As the next of kin, you would have a right to receive that information.'

'What about the body?' the Pastor asked, taking the negotiations more fully into his hands. 'Can we have it brought home for burial?'

'It has been disposed of. This ... accident took place many weeks ago. I am sorry but I can help you no further than that. You can contact the proper authorities in New York,' the official said, shutting his file and rising.

'One moment please, sir,' the Pastor said, rising as well, but with the portentous ceremony of the holy man about to read out the Law. 'That is no way to speak of the departure of a Christian soul. Did he receive the rites ...?'

'I'm sorry. I'm afraid I cannot help you any further. Now I really must ask you to leave. It is an extraordinarily busy morning ...' the man said, shutting his eyes to emphasise the feeling with which his words were spoken.

'You will forgive me, sir,' Reverend Mosiah thundered, puffing his huge chest as if he would knock down the official with an indignant blast.

Why were these men fighting over the corpse of her brother? Dottie wondered. What was it to do with them?

Hudson was their corpse, but they could not think to ask them whether they cared to have his torn and decayed body back. She and Sophie were only two women, too unworldly to understand such things as the disposal of the carcase of a brother who had known no better than to destroy himself by every means available to him.

'Leave him where he is,' Dottie said, turning to Sophie for corroboration. The official was already on his way, and Reverend Mosiah was huffing himself up for a parting shot at his retreating back. He looked at Dottie as if to protest, but the look on her face stopped him. After a moment he nodded and sat down beside them. He glanced at Sophie, but she dropped her eyes. Within a moment, she touched Dottie on the arm and they stood to leave.

5

The Reverend Mosiah of the Sacred Church of the True Christ in Balham arranged a memorial service for Hudson. Jimmy and the other friends Sophie had made turned out in a big crowd. Mike Butler sent a wreath but did not attend himself. He did not want to intrude, he said. Some of Hudson's old friends turned up, swaggering in with deeply sullen looks. The bulk of the congregation was made up of Reverend Mosiah's habitual flock.

The day of the service would have been only three weeks after Hudson's eighteenth birthday, and the Reverend made much of this, lamenting the loss of the young sapling cut down in the prime of its youth. His voice rose and quavered in the cramped church as he begged the Almighty to keep watch on their loved one, embarked on his return journey to his Maker when he was still so young and so cruelly unfulfilled. He called on everyone present to bear witness in the sight of God to the cruelties and oppression visited on black people in modern and ancient times, and to pray for God's vengeance on the Evil Ones.

Forgive them, Lord, one of the congregation cried, and the chant of mercy was taken up by others. Hudson's friends cried out their disagreement. The Pastor shut his eyes tightly then lowered his head over clasped hands, seeking guidance. After several seconds of silent communion, Pastor Mosiah looked up. The Lord's will be done, he cried in a voice of wrath. He called for a hymn and the congregation cried Amen before they burst into song. Tears streamed down faces that were already wet with sweat, hands clapped as bodies swayed against each other in the high flood of their lamentation. Dottie felt herself distanced from such excess. She found herself thinking of Dr Murray, who had fallen dead those years ago only a few dozen feet from where they sat. What he would have made of them, if he had seen this bumbling, clumsy mourning! But perhaps it was her, she thought. It was her own fault that she could not find any comfort in this display, that she had grown too cold inside to be touched by the warmth these kind people were offering her. Sophie was weeping in someone's arms. A hand pressed on Dottie's shoulder, and she thought that she had no choice but to shake her body as if racked with sobbing.

Forty days later, and about three weeks into the New Year, Sylvanus Olympio, President of the Republic of Togo, was killed in his palace. He was murdered by officers of his own army, and became the first civilian head of state in black Africa to fall victim to a military coup. He was fated to be the first of many. Idle armies across the continent were soon to undertake a whole string of coups, at first led by colonels, then majors, lieutenants and even privates. On the same day as Sylvanus Olympio's murder, Sophie told Dottie that she was pregnant. Dottie laughed bitterly after Sophie had gone. How much effort they put into the stupid lives they lived!

Coup and Counter-coup

1

The euphoria that Sophie felt at her pregnancy did not begin to diminish until her fifth month. By then she was swollen to a cumbersome size, and was persuaded that it would be best for her to move back to Balham. The early months, with their discomforts and inner upheavals, were worse than anything she had expected. There really was morning sickness, with vomiting and nausea as rumour and lore had promised! Her guts erupted from the other end as well, making her wonder if there was something wrong with her pregnancy, if the bubblings in her abdomen meant her body was reluctant to play host to the creature which had implanted itself in there. Despite these tortures, the expectation of motherhood made her burst into laughter whenever she talked about it, or whenever Jimmy teased her with thoughts of her own, live plaything. She had started a new job in the New Year, working in the kitchens of a large office block in Waterloo. It was better than the dirty work she had been doing in Victoria Station, better paid and more pleasant. Most of the people she worked with were white. Without thought she saw this as an indication that it was decent work and an advance on her previous job, where the workforce was mostly black and brown. She felt she had been fortunate, and she was determined not to let her pregnancy get in the way. She would work for as long as she could, not only because she wanted to impress her employer with her application and reliability, but because Jimmy said they needed the money.

It was Jimmy who suggested, once she began to grow large, that she had best move back in with her sister. She laughed at him, because he looked so comically worried, telling him that she was a long way off yet, and was not likely to burst out with the baby just like that. He laughed too, conceding that men were notoriously panicky about such things, probably worse than the pregnant women themselves. He would still be happier, though, if she moved in with her sister, who would know how to look after her if something happened. He would miss climbing up her mountainous belly whenever he wanted to enter her, but he would have to learn to live without that for a while. Motherhood was a serious business, and it was better to have another woman around during the later stages. He knew nothing … less than nothing. Hadn't he done his best? And it was not that he minded, but just in case … Look what happened the other night when her back seized up. Suppose it happened again? Also, he had been offered a month's work in Loughborough, on a building site. In her condition she really should not be alone.

Sophie resisted at first, thinking she could cope or that Jimmy would change his mind about Loughborough. Once Jimmy went off on his contract job, and she suddenly began to grow at a spurt, she felt the time had come to give in. Dottie responded readily enough and insisted that Sophie move in with her. It was depressing to stay on in Jimmy's room on her own, Sophie said. She found movement difficult, and doing things for herself was a vexation at times. Her guts felt knotted up, as if part of her had turned to stone and had rolled itself round her insides. She had thought that being with child would be a happy time, but that was not how it was turning out. 'Oh take no notice of me, Sis. It's not as bad as that. You know I just like grumbling,' she said to Dottie when she felt she had gone too far and was beginning to lose her sister's sympathy. Worse was to come, as Sophie well knew, and the thought of swelling even further, and carrying an even heavier lump round her middle, filled her with panic sometimes. She had a dream in which she swelled and swelled, and eventually burst, she told Dottie.

Jimmy called in when he was in London. His manner was more sure with them. He laughed more easily, and once reached to squeeze Sophie's breast without waiting for Dottie to look the other way. Sophie smiled and slightly inclined the other breast towards him, offering it to him, but he chuckled and turned away. Then the two of them burst into laughter, exchanging meaningful looks. When Dottie spoke to her about not letting him take advantage of her, Sophie dropped her eyes and made no protest. In the end, when she had to offer some defence, she would only say that he was *fine*.

'How fine? He treats you like a little thing he can play with,' Dottie persisted. But Sophie's face became set, and she muttered to herself: a good man's hard to find. She said the words as if they were lines from a song, and sometimes varied them, finding different cadences as she toyed with them. Dottie wondered if she was making fun of her.

In Jimmy's absence and at a time of such trials, Sophie found consolation in God and his servant the Reverend Mosiah, who went into raptures over Sophie's pregnancy. At first he scolded her for her sinful ways, but after his pastoral duty was fulfilled he rhapsodised the Lord's wisdom in offering Sophie an irrefutable sign of her election. Praise the

Lord, Sophie cried. Since the memorial service for Hudson, she had become a devoted member of the congregation of the Sacred Church of the True Christ. Her devotion to the Reverend Mosiah was almost complete, held back only by the awe she felt in his presence. Her gratitude for the manner in which he had championed their cause contained no reservations. She even forced Dottie into feeling some guilt that she did not go to the services as well.

Sunday became a time of minor guerrilla wars between the two sisters. While one tried to impose a solemn air about her doings, humming sacred songs while she dressed in her church finery, the other did her best to subvert this. Sophie would burst into *My Lord*, or shut her eyes in a fervent prayer, which would be a signal for Dottie to start cleaning a window or to announce that she was going down the hall to the bathroom. Dottie knew that Sophie prayed for her. At night, when they lay in the dark waiting to go to sleep, Sophie's muttered devotions became longer and longer, and Dottie heard her name frequently mentioned. If she was not worried about Sophie's sensitivities, she would have burst out laughing. She watched with some surprise as Sophie transformed herself. She dressed like other members of the congregation, wearing longer gowns and elderly styles. *Lord* and *Jesus* littered her speech, and every wish or hope that she uttered was followed by a small prayer and the ejaculation of an *Amen*. To someone who did not know her better, Sophie's behaviour might have looked like a parody, Dottie thought. She just could not believe that it would last.

Sophie duly lost some of her fervour in the latter stages of her time, put off by the labour of dragging her cumbersome body from Segovia Street to Reverend Mosiah's tabernacle. She became more preoccupied with the coming birth, and gradually allowed herself to miss some of the church events. Together, the two sisters went out to look for a cot in the second-hand shops. They found a cradle in the ironmonger's yard in Rossiter Road, and asked the man in the front if they could buy it. He looked incredulous, and perhaps assumed they were making fun of him. He was a short plump man, with metal-rimmed spectacles and a cap pushed back on his head. He looked even more surprised when they agreed to pay a pound for it, and his wily, put-upon face melted with melodramatic pity. He had a couple of innocents on his hands! 'It needs cleaning up a bit. You won't be needing it for a couple days yet, will you?' he said with a smile and a nod at Sophie's bulge. 'If you tell me where you want it sent, I'll have it cleaned up and brought round in a couple of days. Don't mention it, love. What are you hoping for? A boy? They're more trouble than they're worth.'

When the cradle arrived, not only was it clean, it was also painted white. The frame consisted of two intricately wrought panels that made up the ends, linked together by four longitudinal bars. At the top of the panels and pointing inwards were two hooks. The basket, which was made of a fine mesh around a sturdy, box-like frame, hung from these hooks. A delicate rod was fixed to the head-panel, from which, they assumed, would hang an awning or canopy to screen the baby at appropriate times. Sophie played with it for hours after they got it upstairs, putting different objects in it and endlessly rocking them.

2

At the very beginning of November, three weeks before the assassination of John Fitzgerald Kennedy in Dallas, Texas, Sophie's baby made his appearance. Dottie was called from the factory and came to lament the arrival of a new Hudson into her unhappy world. The next day she went looking for Jimmy, and tramped from one billet to another looking for him. At the Camberwell address she found two men. They were sleeping, perhaps night workers on the Transport, and she was sorry to have disturbed them. They told her he had moved out, and now was to be found at a place in Stoke Newington. She took a bus to the street they told her, and was met by an angry black woman with dyed auburn hair. She looked Dottie contemptuously up and down then sucked her teeth. She spat out an address in Ladbroke Grove when Dottie persisted, saying she had very important family news. Dottie nearly turned back after that, but the thought of Sophie's misery persuaded her to make one more try. He was not at the address she had been given in Ladbroke Grove, but she left word with the man who was there and went back south of the river.

Jimmy came the following day. Sophie had not seen such a lot of him in recent weeks. In truth she had not seen such a lot of him since she fell pregnant, but in the very last weeks he had not appeared at all. Dottie found it almost impossible to hide her disapproval of him, and this neglect, although she spoke of it with Sophie as a matter of mutual condolence, vindicated the low opinion of him that she held. She had found out from Sophie that Jimmy was no longer his name. He had changed it to something else. When Dottie asked what his new name was, Sophie shrugged and looked persecuted.

When he came to see Sophie at the hospital, he had eyes only for the baby at first. He picked it up and played with it, whispering to it and smiling, exclaiming at its every feature. It was only when the baby was taken away from him because it started to grizzle and grumble that he showed his annoyance for not being consulted about the name. It was his right as a father, and he had been denied it. He insisted that the baby should also be given his brother's name, Patterson, as a second name.

'I didn't know you had a brother,' Dottie said. 'Is he older than you? How many of you are there?'

Jimmy laughed, arching his body and then straightening lazily, affectedly. 'He's not my real brother,' he said.

'You're full of surprises these days. Sophie tells me you've got a new name as well.'

He sang out a long name which was incomprehensible to her but which was unmistakably African. It sounded like Bongbongbong, and she wondered if he was saying it right. When Africans said their names and she could not catch the word, the sound was usually a blur, a hiss and roll of vowels and diphthongs, like a long knife being drawn out of a dry scabbard. Jimmy said the word like a series of clumsy hammer blows. He laughed to see her open-mouthed shock, and explained that it was a Ghanaian name. His adopted brother Patterson, who was himself Ghanaian, had given it to him.

'Oh, it's a Ghanaian name,' Dottie said, and nodded her head patiently as if she was humouring him.

Like someone reciting from a memorised passage, Jimmy told the story of Patterson. His father had been a sailor from Gold Coast in the Thirties, had been paid off at Tilbury at the end of a voyage and had never gone back. He had left a family back in Gold Coast whom he chivvied and nagged until they sent the eldest boy to him when he was old enough. The education here was better, he said. Patterson's family had been reluctant to see him go. They had hopes of their own for him, and put a high value on his quick understanding and his gentle manner. They called him the son of their white man, but they did so with irony, lamenting the loss of the boy's father. In the end they had no choice but to let the boy go. They did so with trepidation, afraid that with the boy they would also lose the remittances that they had learned to depend on from their absent man. The boy was given a new name when he came to live with his father and his new mother in Barking. He was called Patterson.

Sophie had already met Patterson, and had her own reservations about him. But she was so pleased that Jimmy had come that she nodded her grateful consent without a murmur, even though she found Patterson frightening and overbearing. Dottie said nothing, suppressing her disdain for Jimmy and his new African name. For Sophie's sake, she stopped herself from being sharp with him for his high-handed insistence on his rights. She could tell him a thing or two about his rights if he wanted to listen. Patterson was not even his real brother anyway, and in any case what kind of name was that! However much he irritated her, though, she could see Sophie's affection for him. She had seen him being kind and caring with her, and perhaps the child was what was required to make him give more of himself. She remembered one Saturday afternoon in the summer, during one of his visits, when he had gone shopping with Sophie. She had stumbled and sprained her ankle on the High Road, and he had carried the shopping and supported her all the way home. Dottie had boiled some water and poured it into a bowl, and made her sister soak her foot in a mustard bath. While she had some spare hot water, she made him a cup of tea, and was pleased that he stayed a few minutes and cheered Sophie with his conversation. He had come back the next day, bringing a bunch of lilies to cheer the lady who was poorly.

It was not really her business. However uneasy Dottie was made by Jimmy, she felt she should not interfere to spoil things for her sister. Jimmy had a wild way about him. Sometimes his joking got out of hand and he laughed too much and too loudly, like a man who was sick and bitter inside. He would not say exactly what he did when Dottie asked him. Just general labouring, he said. The last time she tried to find out he had frowned and seemed on the point of getting angry, but then he had smiled and wagged a finger at her. He told her that he did whatever came his way, mostly jobs on building sites. He could get a job whenever he wanted because he was a welder by trade. Whatever her worries, she had not imagined him being able to do Sophie any real harm, unless it was to make her fall pregnant.

'You don't worry, girl,' Jimmy said before he left. 'I'm the father and I'll look after you. Just get yourself out of this hospital so I can come and give you some loving. I miss you all this time, girl, and I don't want you to keep them bubbies just for him.'

He had not asked her how she felt, or how she would manage, but Sophie was so pleased that he had come, and had promised to come to her once she was out of hospital, that his lack of interest in her pain only hurt her for a short while.

The hospital asked her to leave after three days, and told her if she was ever pregnant again, she must get in touch with her doctor and attend ante-natal check-ups. They told her about checks and vaccinations for the baby, and frowned at her respectful and confused silence. At last they let her go, 'See you next year, love,' they said. She took the bus back to the room in Balham that she shared with Dottie, glad to be going home. She found the room ready to receive her, even though Dottie was at work. The cradle was decorated with ribbons, and a fragile-looking mobile of satiny goldfish hung from the tapering pole above the head-panel. The wall nearest to it was covered with pictures from advertisements cut out from magazines. Sophie put Hudson in the cradle and painfully stretched herself on her bed beside him.

When Dottie came home, and after her initial surprise that Sophie had been discharged so suddenly, she too sat near the baby, watching her sister ministering to it. Little Hudson seemed to prefer having his eyes shut but, after much cajoling and chucking under the chin, agreed to open them briefly. The two sisters were delighted with their success, but their attempts to repeat it incensed the young lord, who emitted powerful screams of rage that were quite out of proportion to the provocation. And he filled his nappy for good measure, intent on demonstrating that he would not be trifled with. Instead of casting down his new devoted slaves, this behaviour only seemed to delight them, and Hudson sighed to himself as he realised the tasks that lay ahead.

Later, after Hudson had gone to sleep, Dottie watched Sophie stretch herself out on the bed again. She groaned and creaked as she did so, unfolding herself as if flexing a wounded muscle after long misuse. Sophie looked so ill and fat, and so resentful of her condition, Dottie thought. For all her prayers and her religion, the God she worshipped had not seen fit to make her better suited to life, and instead had given her such a heavy lot. Soon they began to talk of what would need to be done. Dottie brought out the exercise book in which she spasmodically kept their accounts. It usually came into use when they had to save money for something. In it Dottie did the sums that showed undeniably that she could not earn enough money on her own to look after all three of them. She had to say it several times, and mention all the alternatives she could think of, which were mostly unavailable to them, before Sophie would reluctantly concede that she had to go back to work immediately.

'I have to go to the doctor. The nurses told me,' she pleaded. 'And Hudson has to have injections. Do you want the baby to fall ill? They'll keep the job for me, Sis. The supervisor told me ... Jimmy will help until we can move to our own place.'

Dottie snorted with contempt. Sophie looked apprehensively at her, fearful that she would lecture her again for believing in Jimmy. But Dottie said no more, looking down at the depressing rows of figures in her exercise book.

'The Lord will provide,' said Sophie.

'Amen,' Dottie said sarcastically.

'It's the burden our Almighty has given us to bear, and we must manage as we can to earn His love. Now He has given us the most wonderful gift we could've asked for. He has given us our Hudson back. Thank you Lord for this little angel.'

'Amen!' repeated Dottie, throwing in a wiggle of the head, the way she had seen the Holy Rollers working themselves up. 'But we have to find somebody to mind him now. I'm sorry it's so hard, Sophie, but we don't have very much choice. We can make a life for the boy, never fear that, but we have to organise ourselves.'

'Jimmy will help ...' Sophie started, and then stopped when she saw the look of irritation pass across Dottie's face. She scowled obstinately and continued. 'Jimmy will come for me and Hudson as soon as he finds a place for all of us. Then you won't have to worry about us. You have no faith in him, Sis, but you'll see.' She picked the stirring

Hudson up out of his cradle and busied herself with the buttons on her dress. Dottie passed her a wet cloth, and she wiped herself gently before putting him on her breast. She leaned back a little against the wall, and watched him as he sucked at her with joyful zest. His eyes were tightly shut, and his noisy, slippery gulps were punctuated by moments of silence. He lifted one tiny leg in the air and held it like that, then gently he swung it to and fro in the air before putting it down again in his mother's lap. After a moment Sophie looked up and smiled at her sister, and wiped away all memory of their disagreement.

3

Hudson spent his days with a woman called Joyce, who had recently had a child herself. She lived in Elmfield Street, not too far away, in a room of her own. It was not difficult to guess what she did at night to make a living. Her costumes were hanging on a rail in the alcove that served as her wardrobe. Joyce had come to see them, saying she had heard from one of the women in church that they needed a minder. She was younger than both of them, tall and slim with a large wide mouth and eyes full of mischief. Dottie guessed she could not be more than nineteen. She laughed a great deal that first time, anxious to win them over. The Reverend Mosiah would recommend her if they wanted to ask him. She needed the money, she said, and another little one would be no bother since she was already looking after her own. Feeding would be no problem since her own was still on the breast and she produced more than her baby could consume. Sophie was reluctant, glaring at her and touching her own breasts. The younger woman looked too skinny to be able to produce enough milk for two babies, and she did not want Hudson catching something from her.

Dottie was also uneasy about Joyce, but her price was so reasonable that they could not refuse. Sophie still whimpered grumblingly as the arrangement was made. She would give Hudson three of his feeds, so Joyce only needed to feed him in the late morning and late afternoon. And she was to change him after every feed, and keep his nappies separate from her own baby's. Joyce agreed to everything, desperate for the money, until Sophie ran out of objections. They agreed that Sophie would drop Hudson off in Elmfield Street every morning, and pick him up on her way back from work. Joyce smiled, leaning down to look at Hudson in his cradle. He reached up and clutched her blouse, and then let out a polite whoop of delight, which finally banished Sophie's lingering unease. The three women joked about the terror he would cause the world's unsuspecting female population when he had grown older.

Jimmy came one weekend, three weeks after Sophie had left hospital. He had been working in Moss Side, he said. That was why he had not been round earlier. He had told Patterson about the little boy who was named after him, and he would like to come and greet them and his namesake. 'Where's the little Patterson?' he cried. He was obviously well tanked-up, and took no notice of Dottie's tight-lipped disapproval. It was early Saturday afternoon, the end of Sophie's first week back at work. She had been woken up several times by Hudson the previous night, and she had been feeling depressed and put-upon before Jimmy turned up. His arrival transformed her, and she clung to him as if she was afraid he would run out any minute. Jimmy gave Dottie some money and asked her to go and do some shopping. 'We're celebrating, girl, so don't you spare any of that legal tender. Get us a slap-up down-home feed. There's plenty more where that came from, honey.' Dottie took the money and went, if only to give them time to themselves and to buy him the rum he kept asking for.

As soon as Dottie left the room, Jimmy threw himself on Sophie, reaching into her dress without many preliminaries. He gave her his mock-satyr laughter as he struggled to pull her pants down. She fought him off playfully, giggling with anticipation of the love-making that she knew would come. Jimmy was very good at giving her pleasure, but at the back of her mind was a nervous worry that this time it would hurt. She helped him take her dress off. He lunged for her huge breasts, making wailing baby noises and tickling her sides at the same time. He overcame her guilty reservations about allowing him to suck her by making a comically crestfallen face. She laughed and gathered him to her breast. Her eyes filled with tears as she watched her man nestling on her, and she suppressed the desire to have Hudson suck on the other side.

He was sleeping when Dottie came back. Sophie avoided her eyes, concentrating on the pain between her legs, feeling the pulse of its rhythm as it beat through her. Hudson started to make small snuffling noises. Dottie reached for him before Sophie could move, rebuking her for Jimmy and for neglecting the baby. When Sophie started to undo the front of her dress, Dottie snorted with derision. 'You'd better go and clean yourself first, my girl,' she said, looking pointedly at the dark stains her leaking milk had made on the bodice of her dress. 'If you've got anything left …'

'There's no need for that, Sis,' Sophie cried, wounded by Dottie's accusation. 'If you don't like him to come here …'

'I'm sorry,' Dottie said quickly. 'It wasn't charitable to say that.'

'The Lord watch over us, Amen,' Sophie said in a hurt undertone.

Jimmy stayed the night, so drunk by the end of the evening that the sisters had to undress him. Dottie would have left Sophie to get on with it, but she did not want her to hurt herself for such a worthless snail as him. They squeezed him up against the wall on Sophie's bed, and Dottie went to the bathroom down the hall while Sophie finished undressing him and tucked him up.

Sophie thought they had had a good evening, and she thought Dottie had enjoyed herself a little. Jimmy had made them laugh so much with his drunken clowning. He even persuaded Dottie to hurl back a rum, and watched with tears of mirth trickling down his tortured face as she struggled for breath. His talk had become dirtier and his laughter less controlled as he got more drunk. Sophie saw her sister shrinking, and saw the moment approaching when she baulked at so much indecency.

'Shut your filthy mouth!' she shouted. 'That's all you men know, you ... That's all! You just shut up that kind of shit.'

Jimmy looked confused, and then was so apologetic that Dottie could not be stern with him any more and ended up laughing a little herself. There was a part of her that was calculating, and, in any case, she had no choice. As he made his affectionate lunges at Sophie, Dottie could see how happy she was after the hardships of the last months. In those months, Dottie would have gladly murdered Jimmy. She would overhear her sister's prayers, tearfully begging forgiveness and asking that her man should be returned to her. She should have been praying for something terrible to happen to him instead. Dottie was under no illusions about his visit, but her sister was. And after all, everything was so hard that an evening of gentle carousing was not that difficult to bear. She had witnessed enough of them in her early years to learn to bear them, she thought bitterly. Long before they had to put him to bed, she was reconciled to him staying the night. He had stayed once before, but then he slept on the floor by the door with his back to them, but there did not seem much point in continuing that fiction when the fruits of their relationship lay playing peacefully in the cradle.

Hudson! She had never known such a baby, not that she knew such a great deal about them. Everything pleased him. After he was fed he let out a few discreet burps, filled his nappy obligingly and slept. When he was awake he maintained a whole symphony of good-humoured whines and gurgles, so sustained that it seemed as if there was meaning behind them. At times, he cried out with a passable parody of his own wail, as if he was making a self-deprecating joke. Once he lay uncovered while Dottie was bent over him, anointing his body with oil, and he released a spume of urine which poured over her arm. She could have sworn that a look of embarrassed mortification crossed his face at the indignity he had imposed on her. She watched him lying patiently while Sophie changed him, and then watched him kick his legs in the air with restrained abandon when he was released. Free at last! He was a beautiful gift!

Jimmy stirred during the night, when Sophie rose to feed and change the baby. She knew that Dottie must be awake too. She always woke for Hudson, and in the late hours they would sit together while she fed him. Sophie was thrilled and a little frightened by the unexpected intimacy of having her loved ones all in the same room, and Jimmy lying in her bed. She had been so surprised that her sister had not made a fuss about Jimmy staying. In the state he was in she could not very well throw him out of the house, but she had even been the one who had propelled him towards the bed, complaining cheerfully about having to put another drunken man to bed. Another? Sophie wondered, and then decided that Dottie was talking about *women* putting *men* to bed, and not about herself.

Sophie hurried over Hudson's feed, and quickly went back to bed. Jimmy reached out and began to stroke her. As his caresses became more intimate and vigorous, she could no longer restrain heavy sighs of pleasure. She tried to stop him climbing on top of her, out of embarrassment for Dottie, but he ignored her. She did not have the will to fight him, and she spread her legs apart with a mixture of excited anticipation and shame that Dottie would despise her for what she was doing. Her heavy sighs turned to groans, making Jimmy chuckle. But even as the pleasure overwhelmed her, she thought of Dottie lying a few feet away, grimacing with disgust at the vision of her bloated body writhing in this sinful ecstacy.

In the morning, Dottie was already up and ready for church when Sophie woke up. If the latter felt any surprise she did not show it. She was filled with guilt at the embarrassment she had imposed on Dottie. Jimmy stayed in bed, one arm folded under his head, dozing intermittently while they made ready to leave. The two sisters both avoided his eyes, and hardly spoke to each other. At last they were ready, Dottie waiting at the door with Hudson in her arms. Jimmy called out that he probably would be gone when they got back, but he would call round in a few days.

On the way to church Sophie tried to say something, but Dottie grimaced and waved her explanations away. What was there to explain? How often had she lain in the dark while Sharon gave herself to some drunk who was paying for her? During the service, Sophie sang with inspired intensity, rocking her child from side to side, and with tears streaming down her face. As the words they sang stabbed her with guilt, she leant on her sister for strength. Dottie put out an arm for her, swaying with her as the words of the songs coursed through them. Pastor Mosiah preached a fierce sermon against the curse of rootlessness, reminding his congregation that they must remain true to their beginnings, and Sophie sobbed as the angry words cut through her.

Jimmy had gone by the time they got back. Sophie found a five-pound note under the pillow. She looked up and caught her sister's eye, and they exchanged the briefest of bitter smiles. Dottie added a philosophical sigh as she reached for the cigarette can in which they kept their miserable hoard of cash. She insisted that Sophie should lie down and rest, because it was obvious that the night had tired her. Dottie guessed also that she was in some pain from the way she was walking. While Sophie slept, she took the nappies down the hall to the stinking bathroom to wash them, leaving their door ajar in case Hudson should wake.

She came back to find the toothless and incontinent Polish woman who lived in the room on the top floor crouching on all fours by Hudson's cradle. Dottie gently put the bucket down and tiptoed towards the urine-stained figure on the floor. She kicked her with uncontrollable rage when she saw what the woman had done. The woman rolled towards the window, yelping with pain. Dottie went after her, lifted her by the lapels of her congealed coat and shook her with violent hate. She dragged her back to the cradle, and, with one hand still holding her, she reached for the blankets that covered the baby, smeared now with the woman's excrement. Ignoring Hudson's howls of fear, she rubbed the excrement in the woman's face, wanting to wrench her neck off or pierce her eyes.

'You dirty mad bitch,' she yelled as she hurled the sobbing woman out of the room.

Sophie ran to pick Hudson up and hush him while Dottie chased the woman upstairs. She heard Dottie banging on the door and screaming violent abuse. In the end she went up to her sister and found her sitting outside the Polish woman's door.

'Come down, Sis,' she pleaded. 'It's no use sitting there.'

'I'm not coming,' shouted Dottie, her anger now out of control. 'I want to break that crazy bitch's face. It's not enough that they spit on us and make us clean up their shit for them. Now they want to shit on us. Well, I'm going to sit out here and wait until that dirty bitch comes out then I'm going to shit in her *mouth*.'

'It's no use talking like that, Dottie. She's only a poor mad cow,' Sophie begged. 'She don't know what she's doing.'

'I think you're soft in the head, my girl. I'm telling you I'm tired of these dirty white scum spitting on us and shitting on us. And I don't care how mad she is, I'm still going to twist her filthy head off.'

Sophie tried to take the dirty blanket from her, but Dottie would not let her. Hudson had stopped crying and was watching his enraged aunt with surprised attention. Sophie lowered herself beside her sister, and the three of them sat in a silence that was only occasionally disturbed by Hudson's weary gurgles. In the end, his good-natured patience ran out and he started to complain, politely at first, then with greater insistence.

The Polish woman had plumbed bitter depths in Dottie, and for the rest of that Sunday afternoon and evening she ranted against the injustice of their circumstances. She was tired of the life they lived, she had had enough of it. The drunkenness of the previous evening, and all that giggling and heaving in the dark had brought Sharon back with such force that Dottie had lain on her own bed weeping at the tragedy of their mother's life. And there was Sophie blindly running down the same alley. After Sharon had lived and died as she had, and Hudson had tortured himself to extinction, here was Sophie setting herself up for her bit of squalor. Dottie had sat in Reverend Mosiah's church that morning and envied the Pastor his certitude and passion, and the congregation their energetic embrace of their words of hope. Something inside her rebelled at the cruelty of the Pastor's austere joy in misery and oppression. Then when she saw the woman smearing faeces on that little baby, it was more than she could bear.

They shared a house with people who were so crushed by their lives that they found relief in losing control, just as she had done. The Indian man downstairs, the dirty old coolie as Sophie called him, was living on his own. His young wife had gone away, perhaps back to wherever she came from. No one visited him in his unkempt loneliness. At night, he wailed with misery, a man in his fifties crying like that, calling out names of people between his cries of agony. Their neighbour persecuted him with parcels of rubbish outside his door, and with tight-lipped stares and muttered abuse. She was a short, angry woman who stared resentfully at everyone, as if she suspected them of laughing at her. She dressed like an office worker when she left in the morning, but as soon as she came home she changed into working rags and a house-coat, and set about cleaning. She was the one who moved furniture in the middle of the night.

On the floor above them, in the cupboard that Hudson had occupied, had moved in a ragged Irish whore. That was how she described herself to them, 'and proud enough of it too,' she told them, swaying defiantly in her inebriation. She had come to introduce herself to her neighbours because she didn't hold with being snooty at her time in life. Dottie had no way of guessing her age, but she could not have been much beyond fifty. Flaccid folds of flesh hung beneath her chin and her under-arms, and lines crossed her brow and cheek-bones in cruel, intricate patterns. They were all immigrants together in this lousy country, she said with a wink. And she always had a special place in her heart for darkies. There was nothing to beat a big, flashy, black punter in her time. Too big? She didn't think their things were too big. She used to swallow them whole in her day. Before she left, she gave Sophie a long, searching look then nodded towards Hudson. 'Somebody's messed your sister up good, hasn't he?' she said, heaving agonised sighs as she rose to leave. 'They're not worth it, my love. None of the fucking bastards are worth it.'

Then there was the crazy shit expert upstairs and her army of cats, flea-ridden monsters that plagued the house with their scrounging and their noisy squabbles. She hid from everyone, and crept about the house when she thought there was no one around, looking for a place to empty her chamber-pot. More often she hurled its contents out of her window, making it impossible for anyone, should such an inclination have occurred, to venture into the wild back-garden. At first Dottie and Sophie had gone up to her and tried to tell her about the toilet. The woman had peeped at them through a crack in her slightly open door, weeping as she listened to them speaking to her in a language she did not understand. Dottie leant on the door, gently, to press her into letting them see her properly, so they could talk face to face. She slammed the door shut with sudden violence, but they had seen enough in the brief moment that the door had opened never to want to try and enter her room again. It was not impossible to imagine what might have happened to a woman like her, to reduce her to the state she was in. Dottie felt remorse for the way she had dealt with the crazy woman, the way she had screamed like a mad woman herself. It was just that it had all been too much.

And they had killed that man in Dallas, because he had wanted to do good for black people, she lamented. And one day they would kill King for calling his people to freedom. Free at last! he had cried, predicting what the future held for them. While he said those words, Hudson was floating dead down the poisoned river.

'It's like living in Hell,' Dottie said. 'Like a kind of punishment.'

'Oh you're just speaking in anger,' Sophie protested. 'The Lord works in mysterious ways, His wonders to perform. We should thank Him for His Mercy and not grumble about our little miseries. He'll keep His eye on us and make sure we'll come to no harm.'

'Yes,' Dottie said sceptically.

'Forgive her, Lord,' Sophie prayed but could not quite suppress a smile.

Later that Sunday night, after Dottie had quietened her feeling of remorse and self-condemnation, she sat for a long time adding up figures in the exercise book. When she had finished, she shut the book and put it down beside her on the floor. She watched her sister feeding and playing with Hudson.

'We're lucky, you know,' she said. 'Look at that little man. We're lucky to have him.'

Sophie looked down proudly at her little baby.

'But this is no place for him to grow up,' Dottie said, wiping the smile off her sister's face. Sophie sighed, thinking that Dottie was about to start again. 'We're going to move out of here, Sophie. I've been doing some sums. I don't know how yet, but we're going to look for a place of our own, where Hudson won't have to grow up with crazies. We'll buy a place of our own,' Dottie said firmly, leaning forward to pick the exercise book up. She waved the book at her sister as if it was proof of the power of her words.

Sophie looked at her with wonder.

'We can do it,' Dottie continued. 'If we put our mind to it we can do it. We saved all that money for Hudson when we had to. We found a way ... Now we'll have to try again, for the young Hudson. It'll be harder this time because we have to get so much more, but we'll find a way.'

Sophie nodded, wanting to believe in her sister's vision, wanting to believe that Dottie would not say they could do it if they could not. 'We can go and see Reverend Mosiah,' she said.

Dottie was taken aback by the suggestion, but after a moment she shrugged. 'We'll talk it over properly when we come back from work tomorrow. All right, we'll go and see the Pastor. I expect he'll know about buying a place.'

'Perhaps Jimmy ...' said Sophie feebly.

'Yes, perhaps Jimmy will.'

'He'll want to help for Hudson too. He will, Sis,' pleaded Sophie.

'Yes I'm sure he will,' said Dottie, smiling to placate her sister. 'We'll go and see the Reverend tomorrow night and hear what he has to say.'

Much later on that night, when Hudson woke up for his early morning feed, and they were drowsily waiting for him to drop off again, they started again about their house. 'What do you think? Where should we buy our little mansion?' Dottie asked. 'Perhaps Hudson has an idea.'

'Where do you think it'll be, Sis?' asked Sophie, laughing with pleasure through her weariness.

'One of those nice houses in Clapham,' Dottie said, thinking of Dr Murray.

'Or a place in Brixton. I fancy Brixton,' Sophie said, smiling.

'It will be a clean, cheerful house, with plenty of room for our little child to play. It will have a living room, and a drawing room and a nursery. And a real garden at the back.'

'Like a dream house,' Sophie said.

They lay talking in the dark after they went to bed. Sophie was asleep before too long but Dottie lay dreaming and planning their new life, pausing now and then to listen to the stealthy sounds of the house.

Bearing Gifts

1

As if suspecting that something was afoot, Jimmy disappeared again, reducing Sophie to tears. Dottie sighed with resignation, but her exasperation was not unmixed with relief. The more Jimmy behaved with what Dottie took to be his habitual cynicism and cunning, the more easily would Sophie be made to understand that she could not rely on this man. For a week or two she was still inclined to defend him and make excuses, and Dottie was forced to be subtle in stoking Sophie's resentment without winning any sympathy for Jimmy. They were well into the fourth week of his absence before Sophie allowed herself an unrestrained expression of her disdain.

'That man is not worth the trouble,' she cried. 'I don't know what he takes me for. I worry myself sick for him, I pray for his return and he hasn't even got time to let me know where he is,' she cried. 'He's probably found himself some slut he can live off. That's the trouble with black men. Just let him come here and I'll show him what he can do with himself.'

Sophie stomped around the room, attending to her domestic business with unnecessary violence, sucking her lips with anger at appropriate moments. Dottie shook her head with commiseration, listening with growing relief and rising glee as Sophie abused Jimmy. Before long, she knew, would come the sniffles and in the end Sophie would burst into tears, but it was a start. All that flapping and shouting was Sophie beating about for air, Dottie thought, as Hudson had done in his pained, arrogant way. Dottie had understood that in some part of herself. In the portion of life they had been given to live, they had to beat about quite a bit for clean air. It was not something they could have at will. If they flared their nostrils and filled their lungs, all that they took in were other people's poisoned, used-up gases. They had to push away and shove off the backsides that were resting on top of them to sniff some real oxygen. But she had never been able to do that. Perhaps she was afraid of the easy and addictive satisfaction of such violence, or perhaps, as she thought, she was afraid and abject before a world that saw no reason to stop torturing her.

Then, out of the blue, Patterson came to see them, appearing on the first-floor landing. It was the first time that Dottie had seen him, and she was at once struck by how different he was from his *brother*. Jimmy was small and restless, always inclined to smile and endlessly clowning. Despite his light airs, though, there was something sad about him, as if he was only pretending to be relaxed and happy, and really harboured feelings of inadequacy and expectations of failure just below the animated surface. It had often seemed to Dottie that his good humour had a trace of frenzy in it, that behind the jokes she could feel a tremor of instability. Everything that Dottie had seen him do was charged with hidden resentment.

Patterson on the other hand was gaunt and lank, with a casual air that gave an impression of indifference. His manner was both morose and tense with checked violence. He would make a very unfriendly enemy, Dottie thought. His face had an ashen look, as if greyed by illness or a poor diet. It was creased with narrow folds of flesh, running from his temples to his chin. It was a face that seemed set and crafted, moulded on an ancient design. He looked around the room casually when he first entered, come into their midst to judge them. When he smiled, the smile did not sit well on his face, perching for a brief and uncomfortable rest before flying suddenly away. He spoke with a gentle growl, a steady monotone full of arrogance and authority. He still had an accent, but he appeared neither aware nor concerned by its African tones.

The sisters were wary of him. Sophie was unashamedly frightened, staring at the floor in his presence. Patterson stood at the door, looking beyond them at the cradle in which Hudson reclined. 'May I?' he asked, hunching his shoulders deferentially in Sophie's direction. As he did so, he dropped his eyes for a moment, and really looked as if he was begging for a favour. The pose only held for a moment and then shifted, as if Patterson was performing a customary politeness. In any case, it seemed incongruous and insincere, a gesture intended to humour Sophie.

It was still early in the year, and the weather was chilly. The great freeze of that winter, which was to cause unprecedented chaos and suffering in the country and along the European North Sea coast, had not yet arrived. If anything it was warmer than usual outside with a bright wintry sun and clear skies. In their gloomy room, though, it was decidedly cold, and Patterson made no move to take off his coat. He was wearing a tailored grey coat, which made him seem tall and flat, adding to his air of unreality and enhancing his ceremonial manner. He held Hudson for a few moments, looking into his face and down his body. He put him back in the cradle reverentially, but with a hint of irony in his manner.

'A fine young man,' he said with a small, polite smile. 'I pray that the Almighty give him a long and active life, and bless him with health and fertility. May I offer the mother my congratulations for such a wonderful child? I understand that you have called him Patterson. Thank you for the honour you do me and my family.'

'Hudson Patterson Balfour,' said Dottie, refusing to be intimidated.

Patterson glanced at her and smiled an acknowledgment. 'A magnificent name,' he said. 'One to do credit to a boy with a bright future. I was only being selfish in mentioning the part connected with me first. Because I was so honoured ...'

'Please, take off your coat and have a seat. I'm afraid it's not very warm but we can put the paraffin on. Jimmy told us that you are from Ghana. The land of Kwame Nkrumah and the Ashanti, and a wonderful warm climate, I'm sure. Here we only have this miserable winter,' Dottie said, conscious that she was putting on airs but unable to silence herself. She hoped she had said the names properly, but Patterson made no response. 'Please, have a seat. Would you like a drink?'

'Please,' said Patterson, declining, 'don't go to any trouble.'

'Some tea, at least,' Dottie insisted, enjoying the firmness with which she was offering hospitality. In her mind, she was making sure she would not offend against the legendary African welcome to strangers.

Patterson shook his head just as firmly and declined. He had come to bring them news of Jimmy, and he discharged his errand while standing inside the open door. Jimmy, he told them, was in jail, serving a five-year sentence, minimum. Sophie's mouth fell open and she put her hand across it as if to stifle a scream. Patterson looked at her for a long moment and then nodded slightly, approving this anguish. He ran his eyes over her and smiled. Dottie watched him with rising unease.

'What is he in … side for?' Dottie asked softly, wanting to force Patterson's eyes away from Sophie but none the less afraid to provoke the aggression that his every gesture hinted at.

'He is accused of burglaries in Manchester. The police arrested him in the street. He had his bag of tools with him but they said he was on his way to a job, a break-in. They said they had prints and witnesses from other jobs he did. It doesn't matter, they'd say anything. I hear they beat him up. And they say they suspect him of other crimes too. Bad crimes. Now they've caught him on these things, they will blame him for something else as well. It's their way,' Patterson said, speaking quietly but with unmistakable bitterness. 'That's where they want all of us. In jail. The way they look at it, all black men are criminals and deserve to be locked up. It's because they don't like people like us in their country. They're afraid of us, and of what they've done to us. If they could, they would kill us.'

That was all the explanation he intended to give. He listened silently while Sophie protested Jimmy's innocence. 'He was working on a building site,' she cried, beginning to sob as the realisation of what had happened began to overcome her. 'He's a welder, everyone knows that. *Didn't anybody stand up for him? Help him?*' Dottie went and stood beside her, and took her arm.

Patterson held a hand up to stop her. After a moment he bowed stiffly, as if engaged in grave ceremonials. Dottie felt no temptation to laugh, for she could see that Patterson took himself seriously. 'If there is anything you need for the boy,' he said, 'you must call on me. Or if you need help yourselves ...' He put a card on the edge of Sophie's bed and left without another word.

'Thank you for coming to tell us,' called Dottie, following him out to the landing.

2

He came again the following Sunday, and brought with him an electric fan heater. He found them eating their dinner of boiled cassava and spinach. They were in the midst of an austerity campaign which was part of the drive to save money for the house they intended to buy. He would not stop for long, leaving the fan heater inside the door and tutting irritably at the gratitude the two sisters tried to express. Before he left, he waved in the direction of Hudson, who replied to his greeting with several hearty chuckles. The austerity measures were not allowed to interfere with his food, and he enjoyed the full attention that a young lord of his age and circumstances could expect. Patterson gave their plates a lingering stare before he left, not quite able to hide his disgust.

They waited until they heard the front door close before they pounced on the fan heater. Sophie giggled with pleasure at her new gift. She took it over to Hudson to show it to him. He reached out for it, smiling at his mother's pleasure. Later, when all was calm again, Dottie suggested that they sell it and add the money to their house fund. They still had the paraffin to keep them warm, and that was quite adequate to their needs.

'Sis, it's a gift!' protested Sophie, turning to Hudson for support.

'If you want to live in this room all your miserable life, that's all right and fine with me. But if you want to find a place for the baby to grow up in, then we have to find the money however we decently can.'

'No, Dottie. Selling gifts is not decent, it's mean. We're hitting hard times, but they ain't so bad that we have to sell gifts that people give us out of kindness.'

Patterson came again the following Sunday, with a bag filled with food: rice, corned beef, spam, biscuits and tins of condensed milk. Dottie was inclined to be ashamed but Sophie's gratitude knew no inhibitions, and she thanked him profusely. He stopped for longer this time, although he still refused to take his coat off. He sat on Sophie's bed, perching on the edge, holding Hudson on his lap. Sophie had insisted on putting a waterproof on his lap, in case Hudson wet himself or worse. Hudson sighed wearily at the indignity but made no fuss. Patterson sat dandling the baby over a sheet of red tarpaulin like a priest officiating at an infernal rite.

It became a regular feature of their Sundays that winter, that late in the afternoon Patterson would call on them. To begin with, they talked about Jimmy, as if duty-bound. Was there any news? No, not much. Patterson could not be too insistent in trying to discover Jimmy's whereabouts and condition because, he told the sisters, the authorities were interested in him as well. Well, no news is good news, and he knew enough to know that if anything happened to Jimmy he would be informed at once. He had his own sources who were keeping an eye on things, so they were not to worry their heads about that. They could not keep the information of where Jimmy was held away from them, could they? Dottie asked. Oh yes they could, Patterson told them. They could do anything they liked, and generally did, especially to black people. They talked less about Jimmy in subsequent visits since there was so little any of them could add to what had already been said.

Patterson always brought a gift, a bagful of shopping, some ornaments, a vase, an ashtray, a china antelope. One Sunday he brought them a folding garden chair to go with the other one that Ken had bought. He gave the gifts to Sophie, or left them by her bed. He did not tolerate any expressions of gratitude, and if Sophie insisted on thanking him, his brow darkened and he quickly departed. If he said anything about the gifts it was that they were for the child.

He had come to them like something out of a fable, appearing to them in the early months of the year, like a promise of new life, Dottie thought. He was not, and she knew that, but she still liked to think of him in that way. He was a magnanimous prince travelling incognito, hiding his kind heart behind a frightening scowl. He had broken his journey among their poor lives and had transformed them with his generosity and friendship. There was no magic in what he did, although it would have been something worth celebrating if Patterson had turned out to be a genie or a gullible fairy with a mighty wand who could change their stinking hovel into a gilded palace, or fill the wildness in the back-garden with blooms and bird-song. The small gifts he brought lifted the gloom of their lives enough, and made them happy.

At first he had terrified her, and made her frightened for Sophie. When she came to know him better, she saw the respect and care he lavished on her, and she envied him his sense of the importance of such things. Jimmy was his *brother* and so he had come by to help out. She still could not understand how the bond between Jimmy and Patterson could have come about, but she could no longer doubt his care for them. Despite his appearance of inflexible rectitude, like something carved out of an ancient hard wood, she thought, there was something quick and warm underneath the ceremony of coldness.

Hudson himself, the young emperor of their impoverished kingdom, had made his feelings known. He was obviously fond of Patterson, and when he began to crawl in the months that followed he would leave what he was doing as soon as Patterson arrived and propel himself cheerfully towards him. Patterson would take his coat off, the coat which always made him look like an undertaker, Dottie thought, and he would get down on his knees despite his Sunday best and play with the child.

Patterson asked about the name. Such a beautiful and powerful name, as muscular as the river itself, he said. Had he seen it? they asked him. Well, it had been muscular when it was in its prime, he said. You could still see that, but the parts of it he had seen looked a little dirty. He had seen the river, the sisters said to each other, their voices hushed as they contemplated the mystical power of the sight. There were dead fish floating belly-up in it, he added, but failed to dispel the beautiful and supple vision he had created. They told him about their brother Hudson, finding new relief in the confessions and recountings. When they had finished, his bitterness flowed unchecked for several minutes, making the sisters exclaim at its passion. Afterwards Dottie felt ashamed of the orgiastic indulgence of racial feeling, but could not deny that she had taken pleasure in the cruel condemnations, and felt a kind of unity and purpose which had filled her with strength and pride.

Yet, something remained unplacated in Dottie, some unease she could not quite overcome. He had been very kind to them. He was always courteous and soft-spoken, but she found herself circumspect in his presence, mistrusting him.

She tried to think of a way of explaining this to herself, but she could not.

A picture that described her feelings came to her in an unexpected way. One day at work someone brought in a calendar that she had received as a gift from an admirer, and the women in the line huddled together, flicking through the beautiful photographs of magnificent landscapes that were touched with romance. The landscapes were simple and uncomplicatedly benign, places where she would be able to sit silently on a log beside the path or atop a rock like a harmless and romantic innocent. They were places she could make-believe were made for her, anyone could, and where she could feel at one with everything. She had even been in such places, or perhaps it was truer to say that she had felt such moments, when the colours and the symmetry of objects had a rightness as if that was how they had always been since the very first times, and always will be. As she gazed at the pictures, Dottie found herself thinking of Patterson. When she imagined him there, she knew he would stir the hidden forces of the earth into turmoil and mischief. Not because of anything he might do, but because they would feel a subterranean antagonism from him. However courteous and soft-spoken he was, she felt his violence bubbling underneath the surface, like the ferment of organs and gases behind a placid smile. In his presence, she found it hard to resist the inclination to efface herself.

He made no sign to her, and Sophie said nothing, but Dottie began to feel that she was in their way. Jimmy was not often mentioned any more. Sophie's affection for Patterson was almost fawning when he was there, and had all the marks of passion when he was not. Dottie knew from her sister's charged movements that there were times when it was all

Sophie could do to stop herself from touching him. She had seen her watch him with her lips parted, longing for him with an openness that was almost comic. He would have had to be blind not to see Sophie's desire for him. Patterson appraised her ample body with undisguised interest, but without the confusion and abandon of the stricken. It was as if she was not there, Dottie thought, although if she hadn't been there she imagined they would have been tearing at each other. Once she had been confirmed in her passion, Sophie seemed to have lost all fear of him. She returned his looks openly, chided him for spoiling Hudson with affection and even teased him about his clothes, which were inclined to be formal in a stiff-necked way. He rarely stayed longer than an hour or so, and he only ever came on Sundays, but Sophie spoke of his visits as if they were the most important events of their week.

Dottie thought she knew what Patterson was up to. When she was feeling charitable, she recalled the gratitude she felt towards him and the many kindnesses he performed for them. At those times she saw him as being protective, guarding his *brother's* cherry tree. More often, as time passed, she knew that his intentions were less selfless. Perhaps, she thought in her cynical moods, it was some African custom. You have the use of your brother's goods in his absence. Just as likely was that it was a *male* custom, she thought, wherever that member of the human species found a woman looking feeble and stricken.

But Patterson made no demands, and seemed concerned that that should be understood. He never allowed his visits to extend beyond the time that a close but not intimate friend of the family would take. He always dressed formally when he came, and thanked them profusely for the kindness they had done in letting him call on them. They made him feel human, he said. He did not burden them with any of his problems, and only hinted at the palpable bitterness that afflicted him when he spoke of Jimmy in prison. He told them once that he had visited him, but adamantly refused to reveal where he was being held. It was too far away, he told them. And Sophie would only feel the need to drag herself there for no very useful purpose. Dottie almost suggested writing but managed in time to hold her breath, without having put Sophie in a position of being forced to admit that she could hardly write. In any case, Sophie did not seem all that concerned, and Patterson gently changed the subject.

For all the importance that the Sunday visits came to assume in their lives, Dottie was uneasy about them. Part of her looked forward to them, and she was not stupid enough to deny the painful tingling in her own chest as Sunday afternoon came near. Sophie was not the only one who found herself stirred by Patterson's presence. She had been a long time without a man, that was all, she told herself. She felt the urges bite in her, as did every living thing. It was almost two years since Ken left her, and although in that time she had been approached by men, she had not been tempted enough to succumb to the kind of brutal invitation they were offering. It was incredible that men were like that, so without mercy. The sheer audacity of their approaches had surprised her. She could not imagine herself being able to make those kinds of blatant assaults if she had been born a man, however desperately urgent her need. And these men had not looked urgent, just desperate and callous. Perhaps men were simply made predatory and did not require any special resolution to behave in that way.

Even now, with Patterson's intrusive presence in their midst, it was not as if she was in the grip of an unmanageable frustration or something brutish like that. She was conscious, and was made uncomfortable, by the desire she felt for him. It was not something she was likely to succumb to, for whenever she felt herself weakening, the air of menace he carried came to sober her and disperse the illusions she had allowed herself to entertain. He was too much for them, she thought, too knowledgeable and worldly. She was afraid that he was playing with them, that he knew what he was doing much better than they did – certainly much better than Sophie did – and that one day he would exact a price that would be too high for them.

3

One Sunday in June, he told them that he would be leaving for a while. He was sitting in the folding garden chair, which had become his ceremonial seat, between Dottie's bed and the window, his hands clasped together in his lap.

'For how long?' Sophie asked, her voice suddenly solemn.

'A month,' he said. It seemed to Dottie as if he would reach out and touch the stricken Sophie, and his own eyes softened with tenderness as he looked at her. She wondered whether she should leave, and she was gathering the strength to make herself rise when he turned his unsmiling face to look at her. 'They're sending me to prison for a month. I got into a fight I should not have bothered with,' he said.

'A fight about what?' Dottie asked.

Patterson shrugged, then managed to look both indifferent and a little irritated. 'It doesn't matter what the fight was about. It is only ever about the same thing, the same battle we have been fighting all this time,' he said calmly. 'How to keep our freedom and how to keep our dignity. I did not want to talk about that, about the fight – there are too many cruel things in our lives already – but having mentioned it I should say that the man in question was severely punished for his bad manners. I wanted to say something else. You have both been very kind to welcome me in your house. You Dottie, and you Sophie … and Hudson Patterson Balfour as well! I want to do something to help. If you will let me.'

He told them he knew about their plan to buy a place to live. He had heard them talking, and guessed from the way they lived that they were saving up. He said that with a smile, as if he had caught them out in a reckless conspiracy. It was a fine ambition, and would help to free them from bullying landlords, he said. He wanted to help. He was a trader and he had money. If they wanted, he would loan them what they needed, and they could pay him later, when they could afford to.

'Think about it,' he said, looking from one to the other. 'When I come out, at Her Majesty's pleasure, you tell me your decision. If you decide to take the loan, I'll help you make all the arrangements you need. I want to help because you've been kind, and because of the boy … and because of Jimmy. You're my family now.' He smiled, broadly, a little embarrassed. He would not stay any longer, saying he still had a lot of things to sort out.

'He's a good man,' said Sophie, her eyes watering.

Dottie was stunned by Patterson's offer and made no reply. She had often wondered what he did, but had never dared to ask him. He ignored the usual polite openings to state his work, and she had been made suspicious by that too. She could imagine him only too clearly barking back an answer to the question she might have asked: I do the only work a black man is allowed to do in this country, I slave for the white man. What a mind she had! Not that *trader* told her such a great deal. Her mind was racing, furiously adding up sums. Reverend Mosiah had told them, when they went to consult him in the flush of their new resolution, that once they had about three hundred pounds they could go to a building society for a loan. Three hundred pounds! He might as well have said a piece of the moon or the Prime Minister's collar studs. If Patterson could lend them enough to bring their savings up to three hundred … She wanted to race down the stairs after him, tell him that there was no need to wait for a month and could they please have the loan now. Could he afford three hundred pounds? How could they ever pay a loan like that back? That was a lot of money. Perhaps he had not meant that kind of money.

It was only after the initial excitement had left her, and with her mind only half on the eulogy of Patterson that Sophie was singing, and which Hudson was accompanying with a pleasant high-pitched chanting, that she began to wonder why he would want to do all this at all. At first she tried to stop herself, telling herself not to look a gift horse in the mouth. It would just be a loan and they would pay back every penny. It must be for Hudson, she thought. He was making up for Jimmy's absence, doing for them the things Jimmy would have done.

The thought made her smile. Jimmy would not have done this, not in a million years. Jimmy was like any other man, leaving his seed where he could without thought of consequences. Perhaps, she told herself, it was because Patterson was an African. Jimmy was just one of the boys, even though he was thirty if he was a day, but Patterson was still an African, and he acted as if he knew that was something. And she had heard people say that Africans took their families seriously.

Perhaps he liked them, wanted to help them. She tried hard but she could not banish the thought that the offer of money was part of a plan, part of the game he was playing with them, and that Sophie was the prize. She knew that he had looked at her too, in a way that made her shudder with excitement and shame that he had guessed her craving for him. She smiled as she thought of the word she had used to describe her feeling for him. She craved him. She wanted him to lie with her, to fondle and love her. And for all that, she knew without knowing much about him that he was a hard, violent man. Would he give them the money and then use them both? Why should he not? If he did, it would only be because Dottie wanted it too. She was not a child like Sophie, besotted with desire for him. The thought made her feel cruel, and she looked at Sophie to see if she had guessed her ill-will.

Sophie sensed that her sister had resolved the battle with her harrowing thoughts, and quietly, without emphasis, she began to sing 'Rock of Ages', always her song of joy and thanksgiving. After a moment Dottie joined her, for the pleasure of singing, and to make her sister smile. They sang together while Hudson stood up in his cradle, staring at them with startled incredulity.

The next day Dottie went to an estate agent as the Reverend Mosiah had advised her. She resisted Sophie's pleas that she should seek out the Pastor and ask him to accompany her. The agent she chose was the one next to the builders merchant at the corner of Bedford Hill and Balham High Road. She passed it in the mornings on the way to the bus stop, and had often glanced at the wares displayed in the window. The office looked small and dull, which Dottie thought would be about suitable for her needs. A smiling young woman there asked her a lot of questions, many of which made Dottie feel absurd. Did she want a terrace, semi or detached? A garage? How many bedrooms would she like? Did she have any particular area in mind? Did she have a property to sell? Around how much was she thinking of spending? She answered the questions diffidently, unable to give a proper answer to many of them, and feeling stupid and conceited for even aspiring to as much as some of her answers implied. Three bedrooms! The woman's smile never faltered, which made Dottie fear that she was laughing at her presumption. She gave Dottie some papers about houses in Brixton, which was what Dottie had asked for, and then sent her to a building society.

At the building society office in Ravenstone Street – the woman had told her which one to go to and what to say – another young woman asked her more questions and told her she must bring all her savings to them. She asked Dottie what job she did and how much she earned. The answer made the woman pause dramatically in her scribblings and give Dottie a long look. She asked whether Dottie had thought of changing her job.

Before she left, she was given some forms to complete. On her way home, walking down Station Road and Bedford Hill, she told herself not to mind about feeling stupid, not to take any notice of the tone of voice with which the young women in the offices spoke to her. It was only that she was poor and they could see that. Perhaps she should have waited for Patterson, or should have asked the Pastor to come with her, as Sophie had suggested ... That was a job that would suit her, she thought. Sitting behind a desk dressed in finery, asking grand questions all day. How many bedrooms would you like? Have you thought of changing your job? It would be best to wait until she had the money that Patterson had promised, then she would go back and wave it under the nose of that woman in the building society. She had wanted to get the house herself, but she would have to wait for help after all.

4

One evening later that week, Dottie arrived home late from work. The summer shifts were in operation again, and there was plenty of over-time. The factory was crowded with casuals, one of whom Dottie had got into an argument with about the Commonwealth, of all things. This man did not want Africans in his precious Commonwealth because they did not share *our way of life*. West Indian people like Dottie were all right, he told her. They were civilised and were subjects of the Queen. *West Indians love the British Empire. They love cricket, and they speak English. They're civilised, or at least they share our values. It's those Kolokolo tribesmen from the jungle we should keep out, walking around with their meat hanging out. How can you give a bunch of primitive savages who think it's smart to eat the dead body of anyone you dislike the same right to make decisions and policy as Australia or Canada, for example?* Dottie had felt herself curling up as she listened to the man holding forth, and was ashamed that she could not think of anything devastating to say to him.

'It's not your Commonwealth,' she said to him. 'Why should they follow your way of life? Or worship your Queen?' *Because we pay for the blooming thing, don't we?* he said. 'And I'm not West Indian,' Dottie shouted. *Where are you from?* the man asked, apparently untouched by Dottie's annoyance. *I could've sworn … Go on then, tell me. I've been to most places with the services.* 'England,' Dottie said, and at least got a laugh against the man.

She arrived home still angry with herself for not having put up a better defence. Perhaps the woman in the building society office was right. It was time she looked for another job. She had stayed at the factory for all the years because she was afraid of having to start again, of having to make new *friends*, if that was what they were. There were more black women working there now, and she had got to know some of them and sat with them at lunch-time. Mike Butler was also still around, with his cheery sermons and his unprovoked, conspiratorial winks. It was the work and the place that were depressing her, repeatedly making her ask herself if this was all she was capable of, if for ever she would remain a plaything of whatever it was that organised lives such as hers. On the bus home, she had almost come to the decision to take herself in hand and clear out of that place. Her dream of going back to school would have to wait now that Hudson had come, but she could do better than packing powdered soup in foil packs or sorting prawns for the freezer bins.

When she got to the house she found Sophie lying on her bed in the gloom, while Hudson had crawled near the open window. He was crouching on all fours and was picking tiny ants off the floor and eating them. He looked up at Dottie and immediately started to grumble. She picked him up and hugged him, murmuring to him. She went to Sophie and peered down at her. Her eyes were shut, and at first she thought Sophie was sleeping. She shook her gently, and the lack of response made her fear that something worse had happened. She put Hudson down, more violently than she had intended, and bent urgently over her sister, ignoring Hudson's angry howls. She shook her and called out to her. Sophie groaned but did not open her eyes.

'What happened, girl? Are you all right? Sophie!'

She opened the door and stood at the landing, uncertain what to do. She should call a doctor, but she did not know one. Neither of them had ever been to a doctor. The hospital had said Sophie should take Hudson for vaccinations, but she had not. She heard a door open upstairs. Sophie groaned and Dottie hurried back inside, snatching up the crying Hudson as she walked past him. She crouched beside Sophie's bed, talking to her and shaking her. She heard the Polish woman at the open door of their room. When Dottie turned round, she recoiled at first, running a few steps in the direction of the stairs. After a moment she came back, and in the evening gloom Dottie saw her grinning. She laughed softly and nodded her head several times.

'Dead,' she said tentatively, unsure of the word. She ran her index finger across her throat and rolled her eyes, gurgling a last breath. 'Dead,' she said more firmly, pointing at Sophie. Then she performed a heavy-footed jig, holding her arms out beside her to mimic someone fat.

'Mad white bitch!' Dottie said. She let Hudson go, and he slid to the floor with a cry, unable to believe that life could expose him to such cruel treatment. Dottie caught the woman halfway up the stairs, held on to her grimy coat and turned her round. She slapped her face with all the strength she could summon, letting her loathing for the life they all led find expression in the pain she could inflict. She butted the woman's head against the wall, and then hurled her away with a cry. The woman was blubbering with fear, tears running down her face. She cringed and crawled backwards up the stairs. Dottie followed after her and drew her leg back to kick her, as she could – anywhere she could – but she could not, and stepped back with an anguished sigh, already overcome with shame. 'Now you go on up there and laugh up your arse hole,' she blustered.

She found Sophie awake when she got back down. Her eyes were open but she had no idea what was happening around her. Hudson was lying on the floor beside his cot, sucking his thumb and snivelling, overcome with self-pity. Dottie went through all the obvious remedies she knew of. She wrapped Sophie in several blankets, but Sophie threw them off, complaining she was too hot. She made her a drink of honey and lemon but Sophie said the lemon was too strong. She chopped up the tripe that she had bought for their supper and boiled it to make stock, but Sophie complained that the smell made her sick. Sophie sobbed intermittently through the night, and even sobbed as she fed Hudson, who watched his tearful mother out of the corner of his eyes as he sucked at her breast.

They went to look for a doctor the next day, walking around the streets of Balham until they saw a surgery. Dottie expected the doctor to tell them that it was typhoid. The newspapers were full of the typhoid epidemic that was sweeping across the country. There had been so many cases of the fever, hundreds of them in Scotland, caused by eating contaminated corned beef. Some of the victims had died, and hospitals were full of patients stricken by it. Sophie admitted to eating left-over corned beef at work the previous day, and Dottie was convinced that that would turn out to be her sister's illness. She expected the doctor to lecture them for bringing the dreadful disease to his surgery. It was one of their kind of diseases, she knew that. Typhoid, cholera, malaria, blackwater fever, blood and pus and vomit and remorseless agues. That was their contribution to human civilisation. She had read in the paper that some people were saying that there might be a connection between the thousands of migrants from India and Pakistan who had entered the country in the last year and the epidemic of typhoid that had hit the country.

She was also afraid that the doctor would be angry with them for neglecting the hospital's instructions about Hudson, and for not having Sophie examined after she left hospital. Perhaps Hudson would get typhoid too, from sucking at Sophie's breast. And even though he would not say so, the doctor would blame them for the military coups that were sweeping across Africa, for the corrupt governments that ruled in Asia and for the thriftless manner in which people in poor countries were using up the world's resources, resources intended for the proper enjoyment of their betters. Altogether, Dottie went into the surgery looking penitent and cowed, expecting the doctor to speak firmly to them while his eyes flashed with hostility. The doctor was a large, red-faced man. He looked momentarily surprised to find two women and a child facing him. He told them that Sophie had suffered a heart attack, that her veins were diseased and that she had to be careful or it would happen again. He wrote quickly on a piece of paper. 'Do you work, Miss Balfour?' he asked, glancing up but looking away from them.

'She works in Waterloo,' said Dottie, her mind still reeling from the doctor's news. Heart! Sophie was not even twenty-one years old yet. She spoke for Sophie because in her eyes her sister had suddenly become an invalid on the very threshold of ... God forbid. 'In the kitchens,' she said.

'Oh dear,' the doctor said, reaching for another pad. 'I'm afraid that won't do. You see, your body can't take that kind of strain. You'll have to find another job, something less strenuous, less on your feet. I want you to take two weeks off, then come and see me. And I want you to lose weight. This is very important. It won't be easy but you must do it. I'll give you a diet sheet, telling you which kinds of food to eat and which kinds to avoid. Do you understand me? You must reduce your weight. I'll arrange for you to go to the hospital for tests.'

Sophie did not keep the appointment he arranged for her. She went back to work as soon as she felt strong enough, long before the fortnight was over. She was afraid the supervisor would sack her otherwise. She had been getting at her again, she said. Dottie begged her, telling her that her health was the most important thing of all, more important than life itself. What was the point of living a half-life, ill all the time, when she could get better by following the doctor's instructions? But Sophie sat in a tense silence, saying nothing for a long time, looking down at her feet. 'I want a house for Hudson,' she said at last. 'It's for him I live. What other reason is there for putting up with this oppression? How are we going to buy a house unless I go back to work? I'll take care, Sis, and the Lord will keep an eye on us. I'll follow all the diet and pills that doctor man gave us. I'll lose weight and I'll get better. I feel all right, true to God, Sis, but we must get the house for Hudson.'

Sophie could not lose weight. Even after she went back to work, although she easily got tired and came home looking sick and grey, she did not get any thinner. She followed her diet at home, but could not resist the tit-bits with resonant names that were sent down to the eaters-of-left-overs. Her milk began to turn sour, to Hudson's disgust. He would go to her, howling with hunger, only to turn away from the swollen breast with a cry of rage as soon as the liquid began to flow. The doctor shrugged and advised the bottle.

'That's what he'd like to do,' raved Dottie when they got back, frightened that the doctor had not seemed to know what was wrong with Sophie's milk. 'Did you see his hand shaking, and his blood-shot eyes. He tries the bottle himself all right. It don't matter to him just how sick you are. Just try the bottle, girl. I don't trust that man one inch.'

Hudson did not like the bottle, but Sophie was now in such a state that as soon as Hudson began to cry she pummelled him without mercy and without any respect for his age. The young prince was well on the road to becoming another battered baby. His frightened howls and tear-stained face filled Dottie with anguish, and made her intervene in the most determined way, despite Sophie's protests. They were not travelling that old journey again, she thought. Dottie took the responsibility of feeding him, ruling mother and son with inflexible insistence. To save Sophie the bother, she took Hudson to Joyce in the morning and picked him up in the evening, and she lectured Joyce furiously when she discovered that the young woman did not bother making a bottle for Hudson but simply put him on the breast. She took no notice of the strange, accusing looks that Joyce gave her, as if she was a bully to all of them. In her mind she snapped her fingers at her. Who cared what a painted-up whore thought? It was painful for all of them but Hudson was forced to accept the bottle. Sophie too found some relief in having Hudson taken off her hands, and she improved a little.

Hudson accepted the new dispensation grudgingly, having forgotten all his elegant good manners. He still pestered his mother for the breast, and when Dottie was not around, Sophie would let him suck. He would snuggle down with contented mutters, only to drop the breast in a howling tantrum once the milk began to flow. Then it would be left to Dottie to enforce the rules. Dottie saw with what ill grace Hudson came to accept her ministerings, and saw how Sophie laughed to see her rejected by him.

'You're a bad boy,' shc would say, unable to stop herself from chortling with laughter. 'Auntie Dottie will smack you for that.'

Dottie accepted the injustice of this arrangement with resignation. What else could she do? What would be the point of saying anything? She was happy that the boy was weaned, and that Sophie was getting better. Hudson will soon forget all this, she thought, and will go back to being the fine-tempered little lord he had been in his younger days. Sophie will get better and they will buy their dream house, and all their lives will be summer and full of joys everlasting. Late at night, or at moments in the dark when she felt by herself despite Sophie's heavy breathing near her, then she was afraid that she had given too much away, that her life was already given to tasks that would never bring her any joy.

The House in Horatio Street

1

On the fourth Sunday since they had last seen him, since Her Majesty had taken him away for her pleasure, the two sisters waited for Patterson's return. They waited for moderately different reasons, and revealed their anticipation in contrasting ways. Dottie sat by the window, preoccupied and a little nervous, toying with a multitude of apprehensions. Her sister had preened herself, wearing her church best. Make-up glistened on her lips and face, and made her seem fatted and dressed for a ceremonial sacrifice. Hudson, though safely past his seventh month, was made to wear a frilly white frock with purple ribbon, an indignity he bore with fortitude, though not quite yet with his old good-humour. But Patterson did not come. Sophie did nothing to hide her disappointment, sulking for hours and shouting ill-temperedly at Hudson whenever he transgressed.

She had looked forward so much to seeing Patterson again, she said, speaking as if to herself. But that was how women were always made to suffer by their menfolk. It was the heavy lot they had been fated to bear. 'What have we done? What have we done to drive him away?' she asked plaintively, growing into her part. When she started to cry, it seemed that she could not stop. Dottie ignored her at first, nursing her own disappointment. She took Hudson out for a walk to the Tooting Bee common near by. She pushed Hudson's chair absently and tried to reassure herself that the loan was safe and Patterson would be there the following week. Hudson chanted his praises of the beautiful summer afternoon, a faraway look of rhapsody in his eyes, utterly oblivious to the quotidian gloom afflicting his aunt. When they got back, Sophie was lying face down on the bed, and her sobs were forlorn and distressing enough to start Hudson bawling. Dottie sat beside her on the bed and tried to comfort her, humming sympathetically as she stroked and massaged her shoulder.

Sophie was not to be comforted, and her tears of disappointment had long since become sobs of self-pity. Hudson had stopped crying and was watching his mother with anxiety. When he tired of the game, he went to play under the sink, something he was not usually allowed to do, inhaling the smell of drains with disgusted wonder.

Sophie got better as the evening wore on, but she could not stop completely. It was no longer about Patterson, Dottie thought. Something had frightened her, and Dottie thought she knew what it was. She often complained of pains in her chest and one night she broke out into a sweat, waking Dottie in terror. She was afraid, she wept. She did not want to die. Whenever anything upset her now, she sobbed and wept, and sooner or later her mind turned to death. Dottie lay on her bed feeling resigned and defeated. She was almost past caring, and whatever would come would come. She no longer felt that she had the strength to keep fighting for all of them.

That night she dreamed of deliverance. Flights of angels, male and glittering in the slanting light, swooped down for her. She rose with them, a warm breeze blowing through her, ruffling the hairs on her body. Later she was on her own, capable of movement in any direction, but she lay instead under an apricot tree that was cream and pink with blossom. In the sudden stillness she knew she would wait there until darkness came. Slowly it dawned on her that she was sleeping and the dream was over. Even before she reached the surface, she knew that the clucking noises drawing near were Sophie's tortured snores.

Sophie was tearful all week. She was so tired. As soon as she came in from work, she collapsed on the bed and shut her eyes tight, squeezing out tears of pain and misery and then letting them run heedlessly down her cheeks. Dottie gave Hudson some mess to eat and his milk bottle and then massaged Sophie's legs while their supper was cooking. She tried to persuade Sophie to give up work, to stay at home and rest, but that only upset her more. She thought of going back to the doctor and asking for his help, but she could not imagine that big, raw-faced man being interested in Sophie's tearful decline. She thought of going to the Reverend Mosiah. He was a good man and he would try to help, but she was afraid that he would demand too much of Sophie, would vex her with sermons and lessons. In the end, she pinned her hopes on Patterson.

'You want Patterson to come and see you like this? What's he going to think when he sees this? He's coming this Sunday, you know. Maybe he'll bring you something.'

'Do you think he's coming?' Sophie asked.

'And I would like to know what's going to stop him,' Dottie said, her voice rising with a maternal quarrelsomeness that was meant to suggest indignant conviction. 'Of course he's coming. Then we can sit down and talk about our house …'

Sophie was diverted for a while, planning the afternoon, but soon she started to worry again, making Dottie groan to herself as she wondered for how long she could bear the snivelling. 'He isn't coming, Sis,' Sophie said. 'We offended him, I know we did. It was that business of money and all, asking him for a loan. Lord knows what he thinks of us now. He isn't coming again.'

Dottie went to church with Hudson on Sunday, to escape the room and Sophie, leaving her sister heaving and groaning on her bed. What that girl needs is a good kick up her pants, she thought. She felt guilty that she no longer had the strength and resolve to outface the miseries that had pursued them all their lives. She sought comfort in the hymns and in the warmth of the child sitting on her lap. Her singing was conducted with such vigour that Hudson began to laugh. Dottie smiled at him through her words of devotion, feeling a familiar pain in her chest as her heart filled with love for the child. She had made mistakes with one Hudson, driving him to his death, unable to make him stop by them for longer. She would try her hardest to help this one to live.

She hurried home, invigorated, filled with schemes of retrieval. The gutter smells in the room, rising with the heat of early summer, weakened her resolve and made her want to rush out again into the clear air. And as she looked at her sister's slumped body she felt her resolution turning into impatience. Hudson cried to be allowed on Sophie's bed and then squeezed himself between her and the wall. He burrowed into her open nightdress and started to suck on her. Dottie bit her tongue. She wanted to tell the boy not to do that, that it was not right, but the matter was between mother and child and nothing to do with her. 'Oh Hudson child,' Sophie groaned. 'You're my baby, you're my handsome man.'

She was no longer producing milk. Dottie could not see that it would cause anything but trouble to let him start sucking again, and on an empty breast. She fought down her irritation and resisted the temptation to bang the pans as she cleared up and cooked their meal. When the sucking noises ceased, she went over and peered down on them, and found both mother and child asleep. She rebuked herself then, calling herself twisted and loveless. She wanted to be fulsome and affectionate, loving and self-sacrificing, yet all she could manage at the sight of a child craving comfort from its mother's breast was discomfort and dirty thoughts. She wanted to be a good woman. She could sense with each passing day that her life was trickling wastefully away, yet all this would be worth bearing if she could achieve something real with what was left of it. She wanted to give herself fully, to find contentment in endless giving and selfless affection. What could she achieve for herself that was grander than that? If her mean ambition for herself were fulfilled, what good would it do her or the world she lived in? But to make life better for others …

Yet she always failed, in her own eyes and in the eyes of those she sought to serve and help. She wanted to deserve the life she had been given, but she failed. Even with the other Hudson, her self-sacrifice was always laced with resentment. She had been ready to deny herself everything to make his dream possible, to help him get to New York or become a sailor or whatever. She had loved him as dearly as life itself when he was her lost little brother abandoned with strangers in Dover. Yet … yet … there had always been a nagging resentment that no one thought to make such sacrifices for her. And she could not completely lay low the thought that she would have made better use of the opportunity if it had come her way. Such grumbling discontent only made her feel that her heart was envious and sour, that she lacked the warmth that put people at their ease and made them warm in return.

She cooked more rice and beans than they needed, in case Patterson should turn up while they were eating. When they sat down to eat, she only had a token portion of the fried snapper, keeping some back for him. She gave up her share gladly, not only because it fitted in with her self-sacrificing mood but because hospitality demanded it. Dottie felt guilty that they had decided not to buy the special food that the doctor had said Sophie should have. She had tried to argue with Sophie, and she was sure in her own heart that she would not have begrudged her the means to regain her health, but Sophie had become difficult, obsessed with buying the house for Hudson.

Patterson came late in the afternoon, later than usual. As if she guessed the nearness of his arrival, Sophie rose from her bed about half an hour before he appeared. She went to the bathroom to wash herself. When she left the room, she was a grumbling, garrulous tangle of prose, but she returned humming and smiling, full of grace. She sat by the window to make her face up, colouring her cheeks with a hint of gaiety. When Patterson arrived she had shed the grey look that had haunted her face for so long. Sophie clapped her hands when the knock came, and was at the door before Dottie could get to her feet.

He looked different. His hair was only just growing again after being cropped. He was conscious of it and stood at the door rubbing his head. His face looked leaner, more tormented. He looked at Sophie's delighted face for a moment, smiling and nodding his head, then ran his eyes over her ample body. Sophie smiled and Patterson laughed softly before opening his arms to her. He looked at Dottie, standing by Hudson's cradle, over Sophie's shoulder, and smiled at her too. Dottie did not want to move, did not want to invite comparisons between the way he had greeted Sophie and the way he might greet her.

'Let me salute my little father,' he said, loosening Sophie's embrace.

'It's so good to see you, I could hang on like this all day,' Sophie said, holding on to him as he walked towards the baby's cradle. 'Say hello to the boy. He missed you so much, didn't he, Sis?'

Hudson answered for himself, laughing and waving his arms and filling his nappy all at the same time. Patterson bent forward to talk to the child, standing only a few feet from Dottie. Her whole body craved for a warm touch, an affectionate pat or a squeeze of the shoulder, but he only glanced at her once, smiling vaguely. When he straightened, Sophie claimed him again and Patterson laughingly returned her crushing embrace. Dottie made some tea, hurrying but trying not to show it. If she was not around he would have expressed his affection and hunger for Sophie without awkwardness, she thought. When she had made the tea, and had changed Hudson's nappy, she suggested that she should take him out. It was what she had intended to do anyway, she insisted, anticipating any protests they might think to make. Sophie smiled gratefully at her while Patterson talked casually to the child.

She took Hudson to the common, her heart filled with resentment. She tried not to think of what would be happening in the room. Poor Jimmy, gone and forgotten. The thought of their passion made her think of Ken, and of how things had been between them. He was still the only man she had been with, and that made her feel bad in some way, as if she should have known more of them. What good would that have done her? How would any of them have been different? But perhaps the knowledge of them would have made her feel stronger, more worldly, and less as if there was something wicked in her aloneness. She forced herself to be cheerful, to smile at everything she saw, to think of herself as just another oppressed working woman. Poor Sophie, who could blame her for turning to him. Jimmy had not sent any word to her since he was sent to prison. She found that it gave her pleasure to beat down her misery, to brow-beat herself out of her loneliness, to contain her bitterness in corners and crevices of her mind.

She stayed out for as long as she could. When she returned, because Hudson was getting hungry again, she found Patterson sitting in his chair eating rice and beans with fried snapper. Sophie was standing at the sink, preparing Hudson's bottle and humming a lullaby. Dottie allowed herself a secret, cynical smile. 'Come and eat some food, little father,' Patterson said, holding out a spoonful of rice and beans. To Dottie's surprise, Hudson perched on Patterson's knee and ate what he gave him.

Later in the evening, when Hudson's gripe and indigestion had abated and he had gone to sleep, the three of them sat talking. It surprised Dottie how forceful her sister had become in an afternoon, keeping the conversation going with shameless flattery and forced hilarity. Patterson accepted the homage without embarrassment or acknowledgment, like an African potentate listening to a ceremonial praise-song. He dismissed Dottie's question about his time in prison, looking angry and distant for a moment. Sophie looked daggers at her.

'We don't want to talk about that business, Sis,' she said, her attempt at a fierce tone managing only to sound churlish and whining. 'We're just glad you're back, honey. Oh it's so good that our big man is back.' All that he would say was that it had been harder this time. As he said this he rubbed his cropped head and looked away from both of them. Dottie wondered if she would be able to raise the matter of the loan.

Sophie reclined on the bed, beginning to tire. Every so often while he talked, Patterson glanced at her and smiled. Dottie found the look frightening. It was a look of ownership, and it made Sophie squirm with pleasure and affection. She found Sophie's manner silly, she decided. Giving herself up like that, at her age. It was Patterson, in the end, who raised the matter of the loan. She told him the exact amount they needed and how far she had got with the building society. He nodded, promising the money next time he came. Dottie saw that her sister was looking tired and worn now, and hardly interested that they were another stage nearer their house. With an effort, she reminded herself that Sophie was ill, and smiled apologetically at Patterson. He looked unsmilingly back at her, making her wonder what the look was intended to mean.

2

Patterson went with Dottie to see the manager of the building society. He was a soft, balding man with glasses, and he listened to them with a grave, hunched-over look, as if they were discussing big business with him. Dottie liked him and felt her confidence growing as she talked to him. She liked the way he took the matter so seriously, and that he had so many questions to ask. Patterson did not say much, but she was glad he was there. It made her feel respectable. Afterwards, they pored over the figures the manager had given them to take away, calculating what they would have to pay back every month.

'You should get another job,' Patterson said to Dottie when he saw how much she earned in a week. He offered the advice as if it were a judgment from the gods. Dottie found herself defending her job, saying that she was reluctant to lose all her mates or something like that. She did not like his tone of voice any more than she liked the smiling young woman interfering in her life.

He came with them when they went to view their first house in Tooting. Dottie knew even before they went into it that it was not the one. It was too near the big intersection between the Broadway and Garrett Lane, and would be both noisy and unsafe for Hudson. Inside the house she found that the rooms were too small, the living room was at the back of the house and there was a bad smell in the kitchen. The garden was only a small piece of concrete with flower-beds around the edge. She did not like the English couple who lived there either. She thought they were laughing at them. They saw another house in Streatham. Patterson was very enthusiastic about it because it had been fully done out with new plumbing and wiring, had been re-decorated and was going at a good price. Sophie kept shivering while they were walking around, saying that there was something there. Patterson laughed at her, saying it was only because the house was a little chilly, not having been lived in for a while. Sophie was not convinced, and behind his back shook her head firmly at Dottie.

The third house they saw was in Horatio Street in Brixton. Dottie felt good about it as soon as they began to walk down the street. It was a sunny day and there were several people standing outside their houses, chatting. They were mostly black women, and they smiled at the two sisters as they strolled past. The person who lived next door to the house they had come to see smiled and spoke to them. She was a short, plump, light-skinned woman who leaned unconcernedly over her gate when she saw them and hailed them over. 'You've come to see the house? It's a good house, and a good price. I live next door ... my name's Laura. You better give the door there a good hard knock. The old boy in there, his hearing not so sharp these days. You're not Jamaican? Small island people, no? I'm from St Ann's Bay, and God helping me I'll go back and die there anyhow. Go on, I'll catch you later on and we have a good talk about the place.'

Dottie glanced at Sophie and they shared a smile. The gentle Irish man who showed them round was politely gallant despite his undisguisable old age. He was full of information about the house. It was a two-bedroomed terrace, two-up two-down with a back extension, but the old man's stories gave it an unexpected dimension, endowing it with mythology and history. He told them when it was built, and who had lived in it through its age. He was forthcoming about its problems and shortcomings, and all the various things it needed doing to it before it could be said to be an appropriate abode for such charming young ladies as them. He showed them the garden, which was nothing grand, but large enough to put a swing in, one of Dottie's secret ambitions for Hudson. Patterson was not with them that time, so they could indulge the old man without feeling that they were wasting time.

'You like the house, Hudson boy?' Sophie asked, and claimed that she could tell from his enthusiastic gabbling that he was delighted with it. The old man seemed pleased too. He wanted to get a smaller place, he told them. It was too big for him on his own, although they had had a high old time when the family was all together. 'I'm a grandfather now,' he said. 'I want to live peaceful and quiet.

A lot of you coloured folk are moving round here. No offence to you, my dears, but I'm too old for that sort of thing. It isn't your fault, I'm not saying that. They treat your people like dirt and you want to get them back for it. Only some of you darkies can't tell the difference between an Irish republican and a Tory Englishman. It's scary to be a white man in this part of the world now. I don't mean no offence, my dears.'

They walked to the office of the estate agent and made the offer immediately after viewing it. Dottie felt a fraud as she agreed the price with the man in the estate agent's office, as if she could even dream of ever having that kind of money, but a part of her was bursting with pride anyhow. She wondered, as she listened to the young man talk, whether he had a house of his own. He did not look it, did not look as if he was the kind of person who would have the strength to eat spinach and cassava for a house. That Sunday they celebrated. Patterson brought a couple of bottles round, one of schnaps and one of rum, and joined in their joy and their plans. He insisted on throwing a glassful of schnaps out of the window, into the back-garden. 'It may not look like it,' he said, 'but there may well be some ancestors under that earth there, and we should never neglect them when good fortune comes our way.' He was not a bit put out that they had made their decision without his assistance, as Dottie had feared. She thought how close he had become to them since coming out of prison. He was no longer the watchful, stiff man always on the verge of leaving, and always with that undercurrent of bitterness and violence.

Sophie began to feel sick after her fourth rum. Patterson insisted she should go to bed, and would hear nothing of her pleas for him to stay. He looked at Dottie for a long moment before he left, unsmiling, as if considering and testing a thought. After he had gone, she stood trembling with the confusion and the pain that the look caused her. He was wooing her! If that was not too grand a name to give to what he was doing … He was not sure how she would take his approaches, and he was waiting for guidance from her. She thought he meant her to understand that it would all be discreet. They would be careful, and Sophie would never know. There was no point in upsetting her.

She lay in the dark that Sunday night, thinking about him and the way he made her feel. She thought of his lean strong body in hers, of the smell of his flesh in her nostrils, the feel of his breath on her neck and her ears. She would have him. She would have him lie with her even if it made her feel disgusting and dirty. She wanted him, but she was afraid to concede as much as he seemed to be asking. She had feared all along that this was how he would want things to be, so he could come to them when he wanted and use them. Patterson and his pen of Balfour sisters. The thought was painful, degrading. Just as it degraded her sometimes to think that Sophie had so completely abandoned Jimmy and taken up with his *brother*.

Perhaps she *would* have him, just once. It had been such a long time, and always she had baulked at the thought of being used, of being degraded and abandoned. Perhaps there was no other way for men and women to be together, and she would have to grit her teeth and steel herself to the indignity that lay ahead whatever she did. Unless she wanted to live without a man. She had seen Sophie run through a string of them, and had seen that to these men, like Andy the landlord and Jimmy, and Patterson too, she was something they took pleasure in. Something that filled their mouths and made their eyes light up with excitement.

Dottie knew, on the other hand, that they laughed at *her* and her awkwardness with them.

It puzzled her what they saw in Sophie, although it made her feel unkind to think that. She was quite big now, cheeks bulging with grease and a body layered with rolls of fat. What could they be attracted to in that? Not that she was anything wonderful herself, all scrawny and on edge, but that was not the point. No one was slavering at the mouth for her. When she was feeling more generous, or more critical of herself, she thought she understood. Sophie was like Sharon. She had a kind of happiness when she was with men that was almost innocent, child-like. She was like Sharon in that way, except that Sharon had been full of bitterness and pain the rest of the time, when the drink had worn off. Sophie took pleasure in everything her men did, and laughed with an abandoned submission at all the affectionate deeds they performed. Dottie could not imagine being able to deny herself that much. But perhaps she would have him once, just to feel that raw joy again.

3

Their affairs with the house purchase proceeded at such a pace that the day of moving was approaching fast enough to inconvenience and fluster them. Andy was flabbergasted when they told him. He was suspicious at first, but when he could no longer refuse to believe, he looked comic-ally tragic. Dottie saw his eyes watering, and understood how Andy's world had slowly been turned upside down over the years. Before he left, he asked Dottie to come out for a drink with him. For old times' sake, he said. When Dottie refused, he took her hand and pleaded. 'I won't do anything, I promise,' he said. 'Just to talk about old times … and if I can help. If you need anything.'

'No, Andy,' Dottie said. 'We don't need anything.'

'Your address. Give me your address in Brixton. I'll come and visit you and we go to the cinema. Or if you need anything or something like that, please.'

Dottie gave him the address in the end, because she could not bear his pleading. He took the paper she gave him and sniffed it, then he smiled in his old, cock-sure way. He ran meaningful eyes over her body and whistled tunelessly to himself. 'Just remember, darling, if you need anything …' he said, making Dottie laugh.

Various of the women at the factory had promised bits of furniture or utensils to Dottie: tables and chairs that were being discarded for the new-fangled wipe-clean veneered suites, an old bed, a Belling electric cooker that was going for free, although they would have preferred gas. She had to arrange for someone to collect all these bits and pieces in a van and deliver them to the house in Brixton on the appointed day. Small items like old curtains and bedding she collected herself and stored in the room, ready for the move. She found some clean boxes at the market and took them home for packing their belongings. There was not a great deal to put in them: clothes, crockery, some ornaments and four boxfuls of books. Dottie was proud of her boxes of books, and heard Sophie's exclamations about them with contentment.

In one of the book-boxes she put the old biscuit tin in which she kept their papers. She looked through it before she packed it away. The last time had been when they had to find Hudson's birth certificate for his passport application. She knew everything the tin contained as if she had learned it by heart. There had been times, between Ken's departure and Sophie's return for example, when she had leafed through the yellowed papers and faded pictures as if she was turning the pages of her history. There was the photo of Hudson on the cliffs in Dover, pretending to be David Copperfield. The sun was still shining on his delighted grin, leaping off the stick that he had jokingly raised over the animal's flanks. Behind him and over the edge of the cliff, the sea still glimmered in the distance, bouncing up sharp splinters of light. The boy who was his friend, his *brother* Frank, was laughing with him, filled with the joy of the beautiful afternoon. Even after all this time, they were still happy. Especially after all this time and everything that had happened. She should have left him there, instead of harrying him to his death. They could not have done much worse with him than she had done, and she could not recall seeing Hudson with such a happy face in all the time she had known him. What had happened to the other boy, she wondered? Like Hudson, he would be twenty now, just about to be a man.

There was another picture in the tin, creased and dog-eared with handling. It showed a woman and a girl standing beside each other in a garden, their backs to the house. The door was open, and in its gloomy and grainy shadows another shape was visible. The woman was smiling shyly, as if reluctant to be photographed. Even in the faded old print, her beauty shone out. The features on her face, her eyes and her lips, were like shadows on the moon. Her right hand rested on the shoulder of the girl who stood beside her. She could not have been more than twelve or so. Her face was contorted with the effort of keeping an unwanted grin from breaking out across her face. The girl was wearing a blouse that was decorated with narrow silver braid across the front. In her right hand she held a lollipop, partially shielded by her palm but none the less visible enough. Although the picture was so pale and creased, she knew that the little girl was Sharon. There was no mistaking her.

On the back, a flowing hand had written the names of the woman and the girl in the picture. It was not Sharon's writing, and Dottie wondered, with an avidity that made her desperate with frustration when she allowed it to, who could have written those two names with such a sure hand. Behind the woman was written the name Hawa, and behind the girl was the name Bilkisu. And underneath them was the date 1933. While Hitler was stepping into the Chancellory in Berlin, about to embark on the historic task of making Germany count in the congress of nations again, mother and daughter were standing shyly in the back-garden having their photograph taken. Hawa and Bilkisu, 1933. Those were their names. Where would they have got names like that? She had known them for years, but had kept Sharon's name to herself, like something that embarrassed her. What good would it do them, anyway? Sharon herself had told her not to submit to the tyranny of times that had passed.

The shadow at the door gave her a feeling of foreboding. She thought she could see from the outline that it was a man, but there was nothing to make her certain of that. Perhaps it was perversity, or a stubborn romanticism, that convinced her that the shadow was Sharon's father. She was not sure why that should trouble her. He was nothing to do with them, and it probably was not him, anyway. Why shouldn't he be the one who was taking the photograph? The shadow could be a neighbour or a friend. And was the house behind them the home that Sharon had told her about? Was that Cardiff? She wished she had listened to the ramblings of her dying mother. On the other hand, perhaps they were better buried. That way they knew nothing of what they were, and there was no one to feel shame for the way they had turned out.

So often, as she pored over the picture, she wished there was more. Sharon's anger with her father had been so complete that she had not even bothered to mention her parents until she was almost overwhelmed by squalor and despair. Then her stories had been full of guilt and agonised regrets. Dottie had had no time for all that, ashamed beyond utterance by their lives, her every feeling and emotion turned to revulsion and self-loathing that they had been found worthy of such punishment. She had only listened to Sharon out of duty, seeing out the unhappy woman who was suffering such torments in her last years.

Could she not have left her something of the man in Leeds who had almost become their father? Not that it really mattered that much! Dottie Badoura Fatma Balfour, what could she do with all that? A hundred pounds or so would have been much more useful to them than that baggage. None the less she wept as she thought that she would never know what those names meant or why he had chosen them for her. For years she had seen an image of him walking a dog, and herself beside him. She had been so sure that there must be a picture somewhere but for all her searches she had not been able to find anything. There must have been a picture, for the image always contained her in it, looking up at him with a smile. It must have been thrown away with all the other bits of junk that Sharon had left behind. All Dottie had kept were trousers embroidered with tiny silver caps, so that at a glance the material looked like sequin or mail. She did not remember ever having seen them before Sharon's death. They were the size of a teenager and she had kept them because she thought that Hudson could have them one day, an idea that seemed more and more ridiculous every time she saw them. Over the years they had grown grubbier and more crumpled at the bottom of the box of old blankets and rags where sometimes she found cockroach eggs and little black droppings. She could not quite bring herself to throw them away.

She packed the biscuit tin in one of the book boxes. There was nothing much in it, really. Bits of paper that attested to their existence, and round which she could weave half-made stories that gave their lives substance and significance. There was more to them than met the eye, after all. Papers and photographs and tokens of abandoned times. The defeated lives they owned did not tell the whole story, did not specify the full extent of who they were.

Expectations

1

Hudson dramatically bloomed once they had moved to their new house. He had learnt to crawl while they were still living in the room in Segovia Street, but he had only been able to crawl into corners and under beds, playing elaborate games with the few sticks of furniture, round which he peered and hid. Within moments of being released in the new house, he was out of sight. Within days of moving to Horatio Street, he was walking without any support, fearlessly exploring the abounding acres of his new home. He had been a demanding baby despite his good nature, always hanging on to somebody, refusing to be left alone, complaining for company, reluctant to go to sleep. Now he played for hours in the room he shared with his mother, singing and calling out when the mood took him, in transports of joy.

The games he played became more detailed and more subtle, requiring imaginative uses of the huge spaces at his disposal. He used his voice with greater variety too, trying out new tones and listening for the old combinations, teaching himself to sing. His cradle no longer restrained him, and he had learnt how to climb in and out of it with ease. For a long time he had been restrained by the cradle's rocking motion. When he clung to the sides, to try and climb in, the cradle followed him and deposited him back on the floor each time. When he tried to climb out, it tipped him unceremoniously on the floor. In the new dispensation he climbed over the ends, crawling hand over foot on the sheer grid, resting between moves like a species of Amazonian sloth.

Joyce came to their house some days now, to save Dottie the journey, but she was not happy about the new arrangement. Very little pleased her, and it was easy to see that times had become harder for her too. She still dressed as if she was on her way to a party, shiny dresses that were too tight and too short, but the costumes had lost their lustre. Her face was always heavily made up. Often the make-up was old, dull and patchy where sweat or hands had rubbed it off. On some mornings, the more bizarre aspects of her face-paint turned grotesque in their half-effacement, and her silver eye-shadow and green lipstick would be running like exhalations from a corpse. Her body smelled of bitter, burnt nuts and sometimes her breath smelled bad, but more with staleness and exhaustion than corruption. Where her appearance before had promised exuberance and happiness, now it only suggested vice. She had a frighteningly tragic air about her, as if she was already resigned to being a victim despite her aggressive manner.

Dottie thought that if she could detect that, so would the men whose fantasies Joyce lived off. They would smell her out without thought, and one of them would fulfil her secret fate. The thought shocked Dottie, and made her see Joyce with new eyes. After that she could not fail to see that behind the pouts and the complaints there lurked trills of fear and dependence, and that for all her foul mouth and fierce looks she was frightened.

Despite the feelings of sympathy for her, Dottie rushed home from work when Joyce was there. Perhaps the new knowledge of her vulnerability made Dottie less quick to rebuke Joyce's remissions, but that did not make her any more trusting. Dottie could not get over the worry that Joyce would use the house for other purposes, carry out her filthy business there. When she arrived home, it was usually to find the house in chaos. The two babies would be running about, screaming with hysterical hilarity. Clothes, furniture, kitchen pans would be scattered wherever they did not belong. She would find Joyce slumped in their scantily furnished parlour, her eyes closed to the chaos, with her bag and coat beside her, ready to go. She always looked at Dottie with a superior smirk, and Dottie had taught herself not to mind it, not to rush into placatory smiles. She was only a young girl, she told herself, made bold and brazen by her life of prostitution.

'It's not worth it for me, coming all the way here,' Joyce complained. 'I'm only trying to help. You know what I mean? Cause we're all in it together. Otherwise I wouldn't bother. Not for the money you give me. And the bus journey from Balham and that. Anyway, I'm thinking of going to sec'tarial college soon, so I don't think I can keep doing this.' If she was still there when Sophie came back from work, she stayed longer to taunt Sophie about Jimmy. She spoke of him as *the boy's dad*: 'Have you had any news from the boy's dad? He's doing all right then, is he?' She used to know him a couple years before, she said. She would grin at Sophie, strutting a little in front of her. It must be one of the small benefits of the work she did, Dottie thought, that she understood the full depravity of men and could sneer at women like Sophie who chose to delude themselves.

'Patterson's helping you out a lot these days, Miss Sophie,' Joyce said, using the term of respect with crude irony. 'He's always around here these days, isn't he? This is a nice house you have here. You're ever so lucky, Miss Sophie.'

It seemed to Dottie that her sister would never hear the sarcasm in Joyce's voice. She smiled at the questions and gushed about Patterson, remarking on his kindnesses and making Joyce laugh. She never answered the questions about Jimmy, and appeared unembarrassed by them. There were many times when Dottie was tempted to ask Joyce how her business was, but she was reluctant to invite further enmity from her. She determined early after their move that she would try and find a minder nearer home.

Their neighbour, Laura, came over to their house every day in the first week, asking them how the day had gone, whether there was anything they needed. They went to her for sugar, or a can opener, the usual little things that get lost with moving. Laura told them to come round for anything if they were stuck, or just for a natter, and not to worry about seeming rude. That was what neighbours were for, she said, especially in this cold country with closed doors. 'I couldn't believe it when I first come to this country, my dear. If you speak to anyone they run away and bang their door shut. My husband said it was because they don't like us Jamaicans, but I think they just like shutting themselves in their little boxes. So you come round when you like, you hear me.'

Those were days of joy for Dottie, rushing home after work to do a little more unpacking, move things from one place to another until she found the right position. She discovered the loft, and put a chair on a table to look into it. Sophie held on to the chair legs, serenading Dottie with a stream of terrified warnings. Dottie put her head carefully into the dark hole and smelt sharp, clear air. She lit a match but that did nothing more than reveal a huge cavern. In a corner of the roof a little moonlight shone in, which Dottie thought was charming, until heavy rains came a few days later and explained the damp patches in the little bedroom.

People she worked with wanted to hear a blow-by-blow account of the house and were quick with advice about curtains and repairs. Mike Butler overheard Dottie's description of her attempt at the loft, and pursed his lips wisely over the glint of moonlight through the roof. He could've told her what that meant, if she'd bothered to ask. Soon enough, when opportunity offered itself, he embarked on a monologue about the life-time knowledge of lofts and their eccentricities that he had acquired in his travels. Why, there was a man who built a pond in his loft, Mike Butler pronounced, working himself into a powerful rhythm. He spent hours of every day up there, improving his pond, adding little refinements. It was an obsession. He missed days off work, neglected his family. One day this poor man went up to his roof-top pond to find it had been taken over by a hideous creature with protruberant eyes and enormous whiskers. 'A creature from the deep,' Mike Butler declaimed, watching with customary incomprehension as his audience deserted him. He slipped in a warning about holes in the roof, and how they could lead to ceilings crashing down on you, but no one was listening by that stage.

Laura brought her lawn-mower over during the weekend and taught Dottie how to use it. Her Alsatian dog, whose name was Daisy, stood on her hind legs and peered at them over the garden fence, barking now and then to capture their attention. To Dottie the dog seemed frighteningly fierce, but Laura spoke to her as if she were a gentle child, and stroked and patted her to soothe her fractious nerves. It was to protect them against robbers, she explained, but the poor animal was more scared than they were. Laura was living alone with her daughter, and she was afraid of some badjohn breaking in and hurting them. Her daughter's father was still in Jamaica, not well enough to travel, Laura said, glancing at Dottie as she said this, to see how she would take it. Later, when they knew each other better, she told Dottie the truth. The man had left them to go back to Jamaica, disgusted with England. The cold, the rain, the endless nights and all the bad-talk he had to accept were too much to him. It was he who had bought them the dog before he left, telling them the three bitches could now live happily together. In any case he had not been much use, Laura said, complaining all the time about colour-bar and about his *rights*.

Dottie expected the daughter to be a young girl, but she turned out to be about eighteen or so. She was a trainee nurse at St George's Hospital, where her mother also worked in the laundry. To hear them talk to each other, and to listen to the authority with which Laura pronounced on medical matters, one would have thought that their situations were reversed. It was the mother who had all the big words, while the daughter stumbled over them. Laura had been training to be a nurse before she came over to join her husband, but she had given that up when she got to England. It had been a difficult decision. She took the laundry job so they could afford to buy their house. Dottie liked both of them, and liked their closeness to each other, and the soft-spoken tones with which they addressed each other. Late at night, she would hear voices on the other side of the adjoining wall, not clearly enough to distinguish the words, but there was no mistaking the even-tempered familiarity of the tones.

The daughter's name was Veronica, and two or three evenings a week a young man walked her home from work. He looked very young and wore a grey suit and dark tie. They stood chatting by the front hedge, laughing and leaning towards each other. If they stood there too long, Laura pushed her head out of the living-room window and called her daughter in. Veronica dressed fashionably and wore clever hairstyles, and to Dottie she seemed fresh and happy.

2

Sophie started to miss days off work because of her illness, which had got worse over the move to the new house. She had hurt her back lifting a box, and complained that the pain made it impossible for her to do anything at all. She could not even sleep. They thought it best that Hudson should move into Dottie's room. As time passed she did less and less in the house. In the end Dottie suggested to her that she should take a part-time job, and rest up more until she was better. Patterson would call in on her during the day. It was all very simple now for Patterson, Dottie thought. He did not bother with the Sunday visits any more. He came when Sophie was available and sometimes stayed the night in her room. He helped out with money for the bills, now that Sophie was not earning enough. If there were heavy jobs to be done he volunteered for them. He had fixed all the water taps, and repaired the broken sashes in the windows. He arranged for someone he knew to fix the hole in the roof. He was part of their lives. He asked questions about what they were spending on, where they went shopping, and even where they intended to buy their new parlour furniture. He knew someone who ran a store, and had just received a very attractive suite that may well suit them. He was free with advice, and did not mind being insistent with it sometimes. Patterson and his pen of Balfour sisters, Dottie thought. As she had always feared.

Some weekends he was there all the time, doing the bits of building work that they wanted done. He wired the loft and helped them clean it out. They found an old trunk full of newspapers and clothes, commemorative editions and old military uniforms. They also found a broken wire bed, twisted and tangled grotesquely on itself. An ancient iron tank had rusted immovably into the beams and side-wall, and would have to stay there until a calamity befell the house. Stuffed into crevices and holes were pieces of rags and strips of soft leather, to keep out draughts and wind-swept snow. All round the loft were scattered the detritus of other people's lives, and Dottie found its presence intrusive and irritating. Her attempts to remove it, though, only created an unmanageable chaos and filled the loft with dust, driving her away in the end.

Patterson was very helpful. He found out about grants for them, and accompanied the buildings inspector from the council when he came to look at their house. The two of them talked like friends, ignoring Dottie, who followed them wherever they went. Patterson brought builders to install an indoor bathroom and toilet which the council paid for. He converted the outside toilet into a shed, ripping out the plumbing and re-laying the floor. He worked silently, with methodical and stubborn violence.

He hardly talked to them most of the time, but when he did he was courteous and firm. He came and went as he pleased. They learnt to ask him nothing about himself or where he went when he was not with them. He taught them simply to accept whatever he chose to do for them, and they learned that he would tell them nothing except what he chose. They knew nothing about his life or what he did for a living other than what they saw or what he told them. Dottie knew that in her own mind she thought of him as an obstacle, as somebody who was often there to appraise and judge what she did. Even when he said nothing it was not difficult to guess his opinion. A sad smile or a weary shake of the head were just as eloquent. She was resigned to his control of their lives. His influence had grown over them and she had known no way to prevent it. In his presence she felt herself diminishing, shrinking.

Sophie gave up all responsibility for Hudson. *Why not have a proper holiday?* Dottie thought. *Why keep a dog and then bark yourself?* Dottie devoted herself to the child. Even though he always ran to Sophie when he wanted comfort, and threw himself at her when she came in from somewhere, to Dottie it was enough that it was she who looked after him. She had to watch that she did not become a tyrant under the guise of her devotion, as she thought she had done to the elder Hudson, assuming that she knew what was good for him. She would make what amends she could to the young Hudson for the ignorant way she had dealt with her own brother. It was the boy who mattered, not Dottie's feelings or what she thought of his mother. She no longer believed in Sophie's illness, and she resented the burdens she had to shoulder in its name. As if to anticipate what grumbles she might make, Patterson looked stern when Hudson was being difficult, and he talked earnestly to Dottie about sacrifice. The Reverend Patterson Bongbongbong is in our midst, she sneered, the Pastor of the Church of the Doomed of Horatio Street.

She found it hard now to listen with any sympathy to tales of the aches and pains that made her sister's life such a living torment. To mortify herself even further, Dottie listed all the other things she would have been doing had it not been for Sophie and Hudson. She could have gone to college to do some exams. Mike Butler urged her to, and even invited her to meet his wife who was a college teacher or adviser or something, and who would tell her about what was available. He had already told his wife a great deal about Dottie, and she would be honoured to meet her. Dottie politely refused. What was the point? Where would she find the time? She had not even visited the library since they moved, and she still had some books to return. And the reason for her lack of time was so that her sister could stay in her room and play dirty games with Patterson.

She hated the bitterness she felt. It made her stiff and awkward with resentment, so that she felt as if all the people she met could tell that she was uncomfortable with them and envied them their quiet, normal lives. The misery made her irritable and clumsy, and made it harder to be sociable in the easy-going manner that seemed effortless in everyone else. People she worked with told her she looked ill, and some advised her to leave the job. With all her brains and all the books she read, they told her, she could easily get a job in an office. She hated the resignation she felt, the slow decline. There had not been much to keep her going all her life, but now it seemed that she was losing heart.

She always found an explanation, a form of words, that prevented her dejection from overwhelming her. At times the words of a song came to her mind, or the memory of a moment of joy, a fragment secreted away against the time of ruin, and for a while the old strength returned as she rejoiced in the miracle of her survival and the sharpness of her faculties. For a while she found again the generosity to make allowances for her sister, and reprimanded herself for her cruelty and selfishness. But then she got back to the house to see her lying in bed in daylight, reeking of perfumed oils and sweetmeats, and she was plunged once again into discontented irritation. To Dottie she seemed to glow with health, yet she was constantly groaning with self-pity. It frightened her that she could be burdened with Sophie all her life, that after all these years they would make a servant of her, a skivvy. It frightened her that she would lose the small independence she had found for herself, so much that her chest hurt with a strange sinking agony whenever she thought about it. It was different when these things were done without bitterness, for Hudson the baby and Hudson the brother, and for Sophie herself.

Some evenings after she had put Hudson to bed, she hid herself in her room, sitting silently listening to Sophie's resentful business when she was left on her own by Patterson. She wanted to leave them, find a place of her own. One evening Sophie came in to her. Dottie had been annoyed by something that had happened at work. One of the foremen, a leathery-faced lecher, had put an arm around her waist and kissed her on the neck. She had turned round on him and abused him, barely able to prevent herself from attacking him physically. But what annoyed her was that she had brought her blackness into it. 'You think that just because I'm black I won't mind being squeezed up by a dirty old man like you,' she had said. She knew that the man was like that with all the women, yet she had said that and heard the other women's indignant grumbles of sympathy grow softer. The words came to mock her with their hysteria. The man had taken advantage, laughing at her. *Oh yeah, oh you poor old coon, you. If you can't stand the heat get out of the kitchen, and piss off back to Niggerland, love.*

She had found it impossible to say anything to her sister when she got home, not only because she assumed that Sophie would be unable to understand her hurt, but also because she could not find the urge to be friendly and chatty, could not be bothered to set the scene for her confessions. She had done her chores with a tired, hostile look, signalling to Sophie, and Hudson as well, that she would not respond kindly to any attempts to engage her in conversation. She made Hudson ready for bed unusually early, and bundled him off into his cot in her room, putting down all his attempts at insurrection with unmistakable firmness. Then she retired herself, after giving Sophie a curt explanation. Sophie followed her into her room, making Hudson raise a cautious eye from the pillow, where he had been pretending to be asleep.

'You all right, Sis?' Sophie asked, standing at the door.

Dottie was sitting on the bed, a book in her hand, pretending to read. She smiled, touched by the look of misery on Sophie's plump features, like a clown's tears. Sophie smiled with relief and came in. She sat on the bed, and, suddenly overflowing affection, she hugged Dottie. To her own amazement, Dottie began to cry. Sophie crooned to her, rocking her as she held her. 'It's all right, honey. Poor, poor lovey. Why do you make yourself unhappy? Oh you poor child.' Dottie nearly burst out laughing through her tears. She lay in her sister's arms and found comfort in the childish endearments, but she also thought that Sophie's was the kind of warmth that was offered without thought, that was given easily. She disengaged herself as gently as she could, so Sophie should not misunderstand her withdrawal. Sophie's eyes were bathed in tears too, and Dottie smiled at her and stroked her cheek.

'I'm fine now,' said Dottie, but thought to herself how little hope there was for them, her and her fat, silly sister. 'I'm just weary.'

Hudson was not satisfied with these reassurances, or he saw the confusion as an opportunity to extend his bedtime for several hours. He raised such a din, howling and complaining, crying real tears and kicking his cot with fury, that there was no other choice but to let the young khan out of his bed and let him roam the room at will. While they waited for Hudson to tire, they talked a little too. Dottie tried to explain why the job made her so miserable. She hated the way it took her whole day away from her, absorbed all her energies, exhausted her and gave her nothing in return. After a while, Dottie knew that Sophie was not listening any more. She looked bored, as if she had heard all this before and understood its futility. And she had, Dottie thought with some shock. This was what she had been saying for years, in some way or another. Even if she had not used the very words she had used that evening, Sophie had understood her meaning long ago.

It amused her, in a wry, self-pitying way, that she should now turn to Sophie for comfort. It was she who always thought herself to be strong. For years she had felt equal to this expectation, had felt capable of carrying the burden of her sister's imbecility and of her brother's naivety and malice. Now she felt tired, weary, irritated by dependence. She suspected that it was all over, that the urge and the zest for anything that she might have wished for was now gone. Hudson and the house had taken it all, and Sophie and Patterson …

It all went back to Patterson, she thought. It was the way he had taken over their lives that made her feel weary. If she was a man, she thought, she would have gone to sea and roamed the world for a year or two, to get the sense of oppression out of her blood. Then she would have returned refreshed and wiser, and put her life to rights. Regained control of it, at the very least. She realised now that the sense of control had been some compensation for the responsibilities she had assumed to be her burden. Patterson had taken that away and had made them dependent on him. He demonstrated to her, wilfully and with ease, how hopeless and vulnerable their position was. They would now no longer be able to afford the house on their own. Dottie knew no way in which they could earn more, unless she found a better job, and she did not know how she could do that. She had looked in newspapers, she had applied, she had even used the phone as some of the ads had asked her to do. The incident with the man made her more determined that she would leave, but her heart was not in any of the jobs she had applied for before. Where would she find the job that would take her away from that factory? She could always ask Patterson, she thought. Or the Reverend Mosiah. A man would know what would be best for her to do.

3

It all went back to Patterson. There was no disguising his tyranny over them now. Dottie knew with every instinct in her that Patterson was too much for them, just as she knew that he led a life of cruelty and violence which he hid from them. Sophie had devoted herself to him because she always devoted herself to someone, and she neither saw nor cared for the finer points. That was how it seemed to Dottie, anyway. How else could she not be alarmed by some of the men who called on Patterson sometimes? Not only were their appearances frightening, but the respect they showed him seemed close on deference, very like homage. Their conversations with him were whispered and urgent, and sometimes packages and boxes were left behind. Dottie had been very ignorant with Hudson, but she was alert enough now to know that Patterson was running some kind of racket, some kind of crime, and was perhaps its leader. Once she saw a long package lying on the floor in Sophie's room, wrapped in greasy sacking and looking suspiciously like a gun. A gun! But it had disappeared later in the day, and Dottie had never been able to work up the nerve to ask Patterson about it, even to enquire if it really was a gun.

Despite all her unease, though, and despite her distress that he dominated and ordered their lives, he was as he had always been with them. He was courteous and helpful, and Dottie still found there were times when she wished he would turn into her room rather than Sophie's. She had nightmarish dreams of Patterson coupling with her, and woke up disgusted with her lust. In the winter months, she could hear their voices as they rumbled through the floorboards, and could hear the bed grumbling and creaking as they made love. She tried not to listen, but when her own need was most strongly on her she could not be as strict with herself as she would have liked, and thrilled with both envy and desire as she heard Sophie's abandoned laughter gurgling through the beams and joists of the house.

4

In the autumn, Dottie enrolled on an evening secretarial course at Morley College, which was near her factory in Kennington. The woman in the library, the one she had asked about Dr Murray and who had smiled at her when she visited the library, had told her about the college. She had been delighted to see Dottie again. 'I wondered what had happened to you,' she said. On an impulse, Dottie asked her about any office courses she could do, and the librarian had brought out leaflets and reference books and had spent half an hour going through them with her. Of course it was not really an impulse, but Dottie would not have asked if the woman had not spoken to her first. She chose the college because the librarian was so enthusiastic, saying it was one of the best evening schools in London, and because it was so near the factory, and therefore she would not have to travel to places she did not know.

The secretarial course was a lot easier than Dottie imagined it would be, and her teacher was delighted with her, exclaiming to the whole class about her astonishing progress. All the students were women, and after class the whole group went out to the pub next door to the college for half an hour or so. Some of the students were very young but several of them were women in their twenties, like Dottie. An older woman who had been coming to the classes for years without making any progress, and who attended for the company rather than out of ambition, mothered all of them and gave them courage when they began to flag and feel discouraged. Her name was Elke and she delighted in reeling out the benefits and comforts that were unavailable in her day, and which her younger class-mates could take for granted. Despite the predictable nature of her inspirational messages, she had an uncanny sense of who it was who was most in need of bolstering over a glass of beer or shandy. She was also the chaperone of the younger women when any unwelcome attentions were forced on them.

Inevitably, people talked about their ambitions and the urgency that had driven them to the evening classes. It humbled Dottie to hear the stories her class-mates told, of uncooperative relatives who put obstacles in the way, of parents who were suspicious of their children over-reaching themselves and tried to hold them back for their own good. There were stories of unfulfilling marriages and lazy, demanding husbands who could not even fry an egg for themselves and who resented the absence of their houris for two evenings a week. Stories of unwanted children. Of the violence and oppression some of the women had to live with daily. Of the spirit with which they vowed to make themselves independent and useful. Yet there had been nothing to stop Dottie, and she had wallowed for years in self-pity and ignorance, and had done nothing for herself.

Their teacher, who was no older than Dottie herself, came with them to the pub. Dottie had been wary of her at first. The notification she had received from the college at the beginning of the year told her that the class would be led by Stella Hoggarth, a name which struck terror in Dottie's heart. It sounded so frightening, and she imagined a large woman with metallic hair and a heroic voice. Stella Hoggarth turned out to be Estella Hoggar, as she explained to them with a smile when she introduced herself on the first day. The office always changed it, even if she spelt it with capital letters, she said. She was neither fair nor large, but dark and slim. Her face was shapely and attractive, the lines of her features clean and precise, perhaps a little on the gaunt side. First appearances suggested a look of fragility, a careful, small woman with obsessive habits, but this too turned out to be untrue. Dottie discovered, when she went to stand next to her in the process of receiving instruction, that Estella Hoggar was taller than her and almost certainly larger in the hip and bust.

When she came to know her a little better, Dottie found out that Estella's parents lived in Birmingham, and that she regularly went to stay with them once or twice a month.

It seemed a wonderfully complete life to Dottie. She had been a school teacher before she came to London to look for work, and was now very glad that she had moved, despite the hard times to begin with. Dottie liked her enthusiasm and her unfeigned good nature. Her way of speaking was strange sometimes, unpredictable and exaggerated, but always followed by a cheerful smile. There was a directness and self-confidence about her that was a little intimidating at first, although the kindness quickly shone through to disperse Dottie's wariness and suspicion.

Estella offered her a lift after classes sometimes. She lived in Wimbledon, so driving through Brixton was not excessively out of her way so late in the evening when traffic was light. 'And I like Brixton,' she said. 'Don't you? It's so seedy.' Dottie told her that she thought Brixton was very likely the cradle of human civilisation, the exact place where God's first garden was built. She had heard people claim, she said after a moment, that it could possibly be the legendary site of the underground merging of all the world's greatest rivers as well, the famous Underground Lake. Estella turned to her with a delighted grin and pronounced her crazy. 'One hundred per cent!'

She drove a noisy and ancient VW Beetle, a sign of fashionable tastes at the time. She was obviously fond of the frightening machine and spoke affectionately to it whenever it seemed to be struggling under the demands made of it. Everything about her intrigued Dottie, but she admired most of all the free life that Estella seemed to lead. She was an attractive woman living on her own in a prosperous part of London. She had a good job and drove a rakish car with some style. Even her name demanded interest. And since that was the safest subject among the many that interested her about Estella, it was with enquiries about her name that

Dottie began her exploration. Estella smiled and said that it was a French name. She said one or two other things about herself, but it was clear she did not want to elaborate, and Dottie was relieved to see her change the subject. That determined her to be patient, not to pry and chase Estella away with her nosiness. It was nothing to do with her, and she herself would be just as evasive if someone she was doing a favour to suddenly wanted to know all about her.

5

The encouragement and praise that Dottie received in her evening classes, and the kindness and friendship with which Estella treated her, made bearable the worsening circumstances under which they all lived. At the turn of the year, Harold Wilson became Prime Minister at the head of a tiny Labour majority in Parliament. Labour had spent thirteen years in the wilderness, and clung to their tiny majority with gasps of relief, plotting to transform it to a more comfortable one in another election within a few months. In the meantime, some lessons were being very quickly learned. During the election, Patrick Gordon Walker, the proposed Foreign Secretary and a Labour stalwart, had lost his seat in Smethwick, defeated by the Tory candidate's slogan *If you want a nigger for your neighbour vote Labour*. When Patrick Gordon Walker was defeated again in a hastily called by-election in another safe Labour seat, the signs could no longer be ignored, and the Labour government was well on the way to proving to the British people that it could be as tough on the niggers as anyone else. In 1962, Labour had fought fiercely against Macmillan's Immigration Act. In 1965, at a time of national catastrophe, it was ready with new measures to make that law even more effective.

After Smethwick, there were beatings and demonstrations of support in Rugby, Coventry, Birmingham and London. Crosses were burnt in the front gardens of houses that were known to be occupied by niggers. A schoolboy in North Kensington, whose parents were migrants from Trinidad, was beaten by a gang of English youths carrying iron bars and broken bottles, and was very nearly killed.

The newspapers carried scary stories of waves of barbarian hordes breaking on the shores of England, as implacable as a force of nature, and requiring drastic vigilance and the classic bulldog qualities of the British genius to roll back into the sea. The police forces of Essex, Kent and Sussex were kept vigilantly on patrol, scouring the beaches of southern England and the streets of the coastal towns. Pakistanis were discovered in freezer trucks, Indians in container-boxes, and all sorts captured by immigration and customs officials, carrying either cooked papers or no papers at all. The entire edifice of civilisation seemed on the point of being dragged down into the primeval mud.

Every week figures were published in newpapers to demonstrate that the epidemic was still raging. The appropriate government departments tried to put these figures in perspective by publishing figures of their own, showing how many Pakistanis or Jamaicans were refused entry, or how many were still languishing in their own countries, frustrated and driven mad by their inability to gain entry into Britain despite the most devilish machinations. People of goodwill organised conferences and seminars, to condemn and express their dismay, and held street parties to show solidarity with the despised immigrant, offering cups of tea and tiny bunches of heather to any dark-skinned person who strolled past their revelry. Dottie learnt to skim the newspaper without allowing her eyes to rest on the horror stories, and learnt not to hear the mean outbursts of her fellow workers. Yet she had done nothing about making her voice heard. She had filled her name in on the electoral register forms when they came round, but she did not vote. Neither did Sophie. And even if they had, who would they have voted for?

Patterson simply shook his head at Dottie's outrage. 'What did you expect?' he said. 'These people have put us in chains and sold us in market places. They transported us worse than animals, and made disgusting use of our bodies. What else did you expect of them? They are being polite now, but soon they will get tired and make us carry passes and live in ghettoes. The only language they understand is violence and oppression, and the only way they will leave us alone is if we scare them enough. We have to make them fear us the way they taught us to fear them.'

Dottie had her doubts about Patterson's cynical summary, but she felt the force of it. The cruel judgments of the newspapers deserved no less, she thought. She could not believe that any people that had talked itself to such a pitch of hysteria could ever listen to anything approaching reason. When she said this to Patterson, he shrugged. 'You could put it like that if you want,' he said, looking at her for a moment before speaking. She knew the look, and she had had it often in recent days, and had felt the unavoidable thrill of excitement at its meaning.

It happened at last one afternoon in the spring. She had taken a week off work to help Patterson decorate the bedrooms. He could have done it all himself, but she did not want him rummaging in her room while she was not there. It was a way of asserting her presence, of clinging on to her own corner, her little space. She had given up the parlour to him and his affairs, and once or twice an associate of his had stayed the night, carrying on with his quiet and unexplained business the following day. The shed in the garden was full of Patterson's boxes and bundles, and was now kept under lock and key. He was the master of the house, the keeper of their fates. She and Sophie were treated with respect by the people who came and went to see Patterson, as if they were his family. Even Joyce had taken to calling her Miss Dottie. There was no disguising that it was Patterson who made this possible for them, who ordered and organised their existence. So when it came to the bedrooms, Dottie took time off rather than have him tramping over her little things.

Despite everything, they worked well together, urgent and purposeful, both keen to get the work done. She sought his approval, pleased by his praise. It was inevitable that working so close to him, sometimes for long periods on their own while Sophie was in another part of the house, she found herself aroused by him and felt her longing for him revive. On the Thursday afternoon Sophie went for her fortnightly check-up with the doctor. Patterson insisted that she take Hudson with her, as he would otherwise be in the way. As soon as the front door closed, he put down the scraper he was using on the wall and approached her. It was not unexpected and Dottie turned to him without any pretence of reluctance or surprise. He pulled off the dust sheet that was on the bed and made love to her without a word.

She thought of it quickly like that because she hated to dwell on what it had aroused in her. She had revelled in the feel of him inside her, the way he had forced himself in without ceremony, without affection. She had clung to him, finding excitement in the knowledge and feeling of being used. She had encouraged him, had squirmed under him in feigned abandon, groaning and sighing, and drowning in the sweet shame of her submission. He had raised himself up, still moving inside her, and looked at her with delighted and startled eyes. When she felt him burst, a cry of ecstasy willingly burst out of her.

Afterwards he sat on the side of the bed, looking at her as she lay slightly away from him, her knees tightly gripped together. She saw his smile of contentment, his contemptuous, knowing look. She saw him rub his stomach with his hand, an unconscious gesture of satisfaction. 'That was some fucking, Sis,' he said.

At that moment, she could have died of shame for having allowed herself to be so misused. He would know that she had lost control, and would know that sooner or later she would do it again. He would know her long hunger and would despise her for it. She had given him so much more than she needed to, and he would know how to use it. He rose and dressed and went back to work without a word. She followed immediately after, leaving him alone in her room while she went to the bathroom to clean herself. In her shame she withdrew from him, and he looked at her now and then, smiling at her torment. She lowered her eyes in his presence and left as soon as she could when he entered a room. Sometimes he brushed against her when he passed, and once he put his hand on her shoulder while they were both standing in the kitchen, waiting for the kettle to boil. Most of the time he ignored her, knowing that he had mastered her.

After that day she sensed him lying in wait for her, waiting to subdue her thoroughly. In a way, she resigned herself to it, although she did her best to avoid being alone with him. It was not that he wanted her, she could not believe it was that. She suspected that to him she was a diversion. In his silent persistent way, he was doing what he wanted with them, and Dottie was appalled that she had allowed herself to fall so acutely a victim of his scheming.

6

In the confusion of that spring, she missed classes for a fortnight. When she missed the first of her two classes for the third week, Estella came to the house after lessons. Patterson answered the door, and left her standing on the threshold while he went to fetch Dottie. They talked outside, smiling at each other in their separate pleasure. Dottie was both ashamed and overjoyed that she had put her friend to such anxiety. She gave some excuse and promised to be there later in the week. Estella was pleased that her busy-body interference, as she had been thinking of it in the process of dissuading herself from calling, had not been misunderstood. 'Are you all right, though? Is everything okay?' she asked dropping her voice a little, hatching a conspiracy.

'Yes, fine. I've just been very busy here at home,' Dottie said, laughing at the melodramatic invitation, deflecting her interest. Estella laughed too, her eyes dancing a little in the light of the street lamps, as if she too was conscious of the way their conversation was hovering on the edges of unreality.

'I'll see you on Thursday,' Estella said, nodding firmly to indicate that this was a serious matter. 'I don't want to lose the best student in my class.'

Dottie watched her drive away in her noisy VW, and waved away Laura's anxious face as it appeared at the next-door window. Laura looked arch, assuming a man had called for her. When Dottie went back in, Patterson called to her from the parlour. He was watching television with Sophie, and looked round the wing of the chair when Dottie would not come further into the room.

'Who was that? What did she want?'

He asked his questions gently, not so much as if he was challenging but rather as if he was commiserating with her for the bother she had been caused. She could hear *these white people* rippling as an unspoken refrain through the words he had not yet said. She was tempted to say that she did not need to give any answers to him. He was neither her father nor her master, but she was afraid of seeming to be over-reacting. 'That was my teacher. She came to check with me because I missed my class,' she said, lifting her chin at him and daring him to say something cruel or mocking.

'Oh Sis, you know you mustn't miss your class,' Sophie said in a pained voice. 'Otherwise you'll never get that office work.'

Dottie was close to laughter at the bizarre scene. She felt like an adolescent who had trangressed and was being scolded by her parents. A half-wit sister and her gangster boyfriend were treating her as if she were a child without a mind of her own. 'She told me I was the best student she had,' Dottie said as she turned to leave. She heard Patterson's soft chuckle and bristled with sudden anger at what she took to be his amusement at her attempt to assert herself.

The arrangement was close to being unbearable. If he would not go, she would have to start thinking of doing so. But so what if she thought about it! This was so obviously an absurd idea – that she should leave a house she had suffered for and planned for – and she could only consider it as an act of desperation, an act of despair. One hundred per cent crazy! Who would look after Hudson? It was her house too. Although most of the money to buy it came from him and the building society, she paid her share of the mortgage. She ate cassava and spinach for it, and went to bed hungry. With each passing day she withdrew deeper and deeper into her resentment, so that she was beginning to find the simplest conversation with them impossible. Some evenings she refused food rather than sit at the table with them, and munched biscuits and raisins that she took to her room. When she came in on them, it was as if she had interrupted them, and they stopped talking or changed the subject. If she was around, Sophie did the simplest things noisily, huffing and puffing with suppressed indignation. She thought they were trying to drive her away, or bring her to heel, like a mad bitch that was beginning to become too much trouble.

The classes were a solace, and her growing friendship with Estella was a godsend. The other students welcomed her back with smiles and ironic cheers, and Elke gave her a stern talking-to for being irresponsible, then gave her a bag of candy to sweeten her rebuke. The teacher presided over the scene with a complacent smile. Later, in the pub, the talk was about the exams and jobs, which made them all laugh self-consciously, as if they were over-reaching themselves and would soon be cut down to size. In the car, on the way home, Estella invited Dottie to see a play that was being shown at a theatre in Wimbledon that Saturday. Some people she knew were in it, and she had been forced to buy two tickets. 'It'll probably be boring. In fact, I'd be completely astonished if it wasn't, but we could go for a meal afterwards,' she said.

Dottie could not remember much of the play afterwards. She had been too interested in looking round as discreetly as she could, watching the prosperous and happy-looking audience as much as the drama on the stage. The hall was small and draughty, and reminded her of school events she had attended. It was not easy to hear what the actors were saying, but she gathered enough from a distant and distracted view of the action to understand that the play was about a detective inspector who has an affair with a woman who has committed a murder. Another murder! She could not understand the obsession. Bookshops were full of people committing murders, and being pursued by a variety of policemen, detectives and sleuths. The cinemas had their murders too, and so did the television and the theatre. The newspapers were always full of them. 'Someone might think that was all we did,' she said to Estella afterwards, when they went for their meal.

Estella took her to an Indian restaurant in Southfields which was called the Regency. It was the first time Dottie had been to an Indian restaurant and she relished the dimmed lights, the starched damask cloths on the tables and the blood-red flock wallpaper. The obsequiousness of the waiters disconcerted her at first, but they soon left them alone while they attended to other customers. The aromas of food were almost overpowering, and Dottie watched with a mixture of incredulity and fascination as the trays of richly-coloured curries and vegetables were conveyed from the kitchen to the scattered tables in the hushed room. She had been buried away for all those years, ever since Ken left, and had forgotten the unique pleasure of sitting in a restaurant, waiting for a meal.

'What would you like? This is my treat, so you don't have to check the price. I got paid today,' Estella said. It was soon evident that the question was beyond Dottie, but Estella was happy to provide advice, and parade her knowledge of Indian cuisine. 'Don't touch the dopiaza. It'll give you indigestion if you're not used to it, all those onions.

And I wouldn't advise anything that contains shellfish. Aside from the danger of stomach upset, I don't think the chef here has got the hang of shellfish. If I could suggest … they do really nice bhaji here, actually, and a beautiful coconut achar. I think I'll have the bhoona ghosht with rice and parathas.' Dottie had the same, and ate every mouthful with delight, until she could eat no more and felt herself bulging obscenely. Without much ceremony, Estella helped herself to what Dottie did not want, talking and laughing with freedom and good humour.

'What you were saying earlier about murder,' Estella said. 'Some people would say that that *is* all we do. Since the beginning of human history we have been killing each other, and have watched while others were killed. It's safer, in a way, to have it all made into a kind of ritual like this play, or a detective thriller. Don't you agree? Or do you think I'm talking rubbish? Our fascination with murder is from so many different angles. To see the murderer caught, because that becomes a kind of morality play. The guilty always get their desserts, and killing people is wrong. Or because of the chase, or the battle of wits between the killer and the lawman. Perhaps also it's a way of living out our own fantasy of being strong enough to inflict that degree of pain. Whole crowds of policemen and pathologists and solicitors and journalists bank on that. I mean that we entertain fantasies of inflicting pain … You think I'm exaggerating, don't you? Well, it is also just simply true that people commit murders, many of them. So perhaps all those books and plays reflect the way we live.'

She paused for a long moment, holding a roughly-torn piece of paratha in mid-air, forcing time to stand still while she considered. Dottie held her breath. 'I'm intimately acquainted with murder,' Estella said, waving the piece of bread for emphasis. Dottie already knew enough of Estella's rhetorical habits to take this observation in without a whimper. *Oh yes, do tell*, she might have said. She waited patiently for Estella to go on with her story, to weave the rest of her web. A small, almost imperceptible smile of pleasure played around Estella's face, a mingling of admiration and disappointment that Dottie was so invincibly calm. 'It's true!' she said, popping the paratha in her mouth, making mock-innocent eyes at Dottie.

'Oh yes, do tell,' Dottie said, smiling.

Then it seemed that all of a sudden Estella began to talk about herself in a different tone, putting aside the extravagance and the gestures, and speaking calmly and truthfully, without embellishment. Dottie listened with a sense of witnessing an important moment, and knew without doubt that this was Estella's token of trust, an opening of accounts of their friendship.

7

Her father was a Frenchman who had come over to Britain after May 1940, shaken and devasted by the collapse of France. He had just been called up when the Germans invaded but the bureaucratic wheels had ground slow enough for him to be still in basic training when the surrender came. He had come over to Britain with hundreds of others, and was billeted in a bleak Scottish wilderness north of Aberdeen. He met Estella's mother in Edinburgh, when he was on war manoeuvres or something. They were always doing military games like that, to keep their spirits up. There seemed nothing else to do. Sometimes they raided the Polish barracks down the road from them, and sometimes the Poles raided them.

Estella's mother was also French, and Jewish, and had fled France with her younger sister, sent packing by a frightened mayor who had chased away all Jews from his little town to avoid the wrath of the approaching Germans. Estella's father, whose name was Marcel, spent all his leave in Edinburgh after that, courting and winning Georgia Simon – that was her mother's name – after only brief and token resistance from her. They talked of marriage, perhaps after the war, for with all the talk of the invasion being imminent there was no point in forcing Georgia to become a widow when they could wait until they were sure of the future. Estella was born while they were still waiting.

Marcel went over to Normandy and survived, and returned to Edinburgh to marry his young love. They moved to Birmingham, where a cousin of Marcel ran a silversmith business. The cousin and his wife invited them to live in their house, and Marcel and Georgia, with her younger sister and Estella in tow, moved in. Perhaps one day, they thought they would go back to France, when the chaos had subsided. But things went wrong for them after that. Marcel took to spending a lot of time away from home, with French friends also marooned in England. Georgia thought they disliked her because she was Jewish but Marcel dismissed this. Some nights he slept out with his friends, or travelled to other English cities. Georgia became distraught and suspicious, and accused Marcel of no longer loving her. She became convinced that he was seeing another woman. Marcel reassured her, and, when he could no longer laugh off her tirades, sought an ally in Georgia's younger sister. All that that achieved was Georgia began to suspect her sister too. She may even have had some grounds, Estella said, but by now Marcel had lost sympathy with his wife and mocked and made fun of her. Slowly he withdrew into an angry and resentful silence, which goaded her into violent fits of shouting and rage. Eventually he started to beat her, and once he started he beat her for everything. He beat her when he was drunk, when Estella was dirty, when he did not like the food or if she spoke disrespectfully to him. He beat her because he could not find work and because he disliked living in England. Her sister Madeline told her it was her own fault and moved out, going to London to look for work as an actress.

Eventually, Marcel's cousin begged them to return to France, to try again there. They could leave Estella with him and his wife in Birmingham for a while, until they had settled. Georgia found the idea of starting again irresistible, especially if they could have a few months on their own without the baby. They went to stay with Marcel's family near a tiny village called Buz, in Provence, which was not what Georgia had expected. The few days extended into weeks, and soon it became impossible to discuss the idea of looking for a place of their own. Marcel was back in his home, and either ignored Georgia's grumblings or put a stop to them in a suitably manly manner. Even his family became disgusted with him, but it seemed there was nothing Georgia herself could do but put up with beatings and abuse. They lived a poverty-stricken life on the tiny family farm, perched precariously on the flinty hillside.

In the end, Georgia took the gun her father-in-law kept in his room and shot her husband. He did not die at once, but staggered round the house like a wounded animal, tearing lumps of flesh out of Georgia's face when he caught up with her. She shot him again. He fell to the floor, panting and heaving with terror and desperation, clinging to life until the very last moment.

Her lawyer got her off on grounds of diminished responsibility, and even the judge secretly sympathised with her for the treatment she had had to put up with from Marcel. The local newspaper was less forgiving, playing up her Jewishness and making open hints about the possibility of Marcel being slowly poisoned or bewitched.

After a year in a psychiatric hospital, Georgia was released, and she went to live with the lawyer as his housekeeper. Estella went to visit her there many years later, when she was nearly fourteen, and found a scarred and dishevelled woman who was unmistakably deranged. Instead of speaking she growled like an animal, and would have attacked Estella if the lawyer had not stood up and started to take his belt off. Estella herself was adopted, in due course, by Marcel's cousin and his wife, who had had only one child of their own when they had wanted more. 'They gave me their name, for which I'm grateful,' she said.

Estella invited Dottie back to her flat after the restaurant, and they sat in her large living room, in chairs that seemed to Dottie to be miles apart from each other. Estella made coffee, and smiled to see Dottie looking with admiration at the furniture and ornaments. 'This is Madeline's flat,' she said. 'My mother's sister. She lets me stay. She's in Canada at the moment, and then after that she's doing a season in New York. Madeline Cooper, the actress, you may've heard of her.'

Dottie shook her head. Estella shrugged. 'I probably wouldn't have either, if she hadn't been my aunt. It's not her real name, you know. She changed it to Cooper because of her work. My parents ... my adopted parents ...' she paused for a moment, and then smiled to acknowledge the confusion. 'I always call them my parents because they are the only ones I know. The other two are Georgia and

Marcel. Anyway, my parents thought it was like a betrayal when Madeline changed her name. I challenged my mother about having to change her name to become a Hoggar, but she waved that away, telling me not to talk nonsense. They are very proud of their name, and cling to it despite attempts to persuade them to make it manageable. Here in England every name is put through the mangle and has to come out with a recognisable shape and sound, like Cooper or Hoggarth. Hoggar … I think it must be after the Ahaggars in Algeria where an ancient ancestor arose, don't you think? Who would want to change that to Hoggarth?'

It was past midnight when Dottie reluctantly suggested that she should go. She could have stayed the whole night. Estella had already invited her to, saying there was plenty of room. But Dottie knew her sister and Patterson would worry, and there was Hudson to look after. Estella drove her home in the noisy VW.

'The car's Madeline's too,' she said with a little shamefaced grin. 'Do you know what Madeline says about Georgia? She says that the reason she became as she did was because she had no ambition. There was nothing she wanted to be, and nothing she wanted to do. Everything aggravated her because there was nothing she wanted for herself. When they first came from France, Georgia had to take responsibility for both of them, Madeline and her, and later for Marcel and me. By then she had got into the habit of offering herself for sacrifice. Life was a burden she had to bear and after all that time she became used to it being like that, became dependent on the misery. I'm not saying she didn't have talents, but she got into the habit of crushing any feeling of aspiration in herself. She thought that would make her selfish. In the end she lost the means and the will to persevere because there was no point in doing so. Nothing to live for except more self-sacrifice and abuse. Even little Estella must've seemed like another one who would turn into a torturer when her teeth were fully grown. That's what Madeline says. I think it makes sense, don't you? Don't you?' she asked, turning to look at Dottie as she drove along Brixton Hill.

Dottie nodded. She wondered if Estella had guessed what went on in her life and was intending that she see the lesson of Georgia's story. That could not possibly be so, Dottie told herself, rebuking herself for her paranoia. In any case, she had already seen and grieved for the poor, deranged woman who had taken on burden after burden until she had turned into some thing grotesque and obscene. Perhaps she *had* done something a little like that too, although hardly on the same scale. Anyway, Estella could not possibly have guessed such things about her life! She *never* talked about the life she led to anyone, and probably would not do so even under torture.

'Have you got an ambition, Dottie?' Estella asked, pulling into the kerb outside the house. She was smiling, turning the question into a joke. 'I'm almost certain I do. I know I don't want to be a teacher, I can't think that anyone does. It's so mechanical and unfair to the students, like a kind of play-acting. I keep coming up with ideas, but nothing sticks. It's worrying. Something should've made a showing by now, don't you think? Anyway, that was a lovely evening. I hope I wasn't too boring with all the stories. We must do it again soon.' She leant forward and touched Dottie's hand.

A Good War

1

She should walk in from work one evening, pick up the gun that he leaves wrapped up in oiled sackcloth in their bedroom and shoot him, she thought. Right through the heart. She had seen the gun there once. If it wasn't there when she went for it, there was bound to be another one in the shed. Gangsters always had guns. And rather than wait for him to pursue her round the house like a headless monster thrashing the last of its life out, she would give him another one to make sure. Take that you eater of putrid flesh! Then she'd like to see him gouge lumps of flesh out of her face with his nails. It would be easy, and in one leaping bound she would set herself free!

Patterson did not like her friendship with Estella and tried to stop it. He drove Dottie mad with his set-piece sermons and his chants of duty. Hudson needed her in the house, he said, or Sophie was not well, and did she not know better than to make friends with white people? Did she not know that the dirty girl intended to use her in some way?

'What are you talking about?' Dottie asked, guessing at his meaning. 'What do you mean dirty girl?'

'You'll find out,' he said.

That was brave coming from a drug-pusher or worse, Dottie thought. 'Do you mean I'm in danger?' she asked, mocking him. 'Is that what you're saying?'

'You'll find out,' he said, getting annoyed.

Despite his disapproval, it was obvious there was nothing he could do. Dottie had not lost all her fear of him, but the intimidation she felt from him had always been more general than specific. It had not usually been precise enough to dissuade her from what she actually intended to do. It was more like an oppression, standing in the way of possibilities, enforcing the limits that Patterson thought they should live by. Nothing like Estella had happened to Dottie before, and the resentment she felt at Patterson's interference with her friendship gave her the courage to defy his bullying. When Patterson said anything about Estella, Dottie ignored him, did not even bother giving explanations or excuses. She went about her business in the house, went to her classes, and saw Estella when it suited the two of them.

Sophie too had turned against her. She was steadily sinking under the burdens of her illness and had become short-tempered and lethargic, spending most of the day in bed or reclining on the settee in front of the television. The drugs were making her like that, but Sophie burst into tears when Dottie tried to persuade her to speak to the doctor. She complained to Patterson, who came to rebuke Dottie for her lack of compassion. 'Do you want your sister to die?' he asked in his gloomy and ancient voice. Sooner or later, Dottie guessed, Sophie would have to go into a hospital. It was not necessary to be a doctor to arrive at that diagnosis. There was no point in trying to make Sophie see that, though, because she would only assume that Dottie was wishing ill on her. To Dottie it seemed as if Sophie was already decomposing, parts of her melting and turning into jelly under that mountainous bulk. When she saw her lying wretchedly on the sofa, with Patterson coming to take bites of her during the day, Dottie almost wept with disgust.

She still could not talk about these things to Estella. That friendship was something that made her feel clean, that uplifted her from the sense of drowning she had felt. Sometimes she thought the feeling of well-being was quite unreal, a kind of a lie. It was not that she pretended, or acted free of worries and full of joy when she was with her, although she did a bit of that too, but that she did not feel hopeless and defeated. Estella talked about extravagant plans and laughed at their grandiose unreality, but she was not afraid of contemplating serious ambitions for herself. The conversation about ambition kept coming back, and Dottie could sense the urgency with which Estella pursued the subject, and admired the need it expressed. She saw Estella striving in her own way not to waste her life, to do something with it, and Estella did not stop at that. She was already organising Dottie as well, chiding her for her self-neglect, laughing at her self-deprecating terrors. With her urging and encouragement, Dottie had been applying for jobs in the most interesting places, laughing with delight as she made an outrageously crazy list: Somerset House had sent her a whole volume of forms, and made dark hints about the Official Secrets Act, the BBC replied with a scrappy, printed letter, telling her politely to take a walk, the Foreign Office sent a much delayed reply regretting the impropriety of her application. Most of the rest did not bother to reply or sent a rejection typed on an intimidatingly thick, letter-headed parchment, enough to chase off and silence any upstart looking to rise above her proper station.

One blessed application yielded a reply. Dottie was invited for an interview at Lever House just off Blackfriars Bridge. She borrowed some smart clothes from Estella and went, expecting nothing. The man who interviewed her looked amused when she walked in, and asked her the question that had earned her the appointment in the first place. *What on earth made you think we would consider you for a job like this? Your background is not at all adequate. You know that, don't you?* Dottie grinned with the pure joy of having successfully pulled off a prank, and the man laughed too and shook his head. I hope you won't just waste my time, he said.

The interview itself was exhilarating. The man did not spare her blushes, and asked her merciless and shameless questions which she deflected or addressed as if she had done this already time out of number. The man shook his head with admiration, remembering stories of other unlikely-seeming people who had been marked by destiny. He could not offer her the job they had advertised, he said, because she needed *experience* for that, but she could join the typing pool on condition that she passed the typing and shorthand examinations. It would be hard work, of course, but it would give her the beginning of her *experience*.

The offer of a job made her stronger, and made it easier to bear the frustrations she lived with. She felt herself at the start of a new time, when she could begin to turn her life around. All she needed to do was pass her examinations. The new confidence made her feel as if she could stroll among the filth and slime at her place of work without being soiled: through the meat drying section, or the fish and shellfish freezing unit, or the vegetable canning lines. Not for much longer would she have to shift for herself in this filth. The money in her new job would be less to begin with, but the man had said there were opportunities, and in any case it would change her life. Estella tried to warn her not to expect too much, but Dottie had no delusions. She wanted to start again, begin anew. Estella nodded. 'And then what?' she asked, but Dottie just shrugged. There'll be time enough for all that later on, for God's sake, she said.

Sometimes she took Hudson with her when she went to see her friend in Wimbledon, and he was at once comfortable with Estella in his good-humoured way. It was through talking about Hudson that she began to tell Estella about the life she led and the things that had happened to her. She told the story slowly, bit by bit, delving a little deeper each time she spoke to her. It was still only the outline, and she only took small steps at a time. There was too much to tell, and perhaps not much to be gained in letting it all out, but she spoke about the elder Hudson, and about Sophie, and about Ken. Estella's eyes grew moist over the story of Ken. 'You should write that down,' she said. 'You tell it so beautifully.' She told her about Patterson, and how determined she was that sooner or later she would rid herself of him, or if she failed that she would leave and start again. More likely than not, she said, she would have to do the latter.

'Didn't you guess any of this when you told me your story in the Regency that night? I thought you must've done, as if you'd taken me by the hand ... I know it sounds unlikely, but we always see our own lives in this dramatic way, don't we? Everything that you said seemed to be about me.'

'What about Marcel? There's no Marcel in your life,' Estella said, intrigued but also made uncomfortable by Dottie's intensity.

'Not about me in every detail,' Dottie said, beginning to feel a little embarrassed, as if she had greedily appropriated Estella's story for herself. 'Of course it wasn't about me like that. Not for real, like that. More to show me how my own life would end. Do you know what I mean? Even what your aunt Madeline said about Georgia not wanting anything for herself, even that was about me, I thought. Did she really say that?'

Estella shook her head, smiling, but nervous of the clairvoyant powers Dottie seemed willing to grant her. 'My aunt Madeline is very useful to me sometimes. I can make her say things I am not sure I can say myself. What I said to you is what *I* always thought about Georgia. It's just easier to blame Madeline for it, seeing as I hardly knew Georgia.'

'Is Estella your real name? Is it your given name?' Dottie asked suddenly, leaning forward, pressing.

'Yes, why do you ask that? I told you how important names were to my parents,' she said, looking surprised and a little suspicious. 'Why do you ask that?'

Dottie shrugged, a gesture that hinted at some disappointment. 'I'm interested in names,' she said quietly, succeeding in sounding evasive. 'I'm interested in how they get from one place to another. Imagine Hoggar, tunnelling its way from the Ahaggars in Algeria to here. Where did Estella come from? And I just wondered if you had found it for yourself.'

'Madeline chose it. Marcel was in France when I was born,' Estella said. 'I was too young to choose a name for myself then. It's the kind of name you'd expect of her, isn't it? She's proud of having chosen it. You know, I've talked about her so much that sometimes I forget that you've never met her. I hope she'll be back after New York. You never know with her. She'll probably fall in love with someone and follow him to Mexico or something. She has lovers all over the place.'

After a silence, Dottie went on with her story of Patterson describing her suspicions in the most colourful and lurid way, and making Estella hoot with laughter. 'Where do you get such pictures?' Estella said. 'You really must write them down.'

Dottie told her about her ritual visits to the library, and how she had not been in recent months. She was not even sure if she was entitled to be a member of the Balham library any more, having changed boroughs. The thought of presenting herself at the Brixton library made her nervous, all the questions she would have to answer and something about her doctor signing her application form, if she remembered rightly. She had faked a signature the first time, when she joined Balham library. Brenda Holly had dismissed the question, waved her hand over the application form and told her to sign it herself. Anyway, she was attached to the old library, with the Sacred Church of the True Christ down the road and the half-dressed women always lounging at the open windows of the terrace next door to it. It was not the place she missed and lamented but the time, when other possibilities had seemed available. Her sadness was not regret that those times had passed, she said, but a kind of mourning for the way things had been, for events and feelings that could no longer be reached or made different. Estella said they should go and visit the library and the street with the church, half-disbelieving the tales of languorous beauties leaning out of windows, but none the less curious.

'We can make a pilgrimage to the shrine,' Dottie said, feeling self-conscious. She must have been too intense in her identification with Georgia, she thought, and must have injected a tone of hysteria in the recounting of her nostalgia. Having no one to talk to for all those years. She had better be careful not to drive Estella away with devotion.

'So long as you don't expect me to go worshipping in a church,' Estella said, frowning. 'I'm an atheist, you know.'

Dottie looked shocked, which made Estella laugh. She assumed Dottie was joking.

2

Dottie's absences from the house in Brixton had become serious irritations to Patterson. Sophie stopped speaking to her altogether, using Hudson as the intermediary for all her complaints. *Your auntie is too busy with her friends to bother with such a naughty little baby as you. Perhaps she's never heard of the saying that pride goes before a fall.* Dottie was not sure what the saying meant. She had heard it used before: why does pride go before a fall? How will this fall occur? Where will I be standing when it happens? She could not mistake the point of her sister's whining, though. Usually she made no answer. She thought of it as Sophie's plaintive meanness. Sometimes she felt guilty about her, thinking that Sophie was only looking for reassurance, but everything had gone too far between them to be retrieved by hugs and kisses and kind words any more. She knew they wanted her out of the house, or at least that they wanted to bring her to order by making her see that defiance would eventually lead to her expulsion. Their resentment had become like an obsession with them, almost laughable in the end.

She told them about the prospect of her new job, and her news was greeted by a moment of stony silence. 'I'm glad,' Sophie said when she could manage the words. That seemed to them the final straw, the last act of betrayal from her. Dottie guessed that they took her to be aspiring higher than was natural for someone like her, and that in due course she would come to grief. Laura and her daughter Veronica showed more pleasure at her news. Even Daisy's approval was appealed for, and she emitted a single, polite bark of congratulation.

With her neighbours Dottie was able to indulge herself at last and describe every moment of her triumphant interview to people who would understand its true significance and daring. Even with Estella she had had to play down her excitement, to make out that she was cool and not unused to ambition. Laura wanted a careful account, and needed to have many details filled in: the colour of the carpet in the man's office, his name – which Dottie did not really listen to and therefore could not remember – the title of her new job, the position and size of the office building. Dottie was required to demonstrate the exact tone that the supercilious porter at the main door used to direct her to the lift, and had to mime the shock of the stricken secretary whose jaw fell open at Dottie's appearance. Laura and Veronica sucked their teeth in a chorus of disdain, and then joined in Dottie's laughter of celebration.

In her own house, though, what she had done was seen as only cause for blame. Patterson and Sophie stopped talking when she walked into a room. They took to eating their meals separately. When she went to call them after she had cooked, they told her to go ahead and they would be along later.

Gradually, the cupboards in the kitchen were divided, one shelf for Dottie, another shelf for them. Sophie cooked their meal after Dottie had finished, and Patterson, who had never bothered about such things, did the washing up. Months before, in the early days of his ascendancy, he had taken over the paper-work for the house, the fuel bills, mortgage payments, rates, and only asked for a contribution from Dottie. Now if there was a bill, he left it on the table in the kitchen with her share calculated on a piece of paper. She left her money beside it. If she was short of money and was forced to delay, the bill and the paper sat angrily staring at her until she paid. At night, she heard grumbling whispers slithering through the floor-boards instead of the gurglings of their former passion.

In the end Patterson's exasperation with her grew so intense that he began to seek her out. When he cornered her in the kitchen or in the dining room, he would place himself at the door and refuse to let her pass until she had listened to all he wanted to say. She learned to laugh in his face when his accusations became too strident, but she could sense him restraining himself.

One evening he approached her and took her in his arms, kissing her angrily and then blaming her for provoking him. In such a small house it was impossible to avoid him if he was as seriously determined to pursue her as he seemed to be. Then, within a few days of starting on his campaign of attrition, he came into the kitchen one night while she was doing the washing and tried to take her by force. She had sensed this would happen, that he would be unable to put up with her diminishing dependence and would try to crush her in just such a way. He had seen how she had once been when he climbed her, had seen her abject loss of control, and how her defiance had turned into jabbering submission.

He was on her before she realised his presence. He put one hand across her mouth to prevent her screaming, using the arm and elbow to pin her against the wall. With the other hand he tried to undress her, but as their struggle progressed he simply tore at her clothes. She fought back with a ferocity and strength that took him by surprise. She made no attempt to call for help, or to scream like a frightened innocent, but clawed and kicked and twisted and bit until he released her. In the end, he raised his arms in surrender and stepped back from her, smiling with a pretence of amusement. He stepped forward once and feigned a blow. She backed against the wall, panting with terror and the effort of putting up a defence. Her eyes were blazing with anger and tears, and her fists were clenched in readiness to continue the fight. He made a noise that was something between a chuckle and a snort, and left.

When her panic subsided, she sat down on the floor, shaking with relief. She could hardly believe that it had really happened, that he had done that. For a long time she sat on the floor, the tight-strung quivering of her sinews running up and down her body, her torn clothes gathered in knots in her hands. Even when the feeling came to her that this could not be real, there was no mistaking the shivers of shock which ran through her.

He had thrown his tantrum because he could not have his way, she thought, could not prevent her from doing what he had forbidden. So instead he would break her on the old wheel, pinion her and draw the cracked reed of her defiance in small pieces. He would dazzle her with his power, overwhelm her with the dread musk of his masculinity. It made her glow with self-delight that she had known to fight back, to see him off. Yet once she had thought of him as something carved out of a noble wood, and felt his presence among them as an eye of judgment over everything they did. Now he was a bully exasperated by his inability to control her, and all he could think to do was to destroy her.

After that, his efforts at seduction became more expressive of contempt than desire for her, to show her that his attempt to force her was only a casual affair, not seriously undertaken. He would come up behind her and put his hand between her legs, groping for her cleft. If he walked past her he would reach out and squeeze her breasts. He growled at her when she was near, and his body exhaled odours of dank earth. Dottie stayed in her room now all the time she could, but Sophie was getting ill again, and there was no helping going in their room to see her. She had to cancel a weekend trip with Estella to stay with friends of hers who ran a golf course in Broadstairs, but she refused to miss any classes however much Sophie groaned at her.

Patterson began to stay away from the house, sometimes for two or three days. His absences were like a reprieve to Dottie, even though he locked the living room and took the key with him. When he came back, he opened a tin of something and ate, asking no questions and paying scant attention to anyone. Even Hudson learned to avoid him. Something in his appearance reminded Dottie of the way he had looked when he came out of prison. His chin bristled with a reluctant stubble, and his mouth habitually twisted into a slight sneer. He slept in the living room when he stayed, leaving Sophie in her sick-bed upstairs. It was as if he was the injured party, Dottie thought, sulking around the house or staying away as he wished. When the bills came he left them alone, and Dottie was forced to plead with him for his share. At least he could unlock the living room so Sophie could come down and watch television, she begged.

Dottie did what she could to cut back. Hudson no longer went to Joyce, instead Laura looked after him sometimes and the rest of the time he stayed with Sophie, the two of them managing as best they could. Dottie went to Social Security, but got very little from them since Patterson was still living with them. Estella came round with advice, but her greatest use to Dottie was as it had always been from the start of their friendship, that her cheerfulness and good sense kept Dottie from sinking under the burdens that had returned as they had habitually done throughout her life.

3

It was about this time that she started her new job. The woman under whose charge she was placed treated her as if she had no idea what Dottie was there for. Mrs Waterson looked through Dottie's file while the latter waited with all appearance of patience. Her stomach churned with nervousness while she sat in a comfortable chair beside Mrs Waterson's desk. The other typists and pool-secretaries who worked under Mrs Waterson were in front of them, bent over their work. The lady pursed her lips over what she read and shook her head gently, glancing sympathetically at Dottie. It was not *her* fault, she seemed to be saying. Dottie was advised to stay close to her for the next few days and pick up what she could. Mrs Waterson was small and soft-spoken, her skin darkened and coarsened by the sun. She told Dottie she had spent many years in East Africa, and had loved it. All the open spaces, the outdoor life, beautiful countryside. The men, of course, had loved to hunt. Her husband had been an engineer with the PWD in Moshi, but he had been retired after independence. 'They wanted to run their own show,' she said, smiling with perfect understanding. Her husband had died within months of returning to London, to their old home in Leytonstone. He could not bear the misery of London after all that time in Africa, she said.

Dottie followed her around the building, went to the cafeteria with her, and found herself nodding and snoozing in the warm office as she sat beside her while she typed or explained the mysteries of the holiday form. After a few days it was clear that Mrs Waterson was beginning to take a liking to the new typist. She told her stories of her two grown-up children, and even brought in some photographs. The daughter was a teacher in Leeds and lived with her family in a very pleasant house just down the road from Headingley Cricket Ground. The son was a mining engineer in Zambia. He had been there throughout all those years of the troubles, and had even gone in to the Congo once or twice to see for himself, into Katanga where all those dreadful mercenaries were causing such havoc. His passion was sailing, and he was at it whenever he could get away. He had sailed all the way from Durban to Mombasa with a couple of friends in some kind of boat, she didn't know what they called them. Catamarine or something like that. They went all round the islands and reefs along the east coast, perhaps places where no man had been before. It was a pity he was a miner, she said, because he had a gift for natural things: animals, the sea, that kind of thing.

Dottie found out also that the man who had employed her was impetuous to have done so, but that no harm was done. In no time at all, aided by Dottie's patience and politeness, Mrs Waterson was able to release her into the office and give her work to do. The other women in the office were friendly but cautious, and for a while longer Dottie remained under Mrs Waterson's protective wing, earning smiles and special greetings from her. The work itself was easy compared to what she had been used to, and she applied herself to it with diligence.

In those same early weeks of her new job, when her whole life seemed transformed by a change from routines that she had lived by for seven years, Sophie was taken to hospital. She received a phone call from Sophie's doctor one Thursday afternoon, after one of Sophie's check-ups. She had to stand by Mrs Waterson's desk to take the call, and was aware of the office manager's disapproval as she listened to the doctor describing Sophie's condition. She had collapsed during the examination and the doctor had had her admitted as a casualty patient. He was now suggesting that she needed constant care and should be admitted to a special hospital. Later that evening, Dottie went to the hospital in Tooting where Sophie had been taken. She was drowsy with the drugs she had been given but was very happy to see Dottie and Hudson. They went back every evening for the next few days, but then Sophie was moved farther away, to a hospital in Penge.

Laura helped Dottie find help to look after Hudson during the day, and she herself looked after him in the evenings while Dottie made the journey on the buses. It was autumn. Chilly winds and torn leaves swirled across the open hospital grounds as she walked from the bus stop to the medical ward. Sophie was lethargic and depressed, sometimes hardly able to keep her eyes open while Dottie was there. Some evenings, when Estella was not teaching, she gave her a lift and waited for her in the wind-swept car park, dozing in the car. The ward sister spoke to Dottie one evening, telling her not to distress herself with the nightly journeys. Dottie burst into tears, sitting at the tiny desk in the alcove where the sister had taken her for a private word.

'There, you see,' the sister said, her own eyes moistening at the sight of this tense young woman so suddenly melting from a touch of kindness. 'Can't you see that all that travelling and worrying is doing you no good?'

How could she explain to this kind woman that Sophie looked just as Sharon had done in those last days, Dottie thought? She could not leave Sophie alone with that, even with the drugs and nurses. The sister consoled her, and told her that Sophie was very ill but that was no reason for Dottie to make herself ill too. Two or three visits a week would be better. 'To tell you the truth, dear, I don't think Sophie would notice in her state.'

Laura agreed with the sister, speaking on these matters with a degree of expertise, being a hospital worker herself. Veronica lent her support, and Estella too was invited to contribute words of encouragement. Her conscience pacified by these women, Dottie began to feel less guilty about not visiting Sophie every night. Patterson found out about Sophie's admission and came to see Dottie. He hardly said anything, but his face was stricken with remorse. He insisted on leaving a large present of money to Hudson, which was only a polite way of offering them help. He went to see Sophie twice, but gave up after that. He appeared now and then to take away the few belongings and stores of his that still remained in the house, but Dottie was still running into his things months after he left.

Andy, their old landlord also came to Horatio Street one Saturday afternoon. He looked very tired but was full of smiles. He told her that he had come once before but Patterson had told him there was no one in. Andy had tried to leave his greetings but Patterson became exasperated and told him to clear off. Dottie saw that he was beginning to lose some hair, and that his eyes looked bloodshot and watery. He was collecting rent from his Brixton house, which was in Saltoun Road, and since that was so near he thought he would come by and ask Dottie to come to the cinema with him.

'Is that the house full of niggers?' she asked him. 'The one your tenants turned into a dirty African village?'

'You remember!' he cried, clapping his hands and laughing.

She told him about Sophie and his voice hushed with sympathy. Would she still like to come to the cinema, though? On one of the evenings when she was not visiting? He looked so desperate and demoralised that she did not know what to say. In the end she touched him on the cheek with her open palm.

'I'm sorry, Andy,' she said.

'It's all right, but if you need anything or something like that,' he said. He shrugged his shoulders and gave her a forlorn wave, his eyes watering with self-pity. 'Give my respects to your sister. You know your house in Balham, it's a dump now. It's full of Pakis cooking their dirty curries.'

4

She went to see Sophie every other day, but the visits soon began to take on a sameness and futility that made the ward sister's advice seem less selfish than it had done at first. Dottie went to see people at the Council to get help, especially in looking after Hudson, and to plead for a rebate on the rates. She went to the building society and explained her circumstances to the bald man who had been so proper with her before, and he agreed to extend the repayment period, reducing her monthly payments. She organised and mobilised and sought out every help that experience and advice could provide. None of it daunted her, to all appearances, and she smiled and charmed where she needed as if it were all that life had prepared her for, all that it had asked of her. Estella watched her with admiration, applauding her cunning and daring.

'Daring!' Dottie said. 'You've got the wrong person for that. Look how long it took me just to learn to stand on my feet.'

In her own secret heart, though, she rejoiced that she had not been found wanting by this latest sadness.

Sophie was getting better in hospital, although she was often unhappy and wanted to be let out. Patterson had disappeared, or only appeared for brief visits, building himself another nest somewhere else. Laura was becoming a good friend, coming round with jokes and little delicacies that she had prepared for her young man Hudson. I've come courting, she would cry as she bustled into the house. When she found her young man, she touched his testicles with the tips of her fingers, sniffed them and then sneezed violently, testifying to the power of young Hudson's manhood. 'My husband!' she would cry in her ecstacy. In order to be obliging, Hudson proffered his loins to her as soon as she appeared, inviting her to have a sniff. The first time he did this Laura took a step back and gave him a long hard look. 'I suppose he does that to all the women,' she said.

But a surprise awaited Dottie, for Estella announced that she had been offered a job in television in Birmingham. She had given her half-term notice at the college and would be starting in the New Year. After the congratulations and commiserations were over, they talked about all the things they had planned but had never got round to doing. They would have to wait for the times when they visited each other, Estella said, feeling treacherous for abandoning her friend. 'I'm not going to the end of the world. You Londoners think anywhere outside your filthy city is the back of beyond,' she said. 'You must come and visit, and I'll show you the delights of real England.'

'I'm not a Londoner,' Dottie said, feeling a little as if she was being ungrateful to the city that had tolerated her for all the years. 'And of course I'll come and visit. I'll have missed meeting your aunt Madeline, though, and that trip to the golf course in Broadstairs that we never got to make.'

'It wasn't a trip to a golf course,' Estella said patiently. 'My friends *run* a golf course. We were going to stay with them at their house, which has a garden, and plants and other normal-sounding things. Just some miles from here and not the other side of a volcanic mountain range on the slopes of which roam sabre-toothed tigers and painted barbarians. Why do you have to talk about it as if it were an anthropological field-trip?'

'And the camping trip to Scotland! I suppose we can still do that,' Dottie said after a moment. 'And the river trip down the Danube as well, and the walking tour around Old Carthage.'

'Did we plan all that? Whose idea was Old Carthage?' Estella asked, grinning at their excess. 'At least we can make sure we stroll past the bordello near Balham Public Library. I still don't believe that, you know. Let's make sure we visit that shrine anyway, where the first faint glimmerings of knowledge struck the youthful Dottie.'

She would not have known how to tell Estella without embarrassing both of them, but she was very sad at her impending departure. With Estella she had learnt to lose her diffident fears, and had discovered that no one minded if she swaggered a little or strode confidently into offices and shops. It was not much to learn, and the surprise was that she had taken so long to do what others did without thought. She had seen young people do things that filled her with envy for their daring and lack of concern. Yet she had worried about so much, about everything, and had done so little, out of fear of seeming ridiculous. Estella routed and despatched those little apprehensions, taking no notice of them, and perhaps was quite unaware that Dottie harboured them. That was the kind of ally she would be losing, shc thought.

It was ridiculous that a woman of her age should be so full of uncertainties. Inside she did not feel as if she had grown at all, even though her mind was continually being enlightened and not a day went past without revealing something to her. The other part of her, the real one buried deep inside her, was still the awkward, frightened girl who had kept watch on her mother, and had forced herself to come near and attend to her decaying stinking body when she was required to. How could she lose that odour of death and squalor? Everyone must have smelt it on her. When she allowed herself to think about it, even now, there was a touch of play-acting about the responsible and adult things she did. She went to see Council and Social Security officials and demanded money and help. No one laughed at her or chased her away. How had she got away with it? How had she got away with walking into that office building just off Blackfriars Bridge and striding into the room so properly occupied by Mrs Waterson and the other women?

Not only had she fooled them all into allowing her into their office building, she gleefully reflected, but she could see that she was impressing them. They even told her how good she was, and some of the people brought their typing directly to her instead of going to Mrs Waterson first. Mr O'Brien, the man who had interviewed her, always stopped to have a friendly word with her when they passed in the corridor. Once he stopped to tell her that he had heard about the excellent job she was doing.

'Who told you that?' Dottie asked, and then wished she had not. It made her sound anxious and desperate for praise, rather than quietly confident. Mr O'Brien beamed and looked comically conspiratorial. He tapped the side of his nose and said, 'A little bird told me.' Dottie forgave him this stupid remark because he had been kind to her in so many ways. He had been nice enough to give her a job, and was always courteous and encouraging. Now and then she was sent to work with his secretary, Mrs Renton, to help out over some rush job, and also as a way of marking out her potential. Mrs Waterson told her this, acting as if it were in her gift that Dottie had been chosen in this fashion. Dottie had already found out from Mrs Renton that Mr O'Brien had asked for her to be given the extra training. She was to cover for Mrs Renton when the latter was away.

There was no reason that she could see for Mr O'Brien to do this, and in every other way he seemed a thoroughly hard and demanding man. He had even had a *good* war, leading his men to glorious deeds in northern France. A captain's war, Mrs Waterson said, although Dottie was not sure what that meant. She was afraid that any day the scales would fall from his eyes, and he would see what an imposter she really was. And what of Mrs Renton? Had he not thought how she might resent Dottie being foisted on her? She was pleasant enough in a chatty, mothering way, but that did not mean she was not laying the foundations of a slow-maturing, nasty plot.

Really, if you looked closely and did not mind the odd distortion, there was not much wrong with her life after all, despite Sophie's illness and Estella's looming departure. She was only half-way there, half-way through her life, as much again lay ahead of her. She thought of herself as living until she was fifty, and at twenty-six years old she had just gone over the hill. She had no grounds for this figure. It expressed both hope and ambition, without conceding to the terror of being cut off that she had felt all her days. Nor did it tempt fate by seeming over-confident or over-ambitious. A round figure, that would let her do one or two of the things she hankered for, and allow her to see Hudson grow into a man.

5

One day in November, on a sunny Saturday morning, Dottie went to Balham with Estella and Hudson. They intended to visit the library first and then go to the market. Hudson was two years old, and inclined to know his own mind about most things. He had little experience of libraries but took to this one at once, settling in the corner with the other toddlers among whom he found a gracious and accommodating welcome. One of the young librarians was reading from a picture book, and Hudson was moved enough by her attempt at *The Owl and the Pussycat* to give her his complete attention. He watched her every move with care, relishing the details of her performance, expecting that sooner or later she would reveal something important about the universe. Dottie and Estella stood with the other adults for a few moments and then drifted to the main library for a look. Dottie wanted to see if any of the old faces were still there. The librarian who had been friendly with Dottie was delighted to see her, beaming with pleasure as she came round the counter to speak to her. As always, her friendship came as a small shock to Dottie.

'You got my letter,' she said, smiling shyly and stammering a little. 'I was afraid ... you might've moved, but I'm so glad ... you've come. I have the address here, and the telephone number.'

'I'm sorry,' Dottie said, bewildered by the woman's words.

'Didn't you get my letter?' she asked, her face crest-fallen and suddenly apprehensive.

'No, I'm sorry,' Dottie said, feeling she had contributed to a crisis. 'I've moved from that address.'

'Oh, but that's all right,' the librarian said, brightening up. 'I can tell you all about it now. If you've got a minute …'

While Estella went back to the children's library for Hudson, the woman told Dottie her story. She had written to her about a man who came to the library asking questions. His name was Michael Mann, and he was looking for people who could tell him something about Dr Murray. 'Do you remember him? The old doctor who used to come here every day to read the paper. You … you were very upset when I told you he had died. I've always remembered you because of that. Mr Mann said he was directed to the library by Dr Murray's GP. I asked him why he wanted to know about the old doctor, and he said he was his grandson. Isn't that incredible? Isn't it wonderful? I told him everything I thought he would be interested in, and I mentioned you. He'd love to meet you. He said he'd love to meet you. He lives at the old doctor's house in Clapham. It's been rented these many years, but now he's back and he's living in it. One of the flats in it, he said. I've got his address and telephone number. He asked if you could get in touch …'

Dottie shrugged, a little apprehensive and reluctant. It was a fine story, but she had known nothing about Dr Murray. What could she tell this grandson? He was a courteous and dashing gentleman, whose smile if she caught it was enough to brighten her whole day. He had a way of lifting his hat to her that made her want to rush to him and embrace him, and soothe the pain that made him dip his head to her as he did.

The woman looked disappointed, and glanced at Estella who had been back long enough to hear part of the story.

She too looked disappointed, and dropped her eyes to Hudson, who was tugging insistently at her, wanting to be taken back to *The Owl and the Pussycat*. Dottie shrugged again. Of course he was not just an old man who had taken his hat off to her, but a stranger who had lavished affection on her and made her feel its absence in her life. What good would that knowledge do his grandson? She would see him if they were all so sure. She did not think there was anything she could tell him.

The librarian looked delighted, almost overjoyed, and Dottie wondered why it should matter to her one way or another. She didn't take his number but left her address for Mr Mann to get in touch, and her telephone number at work in case he chose to call. While they went round the market looking for mullet and some fresh vegetables for their dinner that night, Estella's treat, Dottie told her about the old doctor. As she talked about the kind and gallant old black man who had befriended her, and offered her such casual deference as she had never known in her life, Dottie recalled how important he had been to her in those gloomy days. Estella smacked her on the back of the palm, her eyes flashing with anger. 'And you were going to refuse to see this grandson,' she said.

'It was the first time I'd heard of Algeria,' Dottie said, remembering. 'I knew nothing about the fighting going on there. He was reading the newspaper in the library, and as I walked in he raised the paper triumphantly and pointed to the headline. Something about the French losing control of Algeria. His face was radiant with joy, his finger stabbing the paper gently, making sure I saw. I looked up Algeria in the encyclopaedia ... although I don't remember reading anything about Ahaggars. After that I saw Algeria in the newspapers every day, and saw how the war against the French had become such an inspiration to others who wanted their freedom.'

'Didn't you ever speak to him?' Estella asked.

Dottie shook her head, ashamed of herself.

A Trick of the Light

1

Sophie held her breath with amazement when Dottie described what the librarian had told her. Her jaw dropped open in exaggerated surprise, although she was not intending to seem ironic. She wanted to make sure Dottie understood that she was avid for more. A long-lost grandson had come to look for them! Sophie imagined a rich bequest that the old doctor had left for them, a treasure chest in the deepest part of a cave in Venezuela, or a real gold mine in Australia, or a rich and fertile ranch in the flatlands of Argentina. He must've been secretly in love with them, or wished he was. Or they may have reminded him of someone, a long-lost someone. Oh how incredibly romantic!

Dottie expressed some doubts about the bequest, and tried to argue her case. She saw at once that her words irritated Sophie, but she did not stop. This was not a matter of romance and adventure, she argued, but of guilt and atonement. Sophie's attention began to wander once she grasped that it was going to be a story that was long on description and short on drama. That kind of tale did not appeal to her. It was sure to have too many maybes and perhapses. It was typical of the way Dottie tried to twist everything in her favour, though, so that she could make it seem that she knew everything there was to know in the world, and everyone else was a hopeless dunce.

Sophie was much improved now, a recovery she credited to a handsome young doctor whose name was Newton. It was he who had taken her off the tranquiliser regime and forced her to talk about the feelings that made her lethargic and miserable. He was astonished, he said, that so little had been done for her by her doctor. She told him everything he wanted to know, and after several sessions with him he said that he understood her case much better than he had done at first. He had told her that to her face, stuttering a little and colouring as if he was doing something naughty. Sophie could see that he was inclined to put the blame for her condition on Dottie, for being domineering and reluctant to allow Sophie to grow up and make her own decisions. He said it mostly in questions, but Sophie understood the drift of his case and asked him openly if he thought Dottie was something to do with her sickness. The doctor shrugged, then stroked his chin, which was more than enough meaning for Sophie.

With only minimal encouragement from Dr Newton, she poured out all her grievances against her sister. She had had her brought back from a boarding school in Hastings, a lovely place near the sea where the sun shone on the cliffs and glittered on the water. They had gone for picnics and donkey rides, and once they had gone exploring in the caves under the cliffs. The people at the school were teaching her to swim, and in the new year she was to attend music classes with some of her friends. But Dottie had her removed from there and had her sent to a school for dunces in Wandsworth. They taught them nothing there, just made them do jobs and shouted at them for not trying hard enough. Also Dottie made her go to work when she was too ill, and interfered in her love affairs, chasing away the two men she had really loved. It was that that had made her ill in the first place. Perhaps she wanted the men for herself, but no one would look at her.

For some reason, and without giving the matter any prior thought, Sophie did not mention her child Hudson. The doctor did not ask about him, had no reason to do so. After a few breathless moments of terror when she thought that she would be caught out in a terrible crime, Sophie began to enjoy a new sense of freedom. It dawned on her that, if she wanted to, she could pretend that Hudson was not her child at all but Dottie's, and no one would know. Not the doctor, or the sister or anyone else. For a while, anyway. Then she could start afresh and try to get her life together without having all that to worry about.

Dr Newton wrote everything down in his book, and despite his professional self-control could not suppress an occasional grimace of surprise or prevent an involuntary clenching of the jaws at the story his patient told him. The depravity and squalor of human beings was sometimes too incredible for belief, he thought, and he was the last person to get easily worked up over a little misery. Anyone could see that Sophie was one of life's innocents, and it was incredible that her tormentor should be none other than her only sister. Incredible but quite predictable! Yet for centuries starry-eyed intellectuals and empty-headed *philosophers* had waffled about the nobility of Man. And his Divinity, for God's sake! He would invite them to take a look at this Goddess and her Gorgon of a sister for a start.

Of course, much of what she was saying was an expression of her sense of being victimised, scapegoating her sister and casting herself as the heroine of a melodrama as most sick women do, but the substance was probably accurate. The family history, hints of which the patient gave away, probably lay at the heart of the matter. There was no need to labour the point and give needless ammunition to the political neanderthals, the self-satisfied thugs of the Right, but not much could be expected from such a history of defeat and squalor. The mother, from the bits and pieces he had heard, was probably an alcoholic and a prostitute, half-caste or Eurasian to judge from appearances. The children were neglected and ultimately institutionalised. Predictably enough they were traumatised and hostile.

The doctor persisted with gently probing questions, and was gratified to see that after only a very few sessions Sophie began to lose interest in her sister, and wanted to talk about issues more deeply buried in her psyche. He was not a psychiatrist, or even, Heaven forbid, an analyst, – anal-cysts, as he liked to think of them, with all their obsessions with faeces and sex – so he was not really interested in this line of enquiry. He encouraged her views on the tall, dark orderly who worked in her ward instead. He knew she was interested in him and he wanted to be clear what their relationship was. Of course, her difficulties had not gone away by this change of interest but that was not his problem. At least it was a healthy demonstration of natural appetites, and frankly it was not that surprising for someone of her intelligence.

He was a physician and not a psychiatrist, but he was still one of those required to make a decision on what would be the best environment for the patient. There was not such a great deal they could do for her emphysema, although a good diet, careful practice and medication would keep her going for many years yet. The question was whether she would be better off with her sister, whom Dr Newton had never met but who sounded a total harridan, or whether she was better off in one of the semi-supervised, self-catering units that the hospital championed. The local authority contributed heavily to them, relieving the hospital of the financial burden and also freeing the doctors and nurses for other more important cases. They were a good idea, he thought, and if the hospital did not make use of them they were bound to be withdrawn. Aside from their practical attraction, these units were also a half-way house for the patients, allowing them to become accustomed to the community in a protected environment first before being exposed again to society. He thought Sophie would be an ideal candidate for a place.

That was another reason for the doctor's pleasure at the interest she was showing in the orderly, for the orderly himself had been a patient before being transferred to the intermediate units. He now worked at the hospital and was well on his way to becoming a useful member of society again. Or as useful as he was ever likely to be. For Dr Newton did not hide the fact from himself that the patients he was dealing with were mostly lumpen. He was a warm-hearted man, he knew that, but that did not mean he was a sentimentalist. Lumpen were lumpen, and nothing much could be done about that. But weren't lumpen entitled to their own bit of happiness? On what grounds could he justify returning this unfortunate woman to her hostile surroundings when an opportunity for *some* happiness existed for her? He was the last person to worry about re-claiming the moral authority of the doctor to interfere in patients' lives, all that grandiose self-love and hubris, but if he could ameliorate the sufferings of such unfortunates with a discreet sleight of hand ...

Sophie told Dottie about the doctor, and his caressingly warm voice. She passed on her suspicion that Dr Newton fancied her, and reported the sour and jealous looks the sister gave her as a result. 'He's always stopping by to give me a bit of chat, and he asks such questions! He never wants to go, which makes that Sister Cow-Face green with envy. She'd do anything to get him. You know, I saw her polishing his glasses for him the other day, chatting him up shamelessly. He thinks you're the one making me ill, Sis,' she said, and paused for a moment to see the effect of her words. She laughed to see Dottie look at her sharply with surprise. 'He says you bullied me into sickness, and dominated me ever since I was small. It was because we had no mother to look after us properly. He suspects you interfered with me, I think. And you chased my men away ...'

'He said that!' Dottie exclaimed, feeling the blood drain from her face with shock.

'He thinks you are frustrated with your own life, and so you try to live through me,' Sophie said, speaking the words carefully, as if referring to ideas she had memorised. Some of her vocabulary had come in a package with the orderly, who had taught her to embellish and refine the doctor's tentatively expressed ambiguities, and persuaded her about the virtues of being honest to her sister. 'Why do you do that if it makes me miserable? Why do you oppress me? I asked the doctor to tell me but he didn't. He shook his head and told me to think about it. But I'm asking you, Sis, for both our goods. We can't just go on pretending that everything's all right.'

Dottie resisted the temptation to argue and offer justifications for herself. She deserved all this, she thought, not because she was guilty of these trumped-up wrongs she was being accused of but because for years she had put up with this kind of treatment from everybody, and there was no reason why any of them should stop. She glanced at Hudson to see if he was listening, if he was taking any of this in. He had come visiting as well and was perched comfortably at the foot of the bed, surrounded by real and imaginary toys with which he was deeply engrossed in a complicated game. Estella was there too, listening uncomfortably to Sophie's grumbling.

'The doctor had no right to say anything like that,' Estella said, looking at Dottie and wanting her to make a protest.

Sophie ignored the comment, and after a moment Dottie changed the subject. It was at that point that she began telling the story of Dr Murray's grandson, making Sophie gasp with surprise. Estella already knew part of the story, but she was as avid in her attention as if this was the first telling. It was not only because it would dispel the meanness she had witnessed and allow her to forget her own feeble intervention that she listened so eagerly, but because she thought the story of the old doctor genuinely beautiful, full of surprises that one had no notion of expecting. A man to rejoice in, she thought.

It was to be Estella's last visit to the hospital before her move to Birmingham. Everywhere she went and everything she did made her sad. She was sorry to leave the flat, and she was almost all the time unsure about leaving London. She was afraid of losing the person she had become once she was back in her old home-town, where she would have to work hard to live her own life without distressing her parents. It had been easier away from them, although she had tried to tell them otherwise. They were worried that Marcel or Georgia would surface in her in some way, and when she was around tried to hem her in with questions and rules. Estella liked to think that she resembled the young Georgia, before all the terrors stalking her finally overcame her. Madeline had told her she did, and the thought filled Estella with pleasure. It assuaged some of the guilt she felt that she had no affection or any attachment to her mother.

She found herself already missing Dottie. There was so much she had neglected to ask about her, just as there were so many things she had suppressed about herself, and that made her wonder if she had been too smug and selfish, too satisfied that she was doing Dottie good to worry enough about her sensitivities. She would write it all down in a letter to her after she left, and she had already made Dottie swear to write long letters to her in Birmingham, telling her about everything. Despite all the fervent assurances the two friends had given each other to stay in touch, though, there was an air of leave-taking in the way Estella lingered over the places they had known, as if she suspected that her fervour would be impossible to sustain all those miles away and in the midst of the new experiences she hoped would befall her.

'He rang me at work and asked if he could come to the house in Horatio Street to meet me,' Dottie said, addressing Sophie although it was already clear that the latter was not interested. 'I said no, of course, not knowing who he might be. I was in the typing pool when the phone rang, so I had to take the call at Mrs Waterson's desk again. Not the best place for explanations. The old cow was pretending to be doing her accounts. There's only one phone in that office, and it's on her desk. Guess why! She's got this idea that left to ourselves we would spend the whole day on the phone to all our admirers. I could feel her whole body straining to hear the conversation, especially once it was obvious that it was a personal call and a man was at the other end. When I said that perhaps it would be best to meet somewhere else, a pub or something rather than at home, she snickered with a kind of mockery and rearranged herself on her chair.' As she said this Dottie mimicked Mrs Waterson, busily rocking herself from side to side with self-righteous and matronly dignity. Sophie looked on with an amused smile.

'You didn't say that before,' Estella said.

'A woman of the world like her would've known what to do with such an invitation. That's what her flouncing about was supposed to mean, I suppose. She's all right, really, I think,' Dottie said, giving Estella a small, ironic smile. 'Do you mean I'm making it up? Anyway, we arranged to meet in a restaurant in Clapham High Street called Wilbur ... Do you remember the place, Sophie? Towards the Common end, just by that big furniture store. We go past it on the bus in the mornings.'

Sophie nodded and smiled, then deliberately shifted her gaze away and fixed it on the figure standing by the ward door. She was making a show of her affections, if that was what they were, behaving with a ridiculous lack of restraint like a sulking teenager, Dottie thought, suppressing a sneering smile. Sophie heaved an agonised sigh, sickening with love for the tall, thin orderly who lounged against the wall just inside the ward doors. He was dressed in whites. His long coat, which was a size or two too big for him, was unbuttoned and flapped unheeded about him whenever he moved. Pieces of tubing peeped out of his pockets, intended to be mistaken for stethoscopes perhaps, or other necessary tools of the trade. His face had a weathered tint, as if he was used to spending time in the open. His complexion revealed a touch of dark blood along the way, Dottie guessed, as did his wiry auburn hair, receding to reveal a nobly curved forehead. He wore dark-rimmed spectacles which were pushed hard against his face. There was something unsettled about him. When he spoke, his voice was high-pitched and quarrelsome, grumblingly expecting to be misused.

He was at the beck and call of the nurses and the sister, and performed the tasks he was set with a tight-lipped parody of jauntiness, making a joke of his oppression. The nurses sensed his hostility and tried to evade it with bland endearments. Their manner implied forced tolerance and quite visible condescension. It did not contain the least trace of affection or encouragement. To Dottie he seemed a little damaged, perhaps even slightly dangerous. His head nodded whenever he was about to move, as if relaying a signal from a deeper source. He was positioned on the very edges of the sight lines from the staff nurse's desk in the middle of the ward and the sister's glass cubicle at the end. From his vantage-point, he leaned forward now and then to glance at the patients and their visitors. He gave all of them long, satirical looks and raised his eyebrows dramatically as if he disapproved of something they were doing. Then he slid back against the wall, grinning to himself. Dottie was filled with a premonition that this would be Sophie's next man, and that when she left the hospital she would bring him to Horatio Street. Her apprehensions were for Hudson as well as for herself, and for the danger that would come in their midst.

'Anyway, I met him … the grandson … last night,' Dottie said, tearing her eyes away from the orderly. 'At the restaurant where we had arranged.'

2

She arrived at the Wilbur restaurant early despite her attempts at delay. She had found herself hurrying through the gloomy, ill-lit back-streets by which she had chosen to take a short-cut. When she got to the restaurant, she found that it was too cold to stand outside or to stroll up and down the litter-strewn High Street pretending to be taking the air. She was close to the Bedford Hill meat-market, where generations of sinners had plied their humiliating trade and plummeted to unimaginable depths of degradation. If she lingered too long on the pavement, Dottie thought, some punter was bound to stop and attempt a negotiation. Or a policeman was likely to turn up and bully her with his self-righteousness. So there was nothing else for it but to go into the dimly-lit restaurant and wait. She would rather not have faced on her own the supercilious looks the waiters were bound to give her. She would rather have stridden in gracefully after he had been waiting for seven or eight minutes and was just beginning to wonder if he had got the wrong day. And what if he did not turn up? Would she have enough money to extricate herself honourably? She resisted the temptation to read the scrolled menu in its softly-lit frame. It hung in the recessed doorway, its tiny characters and inflated figures doubled over with mockery at her pretensions. At least she was not too afraid to go in, she congratulated herself, as she would have been not long ago.

The restaurant was a converted shop. Thick dark curtains on brass rods hung across the glass at the front. The tables were arranged in two rows with a central aisle, at the bottom of which ran a counter that served as a bar. The room was lit as if it were a cavern, and was festooned with fishing nets and oiled ropes. Muted and deflected light bounced off tunnels and shafts to reveal a chamber above rock-pools. In the corners stood huge shells and baskets full of shingle and old twine. The cavern's silence was shockingly serene so close to the unresting sea. The tables were all empty, their cream-coloured cloths laid with glittering cutlery and shiny plates. An older woman was standing behind the bar, her head bent over something she was softly reading out. Leaning forward, with his elbows against the bar, was a plump young man who was obviously the waiter. He straightened up slowly when he saw Dottie and approached her with a friendly smile. He was welcoming but not very enthusiastic, and looked as if he would not be surprised if Dottie merely asked him for the time of day and left. His dinner jacket, though obviously shiny and slovenly to the practised eye, struck Dottie with its due magnificence. She lost her thin pretence of calm and stammered her first few words.

'Miss Balfour, we're expecting you,' the waiter said, speaking with a touch of an accent and throwing in a hint of a bow. He did this with his fleshy, embarrassed smile, conceding that she was bound to have seen through his act. 'This way please,' he said with a sigh, and led off as if to guide Dottie through a restaurant overcrowded with throngs of noisy eaters. Hardly had she settled herself down when the waiter reappeared beside her, offering her a drink. She asked for a glass of wine and composed herself to wait. She knew she had enough money to pay for the wine herself if the worst came to happen, although such worries seemed superfluous. Mr Mann had obviously booked the table, and she hoped the restaurant could see that she was the guest. On second thoughts perhaps it was better that she had arrived first. This way she would be calm and he would be the one who was flustered.

In the event he still managed to catch her out, appearing in front of her while she was keeping her eyes lowered to avoid the smiling looks of the older woman behind the bar. Dottie had been watching the waiter and the woman reading, wondering what it was they were so solemnly bent over. She had come to the conclusion that they were Italians and were reading something tragic about the plummeting lira – she knew about these things now that she worked in big business – when the woman looked up and caught her with a radiant smile. In the confusion of her retreat, Dottie did not notice the approach of the man she had been waiting for. He was grinning broadly, leaning forward to shake her hand across the table. 'My name's Michael,' he said. 'And you must be Miss Balfour.'

'Dottie,' she said. Even in her confusion she was struck by the ease and confidence of his manner. There was nothing at all flustered about him. She took him in all at once, just a hasty glance, but she saw that he was very slim and his hair was tinted with red. The waiter was beside him, relieving him of his coat and looking pleased to see him. He spoke now with a trace of an American accent, exchanging pleasantries with a familiar customer. Michael Mann ordered a bottle of wine while they waited for their meal, and moved aside the candle that stood between them so he could lean forward as he talked to her.

'Dottie,' he said, nodding as if he was pleased with the name. She did not see Dr Murray in him except in the eyes, but then she had hardly known the old doctor, and would have had no idea what he would have looked like as a young man. He was nothing like as dark as the doctor, and his beard was more patchy, without the fullness that had given the old man such dignity. That was just as well, she thought, since she had not come to meet the doctor. He would remain the grand old man of her dreams while before her sat only a relative of his. 'It's nothing special but I like it here. The restaurant, I mean. I hope you don't mind fish … It's a family business. They're very welcoming, aren't they? I couldn't resist that after the first time I came.'

He talked like that for a few minutes, smiling and chatting to her. They were like two people in a painting, she thought, leaning towards each other across a restaurant table, deep in conversation. That was how it would seem if you were looking at the picture and trying to understand it or if you were a painter trying to portray life. What could they be saying to each other? He could be discoursing on the power of Art to transform Life, and she could be making a case for the economic reorganisation of the human community. Or they could be debating and lamenting the Hegelian exclusion of their contribution to human history, to humanity itself, or living again remembered moments of tendernesses they had shared. In the painting, the red tint in his hair would be more pronounced, and perhaps his beard would need to be thicker to emphasise the patches. The two elbows on the table hunched his shoulders too much, so they would need to be relaxed a little without losing the urgent, straining posture he had assumed.

She would be altogether more casual, maybe a hint of bemusement in the way she regarded his insistent manner. Her hands were joined together and resting on the table, fingers intertwined to conceal any agitation she might be feeling. She was wearing a dark purple dress, long-sleeved and V-necked, which Estella told her made her look slim and elegant. Round her neck she wore a silver chain, and a dark silver brooch of a single oak leaf was fixed over her heart. Her hair was brushed back, and held off her face with tiny purple clips. In her eyes, which would only be marginally visible in the painting, was a look of mild surprise that she should find herself where she was.

What colour were her eyes? What colour were his? You can't paint the colour of eyes, she thought. You would have to make the eyes stay still to capture their colour, and you would miss the life in them. She did not think any painting would be able to catch the colour of life.

'Did you know him well?' he asked. The smile had faded from his face now that he was ready to talk, and his manner was less agitated. The realisation that he was nervous too made Dottie attend to him more. 'The woman in the library said … you cried when you found out about his death. That you went to ask about him. Were you a friend of his?'

'No, not really, hardly anything like that. I used to see him in the streets … and in the library,' Dottie said, feeling as if she had agreed to meet the grandson under false pretences. She should have refused. There was nothing she could tell this man about the doctor. She had come out of curiosity, and that was not fair to him. 'I don't think we ever spoke to each other. He used to greet me. He was very kind. I thought maybe it was because we were both black people,' she said.

'You never spoke to him!' Michael Mann said, a small grimace of anguish and disappointment crossing his face.

'I'm sorry,' Dottie said. The look of agony on his face made her feel that it was she who had lured him here with false promises. 'I don't know what the lady in the library told you. I should've warned you on the phone.'

He shook his head, and then had to wait while the waiter brought the wine. It came in an earthenware jar, and the waiter evidently wanted to tell Dottie about this style of serving wine. When he had done so to his satisfaction, he took the order for their meal. Michael dealt with all that, making suggestions with evident authority and glancing at her to make sure of her acquiescence. He was the good-humoured host, full of smiles and charm. And she was in the painting again, she thought, having decisions made for her. In a way it was necessary. It would not be much of a subject if the man in the dark jacket and red-tinted hair only requested the odd dish of a favourite vegetable while the slim lady in a purple dress and silver oak-leaf brooch ordered the grand platters for herself. She would have to be painted differently for that, gross and slavering. Anyway, he was paying the bill, she hoped.

'The woman in the library only said that you had cried … It was my fault,' he said after the waiter had gone. 'I'm not surprised that he greeted you. Did he never speak to you? Even once?'

She shook her head. 'Once he pointed to a headline in the newspaper he was reading. It was about the French losing Algeria,' Dottie said, and saw Michael smile and then nod. 'At other times I thought he would've spoken, but I was a little bit afraid of him I suppose, and I did not give him the chance. Whenever he saw me in the library he stood up and lifted off his hat. He went there every day to read the paper. Did the lady tell you that? In the street, he took his hat off and bowed a little. I thought if I ever had a grandfather I would've wanted him to be like that. Sometimes, as I passed him, he dropped his head as if he was … As if he was ashamed or sorry about something. That's how he looked, anyway. But I don't think he ever spoke.'

'Do you have any idea why he was interested in you?' Michael Mann asked. He was smiling broadly now although moments before Dottie had seen his eyes beginning to redden and moisten. 'That's amazing, all that about dropping his head with shame. Did you wonder?'

'My …' Dottie had almost said *social worker*, and stopped after the one word, shocked at herself but none the less surprised at the unfamiliarity of the words. It must have been a long time since she had said those words to anybody. 'My friend Brenda … I told her about it. She thought I must've reminded him of someone, but I think he was being kind. He always seemed such a kind man.'

Michael Mann nodded, a look of pain in his eyes. Yes, Dottie thought, he had the eyes. They would be difficult to paint without making the warmth and understanding in them seem like weakness or self-pity. In the old man, the torment in the eyes had made Dottie want to turn away, to hide from the burden the doctor was carrying. In the younger man she saw that the brightness was the beginnings of tears and she resisted the temptation to look away. They would be grey in the painting, she thought, like luminous pools in twilight, and they would catch all the light but would keep their secrets to themselves.

'It's many years now since he passed away, Mr Mann,' Dottie said, thinking to console him. 'Five, six years? You must have found many people with their stories about him. He'd be delighted if he knew that you were here chasing up all the old trails, I'm sure of that.'

'I doubt it, and please call me Michael,' he said, smiling ruefully. 'I suspect he'd think I was interfering needlessly, hunting him up like this. It's what I would think if someone was doing this to me. But I have no other way of finding him … what his life would have been like in those last years. I'm staying in his house now, did I tell you that? There's an old lady living downstairs, and two women live on the first floor. The old lady looks after the garden. She told me that very firmly. She remembers him well, she says, but I can't get much out of her. I can't tell whether she's past it or whether she's just a wily old woman who doesn't want to talk. She was a tenant there while he was still alive, but she says he had very little to do with her.'

Later, when she could no longer resist it, and when the food and wine had made both of them more relaxed and convivial, she asked him how it was that he had lost touch with Dr Murray in his last years. He raised his eyebrows and said, 'Families, you know what they're like.' She persisted with one more question but he smiled and shook his head, implying that it was too trivial and petty a matter to be gone into. She was not convinced but could not blame him for not wanting to burst out to her with intimate details of family quarrels. He asked her about her job – just a secretary, she said, taking pleasure in the self-deprecation. After a little while she found herself talking about Sophie's illness and the difficulty she was having finding enough people to mind Hudson while she went to work.

'Have you advertised in the local paper?' he asked. 'Try it. It costs hardly anything and you don't have to take anyone you don't like. There could be someone a couple of streets away looking for a little bit extra and who would suit you exactly.' She looked sceptical but he persisted, and in the end offered to do it for her. He worked on a newspaper, he explained, and such things were not as frightening as they seemed.

'Do you work on the local paper?' she asked, beginning to see glimmerings of logic in his offer to help.

'No,' he said, then raised his eyes to heaven for a long moment of heart-felt thanks. 'I used to, but I work in Fleet Street now.'

She sensed from his conversation that he was not going to say anything more about himself, that he was only being friendly. No doubt he was disappointed and regretted arranging the dinner. The thought made her feel silly, as if she was a bore that he could not shake off. She found the fish too strong when it came. There was something wrong with the sauce, she thought, but Michael praised that the most, so she kept her opinions to herself. She left soon after they finished eating, when the first reasonable opportunity presented itself.

3

He rang her at work on Friday afternoon. Mrs Waterson was not amused and made her displeasure obvious, staring at Dottie as if willing her off the telephone. He wondered if she would like to go to the theatre with him. He'd just acquired a couple of free tickets for Saturday night, never mind how, and if she'd be interested ... She said yes without any further thought, surprising herself with her alacrity. She would sort something out about baby-sitters later. Laura or Estella, otherwise she was in trouble. Yes, yes. She had tried to convince herself that she did not really like him. He had only been interested in himself, she thought, obsessed with himself. Something else about him did not appeal to her. Could it be that red tint in his hair? It could not be real, and some puritanical streak in her insisted that people who dyed their hair were cheats. Also, she disliked the way he thought he could avoid saying anything to her by making charming and flattering little comments. Probably a natural-born creep who knew how to evade answering questions. That was why he was a journalist, no doubt. Yet when he rang her she knew at once what her answer was, and heard in his voice the relief and pleasure at her acceptance.

Laura laughingly agreed to baby-sit, teasing Dottie about protecting herself against hungry men. Laura's daughter, Veronica, was brought in to offer her opinion about the proper way to dress for the theatre. Among Dottie's clothes, only the purple dress she had worn to the restaurant earlier in the week failed to draw a look of withering disdain from Veronica. It was out of the question for her to wear that again, of course, Veronica insisted. In the end there was nothing else to be done but to try out some of Veronica's clothes. Small alterations were required but before long

Dottie was decked out in a light-blue gown, glistening with tiny, satiny flowers. She regretted asking for help, but she could not refuse the dress after all the trouble she had caused. The bodice was tight, though not uncomfortable. It made her feel brazen and dissembling.

She was late arriving at the theatre, and her mind was still on the amount she had had to pay out to the cabbie. Michael hurried her to her seat and they sat in stony silence, along with hundreds of other revellers, while the actors and actresses pranced their make-believe life. She could not take it for real, all that anguishing and yelling while people watched. The theatre was stuffy with the smell of carpets and old clothes. Dottie watched the business on the stage but could not keep her mind on it. She had got heated in her rush and anxiety, and had warmed up the dormant life in Veronica's dress. It was giving off its owner's perfume and a tart whiff of old sweat.

A storm was winding itself up when they came out of the theatre. High winds were snatching at everything they could in the streets, hurling crates and litter along the pavements and howling around corners and across open spaces. It was raining heavily, the great downpour of water dimming the street-lamps and making them seem farther away. The vault of the sky seemed to have fallen in, and was suspended now only a matter of a few feet above their heads, churning in inchoate throes. Out of it leaped a flash of lightning so crisp and powerful that it took their breath away. In the sudden brilliance the turmoil of the skies was an image of primeval chaos, the irresistible confusion which was the beginning of life. They waited for the thunderclap with bated breath, hiding under the canopy of a gabled door. The lightning came again, a sheet of light thrown across the sky.

'If it wasn't so freezing cold, it would be like the coming of the first rains,' Michael shouted, laughing even as he winced at the thunder. 'On the savannah. There's too much mud in this land. Out there you waited for the smell of singed earth during a storm.'

They found a cab in the deluge and took a ride home. They were completely soaked, and Veronica's dress was probably ruined, but the exhilaration of the storm and the sudden intimacy of the cab kept them warm. The cabbie dropped Michael off first, at Dottie's insistence. 'I'll call you,' Michael said, picking up her hand and kissing it. She felt her hand burning all the way to Brixton.

4

Sophie had told her that she had been offered the chance of a self-catering place in a hostel near by. It would help her get better, she said. She could move in there in the New Year, make a new start in her life. She broke the news defiantly, expecting to be hectored and dissuaded. 'There I'll be free,' she said, sitting with her back hard up against the top bar of the hospital bed.

'And Hudson?' Dottie asked.

'It'll only be for a while, until I get better,' Sophie said, breathing fast and panting lightly, her voice plaintive and wounded. 'Do you think I'm trying to give him up? You don't understand a mother's feelings, Sis, or you'd never say that. You've never had a baby yourself and you can't know how a mother would rather die than see harm come to her child.'

Dottie looked at her sister's pouting face and resisted the temptation to burst out laughing. How could Sharon's daughter say a thing like that? Could she not remember how Sharon had been so steeped in despair that no thought of *harm* could reach her any more? A mother would rather die, she thought bitterly. We fight these little battles to save our miserable lives, and hide their meanness from ourselves with grand words. 'What does the doctor say about Hudson?' she asked.

Sophie nodded vaguely and then dropped her eyes. Dottie nodded too and guessed that the doctor had not been told. She asked interested questions about the hostel, not wanting to start a confrontation. Sophie was a grown woman and could do what she liked. If her idea of freedom was to live in a hostel with sick people, she would have to find out its truth for herself. Dottie could not deny a thrill of pleasure that she would not have to suffer Sophie's irritating presence for a while. And Hudson would not be taken away from her. But also in her mind was the worry that the Council and Social Security would deny her the various reliefs she was collecting. She would not be able to manage if she lost all that.

Before she left, she went to see the sister in her cubicle at the far end of the ward. It was the same woman who had spoken to her before about visiting. Dottie had then thought of her with gratitude, and had once seen her in a dream, her fair features burnished with the metallic brightness of a sculpted angel. She had hovered near by, her head lit by a beatific smile while the index finger of her right hand, the finger of blessing, pointed insistently to the water's edge. In the end the angel beckoned her, her arm sweeping an arc through the moist air and leaving traces of sparks in its wake. It was only a dream, and Dottie smiled at her fancifulness every time she saw the harried and jaded woman whom she had pictured with a bright and unlined face. Her eyes were red with exhaustion, and her coarsened skin looked dry and hot. The sister sighed heavily behind her limp smile. She told Dottie that the doctor wanted to talk to her about her sister's move, to explain what was involved, and wanted to arrange an appointment to coincide with her next visit to the ward.

'It'll save you a bit of travelling anyway, won't it?' the sister said with a tired smile.

'What are these places like?' Dottie asked. 'Where Sophie's going.'

The sister hestitated for a moment, and a flicker of irritation passed over her face. 'I don't really know, love. The doctor can tell you more about that, but I think Sophie's very keen. Sometimes that's a better reason than any other.'

5

Michael rang her again the following week. It was the week of Christmas and he rang to invite Hudson and her to a Christmas Eve ice-cream on Clapham Common. It was a bright and chilly afternoon when Michael and Hudson made their acquaintance by the pond on the Common. Hudson was inclined to be cold at first. On the whole he was not too comfortable in the company of men any more, not since Patterson had gone berserk on them. He was now inclined to find men opiniated and argumentative. Michael was quick to pay homage to the young lord, though, abasing himself more or less with his knees on the cold, wet earth. When it was clear that the purpose of the outing was to eat ice-cream cones on a bitterly cold day on Clapham Common, Hudson's lingering doubts were swept violently aside. Here was a man out of the ordinary, a man who knew how to make the most out of life. Hudson extended to him his gracious acquaintance, and presently offered to exchange ice-cream cones with him.

'I must meet him before I leave,' Estella said when she found out. 'Why are you being so selfish? Even Hudson has met him and he hardly cares. They've exchanged handshakes and swapped ice-cream cones, and yet you hide him from me. We can go out on a farewell dinner and celebrate.'

'Don't anticipate,' Dottie said anxiously, wary of a fate that had mocked her too often before. 'It might all come to nothing and then I'll feel a fool.'

'Oh yeah, strolling across the Common eating ice-cream on a freezing day – who else but lovers or stupid babies will do that? Holding hands in a storm and you think it'll come to nothing,' Estella scoffed. 'All that thunder and lightning was probably to signal that your destinies are now inextricably linked. He was even talking about hot singed earth ... there's probably some sexual symbolism in that too. Are you sure no birds burst into song as you strolled down the Avenue by the Common? Anyway, I wasn't meaning celebrate about him arriving in your life but about me leaving. Hello and goodbye, that sort of thing. I don't want my farewell to be a glum gathering in the flat. Did I tell you? My parents are rubbing their hands with glee up there in Brummie. They've even found me a flat to rent not far from where they live. And I'm to take my washing round for Mum to do, and if I need any shelves put up Dad will come round, no bother. It's enough to make you want to run away.'

6

Dr Newton knew he had made a mistake after his interview with Dottie. She had been cooperative and intelligent, so unmistakably in command of herself that the doctor had found himself a little bit intimidated by her. Well, perhaps not intimidated, but certainly taken aback. In any case, he rather liked her. And of course he had not known about the child. In a way, he had wanted to assess her himself before completing his notes on Sophie. He was not so blind that he could not see how the situation was substantially complicated by this new information. He would have liked to ask more questions, but when he had tentatively essayed something about their problems in childhood, he had seen her look harden. For a moment he thought she would say something unpleasant. Her lip trembled with obvious anger. He could appreciate her distress and gently shifted the question.

'Of course, it is really Sophie's decision, but I wanted to discuss it with you as well. There is nothing irrevocable in this,' he said, and paused in case Dottie wanted to ask a question. 'She can change her mind whenever she wants. I believe this way she has a chance to make something of her own, especially since she appears to be establishing a relationship ... which will be something new for her, I think. What is the child's name, if I may ask? And his date of birth as well, please.'

He felt a twinge of sadness as he saw her out, and he was not quite sure why. Perhaps he had made a bit of a fool of himself, or that was how he might seem to the young woman. He was not sure that he had been that far out in his assessment of Sophie, despite the existence of the child Hudson. Why did they always go for such grandiose names? The doctor sighed to himself. Even if you were predisposed towards them, as the doctor considered himself to be, you could not fail to note the ridiculousness of the names. Like this boxer, Cassius Marcellus Clay! What a ridiculous hybrid!

Anyway, it was impossible to withdraw the offer they had made. It would damage Sophie and would, in all likelihood, be a mistake. The elder sister may not have dominated Sophie in the manner the latter had recounted, or for the reasons that the doctor had assumed, but it was quite clear that she did dominate her in an unhealthy way. Above all, *that was how Sophie saw it*. What mattered to him, after all, was the well-being of his patient, and not the desire to cut a dash in front of the clever sister. In his patient's interest, it was best that she should have a bit of room to grow without being harassed. Perhaps also, for what could be the first time in her life, she might be on the threshold of a meaningful relationship with a man. Dr Newton had hopes of the orderly Quixall, and was delighted with his interest in Sophie. If what Sophie had said about Dottie's interference in her relationships was true, and surely that was true, or at least contained the seeds of truth ... In any case, such behaviour would be consistent with the condition of an intelligent woman who was frustrated by her environment as the elder sister must have been.

Dr Newton suspected, in the final resort, that Sophie did not have the resources to avoid being institutionalised. Sooner or later she would succumb. He wrote this in his report, but riddled it with enough qualifications and conditions to ensure that it would not have an adverse influence on the treatment she was likely to receive in the future.

7

Dottie and Hudson spent Christmas Day with Estella in the flat. The two women were drunk by the afternoon, to Hudson's huge enjoyment. He was not at all surprised when they decided to go for a long walk on Wimbledon Common in the afternoon. Honestly, you'd have thought they had never heard of self-restraint, he sighed to himself. It was freezing, of course, so he could try out his new gloves and his fur cap. It was an astrakhan cap that he had picked for himself because he liked the way it gave him a bit of dash, made him look heroic despite his rather irritating lack of height. He had also been given a variety of other gifts but none to rival the head-gear.

The next day, after they had gone back to Brixton, Michael called with a tricycle for Hudson. It was his Christmas gift. He had found it in the summer-house in his garden and had cleaned it up for the boy.

'Summer-house! That sounds … romantic, like a fairy-story,' Dottie said. 'It's lucky we're in.'

'You must come and visit,' he said. 'I told you about the old woman downstairs who looks after the garden. Well, she keeps the summer-house in fine shape as well, and insists that we all use it. Even in this weather.'

Dottie nodded, not knowing exactly what to say. 'It's lucky we're in,' she repeated.

'Oh, I would've left it with the neighbours,' he said. He stopped long enough to watch Hudson careering backwards and forwards from the kitchen to the front door, with various furry passengers as company. Dottie had refused to let him wear his astrakhan cap in the house, on the ridiculous grounds of a vaguely remembered old wives' tale or superstition about hats indoors.

'I'm going away for a few days,' Michael said, looking a little embarrassed. Suddenly he smiled, amused at his own uncertainty. Dottie smiled too and stepped forward to embrace him. 'I'll come by when I get back in the New Year,' he said, holding her.

The Wooded Path

1

He was not *completely* truthful with her, that was what Michael said when he returned. She had asked him to stay and have lunch when he came round, and he had accepted with obvious delight. He was sombre after that, but she took her time asking him what the matter was. She was cooking a lasagne for the first time, and total concentration was necessary if a disaster was to be avoided, she thought. She could pick up on his life afterwards. When she asked him if there was anything wrong, he said he was merely exhausted. Nothing much for you to bother with, go back to your pasta and white sauce, signorina, he said. We shall see about that, she replied. He made sure she knew that he had come to Brixton more or less straight from the station, and this mollified her, made her less free with the white sauce, anyway, which was a good thing as she presently discovered. She had not made enough, which is not unusual with first-time-lasagne-makers. He thought to say something about this but held his peace in time.

Hudson was in and out of the house, riding his tricycle in the garden for a few minutes and then rushing in with a treasure-trove from the great outdoors: an incautious spider that had stepped into a wickedly cunning trap that he had set, or a bundle of wet leaves that gave off a peculiarly powerful smell of rot, or whatever else he thought might give the stick-in-the-mud crowd in the kitchen some sense of zest for life. It was a bright, crisp day early in the new year, and to see some people carry on you would not think that life was worth living.

'I was not completely truthful with you,' Michael said afterwards as they sat in the living room. The lasagne had turned out well, and he had redeemed himself by washing up, making the tea and persuading Hudson not to eat the dead spider in his trap.

'Truthful? About what?' Dottie asked. Her mind was already racing with alternatives. He's married. He's married. His family's Catholic and he made a girl pregnant. Now his life is in rack-and-ruin and he is tormented with guilt. He's not really a journalist but deals in drugs and seduces boys. She waited patiently for him to begin and saw him frown as he waited for the words to come.

'You asked why I had lost touch with my grandfather in his last years. Do you remember? You asked me that on the first night. It was something like that, and I didn't answer you,' he said, looking at her unflinchingly, the look of confession. 'I never knew him. I never even met him. Not once. That was why I came to look for him. It shamed me to say that, and made me ashamed for my mother.'

As if what he had said was enough explanation, he turned in his chair and glanced out of the window. After a long silence, during which Dottie had to bite her tongue several times as it was on the point of leaping out with something inane and comforting, he spoke again. The tenor of his words was unexpected, and it took her a moment or two to re-align her mind to them. He spoke slowly, sometimes stopping for long seconds, as if he had finished. 'There are whole continents of things we don't know,' he said. 'Bottomless chasms, vaults of infinite magnitude, multitudes of things ... And even when we think we know, when we think we've got the hang of something, it bursts in our faces and covers our idiot mugs with slime. The ignorance we live with is phenomenal. That shatters me sometimes. We're just such laughable creatures, carrying on as if what we do matters. Out there, in this country too, are events of real importance. History is being made and we are in the middle of it. The whole world is being turned upside down in front of our eyes.

'Have you heard about the coup in Nigeria? And Upper Volta and the Central African Republic? January alone has given us three coups in Africa. Tomorrow it will be Ghana or Indonesia or Argentina. The old barons are being cut down in mid-step, in broad daylight. New bandits are rising from the oppressed, making their gruesome bids for the high places at the very moment that the old robbers are being forced down. It's a time of miracles and grief, history on a mythic scale alongside outbursts of the most gruesome barbarism. Irresistible schemes to transform the wilderness vying with absurd hankerings for corrupt luxury. The works! Yet it's the little things about ourselves that command our attention and our feelings. It's our little aches and pains that we really care about. Our little bits of alienation. It's humiliating ... that it is only our own stories that move us.'

She shook her head uncertainly, a small gesture of disagreement. He glanced at her and his eyes brightened a little with surprise. 'What do you mean? Don't you agree?' he asked.

She would rather not have spoken, in case she had misunderstood him. Estella had told her that sometimes she jumped in when she, Estella, had not finished what she was saying, but Michael waited eagerly for her to speak. 'That isn't true, you know that isn't true. It isn't only our little aches that move us … You can't speak for everyone like that,' she said. She spoke uncertainly, wondering if she was about to make a fool of herself. 'Perhaps I did not understand what you meant. I thought you said that we only care about ourselves. But people give their lives to things, dedicate themselves. I don't mean just the obvious things like freedom or God but to a way of living or to knowledge. How can you say that nothing moves us? Those are just words …'

'I was building myself up nicely to a tragic mood,' he said, smiling but looking miserable and depressed. 'And now you're spoiling it. You're probably right … It's just that I've been thinking a lot about that old man recently. I wanted to say something about that, but everything is so complicated. It's impossible to know just where to begin. You want to say only what you mean, so you can control it and give it shape, so you can keep it neat. But little jagged ends appear, and when you push them in something else bumps up or tears off.'

He sighed and looked away. Dottie waited silently, hearing the noises of the streets and the barking of the Alsation next door as if they were sounds in a dream. She heard Laura shouting at Daisy to be quiet and imagined an ancient scene of a village clearing on a day of rest, with dog and mistress contesting proprieties.

He turned back to her suddenly, resolutely. 'My mother cut herself off from him. She went away and never spoke to him once after that. He married again when he was in his fifties, just before the war. His new wife was only twenty or so. She was about six months younger than my mother. She stormed off, my mother, I mean … disgusted, angry. When I was small she never talked about him, and

I suppose he did not really exist for me. I had some vague idea, but my other grandparents were so solidly there that their ... concreteness made everything about him seem even more unreal.

'We lived in Ghana for most of my childhood, the Gold Coast. My father was an official in the National Bank, and all that distance made it easier too. We came back for holidays but those were busy times ... and we soon stopped doing that, anyway. That was how it went on, year after year, one thing after another until he died. He left her what he had, quite a fair amount of money, and left the house to her children. That's me,' he said with a smile, tapping himself on the chest. 'There's only me. I had a younger brother, but he died in 1948 when we were in the Gold Coast. That was sad. He was so small. I've always missed him. Anyway, it took the solicitors over a year to find my mother. I don't suppose they hurried too much. I was out of the country, on my first assignment abroad. Well, assignment rather glorifies it but I was working anyway. I was sent to the Congo where the attention of the world was focused in gruesome fascination. After that I was really too busy. I spent a year in East Africa, then south to Zambia and Rhodesia. So much was happening: revolutions, wars of independence, forced marriages. Economies were collapsing, prisons were overflowing and the new barons were keeping students of human drama riveted on their tragic soap operas. Whenever I came back to Manchester – that was where we lived, Wilmslow actually – it was only for a couple of weeks or so, and then off to work again. England seemed like a place that was consumed with itself, tardily hugging its inheritance to itself, afraid that unclean hands would soil and pilfer it. They should know, having ransacked everybody else's shrine for the greater glory of their own selves.

England seemed irrelevant, preoccupied with a vision of a world that had passed, constantly huffing and puffing at the indignities heaped on it. My mother told me about the house I had inherited and I told her to have it rented out. I was too busy to deal with it, too involved in real life to want to have anything to do with all that materialism and stocks and shares crap. We idealists talk like that, you know,' he said, mocking himself.

'I don't even remember what she called him. Did she say your grandfather has died or my father is dead? I don't remember what she said. The questions came to me while I was in hospital in Kampala. I had lots of time on my hands then, nearly three bed-ridden weeks, suffering from fever and other interesting complications. I had hoped to do a piece on a rebel group that was operating near the western border with the Congo. Everyone at that time wanted to do a piece on the rebels and the mercenaries. The world wanted to hear the butchers speak for themselves, wanted to get as close as they could to their blood-dimmed vision. A local reporter set it up for me, but everybody got too greedy and angry. We were very nearly shot and were certainly well beaten for our troubles. Not much ceremony or crazy dancing, no unspeakable rites with this crowd of *natives*. Crash! Bang! Take that you bastard! It was more like that. Then we had to make our way through territory neither of us knew. By the time we found help we were very frightened men, and I had picked up some kind of fever. I still wonder that they let us off so easily.'

2

He had thought of himself as making Conrad's journey in reverse. With luck, and if all went well, he would get as far as Kisangani, the old Stanleyville, and Stanley Falls Station before that. Conrad called it the Inner Station. The heart of darkness! It was on an old trade route from the east coast which had been in use for at least a hundred years or more. Slavers and ivory hunters had tramped and marched those mountain paths, and set up their wretched and short-lived kingdoms to harvest the bounty of the land. The upper reaches of the river were dotted with old fortresses and the overgrown ruins of towns the Waswahili robber barons had built for their host. It was only the heart of darkness if you approached it from the other end.

They bribed the border guard, as they would have done almost anywhere in the world. Border guards knew it was their due and would consider that they had been treated with cavalier contempt if their palms were not properly greased. No one told them anything or asked them anything, no doubt assuming they were smugglers or mercenaries, or scientists or Peace Corps volunteers. It hardly mattered in the chaos of that time. They drove their pick-up to the prearranged place and waited for two days. Lemuel Mpira, the man who had arranged it all, was a Luo from Mombasa, working for the Standard. He could not speak the language here, but his Kiswahili was enough to get all their needs seen to, and his French was fluent and perfect. With those two languages he thought they would get by. Michael was really only a passenger, and had only got on the trip because he had struck up a friendship with Lemuel who had kindly invited him along.

They found an assorted bunch of thugs when they got to the camp, which was overcrowded and filthy beyond conception. They were willing enough to talk but Michael could not really take what they were saying seriously. At times he thought he was misunderstanding, that his French was not good enough, but Lemuel translated. Listening to their grandiose talk, it was possible to believe the stories of nuns stripped and raped on the forest floor, and opponents dismembered after death. It was wounded, psychopathic talk camouflaged by words like justice and freedom.

The condition of the republic gave concerned people of good-will no other choice but to take up arms against the tyranny, they said. It was no longer a matter for personal decision. The circumstances demanded only one course of action. Rebellion and retaliation! That was how it had to be.

Until when? How would it all end?

There would be no end, they said, repeating the cry among themselves and then grinning with delight at the celebration of their strength and unity.

They must have sensed his scepticism, or perhaps his questions revealed his dislike.

3

'I heard about your mother, and the young wife,' Dottie said later. 'But I didn't know that was why your mother left. My friend Brenda … she met someone who was an old neighbour of your grandfather's. At a British Legion function. These neighbours used to live in Broomfield Road, not far from you.'

Michael looked at Dottie with an amazed smile. 'What did the neighbours say? Why didn't you tell me this before?'

'She used to be a teacher at the school, and her husband was a banker. She taught your mother, she was her teacher. It's incredible,' Dottie said, pausing to let the thought sink in. 'She said your mother was gifted … a musician. And Dr Murray used to come to the concerts to listen to her. He only had eyes for her, this teacher said.'

'She loved him. When I came back from Kampala I was still ill, and she took time off from her job to look after me. I asked her not to. There was no need, I thought. I needed to be alone at that time. Everything was almost too much ... but also I knew how important it was to her that she was a working woman. She'd worked all her life after she left her father. It didn't occur to me until later that she might have been thinking of the other son, my brother. She was a teacher then too, when we were in Ghana. I don't think she stopped working then. She never mentioned that but it might have been on her mind.

'Anyway, during those weeks we talked a great deal about him. My grandfather, I mean. He was like an emperor, she said. And she stood up tall on her toes with her arms held out and her head lifted. That story about going to the school concerts, she told me that as well. How he came and intimidated the teachers with his fierce adulation for his daughter. She talked of other things about being a child. Her mother, she said, was just a memory of a woman who smelt of medicine and who cried often. She saw a picture of her in the papers my grandfather left, and she realised that she knew nothing about her. She could not even remember how she looked. Most of the time she talked about him. How he took her everywhere and guarded her as if she was a precious possession. How he thundered at her when she neglected herself or forgot to aim high enough. How he encouraged her and how much he loved her. She wept and wept as she told me her story, and made me weep too that I had not known him.

'What else did they say about her?' he asked after waiting for a moment.

'The other children used to tease her because she was black,' Dottie said, and exchanged a smile with Michael.

'But there was no malice in it, apparently. I think the teacher said they used to *rib* her about it. At first I heard that she had been killed in the war. The woman in the library told me that, I think, but the neighbour knew that she had gone north to take a job as a teacher.'

'Carlisle,' Michael said, nodding. 'That was her first job.'

Dottie thought of saying something about Carlisle, mentioning her own history, but decided against it. 'The young wife and her child were killed in the bombing, visiting relatives somewhere on the coast. Southampton or Portsmouth, or something like that,' Dottie said.

'There was a child? I didn't know that. I don't think my mother ever saw them after they were married. She was a nurse in his clinic, you know. The woman he married ... It must've started when my mother went away to college to do her training in Nottingham. The woman ... the nurse ... I don't know what to call her ... she came to stay in the house during term. My mother found out when she came down for her holidays. I don't know what she found out but you can imagine. She confronted him with her discovery and he got so angry, was so livid with rage at the accusations she made against the young woman, that he was unable to do anything but stammer. Then he stepped forward and slapped her.'

Shame on you, he had said. Perhaps it was fear or outrage that made her do it, but she screamed at him that he was the one who was shameful. And he had better not lay hands on her again or she would leave. She was not going to accept that kind of treatment from anyone. Realising what he had done, he tried to speak to her, apologising and uttering endearments. She shrugged off his approaches and refused to talk to him for days. He tried to laugh the argument off, teasing her and pretending to be abjectly contrite.

In an attempt to placate her, he never mentioned the young woman and never allowed her to come by the house. After several days had passed, and his bantering had got him nowhere, he tried to break her silence by having a solemn and serious confrontation with her. Her hostility shocked him, and he became afraid of what might happen, of words said that would be impossible to take back. But she had become reckless with her power, and when she realised that he was pleading for her return she set as her condition the termination of that disgusting affair with a woman less than half his age, and younger than his own daughter. At the very least she should no longer be employed in his clinic. Could he not see that she was only after him for his wealth? She said other things, and in the end he could not contain his anger at the injustice of his daughter's words, and he hit her again in the face.

That's enough of that, you filthy old man, she said and left. She had packed a few things and gone from the house within half an hour. He made no effort to stop her. It was the last time she saw him, when he stepped forward to hit her with a look of disgust on his face. She found out later, from people she was still in touch with, that he was planning to marry the woman. She could not return after that. It made all of them look ridiculous, she thought, like a bunch of hot-blooded foreigners. So she put as much distance between them and her as she could, and took the job in Carlisle because it was the farthest one of all the ones she was offered. Jobs were plentiful then, and she could have found work nearer if she had wanted.

'Can you imagine this skinny black woman storming off to Carlisle to teach music in a school there? That was where she met my father. He was working in a bank, and was a local fencing champion. He claims he could've gone further if he really wanted, but I don't know. One of the teachers at the school was a fencing enthusiast too, so my father used to go to the school gym to practise. From what they say now, I think it was a stormy and passionate courtship. They were married the following year. My father's people came from Cumbria and they were tickled pink by the thought of a dusky bride for their boy. He was a headmaster of a local grammar school and a magistrate, a local pillar of his community. His wife had been a professional actress in her youth and was distantly related to nobility or something. Even until today she refuses to be exact, preferring to keep the game going with innuendo and half-clues.

'During the reception after my parents' wedding, some local dinosaur came to commiserate with my grandfather over the coffee-coloured piccanin that would soon be tramping heedlessly over the flower-beds. My grandfather laughed at him and told him to take himself off. Actually his exact words were "Bugger off out of my party, you unpleasant man."'

'They are wonderful people and they made my mother welcome and helped her to forget him. Then I came and then my younger brother, then the war and Gold Coast. It was easy to make a new life, to start again. Everything was changing, the whole world was different.'

'Was she not tempted? Did she not try to get in touch with him?' Dottie asked. The light had very nearly gone. They had been talking for a long time and she knew they would have to stop soon. There would be other times, she thought, to tell him about herself and about Sharon, and to hear about him and the places he had seen. Hudson was already asleep on the settee beside her, breathing softly in his innocent abandoned way. She would carry him to his bed in a minute, she thought, reluctant to lose the moment.

'I asked her,' he said, sounding very tired. He said no more for a long while, as if preferring not to continue. 'I asked her about that when we were talking about him. She said nothing at all, but you could see how she felt. It was a stupid thing to ask her, insensitive. She thought I wanted her to accept the guilt for what had happened ... Later she told me that she thought about him every day for all those twenty years. Twenty-two years! Over a stupid quarrel like that!'

4

There was a monastery in the village where his grandparents lived. He always visited it when he went to see them. It was mostly ruins but there were many walls and buttresses still standing. When he was younger he used to explore the cellars, some of which were now only wells in the earth because the floors above had gone. In adolescence he had found the desolation of the ruins comforting, and imagined that he could hear the gloomy chants of the monks in the winter winds. He would stand leaning against the walls in wintry sunlight and weave stories round himself, witnessing terrible scenes of injustice and performing heroic acts of rescue. Were it not for his fortunate presence, a charming town full of innocents would be taken and razed by bandits! Invariably he fell in love with a Viking princess. His grandparents teased him about the red in his hair, claiming that it was the Viking in him coming out. When he was a child they used to give him Viking nicknames: Canute the Incontinent or Olofson the Grizzler. His grandmother told him blood-curdling tales of raids and slaughter. How the Vikings swooped down on coastal settlements and river-side villages for loot, pillage and rape. She recounted long stories of incredible journeys from the fog-ridden shores of north-western Europe to all the corners of the known world. Normandy, Sicily, Libya, Anatolia and the Americas.

When he went to see the monastery the last time, it was with his father. They had all gone down to stay for a few days after Michael's return from Kampala. One afternoon his father came with him for a walk, linking arms to give him some support. They were usually easy and comfortable in each other's company, sharing many interests and opinions. Perhaps also they were wary of each other, careful not to offer a challenge or give offence. Michael pointed to electric pylons and cables that cut off the horizon from the monastery site. He said something about the insensitivity of bureaucrats or engineers, or whoever it was that made decisions of this kind at the electricity board. They could've found somewhere else to put them, he said irritably.

'They're not new,' his father said. 'They've been there for ages.' At first Michael did not believe him, but he could see his father was not joking.

When they talked about the old doctor and what had happened between him and his daughter, Michael could not prevent the dejection from overcoming him. He felt his eyes stinging with the beginnings of tears. His father sat beside him on the stone wall and said nothing. He made no attempt to come nearer or to comfort him, but sat with his eyes lowered. It was not just the fight between the old man and his daughter that made him sad, Michael said as tears ran into his mouth, but the waste and loneliness of the last years he must've spent.

'It's the weakness,' he said to his father, excusing his misery. He thought he should wipe away the tears and not look quite so much as if he relished his agony, but a great lethargy had come over him. He felt the wind drying the tears off. 'They did a good job on us in that camp. Everything seems to depress me these days. Maybe I'm just a little bit disillusioned or something.'

They abandoned them on a gloomy wooded path, raucous and mocking as they landed their parting blows. The trees around them were like sheer cliffsides, and in the far distance he caught glimpses of the star-lit sky. He heard their voices recede into the chilly mountain night, and Michael knew that they were lucky to be alive. He heard Lemuel beside him sighing, pain and desolation mingling in his tormented moans. Sigh followed sigh with desolated regularity. Michael could hear his own groans beside the anguish of his companion, and knew that their cries only deepened the low whisper that rose from the land.

He saw a look in his father's eyes that reminded him of the sorrow that came over them when they talked about his younger brother. It was a sunny day as they sat there on the hilly mound, but the wind was still brisk, as it always was. Without saying a word at first, his father pointed at a glittering speck in the far distance. Michael nodded to show that he had seen it.

'The sea,' his father said, his eyes bright with pleasure. 'It must be a trick of the light.'

'A mirage,' Michael said, smiling.

'She talked about him often when you weren't around,' his father said after a long time. 'She did not want her children involved in the squabble, she said. So she kept it all away from you. Sometimes she felt bitter about him, but not usually. She felt it deeply. I mean she regretted their separation, and even when she was angry about what had happened she could not talk about it without pain. There was nothing she could do. After what she had said about the new wife, she did not think she would be welcome. We had no idea that she'd died. We had no idea that for all those years while she tortured herself he was living alone. In the year or two before we received the news of his death, she talked of writing to him. Once when we were staying in London we talked for half the evening about going round to Clapham the next day, to call on him and put an end to the acrimony, but when it came to it she said leave it, another time. She could not do it. It would have been better if she had, but it did not work out like that.'

After a moment his father rose and came over to help Michael to his feet.

5

Dottie took Hudson to bed and hurried down, but Michael left while she was away. She thought she heard the front door click when she was upstairs. Perhaps he thought he had been a bore or had shown himself to be weak. Or talking had made him miserable. She was not tempted to run after him or rush round the following day to claw at him with her affection and her demands. The pains he had described filled her own heart with a kind of lassitude. The picture of the assault he had suffered struck her with force, like a moment she had lived through herself. What was the point of struggling and fretting if this was all that awaited them? Had she got it all wrong? Perhaps all their frenzy and intensity was little more than preparation, fattening themselves up for the slaughterers. She would go to him after a day or two and try to tell him of the comfort she found in his company. She would touch his bruised body with her hand and ask to share the pain with him. But now he had to think what he wanted for himself.

The following evening, soon after she came in from work, there was a knock on the door. Dottie had been thinking of him all day, and as the mood of Michael's dejection lifted from her, so her decision to give him time seemed foolish. Suppose he ran off somewhere again, or took her self-effacement for lack of care? If the fate that awaited them was that confrontation with the killer on the forest path, then it was foolish to delay the brief, genuine pleasures that were possible. In a way that she could not fully explain, she had grasped and understood something of his disillusion, and had felt in it intimations of a kind of despair. As she ran down the stairs to his knock on the door, it was with a determination to resist the temptation, to pull both of them back from the frivolity of their self-dramatisations.

It was not Michael who stood at the door but Patterson, his back hunched up against the winter rain. Dottie felt resolve draining away from her, and would have loved nothing better than to stamp her foot with outraged disappointment. She invited him in with cheerful exclamations even though in her heart she cursed his very existence. He had brought a belated present for Hudson. Dottie thought he looked better than the last time she had seen him, less angry perhaps. He accepted her offer of tea with smiling gratitude and sat in the living room talking to Hudson while she went to make it. She sensed that he was not going to stay for long and that brought her some relief. She could not suppress a small twinge of disappointment that Hudson seemed pleased to see him. She found him on the floor at Patterson's feet, playing with a lorry.

'How've you been?' she asked Patterson, after she had chased Hudson away from that abject position beside his feet. He smiled ruefully but not unhappily, and tilted his chin towards Hudson.

'He looks well,' he said. 'And so do you. I hope the news of Sophie is good and that she is recovering.'

His formality and the gift reminded Dottie of the Sunday visits he used to make. She smiled at the memory and Patterson returned her smile with greater tenderness than Dottie had bargained for. 'This weather's terrible, isn't it?' she said.

She heard him chuckle in agreement. 'This England! I have my family here now, and in their first days they thought they would freeze to death. My wife had cramps in her legs and then woke up sweating in the middle of the night.'

'Your family's here!' she exclaimed, feeling sudden relief and undisguised pleasure.

'It has become very hard now back at home. Food is scarce and very expensive, and the children's schooling is impossible. These politicians and the soldier boys between them have done this. Ten years ago our country was rich and now the people can't eat. We won't let them forget this. They tell us to tighten our belts and make sacrifices for the future. For themselves they build mansions with tennis courts and swimming pools, and send their children to private schools overseas. All over Africa they've done this, and before they've finished they will make all of us into paupers and beggars.' His face was set with anger as he said this, but after a moment he smiled. 'They're very glad to be here. The children want to watch TV all the time, and my wife tries to buy everything from the supermarket. I tell her there are no shortages here but she can't get used to it. If I give her fifty pounds for the whole week she goes to the shops and spends all of it. Sacks of rice and sugar, gallon tins of oil, boxes of canned tomatoes ... two days ago she came home with a crate of orange juice cartons,' Patterson said, laughing softly.

'You must be glad to see them, though,' Dottie said. 'I didn't know …'

'What is a man without his family?' Patterson interrupted gently. 'What news is there of Sophie? I hope she will soon be able to come home.'

He listened carefully while Dottie explained about the self-catering room in a hostel. She was aware of his scepticism even though he said nothing at first. 'It was what she wanted,' Dottie said.

'Those places are sometimes very bad,' he said in the end.

'What do you mean bad?' she asked. 'This is a new scheme, to release the patients slowly so they get used to things again. The doctor himself told me. Sophie said she wanted to go there until she was completely better.' Despite her protests Dottie felt pangs of guilt about Sophie, had felt them as soon as she realised the relief she felt that Sophie would not be coming back to the house for a while. Especially with that strange-looking orderly in tow. His name, she had discovered, was Vernon Quixall, which seemed adequately bizarre. What choice had Dottie had? Sophie blamed her for all the ills that had befallen her, and accused *her* of being envious. She did not intend to discuss all that with Patterson, though, so he would just have to carry on and disapprove.

'Perhaps she'll be back home soon, anyway,' he said. 'Perhaps next time I call I will find her home.'

When he was ready to leave, he called Hudson to him and gave him a five-pound note. He waved away Dottie's protests and closed Hudson's palm over the money. He shook hands with her at the front door. 'It was very nice to see you again, Sis,' he said softly, hesitating briefly before saying the final word.

Michael did not call her at work the next day, but she was convinced he would come to the house in the evening.

It was a bright, sunny day, so that despite the cold wind and the skeletal trees there was something of spring in the air. She walked along the Embankment at lunch-time, watching the shimmering light on the river. The weather had turned dirty by late afternoon, and as she took the bus home her conviction that he would come had changed to hope. How she wished she had a telephone at home! She would not blame him if he decided to stay in and toast his toes in front of the fire on such a night. If she did not have to stay in for Hudson … She thought of trying Laura, but the nearer she got to Brixton the more uncertain she became. He would think her ridiculous if she turned up at his doorstep on such a filthy night. After such slavishness, he would know full well how to make use of her. Anyway, he was probably not interested in her that much.

By the time she had given Hudson something to eat, and had toyed with some food herself, she was sure he would not come. When his knock came on the door, she rose from the kitchen table with an incredulous grin. She gave Hudson the thumbs-up and tried not to run. To her amazement and profound disappointment, instead of Michael she found Patterson again standing on her doorstep. She saw behind him that the rain had turned to sleet and that the pavement was covered with slushy snow. He hesitated for a moment and then made to step forward. She had no choice but to let him in. He sat with them in the kitchen while they finished eating and then joined Dottie in a cup of tea.

'I was near by, and I thought I'd call,' he said, coming to stand nearer to her now they were on their own. Dottie was filled with alarm. They had met on this path before. It was at this place that he had tried to force her. 'There was something I forgot to say yesterday. If there is anything you need, or if I can be of help in any way …'

Dottie turned away towards the sink and felt him instantly on her, brushing himself lightly against her. He moved away at once, but he was smiling, certain that he had made his meaning clear to her. She stared at him in disbelief, unable to credit what had happened. 'How can you do such a disgusting thing!' she said, her voice shaking with anger and shock. That it should be him standing in front of her instead of Michael! 'After everything that has happened, and your family …'

Patterson smiled contemptuously and put his card on the kitchen table. 'In case you need to get in touch,' he said and left.

6

'You look a little like her, I think,' Michael said.

He had rung her at work earlier in the day and asked if he could call in the evening. He would bring records and some wonderful pastries he could get on the way, from a Lebanese patisserie in Brixton Road. There was only one condition he wanted to make, that she did not allow him to talk about himself.

Mrs Waterson had made an inquiring face. She had seen the long looks and heard the drawn-out sighs, and was too worldly not to understand Dottie's unhappiness. *Is it him*? When Dottie nodded, Mrs Waterson smiled and discreetly withdrew out of earshot. She glared around the typing pool, in case anyone should misconstrue her politeness for something softer or kinder.

Dottie told Michael that his condition appeared harsh to her, even absurd. Also she did not have anything on which to play his records, but if he would bring the pastries then they could discuss the options available to them. If the worst came to the worst perhaps they could talk about religion or agronomy.

'I look like who?' Dottie asked.

'I didn't want to tell you,' he said. 'In case you thought there was something odd ...'

'Like who?' she asked, exasperated with him.

'Like the old doctor's daughter ... as she used to be,' Michael said, smiling broadly but none the less feeling apprehensive. 'It's the way you carry yourself, and she used to be slim, just like you. I've seen pictures of her when she was younger. He used to call her a nomad, because she was like the Berber or Fulani women he had seen in his travels. He came from Martinique, and so did my grandmother. You remember that headline he pointed to in the library, about the French losing control in Algeria? He had worked there, and in the French Sudan as they used to call it. But he could not abide being part of the civilising mission, so he came to England where he was only a foreigner. When people asked him where he came from, he said he didn't know. Slavery had deprived him of his home, he said. My mother's got all his papers now. I'll get some old photos and show you. It's only occasionally, from certain angles, that you look like her but it must have been strange for him nevertheless.'

'Why should I think there was anything odd in any of that?' Dottie asked. She had suspected something like that, or sometimes wondered if it was the young wife she had reminded the doctor of. She had not dared ask Michael in case her question sounded presumptuous.

Michael shrugged. 'It doesn't matter. At first I thought you might be related to him.'

'I have my own grandfather, thank you,' Dottie said. 'And my own name. Have I told you my full name? Dottie

Badoura Fatma Balfour,' she said, with the exaggerated flourish she had taken to putting on her names, as if they were grand jokes.

'Badoura,' Michael said, frowning a little. 'Where does that come from? It sounds familiar,'

'I don't know,' Dottie said, and told the story of the man who had given her those names for her christening in the Church of Our Lady of Miracles in Leeds. 'Or sometimes I think it was Our Lady of Sorrows.'

'We could easily check,' he said.

'There's no need,' she said, shaking her head. 'I see him sometimes, but only vaguely, like a figure in a dream.'

'Was he your father?' Michael asked.

'No, I had no father. He would have stayed with Sharon, my mother ... he wanted to live with her. His name was Jamil, which means beautiful. His people chased her away. They made her leave Leeds and we went to live in Carlisle.'

Michael made as if to speak then held his peace. Dottie smiled at him, laughing at him a little. 'I don't think she'd have met your people. Sharon did not frequent banks or music classes. She made her living from the American soldiers quartered there.'

'That was late in the war. My parents left Carlisle in 'forty-one,' he said.

She nodded. 'Well, they certainly wouldn't have run into each other then. Her name was not Sharon, actually, it was Bilkisu. And Balfour was not really our name. She took that name when she ran away from home, from Cardiff, before I was born.'

'Bilkisu,' he said, trying the name. 'What was her other name? Your real name.'

'I don't know,' Dottie said, glaring fiercely at him.

'Do you know why she changed it? To Balfour?' he asked.

She shrugged, then shook her head. 'To cut herself off, I suppose,' she said, frowning angrily.

He saw the angry look and wondered if he should keep quiet. 'Why did she leave her home?' he asked, unable to resist the temptation, wanting to know at least why she was getting angry.

Dottie thought for a few moments before she spoke. 'She told me all these things when she was dying. She used to drink a lot, and sometimes it was difficult to know what to believe. She was very ill and in a great deal of pain. I didn't really want to hear the things she wanted to tell me.'

'Don't you want to tell me?' Michael asked.

'I'm ashamed,' Dottie said.

'It's not your shame.'

'Sharon told me so I would know. I think she told me so I should send word to him … her father in Cardiff. She told me his name but I didn't listen because life was complicated enough as it was and I did not want any more … When she was younger Sharon used to tell us not to listen to old people. They were tyrants, she used to say, who wanted to suck the blood of their children so they could go on living. Then when she herself was dying, she could not go on saying that. She had lost her name, she said. She had dishonoured herself so completely that she was afraid to return even in death. My shame is that I did not listen or pretend to give her comfort. And when she said the names and the places so I would remember them, I deliberately wiped them out. The only thing of hers that I have, survived by chance … an old photograph. That's all the papers she left.'

That weekend they went to visit Sophie in her self-catering hostel. She was sitting in her room, lonely and tearful. Michael and Hudson went out for a walk, and Dottie persuaded Sophie to sob out her story. Her orderly friend from the ward no longer came to see her. The warden was very rude to her. He came into the room and threatened her. He locked the door and told her that if she did not do what he said, he would put some powder in her water. What powder? Dottie asked, but Sophie only shrugged. Her room was never cleaned and some of the other patients made her do jobs in their rooms. They warned her that if she told the doctor then she would never be allowed to leave. *So please, please, Sis. Don't make any fuss!*

There was no question that she was sick again. She was tearful and weak, and had returned to her child-like manner. Even if there were no other grounds than that simple, uninformed diagnosis, Dottie thought, it was good enough to get her out of that pig sty. She had not asked Sophie for any details, but she could well imagine the humiliations she had been forced to submit to. There was nothing very much that she could do with the animal they called Warden. He was probably protected by the whole panoply of the labour laws of the land, but she would deal with Dr Newton in due course. For the moment she helped Sophie pack all her belongings while the latter alternately gasped with fright and spluttered with joy that she was being rescued in such outrageous fashion. It made Dottie cringe with shame for her own neglect to see her sister reduced to such infantile twitterings again.

'We'll go to another hospital next week,' Dottie said. 'And if we have any trouble from any of these swine, we'll get the Reverend Mosiah to come along with us. I'd like to see any of them take any liberties with that reverend gentleman.'

Dottie had mentioned the name of the Pastor of the Sacred Church of the True Christ at Balham as a joke, but she saw a look of the terrified sinner cross Sophie's face.

Dottie's name troubled Michael enough to make him search it out. He came to announce the results, grinning at his own cleverness. 'I've found it. I knew I'd heard it before. Princess Badoura and Prince Qamar Zaman, one of the stories in "A Thousand and One Nights".'

'What did she do? Was she brave?' Dottie asked.

'It's a long story, but I remember that the Prince was imprisoned in a tower by his own father, Shah Zaman. The king wanted his son to marry, to secure the succession, but Qamar Zaman said he would only marry for love. He was put in the tower in an effort to bring him to his senses. Only ... a beautiful genie lived in the tower, and she was so overcome by Qamar Zaman's beauty that she boasted to other genies and an argument started. Another genie said there was a beautiful princess of China called Badoura, and there was no one in the world to compare with her. So the genies put the two young people in the same bed, thinking that if they put them alongside each other they would be able to judge more easily. Princess Badoura and Prince Qamar Zaman woke in the night and fell in love with each other, but by the morning they found themselves in their separate beds, not knowing who it was they had spent the night with. The story is about how they find each other again. I'm sorry, I'm not telling it very well.'

Dottie made a face but she was really quite pleased. How he must have laughed at the thought, the man who gave her the name, that in the midst of the squalor they lived in should be a child called Badoura, Princess of China. 'And Fatma?'

'Fatma was the daughter of the prophet Mohammed, I think, wife of Ali and mother of Hassan and Hussein. Oh, that is a grand name. Dynasties and crusades were named after her,' he said. 'It's an odd name for a christening, though.'

She waited patiently while he pondered, and she took pleasure in the calm persistence with which he searched his mind. In his grey eyes she saw flickers of times passing and saw the flash and fading of tempting moments. 'It could've been Fatima after the shrine, the town in Portugal, where three children saw a vision of the Virgin ...' he said uncertainly.

'Whenever I asked Sharon she said Fatma was the name of a wicked queen who lived in the mountains. She was incredibly beautiful, like me,' Dottie said with a grin. 'She loved to sit by the road and pretend to be lost, and lure into her dungeons any travellers who took pity on her.'

'You go on calling her Sharon when you know her name is Bilkisu,' Michael said. 'It must be hard to begin calling someone you know by another name.'

'It isn't only that,' Dottie said. 'It is the Sharon side of her that I know. Not to call her that, and to give her that other name, seemed like a sort of ... escapism. As if I would be lying about the way our lives had been.'

She said no more, and perhaps would have left things there but she sensed that was not where Michael intended to leave them. It was not that she minded his insistence, not at all. The gradual learning about each other was the most surprising pleasure of all. There is something sensual about it, she thought, as the awareness arrives that you are on the verge of knowing something new. They were sitting on a bench by a window in his flat, looking across to the Common. Earlier, they had gone to tea with the old lady who lived on the ground floor. Her living room was cluttered with parcels and bundles of clothes.

A row of bird cages stood on the floor under the window, occupied by budgerigars in different shades of blue. The old lady mumbled and muttered at them, and told them about the times she had spent in Romania and Russia. She said very little, but the very thought of such a frail and confused creature in those far-away places seemed incredible enough to Dottie. When Michael mentioned the doctor, the old lady smiled. Then her smile grew into soundless laughter, only her body shaking while her face beamed.

'The garden. He loved that,' she said, and told them of all the plants and bushes she had put in and tended. Sometimes they needed special soil, and she had to go to the woods or to the Downs to find exactly what she needed. But then she had got tired. Had they seen the garden?

'Yes, Aunty, we have,' Dottie said, even though it was still winter and the garden was full of skeletons and sodden evergreens, and the paths were littered with dead leaves and stained with dark mud.

'Aren't you tempted now to try and find out about the other name?' Michael asked. 'And about the man in the picture who might have been her father. Or to find out if the woman Hawa was her mother. They might still be there, in Cardiff. Aren't you tempted to go and find them?'

She shook her head. 'It's taken me all these years to begin to find myself, to begin to know what to look for. One day I'll go and look for them ...'

'One day they won't be there,' he interrupted, frowning a little.

'Nor will I one day, in the long run,' she said.

'It sounds like selfishness to me.'

'How kind!' she said lightly, but winced involuntarily at his accusation.

‘What harm will it do?’ he persisted. ‘And it will be terrific to find out.’

‘One day … maybe. You’re just being a journalist,’ she said, refusing to give in to him. ‘You want to get to the end of the story. If the condition of our lives is not that moment on the forest path that you described to me, if we don’t just have to wait until the killer finds us, then it must be about what we do, how we live. That’s what matters. I know it’s only part of what matters, that there are others, but it’s the part I’m living now. And if he’s not there when I go to look for him, I can only pray that he’ll have lived his life well.’

Their voices droned on in a conversation that it would take many attempts to resolve. The light outside was beginning to die, and the shadows in the Common were beginning to thicken and solidify under the trees and against the walls of distant houses. Lines of cars dashed busily by in the Avenue and along the main road. Beyond the Common the immense city spread away into the dusk, lit by strings of small lights and the phosphorescence of the nearby river.

Also available by Abdulrazak Gurnah

Afterlives

SHORTLISTED FOR THE ORWELL PRIZE FOR POLITICAL FICTION 2021
LONGLISTED FOR THE WALTER SCOTT PRIZE 2021

Years ago, Ilyas was stolen from his parents by the German colonial troops. Now he returns to his village to find his parents gone, and his sister Afiya given away. Hamza returns at the same time. He has grown up at the right hand of an officer whose protection has marked him for life. He seeks only work and security – and the love of the beautiful Afiya.

As fate knots these young people together, the shadow of a new war on another continent lengthens and darkens, ready to snatch them up and carry them away…

‘Riveting and heartbreaking ... A compelling novel, one that gathers close all those who were meant to be forgotten, and refuses their erasure’ *Guardian*

‘A brilliant and important book for our times, by a wondrous writer’ *New Statesman*, Books of the Year

‘A tender account of the extraordinariness of ordinary lives … Exquisite’ *Evening Standard*

Gravel Heart

For seven-year-old Salim, the pillars upholding his small universe – his indifferent father, his adored uncle, his treasured books, the daily routines of government school and Koran lessons – seem unshakeable. But it is the 1970s, and the winds of change are blowing through Zanzibar: suddenly Salim's father is gone, and the island convulses with violence and corruption in the wake of a revolution.

It will only be years later, making his way through an alien and hostile London, that Salim will begin to understand the shame and exploitation festering at the heart of his family's history.

'The elegance and control of Gurnah's writing, and his understanding of how quietly and slowly and repeatedly a heart can break, make this a deeply rewarding novel' Kamila Shamsie, *Guardian*

'Riveting ... The measured elegance of Gurnah's prose renders his protagonist in a manner almost uncannily real' *New York Times*

'A colourful tale of life in a Zanzibar village, where passions and politics reshape a family... Powerful' *Mail on Sunday*

The Last Gift

Abbas has never told anyone about his past; about what happened before he was a sailor on the high seas, before he met his wife Maryam outside a Boots in Exeter, before they settled into a quiet life in Norwich with their children, Jamal and Hanna. Now, at the age of sixty-three, he suffers a collapse that renders him bedbound and unable to speak about things he thought he would one day have to.

Abbas's illness forces both children home, to the dark silences of their father and the fretful capability of their mother Maryam, who began life as a foundling and has never thought to find herself, until now.

'Gurnah writes with wonderful insight about family relationships and he folds in the layers of history with elegance and warmth' *The Times*

'A story replete with black humour and contemplative politics, told with great generosity' *Times Literary Supplement*

'At a time of forbidding public rhetoric about immigration, Gurnah's sensitive and sympathetic portrayal of his cast feels welcome' *Sunday Times*

Desertion

SHORTLISTED FOR THE COMMONWEALTH WRITERS' PRIZE

Early one morning in 1899, in a small town along the coast from Mombasa, Hassanali sets out for the mosque. But he never gets there, for out of the desert stumbles an ashen and exhausted Englishman who collapses at his feet. That man is Martin Pearce – writer, traveller and something of an Orientalist. After Pearce has recuperated, he visits Hassanali to thank him for his rescue and meets Hassanali's sister Rehana; he is immediately captivated.

In this crumbling town on the edge of civilised life, with the empire on the brink of a new century, a passionate love affair begins that brings two cultures together and which will reverberate through three generations and across continents.

'A careful and heartfelt exploration of the way memory inevitably consoles and disappoints us' *Sunday Times*

'An absorbing novel about abandonment and loss'
Daily Telegraph

By the Sea

LONGLISTED FOR THE BOOKER PRIZE 2002
SHORTLISTED FOR THE *LOS ANGELES TIMES*
BOOK AWARD

On a late November afternoon Saleh Omar arrives at Gatwick Airport from Zanzibar, a far away island in the Indian Ocean. With him he has a small bag in which lies his most precious possession – a mahogany box containing incense. He used to own a furniture shop, have a house and be a husband and father. Now he is an asylum seeker from paradise; silence his only protection.

Meanwhile Latif Mahmud, someone intimately connected with Saleh's past, lives quietly alone in his London flat. When Saleh and Latif meet in an English seaside town, a story is unravelled. It is a story of love and betrayal, seduction and possession, and of a people desperately trying to find stability amidst the maelstrom of their times.

'One scarcely dares breathe while reading it for fear of breaking the enchantment' *The Times*

'An epic unravelling of delicately intertwined stories, lush strands of finely wrought narratives that criss-cross the globe ... astonishing and superb' *Observer*

Admiring Silence

He thinks, as he escapes from Zanzibar, that he will probably never return, and yet the dream of studying in England matters above that. Things do not happen quite as he imagined: the school where he teaches is cramped and violent, he forgets how it feels to belong. But there is the beautiful, rebellious Emma, who turns away from her white, middle-class roots to offer him love and bear him a child. And in return he spins stories of his home and keeps her a secret from his family.

Twenty years later, when the barriers at last come down in Zanzibar, he is compelled to go back. What he discovers there, in a story potent with truth, will change the entire vision of his life.

'There is a wonderful sardonic eloquence to this unnamed narrator's voice' *Financial Times*

'I don't think I've ever read a novel that is so convincingly and hauntingly sad about the loss of home' *Independent on Sunday*

'Twisting, many-layered ... Explores themes of race and betrayal with bitterly satirical insight' *Sunday Times*

Paradise

SHORTLISTED FOR THE BOOKER PRIZE 1994
SHORTLISTED FOR THE WHITBREAD AWARD

Born in East Africa, Yusuf has few qualms about the journey he is to make. It never occurs to him to ask why he is accompanying Uncle Aziz or why the trip has been organised so suddenly, and he does not think to ask when he will be returning. But the truth is that his 'uncle' is a rich and powerful merchant and Yusuf has been pawned to him to pay his father's debts.

Paradise is a rich tapestry of myth, dreams and Biblical and Koranic tradition, the story of a young boy's coming of age against the backdrop of an Africa increasingly corrupted by colonialism and violence.

'A poetic and vividly conjured book about Africa and the brooding power of the unknown' *Independent on Sunday*

'Lingering and exquisite' *Guardian*

'An obliterated world is enthrallingly retrieved' *Sunday Times*

Pilgrims Way

Demoralised by small persecutions and the poverty of his life, Daud takes refuge in his imagination. He composes wry, sardonic letters hectoring friends and enemies, and invents a lurid colonial past for every old man he encounters. His greatest solace is cricket and the symbolic defeat of the empire at the hands of the mighty West Indies. Although subject to attacks of bitterness and remorse, his captivating sense of humour never deserts him as he struggles to come to terms with the horror of his past and the meaning of his pilgrimage to England.

'Gurnah etches with biting incisiveness the experiences of immigrants exposed to contempt, hostility or patronizing indifference on their arrival in Britain' *Spectator*

'A vibrant and vivid novel which shows human beings in all their generosity and greed, pettiness and nobility' *Herald*

'An intricate, delicate novel, vitally necessary'
New Internationalist

Memory of Departure

Poverty and depravity wreak havoc on Hassan Omar's family. The arrival of Independence brings new upheavals as well as the betrayal of the promise of freedom. The new government, fearful of an exodus of its most able men, discourages young people from travelling abroad and refuses to release examination results. Deprived of a scholarship, Hassan travels to Nairobi to stay with a wealthy uncle, in the hope that he will release his mother's rightful share of the family inheritance.

The collision of past secrets and future hopes, the compound of fear and frustration, beauty and brutality, create a fierce tale of undeniable power.

'He guides us through seismic historic moments and devastating societal ruptures while gently outlining what it is that keeps those families, friendships and loving spaces intact, if not fully whole' Maaza Mengiste

'As beautifully written and pleasurable as anything I've read … The work of a maestro' *Guardian*

Order your copy:
By phone: +44 (0) 1256 302 699
By email: direct@macmillan.co.uk
Delivery is usually 3–5 working days.
Free postage and packaging for orders over £20.
Online: www.bloomsbury.com/bookshop
Prices and availability subject to change without notice.
bloomsbury.com/uk/author/abdulrazak-gurnah